CROSSROADS

CROSSROADS

To Lynne,
It's great working
with you! Happy
Reading!
Kelly K. Scott
Kelly

Kelly Scott

Library of Congress Control Number:		2009908645
ISBN:	Hardcover	978-1-4415-6664-5
	Softcover	978-1-4415-6663-8

To order additional copies of this book, contact:
Xlibris Corporation
1-888-795-4274
www.Xlibris.com
Orders@Xlibris.com
67883

ACKNOWLEDGEMENT

I would like to express my deep thanks to my family for believing in me, to my kids for listening patiently to many scenes and dialogues and especially to my husband for always supporting my dreams even when it isn't in our best interests financially.

I would also like to thank my brother-in-law, Bob Scott who, aside from being my cheerleader, idea go-to, and sounding board, allowed me to use his name as a fictitional character. (He never was really in the Air Force . . . he was a Navy submarine guy . . . . Go Navy!)

I would also like to thank one of my best friends from high school, Joleen Marquardt, who volunteered to edit for me! (Is that self sacrificing or what?!)

Oh, and thanks Mom, for not keeping my feet on the ground this time, but instead encouraging me to go for it!

CHAPTER 1

Radical Changes

Luke woke to sirens and flashing red lights-seen only through his closed eyelids-that seemed to reverberate quite uncomfortably through his head. He could hear voices but he couldn't quite make out just what they were saying. He thought they might be calling to him, but he couldn't understand anything. He couldn't seem to get his mind to focus. The voices seemed disjointed as if the words were just large birds honking to one another in their own form of communication. Opening his eyes carefully, cautious of the pain shooting through his head, he wondered just where he was. What had happened? He tried to remember to but no avail.

Moving only his eyes at first, he began to take in his surroundings. He was in his car . . . well, it looked like his car. But there was someone kneeling on his ceiling! A very bright light flashed in his eyes. He thought he told them to turn it off, but as the light remained on and fixed on his face, he had to assume that either they didn't hear him, or he hadn't said it. Maybe they just didn't understand, after all, they were still honking away. If he couldn't understand them, perhaps they couldn't understand him. His head pounded. He wished they would turn off the light! He thought he might be sick.

There was a click. It barely registered amid the muddled confusion of his reality. Seatbelt maybe? And then he felt hands all around him. The movement reminded him that he had legs and they were screaming in pain. Or was that sound coming from him? He was being moved. It was agony. Why wouldn't they just leave him alone? His vision began to darken around the edges. It faded into what looked like television snow and then everything went black. When he regained some semblance of consciousness again, he was laying on a softer surface, but unable to move. Everything was strapped down. The only movable parts of his body were his eyeballs . . . and maybe his fingers and toes, but he didn't feel like trying them out.

The sirens had stopped but the flashing red lights continued. They were just as bad! Every pulse of red light felt like another solid hit to his head. How could light hurt so much, he wondered. He closed his eyes. That helped, but the pounding was still there. And then there were the voices again! He chanced a peek from under his eyelids for just a moment.

A young man in a dark blue uniform was leaning over him. Luke could tell from his facial expressions that the man was asking something, but he still could not understand *what* it was. They were working on him. He thought he saw a needle and there was suddenly a bag of clear liquid suspended over his head. But the pain in his head would not allow him to register much else.

Luke could see that one of the men working on him had a silver thing in his hand. He thought he had seen something like that before. What was it? What was it? He tried to get his mind working. Scissors! It was scissors! That was his last thought for quite a while.

"Luke, can you hear me?"

That was a familiar voice. Luke knew that voice. He knew a name for it . . . what was the name? He thought for a moment as his eyes fluttered open.

"Mark!" the name came to him suddenly. "What happened?"

"You were in a very bad car accident! You swerved to miss a semi whose driver had fallen asleep at the wheel and veered into your lane. Fortunately, you missed the semi! Unfortunately, you rolled down an embankment and wrapped your car upside down around a telephone pole. It nearly killed you!"

"Did you save me?"

"Well, yes, me and about four others! You woke up at the scene after the paramedics got to you. Do you remember any of that?"

"I remember the sound of large birds honking at me and a man in a blue uniform that could speak their language. And I remember scissors coming at me."

"OK, so you don't remember much. That's probably because of the brain injury."

"I have a brain injury?"

"Yes! You were . . . you shouldn't have lived! But I am an awesome surgeon!" Mark said with exaggerated seriousness. "A renowned, amazingly awesome surgeon! Don't worry; I'll work with you on the bill! You can make monthly payments."

Luke was trying not to laugh, just in case it hurt. "Thanks buddy! I guess I'll be paying for . . . what? . . . The next hundred years? I have insurance . . . I think."

"Oh, no. More like the next two hundred years, even *with* your insurance! Remember the part about 'you shouldn't have lived' but a renowned, amazingly awesome surgeon saved you?"

"What are friends for?"

"Get some sleep, buddy! I'll be back to check on you soon!"

The next time Luke woke up a very beautiful woman stood beside his bed. Though her blond hair was long and shiny with a beautiful soft wave to the long strands that fanned out over her shoulders, and her complexion was perfect, the color of peaches and cream, and her teeth were white and perfectly straight; it was her eyes that captivated Luke. They were a deep, unbelievable blue-green. He had never seen eyes quite like those. He couldn't seem to look away. She was smiling at him.

"Hi! My name's Regina."

"Hi! Uh, Luke."

"Yes, I know. Is there anything I can get you?"

"Well," Luke started to tell her that he could really use an ice cold glass of water with a long straw, when there in his hand was an ice cold glass of water complete with straw! He was so surprised that he spilled it all over his top cover! Wow! It was cold! He dragged the blanket from the bed one-handed and tossed it weakly to the chair beside him. He was stunned for a minute. How had that happened? Luke stared at the beautiful lady as he buzzed the nurse for a new blanket.

While he waited for the nurse to appear he took time to survey his injuries as best he could. He wasn't able to sit up quite yet but even if he could, his legs would not have allowed it. They were both encased in casts from his feet to his hip. They were also suspended from the ceiling, his cold toes peeking out at the ends. One arm was also in a cast from his hand to his shoulder but at least it wasn't suspended from the ceiling. He could wiggle both toes and fingers without any pain. That pleased him. Perhaps it all looked worse than it was. His head was bandaged also. But he thought the worst of it was at the base of the back of his head. The right hand side of his face was also bandaged up pretty well, from his jaw to his hair line.

Luke was still confused by the cold water, but decided it must be due to the pain killers Mark had him on.

"I wonder why they charge so much to stay in a hospital, but they can't seem to turn up the heat?" Luke complained as he tried to wiggle some warmth back into his toes.

"Luke, if you want a blanket, concentrate on the one you want."

He thought she might also be part of his pain killer hallucination, but since she was a very nice looking hallucination, he thought he'd humor her. "OK, I'd like my . . ." he didn't even finish his sentence before one of his favorite blankets from home fell on top of him. "Oh my . . . . ! Where in the heck did that come from?" he looked up at Regina. "How did you do that?"

"I didn't do that." She shook her head smiling. "You did! Luke, you are no longer just a man. I think I was drawn here to you to tell you that you are a telepath! I don't know how it works, but I'm one too. I was . . . well, for lack of a better way to explain it . . . I was drawn to you. For some reason, you and I are connected. I can do that conjuring thing too." She demonstrated by producing a hot cup of coffee. As Luke stared at the coffee he noticed that the fingers wrapped around that coffee cup were well manicured. Each finger was painted in a diagonal design with blue polish on the bottom and clear on the top with a sliver of a moon on each one. Each little moon sported a small rhinestone within it's inside curve. He wondered how much it cost to get your nails done so extravagantly. This was a very detailed hallucination!

"Do you care for one?" she asked, referring to the cup of coffee.

"No thank you, I'm still just interested in a glass of ice . . ." the ice water appeared again and this time Luke was careful not to spill it. "Wow, I must be having one heck of a reaction to my pain killers. Or maybe that brain injury is causing this."

"Yeah, that's what I thought too. A similar thing happened to me. Only, it wasn't a car wreck for me it was a tumor that I had removed from the base of my brain. I went in thinking I might die. I came out in better shape than when I went in and with a few surprising little extras."

"Extras?" Luke inquired.

"Yes! Your body will heal faster than a normal human's would, too, which is a nice perk. Your legs will probably be all right again in a day or two!"

"A day or two, huh?!" Luke smiled in disbelief. "You were pretty young to have a brain tumor."

"I was thirty-eight!"

"Yeah, right! You look like you are about twenty-three at the most!"

"No, I'm thirty-nine now!"

Luke looked doubtfully at her and was about to voice his doubts when the door was suddenly pushed open.

Mark walked briskly in looking down at his clip board, jotting notes as he walked. "Luke your family is in the hall. I told them that I wanted to check on you first and then they could come in and see you." He stopped walking and writing at the same time, clicked his pen closed and tucked it in his pocket. Only then did he finally look up and take in the beautiful woman standing beside Luke. "Wow, who's the pretty woman, Luke?"

"You can see her?!"

"Well, yeah!" Mark looked at Luke as if Luke was playing with half a deck.

"Oh, well, this is Regina. Regina, this is my very good friend and also my surgeon, Dr. Mark Johns." Now Luke looked confused.

"Very nice to meet you, Regina! Where did you meet Luke?" Mark asked as he took out his pen light and began an examination of Luke's eyes, but he didn't wait for her answer. "Wow! Luke! Your eyes! Are you wearing contact lenses? You shouldn't wear those until . . . You . . . aren't . . . wearing . . . ! Damn!"

"What's wrong, Mark? What's wrong with my eyes?" Luke began to get a little nervous.

"Well, they're . . . they're . . . . blue!" Mark continued to shine the light and stare into Luke's eye.

"Well, yeah!" Now it was Luke's turn to look at Mark as if *he* were playing with half a deck. "Are you feeling all right, Mark?"

"No, yes, I mean . . . I've never seen anything like it! Luke, they're contact-lens-unbelievable-blue!"

"That's nice. Would you mind getting the light out of my eyes?"

"Oh, yeah, sorry." Mark turned off the light and straightened up with a troubled look on his face. He finally shrugged it off and continued checking Luke's vitals. "Well, you are doing very well!" Mark dropped his hand down on the bed beside Luke. Only then did he realize that Luke no longer had a hospital blanket over him.

"Hey, where did this come from?"

"I was going to talk to you about that. I just thought about this blanket and it just appeared!" Luke told him. "I thought maybe I was hallucinating. Actually, I thought Regina, here, was part of the hallucination. But you can see her . . . . maybe *you're* part of my hallucination! What kind of pain killers do you have me on?"

"Luke, I'm really here so it couldn't be the pain killers or *I* wouldn't be able to see the blanket too. Now where did it come from?"

"I . . . I . . . brought it in for him!" Regina said quickly.

"No, you didn't! I thought about it and it appeared . . . same as the water! It was the weirdest thing, Mark."

Mark didn't look convinced. He turned to the pretty lady who by now was standing at the foot of the bed and smiled weakly. She smiled back.

"He just woke up. Give him a little time." she said. "I'll be back in just a minute. Girl's room?" Regina asked.

"Head down the hall toward the nurse's station; you'll see it on the left about three doors down."

"Thanks!" she said over her shoulder as she left the room.

"Wow, Luke! Where did you meet her?"

"I don't know! She was just here when I woke up. She told me I was a telepath. She said I could telepathically move things. She said all I had to do was think about something and it would appear. So I thought about some water and it appeared. I was so surprised that I spilled it and then needed a new blanket. She told me to think about the blanket that I wanted. I thought of this one and it appeared! See? Hallucination, right?!"

Mark was looking at Luke with a very worried expression on his face. "Luke, maybe you should try to get some rest!"

"Mark, if you really saw her and the blanket, you have to believe me. Unless you really aren't here and you are also a part of this weird trip."

"Luke, Regina just said that she brought this to you!"

"She lied. I don't know why, but she did!"

Their argument was interrupted by two men who entered the room. The first one introduced himself as a Dr. Todd LeBeau and his companion as his friend Mr. Ron Donovan.

"I was told that my sister was in here visiting with you. Her name is Regina. Have you seen her?"

"Your sister? Well, there was a woman in here who called herself Regina, but she didn't tell us her last name. She's in the restroom."

"Did she seem all right to you?" Mr. LeBeau asked anxiously. "She isn't well. I really need to take her back to the hospital. She walked out when no one was looking the other day. It's taken me two days to track her down."

"She seemed just fine to me! Of course, that's like the pot calling the kettle black! She looks great, especially when you consider the tumor she had! What a speedy recovery!" Luke told the man.

"Yes, well, she does come across well at first, but then she tends to say things that don't quite add up. The longer you are around her the more clear that becomes. Did she happen to mention anything about being a telepath?"

"Well, yes she did!" Luke replied.

LeBeau looked rather sad. "That's the way it starts. Then she starts talking about how she's thirty-nine. She's only twenty-four. Damn tumor! I sure hope she gets better."

"Me too," said Luke. *"I hope we both do,"* he thought. "She'll be back in just a ..."

At that moment, Regina reappeared in the doorway. She walked over to Luke's bed and sat down in the chair beside him. There was no recognition registering on her face at the sight of LeBeau.

"Regina, do you know this man?" Luke asked.

"No."

"It's Ok, Mr. Matthews. She might not remember me."

"Have I met you before?" she asked LeBeau.

"I understand that you are a telepath." LeBeau shook his head slightly to signal Luke not to interrupt.

"Well, yes." She looked uncertainly from Luke to LeBeau.

"Ah, well, my colleague and I would like to talk to you about that, if you wouldn't mind coming with us. We have a research facility devoted to the study of telepaths and we would greatly appreciate any help you could give us." LeBeau caught Mark's eye and gave him a reassuring nod.

"Do you have any identification on you? Obviously, I don't know you from Adam. It would be unwise to go with you, don't you think?" Regina asked.

"Of course," LeBeau reached into his coat pocket and took out his identification. He showed her his ID and gave her his card. It read, Dr. Todd LeBeau, Director of Research, Institute of Telepathic Research.

Luke just stared at her. He was trying to figure out what was going on and it was making his head hurt again. Mark noted the distress on Luke's face and decided it was time to get his patient a little rest.

"Dr. LeBeau, would you mind taking this discussion outside the room? My patient needs his rest."

"Of course! Regina, may we talk with you out in the hall?"

"Well, I suppose that would be all right. Luke, I'll be back after awhile to see how you are doing. Have a nice rest."

"I will. Thanks for stopping by."

She flashed him a dazzling smile and followed LeBeau out the door. Mark turned back to his patient and gave him strict orders to get some sleep as soon as his parents and his brother left.

"And Luke, don't go telling your parents about this telepath stuff. It might scare them. Let them get used to the idea that you're going to make it first!" He checked his vitals and his wounds, exclaiming over the speed with which Luke was healing, reminded Luke once again just how incredible his surgeon was and headed out the door promising to come back and watch a little TV with him later.

Mark never got that chance. When he re-entered Luke's room around eight o'clock that evening, Luke was gone. Mark turned quickly and headed back down the hall to the nurse's station.

"Margaret! What happened to my patient, Luke Matthews?"

"My name is not Margaret! Call me Dedre, please Doctor! That *is* my name!!"

Mark had a habit of naming his staff after characters in movies and television shows. Clearly, not everyone thought it an endearing habit. But then, Dedre's extreme exception to the name was one reason why he called her, Margaret! She had long platinum blond hair, blue eyes and attitude! She was also head nurse and ran her staff with efficiency and competence. She was *so* Margaret from the old sitcom M*A*S*H!

"Sorry, Hot Lips! Where's my patient?"

She gave him an exasperated scowl and replied, "He was moved earlier this afternoon to another hospital at the request of his parents." She read from a clipboard hanging from the wall beside her desk. "He was picked up by Mountain View Medical Center staff about three hours ago."

"Why wasn't I consulted?"

"It says here that you were paged, but you didn't respond. So the ambulance crew went ahead and took him. They had all the right forms, signed, sealed, and delivered! We didn't have any choice but to let him go. Maybe you should try talking to his parents. I have their number right here."

"I don't need it, I already know their number. Luke and I have been friends since college. I just don't understand why they would have him moved without talking to me first!"

"Emergencies do strange things to people."

Mark stood at the desk for a minute longer, turning things over in his head. It just didn't make any sense. Then he asked, "Did you happen to see a strikingly beautiful woman—long, blond hair, blue eyes, perfect smile, super-model material—around Luke's room?"

"No, but I don't usually notice things like that."

"Even *you* would notice this girl!"

"Then, no, I did not see a strikingly beautiful girl hanging around his room. But I only came on at two. I don't know what happened before then."

"Thanks! I'll give Luke's parents a call."

Mark called, but his parents had not requested a change of hospital for Luke! They were frantic and began an energetic search. Further investigation turned up no sign of his patient. No ambulance had picked him up. There was no Mountain View Medical Center within five hundred miles. Mark checked planes, trains and busses. There was no record of Luke Matthews or anyone fitting his description going anywhere on anything! Mark was pretty confidant that Luke would have been remembered with casts on both legs and one on his left arm, not to mention the bandages around his head! And how could his abductors have managed even to get him out of the hospital without an ambulance?

Mark and Luke's parents filed a missing person's report with the police and went home to pray and to wait.

Luke woke up sweating. It was just a little too warm and his blanket was sticking to him. He realized at the same moment that the blanket was sticking to his bare legs! They were no longer encased in their casts! Neither was his arm, for that matter! He felt wonderful! As a matter of fact, he felt better than he had in the last few years! Wow, Mark must have him on some wonderful pain killers. To bad they were probably addictive and now he'd have to wean himself off them!

As he began to look around the room he noticed that someone had moved him to a much nicer suite than the one he had in ICU. The walls were a light tropical green and there were two small palm trees growing in a pot by the window. All Luke could see out the window from the bed was a cloudless blue sky. The entire theme of the room seemed to be tropical, with sea shells and fishing nets adorning the walls. There was a night stand beside his bed and the clock read ten. It must be ten in the morning since the sun was definitely shining outside.

Well, Luke thought, hallucination or not, as long as I feel so good, I might as well get up and look out the window. He sat up and stretched tentatively. Everything felt wonderful! He felt his head. There were no bandages! How long had he been asleep? He stood and walked over to the window. One glance out the window and Luke nearly fainted. He was not in a hospital at all! He wasn't even in the same city! Actually, he wasn't even in a city! It looked like a tropical island!!

There were clothes laid out for him on a small dresser in the corner of the room. Luke grabbed the shorts and t-shirt and slid into them quickly. The quick glance in the mirror prompted a double take. Luke stared at the image in the mirror with utter fascination. Wow, this was a great dream! His hair was darker than he remembered it and it was all there. There was no shaved part where the incision had been. It was as if he had walked backward in time. And his eyes were . . . well, just like Mark had said before, they were very blue, as if he were wearing colored lenses. But he wasn't!

When Luke got past the eyes, he began to notice other changes. His skin was younger looking. It was firm and tan! He had muscles that hadn't been there before! He looked as good as he had in . . . . college!! Tearing his eyes away from the mirror, he looked around the room again, trying to ascertain if this was real or just a dream. It sure felt real! He saw a pair of new flip flops on the floor in front of the dresser. He put them on and turned toward the door. It opened just then and a man stood in the doorway. His eyes were the most noticeable thing about him. They were intensely sage green. They stood out, just like Luke's only a different color, of course. He was probably in his mid twenty's with a strong angular face, softened by a pleasant smile. He stood not quite as tall as Luke but he was clearly in excellent shape. His clothes and relaxed attitude brought the description of beach bum to mind, but there was more to him than that. Maybe it was the fact that he looked like he worked out using Navy Seal routines! Luke new there was more to this man than met the eye, he just couldn't quite put his finger on it at the moment. Somehow, though, he expected the first words out of his mouth to be something like "Hey, dude, care for a swim?"

"Oh, good, you're up and I see you found the clothes!" noting Luke's confused expression the man quickly assured him, "You're among friends! I'll explain everything to you. My name is Rick Dasher. My wife will be along in a bit. Her name is Sophia. You're safe here."

"Wasn't I safe at the hospital?"

"No, but I'll explain it all as soon as Sophia gets back."

"How long have I been here? It must have been a while; I don't have any casts anymore. Of course this is all probably a drug induced hallucination."

"I can assure you that this is not a hallucination. You have had no pain killers since you left the hospital. Oh, and you haven't been here as long as you think you have. It's only been a couple of days. Sorry, we kept you asleep so you would be completely healed before you had to deal with everything else." He swept his hands around indicating the room and the island.

"Are you hungry?" Rick asked. "We could eat out on the deck and talk there. I know you have a lot of questions. You could eat and I could get you caught up."

"Only a couple of days?!"

"Yes, you have become quite a quick healer. We all are, but I'll explain that later."

"Where am I exactly?"

"You are on an island in the South Pacific. Sophia and I own it. We live here."

"Why and how was I brought here?"

"Let's eat first. It's a long story and I'm sure you are hungry." Rick led Luke out of the room and down the hall. They entered a beautiful living room also done in a very tropical motif. They turned left in the living room and headed outside onto a deck.

The deck was beautifully situated to over look a small cobble stone path leading down to a sheltered beach. From the railing, Luke could see two sun chairs down on the beach under a large umbrella. The deck, itself, was large and furnished with a table and four chairs. The awning and chair pads were done in blue and white stripes and flowers in planters adorned the corners and railings.

Luke took an offered chair at the table and was presented with an iced down Coke. He noticed that Rick was drinking a Dr. Pepper, but he had not seen from where the drinks had been retrieved.

"Sophia will be along in a moment for lunch," Rick said.

"Thank you. How did you know I like Coke?" Luke was reminded of Regina and her revelations and was beginning to get very curious.

"Well, I guess we better start at the beginning, Luke. First, I know this might be a little hard to believe, but I am a 'path', actually, so are you. Well, that's what we call ourselves. We are a small group of people with some very unique abilities; telepathic abilities. Every last one of us underwent some sort of trauma to the head. When surgically repaired, by some freak of science, our latent mental capacities were released. We have abilities that most people don't have. For example, when you were in the hospital recovering, did you wish for anything that just sort of happened to be there in the next instant?"

Luke's face went pale. "I was hallucinating!"

"No, you weren't. Try it now! Think about what you would like for lunch. Think of anything. Be extravagant if you like. But think of something that you would guess that I would not be able to produce on short notice."

Luke was thinking about sweet and sour pork from his favorite restaurant. In an instant it was there! He added an egg roll at the last moment and it appeared a second later on the same plate! The plate even looked just like the plates at the restaurant that he frequented! His eyes nearly bugged out!

"Good choice!" A second later, a plate arrived in front of Rick. "It's Kobe Beef! It's one of my favorites! I used to get it when I lived on Okinawa back when I was in the Marines. There was a place on Kadena Air Force Base called Jack's Place. I would go there with my buddies after work and have this! The beef is so tender that you could cut it with a dull chop stick!" Rick picked up his chop stick and began to pull the meat apart and eat.

Staring in disbelief, it took Luke a minute before he took a bite. *"This is one heck of a trip!"* Luke thought.

Sophia did join them a few minutes later, introduced herself and welcomed Luke to the island. Luke stared at her with his mouth hanging open. Sophia was one of the most beautiful women he had ever seen. She had dark olive skin, blue eyes that like his were a brilliant but lighter blue and every inch of her body was perfect. She and Rick ignored his rude stare. She just looked at what they were eating and in the next moment, Luke saw her produce a Big Mac and fries. She looked up and saw him still staring but now it was at her meal in disbelief. She smiled and said, "So, I'm a cheap date!"

For the duration of the lunch, Luke mostly ate, while Rick filled in the information. "OK, so here's the skinny. Most humans never use a good part of their brain. It is inaccessible to them. A few fortunate ones have that power released. As a result we are able to heal very quickly. I'm sure you noticed that your legs are no longer broken, and your arm is healed as well. You don't even have a scar from your surgery though you have only been here a couple of days. We can also teleport items. For example, you didn't just conjure up that meal, someone made it. All you did was teleport it from there to here."

"*All* I did was teleport it!" Luke repeated sarcastically.

"Yeah, well, it gets better! Once you have a telemate, you will be able to do a lot more than that!"

"Telemate?"

"Umm, yeah, let me explain. The telepathic life has a few constraints. You will not be able to access all your talents until you are connected with a mate. My mate was Sophia. I was drawn to her crossroad."

"Crossroad?"

"A crossroad is the point when a person meets that disaster that propels them into the telepathic life. Usually another person is drawn to that point. They are there to help the telepath work through the injury and recovery. That's the best way I can explain it. The draw is very intense and as far as I know, impossible to ignore. But once your minds connect it really gets interesting. For one thing, you are very attracted to each other. It's like chemistry between you working over time and on steroids. Your minds connect and you find that you can read each other's thoughts. You become one with another brain." Rick was watching Luke closely to see how he was taking all this information. Luke looked like a concerned relative listening to a senile old uncle as he explained why he was found stark naked in the yard crowing like a rooster.

"I know it sounds pretty far fetched but pretty soon it will all sink in. You'll find that the telepathic life has quite a few very nice perks . . . after you get over having a mate that can read your mind."

"So can you read my mind too?" Luke asked incredulously.

"Well, when I'm close enough to Sophia, I can. It takes two paths to do it. You could read my mind if we were touching, or you were touching Sophia. Once you have your mind mate, though, it'll eventually work without touching."

"Well, what am I thinking right now?"

"You're wondering just what kind of a cuckoo house you've landed in!"

"That's too easy! What else am I thinking?"

"You are wondering why you didn't have a 'mate' with you if they are called to a crossroads. I got it word for word, didn't I?"

Luke looked stunned! He recovered and started to ask the next question, but Rick answered before he could get it voiced.

"Your mate is Regina. I saw her in your memory, forgive me for probing, but sometimes we don't discover a path in time to bring them here and warn them. We missed Regina, but unfortunately our enemies didn't. The good thing is that they missed you! And because of that, we may be able to get Regina back."

"We have enemies?"

"Yes, a man named Todd LeBeau came after Regina, remember?"

"He said he was . . ."

"her brother. Yeah, that was a new one, he's getting more creative. Anyway, we need to get her back as soon as possible. LeBeau does not play nice! She is in very great danger."

"OK, how do we go about doing that?" Luke had no idea whether or not he believed any of this, but he didn't see any choice but to go along with it until he found a way back home.

"We are going to put all of our abilities together and concentrate on her. Maybe we can get to where she is by zeroing in on her thoughts. We're hoping that you can help with that. She was there for you; you must have connected at some point. And don't worry, Luke, we'll get you back home as soon as possible. You are not a prisoner."

"Uh . . . thanks." Luke was obviously shaken. "Then what? We are still probably hours from her by plane if we are really in the South Pacific. And once we find her, I'm . . . what . . . stuck with her?"

"Yes, but I wouldn't call it 'stuck' with her! You won't be able to stay away from her once you've connected mentally. She'll be intoxicating to you."

"OK . . ." Luke said sarcastically. "And how are we going to get to her quickly from way out here?"

"Well, we won't be going by plane. Paths can also teleport as long as they have a mate. Sophia and I will teleport ourselves and you to her."

"You can do that?" his unbelief was palpable.

"Well, you'll be able to do it to, once we get Regina back. You have to mind mate with Regina first, though. Now, don't look at me like that Luke. It just means that you have to have a mental connection with her. You probably already have it. Did you see her in your thoughts before you were conscious in the hospital?"

"No!"

Rick looked disappointed. "Oh, that's too bad. But maybe you made some kind of connection. Did she touch you?"

"No. Well, not that I know of."

"Oh, I think you'd know. Well, Sophia, I guess we're no better off than we were before in the rescue department. I think we probably better just try to get to her as soon as possible." He turned back to Luke. "We'll need your help; maybe you have some connection that you are not aware of yet. Take our hands, Luke."

Well, I guess is can't hurt to humor them. Luke thought. As soon as Luke touched them he could hear their thoughts as if they were standing in his head.

I heard that!! And now so can you! Rick thought back.

Holy . . . . !!

Try not to think cuss words, Luke. Sophia doesn't like them!

"Sorry, Sophia. It's just that . . . ."

"Yeah, I know. I felt the same way the first time I heard Rick's voice in my head too!"

"You're funny, Sophia! Get serious now, we need to work. Concentrate on Regina, Luke. Listen for her voice."

"OK" Luke thought. At first they couldn't hear her, but then Luke caught the faintest whisper. It got a little louder when he called out to her, but not by much. As soon as they had it, Luke felt an electrical pulse begin to seep up his arms and throughout his body. It was an incredible sensation. The patio began to shift under his feet. He felt as though he'd had one too many drinks at the bar and the smile that spread across his face was impossible to extinguish. He thought he must look like a goof ball.

"Yeah, you do! Concentrate, please!"

The next instant all three of them were standing in some sort of laboratory. Luke glanced around him. "Where is she?"

"She should be right here! Usually when we concentrate on someone, we land right in front of them. But she's not here! That's odd. Can you hear her, Luke?" Rick asked.

"No, not a thing! Lets look around, maybe we'll find her."

"I don't like this, Rick. It's never been like this before." Sophia said nervously.

"Yeah, we better stay close to each other incase we need to make a speedy exit. If that happens, Luke, you'll have to be thinking of the deck at our house, OK?"

"OK" They left the lab and wandered down the hallway, peeking cautiously in each room as they went. Rick thought they might be in a bit of trouble when he opened a door to a computer lab and saw technicians at their stations, but not even one of them stopped to look up at him. They had made it almost to the end of the hall when they finally found her. Luke was the first one in the room. He saw a gurney with a body on it and a sheet draped over it. He stepped further into the room. What caught his eye was an arm hanging down from under the sheet. The fingers attached to that arm had long nails that were very well manicured displaying a diagonal design with blue on the bottom, clear on top with a sliver of a little moon on each one. Little rhinestones glittered in the soft light of the room. He knew those hands in an instant.

"It's her!" his voice was shaky. Luke ran to the table and pulled the sheet back. She was lying on her stomach, her head turned to the side. Her brain had been cut open and some sort of surgical procedure had ensued. What was left looked like Frankenstein had been rummaging around for parts. Luke was sick. He turned to exit the room, but Rick caught him.

"Someone's coming! We have to go! Grab Sophia's hand." Rick whispered quickly.

Luke took her hand; Rick already had his other hand. The sensations began again. They weren't as intense this time, perhaps because they were over powered by the nauseous feeling in his stomach. Once again the floor began to tilt oddly and within a couple of seconds they were standing on the deck of the Dasher's beach house.

"Luke, are you all right?" Sophia put her hand on his shoulder and looked up into his blue eyes.

"Yes, I'm fine, just a little nauseated." Reality was hitting Luke square in the face. He was a telepath. He had healed way too quickly, he had teleported, heard other's speaking in his head and he could not look in a mirror without being reminded of all the changes that had bombarded his quiet life in the last few days. Seeing Regina on that gurney had brought the entire fairytale to life. He swayed on his feet, but caught himself. "I'll be fine in a minute. How could they do that to her?"

"She's not the first path to go into that place and never come out. But, Luke, I'm worried about you. Paths have a very deep connection. Are you all right?"

"I'm fine, I don't think Regina and I ever made that connection. I don't feel anything, except very sorry that Mark and I ever let her go with that LeBeau guy. He was very good at spinning a tale. What a horrible waste!"

"Well, it won't be long before he finds out about you, so we better make sure you know everything about paths that we can tell you. You are not going to be safe in your old life, Luke. You are going to have to make some changes, I'm afraid."

"What kind of changes?"

"Well, if I were you, I'd sell my house, car, and any other investments you have and go into hiding. You will need a safe house like this one; a place where LeBeau can't find you. We can help you with that. Can you change jobs easily?"

"I'm self employed but I've made good money over the last few years and I have a pretty good nest egg from my investments. I can hold out for quite a while. If my investments pay off, I'll be all right as long as I can live on the interest earned."

"Good, because as of now you are in Rick and Sophia Dasher's 'Becoming a Path 101' class. Any questions so far?"

"Yeah, about a million. The first one though, is why are you guys doing this?"

"Because we don't like LeBeau, for one. Also, we feel we should try to help as many paths as possible. If it hadn't been for a little help we got along the way, we might also have been guests at LeBeau's little house of horrors. We're passing it on."

Time flew by for Luke. He learned a lot. Actually, most of what he learned could have been learned in a lot less time, but when he assured them that he couldn't just disappear from his old life and his old friends, the Dashers argued at least that it would not be a good idea for anyone to see him too soon. It would be too hard to explain why he had recovered so quickly and it was going to be hard enough to explain why he looked so much younger. They suggested that he go back to his friends at the end of six months with a story about being in a special research hospital in Europe. He was not to stay at his old house, or with his friends. He was only to report that the hospital he had been in worked not only to heal the body through the use of state of the art medical care, but also state of the art physical training, dental and skin care; the body being viewed as a cooperative unit that needs care on all levels to achieve complete healing.

"What if someone asks me what I learned?"

"Be vague!"

During the six months, Luke sold his house and his investments. He then put all his money into new accounts under a false identity that the Dasher's helped him to set up. He bought a piece of property in Wyoming under the same assumed name and began construction on the log cabin up behind Granite Lake that would be his new home. He purchased two Jeep Cherokee's under two different names. They were not traceable back to him. All of Luke's identification had to be replaced also. All of this work took most of his time during the six months.

The cabin had been built over quite a large unfinished basement. Rick and Luke proceeded to finish off the basement once the construction workers who had built the main cabin had finished. It took them quite a bit of time, but it was worth it. The basement was attached to the cabin by one secret passage and to a very well concealed garage by another secret passage. It was ready to move into at the end of the six months.

Luke had been very excited to get the chance to see Mark again. The day he walked into his old buddy's office was emotional for them both. Using Rick and Sophia's fabricated story about the specialized research hospital in Europe didn't sit well with Mark. He wanted to know everything. He was so amazed with Luke's healing! Luke told him that he had gotten the chance to be a guinea pig for the European hospital only if he promised not to reveal its where-abouts or to tell too much about the treatment. They were still in the research stage and didn't want trade secrets to get out. It was the price he paid for their expertise. He also told Mark that he had not been allowed to tell anyone that he was going. "I had to make a split second choice," he lied.

When Luke would not tell him anymore, Mark grudgingly let it drop. He was so happy to have Luke back safe and sound that he didn't have the heart to complain. He was extremely curious about how Luke could look as good as he did, but when no answers were forthcoming he let that go, too. Mark thought that perhaps he would learn more about it the longer they were together. Sooner or later, Luke would let his guard down and let something slip. But as the months passed, Mark realized that Luke would never talk about the time he'd been missing at all and as closely as Mark watched him, he could discover no radically different behaviors that could account for the healthy glow Luke seemed to exude.

Mark noticed one thing that had changed though. Luke had moved. He had taken a job quite a ways away from where Mark lived and the two only got together about twice a month. They would meet halfway in between and catch a ballgame or an IMAX movie and go for dinner after. It was odd, but Luke didn't wish to talk about why he had given up his business and taken a job . . . in Timbuktu for heaven's sake! He also noticed that Luke seemed distracted a lot lately, as if he was always looking over his shoulder. He had become even more elusive and hard to pin down. When ever he asked Luke what was wrong, he got the strange impression that Luke wanted to tell him something, but then he'd smile at Mark and tell him it was nothing. Mark decided that he would allow his friend his secrets, but keep his eyes open.

This weekend the two were going to catch a basketball game in Denver. The Nuggets were playing the Lakers and Mark couldn't wait to see the game and catch up on the latest and greatest with Luke. They had purchased their tickets and were going to meet in their seats at the game. Mark arrived a little early and bought a drink before taking his seat. Unfortunately, he ended up drinking by himself. As a matter of fact he ended up watching the game by himself. He checked his beeper, but he hadn't been paged and he hadn't gotten a message on his cell phone. He was very worried and had a hard time concentrating on the game. It wasn't like Luke to do this. The only time he had ever not been where he said he'd be was when he was taken from the hospital. Mark left the game before it was finished, frantic to discover what had happened to Luke.

The authorities found Luke's rental car later that night. The accident had been brutal. They thought the driver had been trying to call someone on his cell phone, lost control of the car, driven off the road and rolled down a steep mountainside. It had wrapped around a tree and burst into flames. There wasn't much left of the car or driver, but Luke's cell phone was found about halfway down the mountain side with a partial number dialed into it. The first five digits had been dialed and they were the same numbers as the first five of Mark's phone number. Maybe he'd been running late and tried to call Mark. He wasn't sure. All he knew was that there was a large Luke sized hole in his chest that would likely never heal.

CHAPTER 2

Lazarus

He was forty-seven now, but no one would ever guess it. To look into his gentle, intensely blue eyes; a striking contrast to his square jaw, strong cheek bones and coal black hair, one would think he had barely made his twenty-fifth birthday. But to Luke, the last ten years seemed like a lifetime in itself.

Now, as he sat on the hill over-looking Laramie, Wyoming, he thought about the life somewhere down there that was about to change forever for better or worse, maybe beginning anew or maybe ending abruptly. He hoped it was a beginning. He wasn't sure who it would be, only that he was drawn here by some inexplicable force to witness, and maybe to protect the new one.

He figured the fated person would be a woman. He had never in ten years run into a path connection of two guys or two girls—always one guy and one girl. He felt a little freaked out to have been drawn here now, after ten years. He would much rather choose his own mate than have his mind be trapped by the unwritten but very binding laws of the telepathic mind, though he had not found anyone to fit that bill in his forty-seven years of life. Maybe he *needed* a little help. Still he'd tried not to come, delaying until the last minute, but in the end, he couldn't resist the pull. Heck, he'd even broken his own safety rules and called in an old friend on this one. He figured that if he was going to be drawn in, he might as well throw in completely and try to keep her alive long enough to become the mate he needed despite the resentment. Calling in Mark seemed the only way to give her a fighting chance.

His mind wandered back a few years. Mark Johns was a tall man. He had a perfect beautiful smile, the result of several years of braces as a teenager. He had shoulder length strawberry blond hair that he let hang loose most of the time. His large blue eyes seemed always to betray a twinkle of mischief. Mark had been his best friend in college. But when Luke finished his business degree, Mark had gone on to med school. He was the most talented brain surgeon west of the Mississippi, maybe in the country by now, despite his large hands that seemed more suitable to basketball than delicate surgery. Luke hadn't talked to Mark in eight years. That was because Mark, having been a pall bearer at

Luke's fabricated funeral eight years ago, assumed the relationship had hit an abrupt end.

It had been very hard to fake his own funeral and leave all his family and friends behind. But he'd had to do it. Rick and Sophia had been right. The lab boys were always breathing down his neck, he was running all the time. The funeral had afforded him a quieter life. Still he had made sure that he had avenues for escape should they discover their mistake and come after him again.

He was endangering his own way of life by calling in Mark, but what else could he do? If he left the new one's life in the hands of anyone short of a top notch brain surgeon, she would probably die. He had to try. They would just have to be careful. The lab boys seemed to have given up on surveillance on Mark. Luke knew that because he had spent many an hour staking out Mark himself, trying to catch a labbie to interrogate. Information would have been nice, but Mark was apparently off their hot list. That turned out to be a good thing, since he needed him now. Still, if they noticed that he just happened to be in a small college town the same day that a near death brain injury occurred, they could become suspicious and come to investigate. Deep down, he knew they would come, suspicious or not. The trick was to make it all look as coincidental as possible.

Fortunately, UW had a nursing school that was very excited to welcome a visiting brain surgeon to speak to their students about going on to become surgical nurses. Now Mark had a cover, though if they looked closely enough, they would discover that Mark had set it up himself. What brain surgeon in his right mind would leave his practice on purpose to go speak to a nursing school without being asked? Luke hoped the lab boys would miss this little hole in his plan.

Luke chuckled as he remembered his buddy's face that morning when he looked up annoyed at an insensitive stranger who sat down at his table, uninvited, during his morning ritual of coffee and a newspaper at KeKe's. KeKe's was a little coffee shop that Mark frequented near the hospital where he worked. Luke had watched him enjoy this ritual more times than he cared to count as he waited and watched for the lab boys to enter the scene. Mark was just about to tell the stranger to 'blow' and lie about expecting someone to join him, when his eyes popped open to about the size of the hub caps on Luke's jeep, his face drained of all color and his coffee poured right down his two hundred dollar silk shirt. He didn't even notice the hot liquid running down his chest as he stood in unbelief staring into the face of a long dead friend.

Luke felt a little bad about the shirt, but Mark's next reaction was more than enough pay back. Mark stood, took one step toward Luke and caught him off guard with a solid left hook to Luke's jaw. He then turned and walked out of KeKe's without a glance back. Luke found himself sprawled flat on his back, still in the chair with his feet flapping in the air. Wow, that hurt! Luke rubbed his jaw again, just thinking about it. Mark must work out . . . . a LOT!!

By the time Luke had recovered enough to chase after him, Mark had put about four blocks between them. But Mark only made it to that fourth block before he turned around. When Luke caught up, Mark was pacing back and forth at the corner and Luke braced himself for the argument that he knew would ensue.

"Where in the hell did you come from?" yelled Mark.

"Well."

"All this time . . . why didn't you tell me? Do you know what I went through when you died?" Mark continued to yell.

"Mark."

"Shut up and let me finish!"

"OK"

"So answer me, blast it!"

"Well, make up your mind, should I shut up, or would you like to know what's going on?" he asked quietly, hoping that Mark would follow suit. He didn't.

"You selfish, inconsiderate . . . . you were my best friend, we shared everything! I know what your ungrateful brains look like for heaven's sake! Where have you been?"

"Mark, wait just a minute."

"And how in the heck do you still look like you're 25?" Mark stopped pacing back and forth and stared at Luke. "Holy smoke! You look like you're still 25!" Mark's ranting stopped immediately and the look of shock he'd sported in the coffee shop returned to his face now. "What happened to you, Luke?"

"Mark, I want to tell you everything, but standing on the corner of a busy intersection would not be prudent or comfortable. I have a hotel room just down the block from KeKe's, in the other direction! Let's go there, if you have some time. You need to clean up anyway." Luke pointed to Mark's once beautiful shirt.

"Shoot!" Mark looked down at his shirt and grimaced. He pulled his cell phone from his pocket and punched in a number. He waited for the party to pick up. "Hi, Moneypenny!"

"Moneypenny?!" Luke inquired.

He waved him off and continued the conversation. "What's my schedule look like for the next couple of hours?" he paused as Moneypenny answered. "Reschedule that for later this afternoon." After another pause he continued. "I can't make it, I have an apparent emergency, something's come back to haunt me." He looked directly at Luke. There was another pause, he chuckled, "No, it's not the IRS, those deductions *were* legit! I promise I'll be in the office after lunch" another pause, a deep sigh left his lips accompanied by a smile. "Yes, I'll tell you everything then . . ." he chuckled again. "Yes, I'll even describe my cell mates in minute detail! Thank you, Moneypenny. Bye!"

"Moneypenny?" Luke enquired again. He remembered Mark's greatest hobby. After long hours in surgery, his favorite pastime was watching movies. He had a movie collection at home that rivaled Block Buster's. Often times during surgery, he would challenge his surgical team to try to stump him by throwing out lines from movies. He had not failed to guess the movie of any line they had given him to date. So it did not surprise Luke that he had taken up nicknaming his employees after characters in his favorite movies; Moneypenny stolen from the screen of the James Bond movies.

"So, why Moneypenny?"

"Moneypenny is in love with James, and I think he loves her too, but they never get it together; each somehow afraid to mess with the relationship for fear of losing it. Lisa, my secretary, and I have the same situation. I don't want to lose the best secretary I've ever had by dating her and possibly messing the whole thing up."

"That's the stupidest thing I've ever heard. If you love her, go get her." Luke blurted out.

"You haven't been back in my life long enough to get to have an opinion about my love life. Now tell me what's going on as we walk to that hotel room of yours."

"Ok, but later you have to tell what the whole, deductions, IRS, and cell mates thing is about."

"Fair enough."

Luke wrinkled his brow and scratched the side of his cheek as he asked, "Say, why didn't you ever give me a movie nick-name?"

"You, Luke, already have one!"

"I do?"

"The force you must use, Luke. Come to you it will!" Mark replied in a very close imitation of Yoda.

"Oh how original, Yoda!" Luke returned to their previous conversation. "Well, as you already know, I didn't die in that car wreck eight years ago."

"Mmmm," Mark acknowledged the obvious.

"I was being chased, Mark. I'm not the same person as I was before the life saving brain surgery you did on me. Something changed. You remember all the things that kept appearing in the room. I was thirsty and suddenly a large, ice-cold, water appears on my bedside table? Then I complain that I'm cold and poof, I have my own blanket from home? Do you remember all that? It was like having my very own fax machine but it transported three dimensional things too. I know you thought I was nuts, but you couldn't figure out where it came from either."

"Sure I did. That beautiful girl brought it to you . . . by the way, what happened to her?"

"She didn't bring anything and you're getting ahead of me. Let me finish!"

The two had reached the hotel and Luke paused his narration as they walked through the lobby, took the elevator up two floors, turned right, walked down the hall and stopped in front of the third door on the left. Luke dropped his key card into the slot in the door and opened it. It was a nice room with a refrigerator and a small bar. There was a small table and two chairs by the front window as you entered with a couch, end table and easy chair all against one wall facing a large TV. This room connected to a hallway leading to the bathroom and a separate bedroom. Luke hurried to the back bedroom and came out with a clean shirt for Mark.

"Cotton for silk? It hardly seems fair." Mark changed but didn't miss a beat in the conversation. "OK, keep going with the story . . . . uh, things appearing with no explanation."

"Yeah, well . . . . then some girl comes in and explains it all away for you by saying she did it. But you didn't see what I saw. I knew she didn't bring all that stuff. I thought something and it was suddenly there. Then she steps out for a minute and some guy shows up asking questions about the girl and telling us she's his sister. When she walks in she obviously doesn't know him from Adam. But we think she's just some wacko off the street and we let him take her. Remember?"

Mark made no attempt to stop him or to interrupt, so Luke kept going, "Mark, that guy *was* from a scientific lab that researches telepaths. That girl was a telepath. She was drawn to me telepathically because I had become a telepath during your miraculous surgery. She didn't know they were after her or she would have taken other precautions. They got her, but they didn't realize that she was visiting me because I had become a path also. They missed me somehow. It was an accident that they realized and tried to rectify about two days later. The girl must have said something that finally led them back to me. But by that time I had been whisked away by another pair of paths."

Mark was mulling all this over in his head. He remembered Luke telling him about things appearing and disappearing, but he didn't believe it then and he didn't believe Luke now. He didn't seem to notice when Luke, looking frustrated with the way things were going, handed him another cup of coffee from KeKe's. Mark took a sip before he realized that the coffee had appeared out of nowhere. Mark did a double take.

"Where'd this come from?" Luke just smiled. Mark's eyes widened to twice their normal size. "You can really do it?!" he said, more a statement than a question.

Luke rolled his eyes, "That's what I've been trying to tell you!"

Mark nearly spilled the rest as his hands began to shake. Then he looked into Luke's eyes, eyes that were too blue. He looked at his face and saw the forty-seven year old who looked not a day over twenty-five. His hold on reality got as shaky as his hands. Something had definitely happened to Luke. No amount of plastic surgery could keep a guy looking this good. He started to believe. It was hard not to believe when he held the evidence in his hand. It had been a long time since he had a friend that was as good a friend as Luke . . . actually; it had been exactly eight years. Luke had never lied to him before, about anything. Well, unless you count the whole, fake death and making Mark suffer through being a pall bearer, and not telling the truth for eight years thing.

After taking another sip he finally asked," What happened to the girl, Luke?"

"Her name was Regina. She's dead. The lab boys thought they could open her brain up and see how it had been changed by surgery. There are no paths that have not been through some trauma and subsequent brain surgery. She was their guinea pig. They wanted to know what caused it. Tests didn't reveal it, they opted to open her up and look. She never made it off the table."

"How do you know that?"

"I've been inside their facility with Rick and Sophia Dasher."

"Who are they?"

Luke began to tell Mark all about his time with the Dashers, starting with his abduction, describing their attempt to rescue Regina and ending with his trip back home. Mark listened patiently, taking sips of his coffee as they went along. During a pause in the narration, Mark glanced down into his cup.

"You wouldn't want to whip up a croissant from the Champs d'Elysees, would you . . . for an old friend?"

"For an old friend, anything!" Luke produced a fresh croissant.

Mark admired the fresh flaky French crescent. One bite sent him into his own world of culinary ecstasy. His eyes rolled up into his head and he closed them to enjoy the bite as memories of Europe flooded his mind. He did not linger long there, however. After chewing for a moment, he swallowed, took a deep breath and a sip of coffee. He looked back at Luke and said, "OK, go on."

Luke told him all about his new place and the hideout beneath it. Mark asked questions as the conversation evolved. Finally, Luke had finished and Mark was left to ponder for a few minutes.

"So, if I believe all this, why are you here now? And you never answered the question about why you look like you're about twenty-five rather than forty-seven."

"First the easy answer, another path quirk is that the mind begins to fix things about the body that it always wanted to fix but didn't have the power to fix before. I happen to like very blue eyes. Shortly after my surgery, my eyes started to deepen in color. They are a shade that I like. I also noticed that my skin improved and I began to see improvement on other things, my abs and the muscles in my legs. My hair started to change too, all of the gray just started to melt away the same way it came. Before I knew it, I was looking like a lean, mean, college machine. Physicals I've had since then have also indicated a younger health age. My blood pressure is down and my cholesterol is perfect. What a hoot! You should see Rick and Sophia, they're in their sixty's but they look as young as I do."

"I had noticed some of this after your first surgery, but I assumed that it was the result of the research hospital you had supposedly been to. But I figured it would wear off sooner or later . . . . I guess it doesn't wear off, huh?!"

"I don't know if it will sometime, but it hasn't yet!"

"I should have charged you for that surgery! I should have charged you a lot!! So all I have to do to look like you is ram my BMW into a light pole, injuring my head and then do surgery on myself to unleash this effect in my brain?"

"Yeah, something like that. Which leads me to why I'm risking my life to see you. Another little gift that paths have is the ability to feel when a possible mind mate is coming to the crossroads of becoming a path. We are drawn to our mates in a sense. My mate is drawing near to that moment. She will be injured somewhere in Laramie, Wyoming. At least that's the town I keep thinking about and dreaming about. I am being irresistibly drawn there. I think it will happen in the next couple of days. I need you to be in that town when it happens. If you aren't there to operate on her, she may not live through the experience. If she does live through the experience, I may need you to help me get her out of there before the labbies get a lead on it. It won't take them long. Once they know there has been a severe brain injury, they'll come. They check them all out as soon as they hear about them. If we're lucky, there will be an accident somewhere else first. They'll check it out before us."

Mark winced and Luke realized how callous he sounded. "Sorry," he said, "but I'm just thinking of getting in and out without lab intervention. Are you in?"

"Leave my work for two days for a possible wild goose chase? You know, if I wasn't looking at you and seeing your twenty-five year old face, drinking coffee and eating a croissant that you acquired out of thin air, I'd swear you had jumped off the deep end. Everything you've said is so wild. It's so difficult to get my mind around! But I can't help being curious. I'll be there. Should I have a cover story? Just in case?"

"Yes, I thought about that, UW has a nursing program. Care to go enlighten them on the benefits of becoming surgical nurses?"

"No, but I will, just to see what this 'mate' of yours looks like . . . . if it happens at all!" The thought had occurred to Mark that Luke may end up being pulled into a relationship with a woman who could possibly end up looking like a bull dog in drag. What if she was really fat? Or super skinny? Of course, all those possibilities could be overcome by path acquired abilities but what if she was a nagging whiner? Or what if she were an 80 year old woman . . . OR A TODDLER! This he had to see, even at the risk of wasting a fair amount of time. "Oh, and, Lazarus, if it doesn't happen, you owe me a return trip to Europe!"

"Lazarus, the man who returns from the dead . . . . funny. You got it!" Luke replied as his mind brushed quickly through some of the best memories he had. Memories of their college days and walking the cobbled streets of Paris and later Rome, all the while looking for French or Italian 'honeys' with whom to spend their evenings strolling and dancing. They would both need the trip before this adventure was over.

CHAPTER 3

Invaders

Luke stood there for one more moment looking over the town from the top of Pilot Peak road, turned and headed for his navy blue Jeep Cherokee. He climbed in and headed down to town. It would happen today he thought. Maybe tomorrow, but he was beginning to feel a pull to a specific place. He drove into town until he found himself turning into a corner parking lot. There was a little school right in front of him. The name on the building read Snowy Valley Elementary School. There was a small convenience store across the street and directly in front of the little school's parking lot. Across the street to the right of the school, with a small field between them, stood a large hotel. The school faced Grand Avenue, the main road through town and the playground took up the western side of the building and was plainly visible from the parking lot. Luke pulled into a parking spot and stopped. It felt like the right place. Now what? Just wait?

Kassidy Dover was a wonderful teacher. She was the kind of teacher that her little second graders were just sure the sun rose and set on. The boys doted on her and the girls tried to be like her. She was tall and lean, with long dark hair and green eyes. She had a cheery, playful disposition to which children responded well. She had a large class of twenty-five students, but she had a very diligent aid in her classroom that helped to keep papers graded, attendance taken, pencils sharpened, and who stepped in anytime she was needed. She felt very lucky to have Shelby Pierce as an aid in her classroom.

Today had proven to be one of those rare warm spring days in Laramie. It was May 20, and Kassidy and Shelby had decided to skip spelling today and take the kids out for an extra recess to celebrate a day without wind or snow. It was about forty-five degrees outside . . . positively balmy, relatively speaking, and the tough Wyoming children were all begging to be allowed to take off their winter coats to play. Kassidy finally gave in but opted to keep her own coat on. She had lived all over the world as a kid. Her father had been in the Air Force and had taken their family to Germany, Guam, Hawaii, Idaho,

Japan and finally back to Germany for her last three years of high school. She had graduated from Ramstein American High School on Ramstein Air Force Base near Kaiserslautern, Germany in 1999. She had then gone to college at Oregon State University in Corvallis, Oregon graduating in 2003 and finished her Master's Degree from the University of Phoenix in 2005. Having had no real hometown to speak of, she had decided to come to Laramie and live with her parents until she secured a teaching position here. She was picked up the next fall by Snowy Valley Elementary and had moved into her own house the very next year. Having spent so much time in mild climates, she hated the weather in Laramie. She was also not very fond of the good-ole-boy system that seemed to permeate the small town, but she loved the people she worked with and the children in her class were her extended family.

Totally unaware that trouble was brewing, Kassidy had gone to work dressed in her favorite sage green brushed jeans, her matching sweater vest with the linen shirt with the little sprig of lavender flowers embroidered on the top center of the blouse. She had added a green stoned jewelry that her father had picked up in Iraq when he was there, but she could never quite remember the name of the beautiful stone. It resembled turquoise except that it was a forest green instead of blue. She topped the whole ensemble with her black, down coat that hit her just below the knees and sported faux fur around the hood. She loved that coat, especially on really cold Wyoming days when she had recess duty! Today, it was almost too warm for it . . . . almost.

Little Kenny ran up to her on the play ground breathless and in need of a playmate. He was a skinny little kid with short blond hair and bright blue eyes hiding out behind a set of smudged glasses. He was already missing one front tooth, making his smile all the more endearing. His pants were too short revealing socks that almost matched. His sweatshirt was a little too big, allowing the sleeves to completely cover his hands. He was one of her favorites, though she tried not to have favorites. He was very smart but with little to no parental support. His dad was non-existent except for a note on his registration paperwork that had said, "Kenny should never be allowed to leave the school with his father under any circumstances." She guessed that said it all.

"What would you like to play, Kenny?" Kassidy asked.

"I want to play space invaders." Kenny looked up expectantly.

"Are we the invaders or the invadees?' Kassidy asked, though she already knew the answer. They had played this game before and he always chose the same way.

"The invaders. I want to be the diabolical bad guys!" he smiled up at Kassidy.

Kassidy was amazed that a second grader would use 'diabolical' and asked him where he had learned a word like that and while she was at it, she wondered why he always wanted to be the bad guys.

"I learned that word by watching Sponge Bob," he beamed. "and I always like to be the bad guys because bad guys really kick butt!" His eyes twinkled as he described video battles he'd fought and won on his PlayStation II. It took him a while to actually describe the battles because he had to add sound effects as he went.

Kassidy listened intently to every word until they were interrupted by little Julie Snow, the smallest girl in the class. She had short straight black hair, light blue almost gray eyes, chubby cheeks and a dramatic take on life. She snuck up behind them and grabbed Kassidy around the legs hugging her close. "Guess who, Miss Dover!" she squeaked.

"Hmmm, could it be Joe Joe?"

"No," she giggled.

Principal Martin?"

Julie broke out in a gale of laughter, "No, no, no!"

It was at that moment that Kassidy noticed the man walking toward the play ground. There was something not right about him. What was it? His hands were stuffed deep into the pockets of his bomber style leather jacket and it looked as if he hadn't shaved in a couple of days. He had some good bed head going on but his clothes looked clean, if rumpled, and of high quality. She continued to stare. Shelby was only a couple of feet away from her and Kassidy called to her to please take the children in. The man continued toward them his cold hard eyes fixed on Kenny who played at her feet, still making the sound effects for his own private war with aliens.

"Shelby," she called again, "hurry!" Her eyes had not left the man's though his remained locked on Kenny.

As she said it, Kenny looked up into the face of the man. Kassidy looked down at Kenny at just that moment and saw real fear flood his face. She grabbed the boy and pushed him behind her as she stepped toward the man.

"May I help you, sir?" Kassidy asked, trying to muster courage as she remembered the note scribbled at the bottom of Kenny's registration papers. At the same time she motioned toward the door behind her back, hoping that Kenny was already following the other children toward the school door. When she felt Kenny grab her coat and pull her toward the door too, she knew they were in trouble.

"Get to class, Kenny!" she commanded firmly. "Sir, you are on school grounds without having acquired a pass, please enter through the front door and check in before approaching any students."

The man said nothing but pulled his hand out of his pocket. He was holding a hand gun. Kenny hadn't moved and was now screaming for his teacher to run with him. All Kassidy could think about was how to get Kenny out of this alive. She made a split second decision. She dove at the man, trying to take him down hard enough to hit his head on the pavement and possibly knock the gun from his hand, but Kenny was still holding tight to her coat and the man was about two yards away. She saw or maybe she heard the gun go off and then she heard nothing at all.

Luke had been watching the pretty teacher conversing with the boy and enjoyed her smile as she was attacked from behind by the little wisp of a girl whose laughter he could hear from his open window. He didn't notice the man approaching until he heard the teacher command Kenny to get to class. When he saw the man approaching as if on a mission, he knew he was in the right place and in that minute, he also knew who he'd been drawn to for the last few weeks. Still, he jumped from the car to try to avert the event he knew was destined to happen. He saw as he ran toward the man that the small boy was still behind his teacher and was pulling earnestly on his teacher's coat, begging her to run with him. He saw the man pull something from his pocket and point it at the teacher. Her eyes flew open wide and then filled with determination. He watched in amazement as the pretty teacher lunged toward the man. What was she thinking? Why didn't she run, for heaven's sake? Luke was almost there. He heard the shot at the same time he lunged for the shooter. He saw the teacher crumple, the boy still clinging to her coat, as he hit the gunman dead in the back. They fell, the gunman crashing forward hitting with his full weight on his jaw. The concussion stunned him and gave Luke the time he needed to kick the gun from his hands, roll him over and punch him once, twice, three times in the face.

After confirming that the gunman was indeed unconscious, Luke was up and running toward the teacher in a heart beat. He pulled his phone from his pocket only to discover that it had been crushed when he tackled the gunman. He slid down to his knees beside the teacher and pulled the sobbing boy from her body. "Son, go get the principal to call 911! Now!! Run!"

Kenny nodded his tear streaked face, looked back at the teacher he loved and then ran like a bullet toward the door, moving so fast that he nearly barreled through the principal in his race for the phone. But the principal caught him and held him tight.

"I gotta call 911 for Miss Dover!" he sobbed. "The man said I gotta get the phone! Please, let me call, I gotta call!"

"Kenny, I have the phone, we already called 911. They're coming! It's all right now; you go sit in the office. I'll be right in." the principal handed him over to the secretary who was standing behind her. Then she proceeded as fast as her heals would allow her to move to Miss Dover's side.

"Get away from her now!" she screamed at Luke misunderstanding the situation.

Luke wondered at that statement. If he'd been the gunman, the principal would now be on the ground with a bullet in her too.

Then she saw the gunman laying unconscious on the ground. She recognized him at once and surmised what had really happened. "Oh, sorry, how is she?"

"She'll be dead if we don't get her medical attention now!"

"I've called 911. They're on their way."

"Give me your phone! I know a brain surgeon who is in town. She's going to need him."

The principal handed him her cell and he punched in Mark's number. "Meet me at the hospital emergency room. Now!" He clicked off the phone and handed it back to the principal. As he looked up willing the ambulance to arrive, he noticed that several of the school staff had emerged from the building. One of the male teachers took to watching the gunman to make sure he didn't move before police arrived. The teacher seemed to take great satisfaction from sitting in the middle of the now awakening gunman's stomach. Every once in a while, he'd bounce just to get a reaction, while seeming to ignore the fact that he was intentionally keeping the man uncomfortable. All the while, his eyes never left Kassidy. "How is she?" He asked.

"I've got pressure on the wound, but if they don't hurry . . . ." Luke trailed off as he saw the ambulance approaching. Relief swept through him. He glanced down at the pale teacher, wishing her to move or blink, or something, but she didn't. The only evidence of life was the shallow breathing just perceptible in her breast as he held her.

As soon as the emergency technicians had her loaded in the ambulance and headed for the emergency room, Luke was in his jeep following closely. He pulled in seconds after the ambulance and beat them inside, glancing quickly around for Mark. Mark was already there and briefing the emergency room staff on what he would need. The surgical room was already being prepped for the operation.

"Thanks, Mark. I owe you." Luke said.

"My pleasure, is she a dog, old, fat, skinny? I can't wait to see who your mate is going to be!" He was chuckling at the thought of his old buddy being "mind mated" with a woman as plain as dirt for the rest of his life as he watched them wheel the teacher into the ER. The uglier she was the harder he would work to keep her alive, he thought mischievously. He grimaced as he looked at a very beautiful woman even drained of color, and near death. He would have had to eat his words, but duty called and he raced down the hall with Kassidy to begin the tricky surgery. He called over his shoulder to Luke, "Go get cleaned up, you're a mess!"

Luke looked down at his shirt and jeans, which were covered in blood and headed for the nearest bathroom. He washed his hands and removed his shirt. His jeans also needed replaced. He concentrated on a clean pair of jeans, T-shirt and a pullover sweater from his closet at home. The things appeared in his hands and he changed clothes. He concentrated on sending the bloodied clothes back to his washing machine and they disappeared.

Luke spent the next few hours running little errands. He stopped at the school and sweet talked the aid in the second grade class into giving up the teacher's purse for him to take to the hospital with him. That proved to be easier than he had anticipated. But then again, he had saved the teacher's life by taking the guy out before he could get another shot off. What's not to trust? He also gave her the story of having to have her purse for insurance and medical history checks. He assumed that had done it. Had he been able to read minds, however, he would have discovered the real reason was that he had very kind eyes, a trustworthy face, and the aid had a photographic memory and paid close attention to his license plates as he drove out of the parking lot.

His next stop was Kassidy's house. He discovered her name on her driver's license along with her address. She lived in a cute little two bedroom house a couple of blocks from the high school. It was lemon yellow with white trim. She had no flowers but a nice lawn looked to be thinking about turning green. The front door was forest green with beveled windows decoratively inlaid in the frame. The inside was decorated cutely, but Kassidy was not a neat nick by any stretch of the word. She was a stacker and a bit of a pack rat. Still, the dishes were done and the bathroom was clean. The bed was odd. It was queen sized, made up in a European style with a green fitted sheet on the mattress and only a big feather blanket decoratively covered with a sort of two sided white, green and blue sheet, like a blanket sized pillow case around it. There were two large feather pillows covered with the same sheet color as the blanket and two normal pillows with cases the same color as the fitted sheet. "That's interesting," he thought, "she's been to Europe too."

After that observation, he began to notice other things in the house from different parts of the world. Her jewelry box in the shape of a gondola with inlaid wood designs was obviously Italian. She had framed pictures on the wall opposite her bed that depicted scenes from the Middle East. There was a beautiful set of Japanese dolls in traditional dress protected within a glass case. A small china cabinet in the kitchen/dining room area contained an array of Polish pottery, a set of German crystal wine glasses and a beautiful glass ball hanging from an ornate silver stand with a small German village painted on the outside. The inside of the ball was designed to hold a small candle that when lit would illuminate the little village. In the center of the china cabinet there was a white figurine of Jesus with little children all around him. Luke wandered back to the bedroom and grabbed a small suit case from the top shelf of her closet and began packing a few essentials, jeans, socks, underwear . . . she was not going to be happy about that, some T-shirts, her tooth brush and tooth paste and a hair brush. That should get her by until it was safe to drop in for a repack.

All that was left before retuning to the hospital was to check into how much publicity the incident at the school had picked up. He was hoping that the press had been delayed at least for travel time but sure as spring skips Laramie every year, the press had already descended on the little school only two hours later. Students had been evacuated and sent home but some of the staff was outside huddled in an impromptu press conference. By this time, the police were there in full tilt; snooping around everywhere. Luke thought it a good idea not to even pull into the parking lot. He needed to keep his face out of the lime light and he hadn't delivered the purse to the hospital yet. Those were two good reasons to lay low for now. He left the area and returned to the hospital. He knew that the surgery would not be over for quite a while, but he was not prepared for the number of people in the waiting room already. He had to squeeze his way around them to get to the door to the corridor. He was stopped at the door by a policeman who wanted to know his business down the hall. He held up the purse and said that he was to deliver Kassidy's purse to the ER staff as soon as possible.

"I'll deliver it for you." said the policeman.

Luke decided to hand it over without a fuss to keep his anonymity. He made his way out of the emergency waiting room and around the outside of the hospital to the front entrance. He walked in and followed the information maps on the walls to the surgical wing. He found a little surgical waiting room and informed the attendant there that he was waiting for his friend Dr. Mark Johns.

"Oh, he must be the visiting surgeon the family called in for this one." she said.

"Uh, yes, he is." replied Luke. That was a little tidbit that he didn't know. Mark must have arranged that one. He'd ask him about it when he could. As he looked around he saw only two other couples in the waiting room, they were huddled together and one of the gentlemen carried an open Bible in his hand and was praying with them.

"Are they related to the teacher?" he asked.

"Yes, the gentleman and woman in the corner are her parents and the other gentleman is Pastor Don Forbes and his wife, Marilyn. He's the pastor of the

United Methodist Church here in town. What a message that man preaches on Sunday; straight from the Bible. I try to never miss, but when I have to work, I can catch it on the internet. The Dover's attend there also. What a tragedy it is that Kassidy was shot. We're not sure just what happened yet. Have you heard anything?" she looked hopefully up at Luke who was still standing at the desk. He would love to have told her about the heroic actions of the incredible woman lying in that operating room right now, but he didn't wish to encourage any confrontations with the press, so he shook his head regretfully.

"Well, you might as well get comfortable because I'll probably end my shift before that operation has finished." She smiled up at him pointing to the fluffy chairs in the waiting room. "There are some refreshments over in the left hand corner of the room and some coffee on the stand beside it. Help yourself."

Luke sat down opposite the worried couple. As he watched them from behind a magazine he found on the table beside him, he couldn't help but notice the family resemblance between the woman and Kassidy. Well, hair not withstanding. She was probably in her fifties's now, but was still a handsome woman. She had dark brown, shoulder length hair, graying around the temples with green eyes and an intelligent, kind face. She had a little more weight on her than her daughter, but it looked good on her and her choice of clothes indicated a comfortable pride in her appearance. Her eyes were brimming with worried tears and she clung to her husband as she strained to grasp whatever hope the pastor was offering.

Her husband was tall and lean, with the look of the military about him. He seemed calm in the face of this very stressful situation, but clearly worried about his daughter. Luke thought he must love her very much. It was going to be hard to take her away from them suddenly as he knew he would have to. He'd try to make it a short time, but there were no guarantees. He'd have to console himself by remembering that by taking her, he'd be saving her for them. It wouldn't be much consolation to them at first. They wouldn't know where she was, or if she was all right for a while. Maybe he could get word to them secretly. He would try.

CHAPTER 4

The Black Fight

How long had it been? Luke wasn't sure. He should have checked his watch when he came into the room. He'd been dozing, put to sleep by a silly magazine article on the life of some celebrity. His eyes cracked open sleepily. Then he saw her, the principal from the school. She was talking to the Dovers in the corner. When she turned to take a seat beside them she noticed Luke.

"Oh, you're here!" she said. "The police have been looking for you. They have some questions that they think you may be able to shed some light on. I couldn't even give them a name."

"I've been here for quite a while." Luke responded limply. He purposely skipped giving a name. He was thinking how glad he was that no one at the school had thought to ask him that, in all the excitement, he might have given them one.

"You were there?" asked Mrs. Dover. "Tell us what happened . . . please," she pleaded. "All we have been told is that she was shot by a parent who was after a student."

It was the least Luke could do. Luke looked over to the attendant's desk, relieved to discover that indeed her shift had ended and a new face now occupied the chair behind the desk. He said a quick prayer that the following story would wait a few more hours before it hit the front pages. Then he began. Luke told them of the impending danger, the recognition of that danger in Kassidy's face. He told them about her effort to get between the child and the killer. He described the look on her face as she made up her mind to take the man out or go down trying. Luke thought it prudent not to describe the shot and watching her drop as he dove for the man himself. He did tell them about knocking him down and rendering him unconscious before running to her. Luke finished by describing the bravery of the small boy and his race to the principal. When he finished, he looked up into the grateful eyes of Mrs. Dover though her eyes had overfilled with tears that were now streaming down her face full of pride as well as worry.

Even the principal had not heard the full story. She sat there mesmerized. Her eyes were frozen on Luke, seeing him and the whole event unfold before her mind's eye. It could have been disastrous . . . well, more disastrous than it had been. All the children had made it back in the school except for Kenny before Kassidy was shot. None of them were hurt and most had never known anything was wrong until they were dismissed from school into the care of nervous parents. As she thanked God for Kassidy's fast thinking a funny thought worked its way into her head. What had this handsome young man been doing parked in the parking lot? He wasn't a parent. She'd have remembered a face like his. The closest store was across the street and had its own parking lot. Why did he just happen to be there at just the right time? She decided to ask him.

The question blindsided Luke. He hadn't thought to come up with a reason for being there. His mind scrambled for a plausible answer. What was he doing there? He couldn't very well tell them that he was waiting for someone to have a tragic accident now could he? Then he had it. "I am new to town and I pulled into the parking lot to check my map. I was looking for the main streets in town when I heard a child laughing and I looked up to see Miss Dover with a little girl wrapped around her legs. The two were having such a good time that I continued to watch. Then I saw the man and the rest is history."

"Wow, we were certainly lucky today. Well, luckier than we could have been," the principal corrected. Luke was relieved that he saw total belief in her face.

The hours continued to tick by. Luke wasn't sure how long they waited, but he was glad that he at least had time to get to know Kassidy's parents a little. Of course, they probably weren't at their best, strained by the weight of the situation. But it was a unique look into her life as he watched them and their friends dropping in by two's and three's and listened to small talk and well wishes.

He had dozed off again when he felt someone sit in the seat next to him. He shook himself awake and looked to see who it was. It was Mr. Dover this time.

"Don't take this wrong, but why are you still here?" Mr. Dover asked more curious than anything. "Everyone else comes and goes, but you have stayed right here. Why? And while I'm at it, who are you?"

"I'm a very good friend of Dr. Johns. We were going to meet in Laramie since he was speaking at UW this weekend. We were going to catch up and grab a meal together. It's been a while since we've had the opportunity to see each other." The lies were getting easier. Luke wasn't sure that was a good thing, but he had no choice at this point.

"Oh. Well, I didn't get the chance to thank you for everything you did, Mr . . . ." Mr. Dover waited for Luke to supply a name.

" . . . uh . . . Thomas, . . . Paul . . . Thomas." Luke lied. Mr. Dover had been holding a copy of a Bible in his hand and had been playing with the little ribbon attached to the top of the binding that is used for a marker, sliding it in and out as he talked to Luke. So, it was a natural thing for Luke to choose a couple of names from the Bible for this little lie.

"Nice to meet you, Mr. Thomas." Mr. Dover chuckled lightly. "It occurs to me that I have Mark Johns doing surgery on the daughter that Paul Thomas just saved. All very prominent Biblical names. Must be a God thing." His eyes had wandered down to the Bible as he thought about that and Luke got the impression that he could see right through that false name. He thought about what Mr. Dover had said and realized that even if he'd given his real name, Mr. Dover would still be having the same little chuckle. Mr. Dover interrupted Luke's thoughts as he continued the conversation.

"Mrs. Martin, the principal told me that you called Dr. Johns in for us. We can't thank you enough. They didn't want to let him operate here, insurance purposes and everything, but when he explained to me that he had been called by someone at the scene and that his specialty was brain surgery, I consented. I asked for proof, of course, and as luck would have it, he had brought his credentials for his UW speech and pulled them out of his brief case. He even had his own insurance. After that, the hospital didn't have a problem with it. What a miracle! God is so good." said Mr. Dover.

"Yes, He is." replied Luke. Smart thinking on Mark's part he thought.

Another hour seemed to drag slowly by and Luke had found another boring article to lull him to unconsciousness when he felt a nudge on his shoulder. It was Mark, still in his scrubs. The Dover's hadn't noticed him yet as they were surrounded by another group of friends and they all had their heads bowed in prayer yet again. He gave Luke a silent thumbs up and whispered a room number to him. He was giving Luke time to get there before the family. Luke took it.

Mark caught him by the sleeve before he got out of the room and whispered "I won't be able to hold them long, check her, try to connect and get out of there . . . good luck, she'll be unconscious, I doubt you'll get anywhere." Luke nodded and left.

Luke hurried down the hall looking for the intensive care unit. When he found it, he scanned the room numbers before he found the one he was looking for.

"Excuse me," said a voice coming from the nurse's station. "May I help you?"

"Dr. Johns told me that I could spend a couple of minutes with Kassidy Dover," Luke said truthfully.

"Well, if Dr. Johns said it was all right, I guess it's OK. You know she won't be able to respond, she's still unconscious. Oh, and this is the part where I tell you 'only five minutes'."

"Yes, thank you, ma'am."

Luke entered the room and walked to her bed. She looked just as pretty as she had on the playground before the accident even with the white bandage covering most of one side of her head. He wasn't sure what he should do, but somehow he needed to connect with her. He wanted to have that connection before the lab boys made the scene. Once they were here it would be much more difficult. They could recognize him so he would have to stay out of sight. Luke took her hand and instantly let it go. He'd felt a pain in his head as if he'd been shot! What was that? He rubbed his head in the same place as the Kassidy's injury. Was this part of the connection? Feeling her pain? He braced himself and took her hand again. The pain was back again but he fought to keep his hand clasped to hers. He could no longer see the hospital room, only a dark corridor and a very dark blackness down the corridor.

"Kassidy," he called her name.

"Ohh . . ." she responded lightly.

When he heard her response, he seemed to turn toward the voice in his mind and toward the utter blackness and for just a moment, the pain lessened. Luke caught the difference even though it was only fleeting. Could he lessen the pain again? He turned again focusing all his attention on turning toward the blackness to face it. The closer he got to the blackness the more control he seemed to have over it. It was changing, it was moving away from him. He ran toward it in his mind . . . no in Kassidy's mind. Was that possible? Then he saw her. She was facing the pain and blackness right in front of him, but she seemed to be having trouble just standing. Her concentration was completely focused on the center of the blackness that echoed in both of their minds now as Luke moved forward and they stood side by side fighting together. Luke wasn't sure how they were fighting it, but he could feel the energy that it took. He could feel Kassidy's energy level dropping tangibly beside him. He fought harder, pouring himself out toward the blackness.

How long did they stand together? He wasn't sure. He felt her stumble beside him and he worked harder to fight the blackness for her. He wanted to take it all on for her. He reached out and took her hand in the blackness. Their energy doubled with the touch. He pulled her close to him, trying to support her as the energy poured forth from them both. The closer her body slid to his the more the energy between them intensified. It seemed as if electricity encircled them. It began to pulse, the beat intensifying with each touch. When he turned and took her other hand their hair began to fly in all directions. Though their bodies faced each other, their faces remained fixed on the fading blackness. Their bodies glowed in the darkness. Now he could feel the blackness receding and he chanced a look toward her. She, too, looked at him. He felt his breathing stop completely. She was glorious! Her eyes were an intense green like that of tropical ocean waters splashing on the soft white perfect sand trailing off into the depths. Her hair had found its way back down to her shoulders and had taken on a shine that invited an errant hand to slip through it. Her skin was rosy and creamy smooth. Luke would have reached up to touch her cheek, but he was afraid to let go of either hand. Her smile lit their minds with a blinding light, chasing the last of the blackness far from them.

"Luke! Are you all right? What's happening, Luke? Answer me!" Mark shook his friend, and Kassidy's hand fell from his. Luke was staring at Mark. A smile was still plastered to his lips as he remembered the radiant smile she'd given him. "What's going on, Luke?"

"She's fine Mark. In fact, she's better than fine and wait till you see her eyes!" Luke was weak but very excited. The combination was perplexing. He wanted to dance, to pick her up and float her around the room. He was so elated. But the fight within the blackness had taken everything out of him and he barely made the chair in the corner before he was completely unconscious.

Mark made a mental note to thank his lucky stars that he had told the family that they would not be able to see her for a couple of hours yet. He sent them for dinner in the hospital cafeteria with a promise to send for them if anything changed. Now he had a passed out friend in the chair next to her bed. What was he going to do with him? He turned back to check his patient. She was smiling! It was the same silly grin that Luke still had on his face. He thought she looked better in the silly grin than Luke did and made a mental note to tease him about that later.

He checked her vitals and was quite pleased to find she was recovering nicely despite the short time she'd been in ICU. He wondered what had gone on between the two of them. Actually, he wished he could have experienced it himself. Then he called in one of the orderlies to help him move his unconscious buddy to the bed in the next room.

CHAPTER 5

Clark Kent

"Hey, is anyone there?" Luke heard the voice . . . or did he just think it? Where was he anyway? He looked around. He was in a hospital bed. What happened? How did he get here? Then he remembered the ICU and his experience with Kassidy. He must be in a spare bed. *"Thanks, Mark"* he thought.

"OK, yes you heard me. I don't know where you are . . . actually, I don't know where I am either, but you must be in a hospital because that's what it looks like from here. I don't know what happened or how you got there but I remember the same black fight you do. Who's Mark? Oh, and, what is your name?"

"Kassidy?"

"Yes?"

"You 'heard' all that? You can read my mind?"

"Yes. I think you are reading my mind too, or listening to it anyway. Do you know where I am?"

"Just a minute, I'll come find you."

Luke got up off the bed, crossed the room and looked cautiously out the door. *"Are you alone in your room?"*

"I don't know, I think I'm still unconscious because I can't seem to open my eyes and my body feels too heavy to even think of moving. Name, please?"

"You're name is Kassidy." Luke responded distractedly. He was concentrating on scoping everything out, making sure there were no lab boys in the area yet.

"Wow, good thing you shared that little tidbit with me, I've been alive for about 26 years and I always wondered why everyone expected me to respond to them when they used the word Kassidy. But now I know . . . thanks to you . . . you're a life saver . . . are you still there?"

"Sorry, I'm a little distracted. Kassidy, I hate to break it to you before you are even awake and I appreciate that you are taking this mind reading thing so well, but we're in trouble and we have to get out of here . . . soon!"

"Sure, but I'm not going anywhere until I know who it is I'm going with. Of course, it would be very nice to see your eyes again . . . wow! And as for the mind reading thing, I'm still unconscious so this is probably a dream and dreams

don't usually scare me. I just enjoy them. I discovered a long time ago that I could manipulate dreams and change them if I don't like them."

"Ah, that explains it." Luke was in the room now and walked over to take her hand again. *"Can you see me now?"*

"Yes! You look just like you did last night, except you aren't smiling."

"We're in danger Kassidy. How are you feeling? Do you think you could be moved? Do you need anything? Do you think you could wake up yet?"

"No, I like this dream. I'm full of pain killers, you're holding my hand and you are gorgeous!" She looked into his blue eyes-incredibly blue—and smiled shyly. *"Wow, he is beautiful!"*

"You may be sorry you said that when you wake up and find me still beside you and in your head."

"I'll take my chances." She smiled at him. It took his breath away again. He could have stayed there forever but Mark had entered the room and pulled their hands apart. It was like losing a visual lead and Luke was irritated.

"Mark! What are you doing?"

"We have to get out of here. Now! They're coming down the hall, I recognized the guy from Regina's disappearance. They didn't see me, but they are bound to put it together, I'm going with you. Let's get her out of here. We'll have to roll her out in her bed. She can't be moved . . ." Mark quickly checked her recovery. "How is this possible?" Mark looked relieved but confused. "She's about a week into recovery already!" He disconnected her IV and the other machines hooked up to monitor her progress. "Guess we don't need to take the bed after all. We can just carry her!"

"What's going on?" Kassidy was irritated about the lost 'video lead' too.

"Just a minute, Mark, let me try something with Kassidy; maybe we can all get out of here together without carrying her past the hospital personnel or the press. Take my hand, Mark." Luke picked up Kassidy's hand again.

"Hi again!" he said when he saw her. Her smile was immediate. "Kassidy, I want you to think of a favorite place you'd feel safe in, but not your home, or your parent's home. Somewhere far away, OK?" He spoke the words for Mark's benefit.

Mark interjected, "Why don't you just think of your place Luke. We could get out of here sooner."

"Because, Mark, Kassidy's mind is still mending, it might be easier to go with her than to get her mind to go with me."

"This is fun! I'll show you one of my favorite places." She began concentrating and Luke saw many places spin by in her memory. The electricity they felt the night before began to build. It pulsed through them, intensifying with each breath. It was intoxicating. It felt like the room was shifting, Kassidy began to

giggle with the sensation. Luke felt the same elation he'd felt the night before and began to draw Kassidy closer to himself, partly thinking to increase the power, partly because he enjoyed the electric sensation that sizzled between them. It took Kassidy's breath away and she stopped giggling. She stopped breathing. Luke 'kept his fingers intertwined with Kassidy's in the hospital room as the electricity engulfed them and Mark.

Mark began his own little chant as the electricity reached his hand, flowed up through his arm and spread through his body. "Oh my goodness, oh my goodness, oh no, oh no, wow, oh WHOA!!"

When the spinning stopped, Mark and Luke found themselves trying to catch Kassidy before she hit the cobbled stone of the courtyard they were standing in. It was pitch black except for the door light at the entrance to the courtyard. Luke caught her under her shoulders and swung his arm under her knees, to cradle her in his arms. Her head rested on his shoulder. She smelled like hospital antiseptic and lilacs. Luke would have enjoyed the lilacs, but he wasn't sure where the three of them had landed. Mark let go of them and looked around to get his bearings.

"Kassidy, where are we?" Luke asked.

"*Rothenburg, Germany. We are in a little café courtyard. But it's dark. Why is it dark?*"

"*You have your eyes closed.*" Luke replied. To Mark he said, "She says we're in Rothenburg, Germany. It's her favorite place."

"*But I can see what you're seeing. Why is it dark? I've never been here in the dark. I was hoping for some espresso and a brotchen.*"

"*You going to eat it while you're in an unconscious state?*"

"*It's **my** dream.*"

"Kassidy, we are really here and it was 7:00 p.m. when we left Laramie. What time would that make it here?"

"*Uh, about 3:00 a. m.*" she replied. "*Do you even* have *a name?*"

"Kassidy, we need someplace inside. You are still dressed in your hospital gown and we need to get you into a warm place."

"*Yeah, this dream is making me cold. I wish I had my feather blanket about now!*" The blanket appeared out of nowhere landing squarely on top of her and Luke.

"That's great, Kassidy, I can't see anything and my hands are full of you. You are not helping."

"*Yeah, but it sure feels good. I like this dream. In the arms of an angel with a fluffy blanket, all I need is . . .*"

"Stop it Kassidy, we need to get inside, please!"

Mark was pulling the blanket off of Luke and helping him wrap it around Kassidy. He couldn't believe what he was seeing. The blanket *had* appeared, just like Luke had told him when he was the one recovering.

"Holy smoke, it happened just like you said! Man, I'm sorry I doubted you! I saw it in the hotel room, and I see it now and I'm still having trouble believing it. Wow, thank heaven's we got her out of the hospital before that happened. At least the labbies didn't get to hear about that!" Mark exclaimed.

"Kassidy, we need to be inside. Do you know of an inside place that is not public right now at least? Mark, grab hold."

"Oh great, here we go again!"

She began to concentrate and before long they found themselves in what looked like a small room with about eight student desks, and a small teacher's desk in the corner. There were bits and pieces of student work hanging from the walls. They could see pretty well because of the street light outside the window. They were on the second floor of a school building, overlooking a cobblestone parking lot, situated in the middle of a quaint little German neighborhood.

"Mmmm, I love this place." Kassidy thought and snuggled closer to Luke in their minds though her body stayed relaxed and unconscious. She was very tired but unwilling to let go of the connection with . . . . oh what was his name anyway? She guessed she'd just have to make up a name for that lovely face. What should she call him? Maybe . . . Clark . . . . Kent. She erupted in silent giggles.

"What are you so amused about? . . . Clark Kent? You're going to call me Clark Kent? I hardly find that amusing. Why not just call me by my name?"

"I might, if you'd ever reveal your true identity."

"Oh, sorry! Luke, Luke Matthews."

"Oh, I like that. What is your side kick's name?"

"Mark Johns. And he is the real reason you are alive, so I guess that makes me the side kick and him the true super hero."

"So Luke Matthews and Mark Johns, have you two seen any of the apostles lately?" Kassidy broke out in another fit of mental giggles.

Luke sighed, *"Where are we now, Kassidy?"* To Mark he quipped, "You may have given her too many pain killers!"

"We are at Kaiserslautern Christian School. My mom worked here when my dad was stationed at Ramstein. She taught fourth grade. It's also a church. The school is up here on the second floor. The church and some Sunday school rooms are downstairs. They also have a preschool downstairs. The playground is outside in the courtyard. My brother put the woodchips under the playground for his Eagle Scout Project." Kassidy's mind wandered and she sighed," *I spent a lot of happy times here."*

"Mark, help me figure out where to put her."

"There are some lovely couches in the youth room in the basement and it's not used on weekdays, so we could catch a little nap. All this traveling around in my dreams is making me tired."

Luke relayed the message and the two men headed down the dark hallway and found the stairs that were light enough to see because of the same outside light reflecting in through another set of windows. The basement, however, was pitch black and they had to turn on a light to get settled.

"Find the light switch Mark"

"I'm looking for it, but it's not where it should be."

"Well hurry, she's getting a little heavy."

"Thanks a lot!"

"Sorry, Kassidy, but I've been carrying you for a while now."

"You're forgiven. The lights switches are about halfway down the wall and they are wider and longer than American light switches."

"Thanks," Luke thought, and then he relayed that message to Mark.

The lights flashed on and revealed a youth room with couches lining the brightly colored walls. There was a small stage in the corner with microphones, stands, amplifiers, drums and a keyboard. This youth room looked like a fun place to hang out . . . for a teen. Luke found a soft couch for Kassidy and laid her carefully down covering her with her blanket. He let go of her and was sorry as soon as he did. He already felt a little lost with out the close contact. But she needed to sleep. She also murmured a small protest, but slipped into sleep too quickly to pursue it.

Mark checked her wound and exclaimed at how much it had healed. She didn't even need the bandage anymore! She still had no hair on the spot, but if she had healed that much in only about a day and a half, she would probably have hair in place by lunch time tomorrow. Too bad all his patients didn't recover this quickly. Speaking of his other patients, he was going to have to get back to his practice very soon. They were expecting him back by . . . . he wondered what day it was today anyway. Now that he was in a different time zone, he was all messed up. Maybe he had jet lag. No that couldn't be it . . . no jet! He laughed at his own little joke. He found a comfortable couch, turned around to see that Luke was sleeping on the couch right next to Kassidy's, reached up and turned off the lights and went to sleep himself.

CHAPTER 6

Rerun

It was about five in the morning when Kassidy began to break out of unconsciousness and into normal sleep patterns. The first visual evidence was when her right hand flipped up over her head and across the armrests of both her couch and the one Luke was sleeping on. Her hand hit him square in the nose. It startled him for a moment, but he smiled and moved her hand to his cheek. He continued to sleep, feeling the warmth of her hand next to his cheek.

Kassidy was at school again. She looked around at the children on the playground. She was searching for him. There he was, still wearing the pants that were too short, showing off his almost matching socks. She was relieved that he was all right. She caught his eye and he came running to her.

"Want to play with me, Miss Dover?"

"What are we playing, Kenny?"

"Space Invaders!"

"Are we the invaders or the invadees?"

The dream progressed just as that last day in school had. Kassidy watched it move from moment to moment until she saw the man. The fear was back and the determination to keep Kenny safe. She knew what would happen, but she couldn't manipulate this dream as she usually did. She tried to scream, but she was stuck in the dream. Her body began to sweat and toss and turn.

Mark woke up when he heard both Kassidy and Luke moan at the same time. He reached up to turn on the light at the same time that Luke jumped from his couch and slid over to Kassidy's couch. He caught her as she lunged in her dream. She'd have fallen off the couch, if he hadn't been there to catch her. She fell limply into his arms. As he wrapped his arms around her, he turned and slid into the couch holding her on his lap and stoking her hair.

"Kassidy, it's OK. Everything's OK. He's gone."

Kassidy woke up completely, her eyes wide with terror. She tried to breathe; unable to let out the scream she felt building within her. Uncertain of where she was, she tried to push away from Luke. But Luke was not letting go. He seemed to know what she needed instinctively. She looked up into incredible eyes. Her face registered recognition, and then it was gone. She tried to remember from where she knew him. He looked like . . . . who . . . oh, yeah, Clark Kent. Why was Clark Kent holding her? The dream rushed back to her. Her hand went to her head injury and realization dawned on her. It wasn't just a dream. It had been real. Panic swept through her. *"Kenny, what happened to Kenny?"*

"Kenny's fine. Everything is all right." Luke assured her.

Kassidy began to cry, then to sob. Luke held her close, feeling all the worry and fear as it rolled down her cheeks and slowly out of her system. He breathed in the lilac scent of her hair. What had he been so afraid of way back when he had resisted the call? Oh yeah, the decision. He wanted the decision of a mate to be his. But somehow, he couldn't imagine not listening to her every thought, though he was a little resistant to her listening to his every thought. Still, it saved a lot of time!

The tears subsided and she began to think again. "How do you know Kenny's all right?"

"I was there."

"I thought I was dead."

"No, Mark, here, saved you. He's a brain surgeon."

Mark smiled as he checked her wound again and took her pulse. "Yeah, but don't worry, you don't owe me anything, Luke is picking up the tab!" He winked at her.

The thoughts began to come too fast to voice them. *"Who saved Kenny? What happened to the guy with the gun? I think he was Kenny's dad. Was he Kenny's dad? Did Kenny see him shoot me? He must have! Oh, poor Kenny. Does he think I'm dead? I have to see Kenny!*

Luke kept up with her thoughts. *"I did. Police got him. Yes, he was. Yes, he did. Kenny was brave. He ran for the phone to call 911. He knows by now that you are alive. NO WAY!*

That brought her up short. "What do you mean, No way? Why can't I see Kenny? Of course, I'm going to see Kenny. Who do you think you are, . . . Clark Kent? Let go of me!"

"You must still have your way with words, Luke. So what did you say to her to produce that response?"

She pushed away and stood up. *"What was he talking about? He was sitting right there. How could he have missed that whole conversation?"* She was still wondering about that when she realized she was still in her hospital gown. She turned at least three shades of red, grabbed her blanket and pulled it around her. "Where are my clothes?! Who are you guys?!"

Mark fielded that one with a bow. "Mark Johns brain surgeon extraordinaire, at your service. And this is my good friend, Laz . . . . Luke Matthews . . . . uh, what is it *you* do Luke?"

Luke gave him an unamused stare. Kassidy took the first real look at her surroundings. "I know this place. How did we get here? What are we doing here? How long have I been out?"

"You brought us here. We're hiding out. You've been out for about two days."

"What?!"

"Kassidy, let me show you what you missed. It'll be easier. But you have to trust me for just a minute." He crossed to her and held out his hands. "Take my hands."

She threw her hand up to stop him from approaching. "No. Just stay away from me!" Panic was beginning to rise in her again as she realized she was in a foreign country, in a hospital gown, with only her blanket and two guys she didn't know. "How did this happen?" She wondered.

Luke looked deep into her eyes and spoke to her telepathically as loudly as he could. *"Take my hands, now, Kassidy!"*

She flinched at the vibrations in her head . . . . he had yelled at her! She couldn't believe he actually yelled at her! No, *he* hadn't yelled, he hadn't moved his lips! *"How did he do that?"*

"You can do it too. You are the one doing it now actually, you are reading my mind. But it's easier if you take my hands."

Kassidy quickly assessed the situation. She was clearly at their mercy anyway, so she guessed taking his hands was not too much of a stretch. She took his hands cautiously. She 'saw' him walking toward her. The memories came crashing back to her. The fight with the blackness, the way he stood fighting with her, pulling her close to him, the trip to Rothenburg, and then here . . . . what had she called him? A gorgeous angel? Now embarrassment flooded through her. She saw the laughter in his eyes before she heard it with her ears. She decided that now was the time to exercise a good defense with a great offense.

"Tell me everything I missed."

Luke allowed her to 'see' everything that had happened. It was sort of like downloading a book onto your computer. He watched her face change expressions with each scene. It could have been funny, if the situations hadn't been so grim. She had to watch it all from his point of view, of course and for the first time saw the whole shooting looking at herself as he had. She looked amazed when she saw Luke punching the guy in the face, and then running to her. Her worry and sorrow were evident as Luke pulled Kenny off of her. She was mortified when she got to the part where he packed her bag, rummaging through her drawers, picking out clothes. When he got to that part he saw her eyebrows crunch together and a definite scowl cross her face. He tried not to notice. He thought about going back to the 'punching out the bad guy' scene but time really didn't allow it.

"You went through my drawers?!" she still looked horrified and very angry all at the same time. "Where *is* my bag? At least I can change out of this thing." As she continued to hold his hands, she discovered the answer to that question also. "So, you don't even have it here! What am I supposed to do? Run around Europe with a big feather blanket wrapped around me?" She continued to talk out loud having still not figured out that Luke could hear each thought before it left her lips. But Mark was enjoying the whole scene even though he was only getting half of it.

"I can't wait to hear the answer to that question," piped in Mark

Luke glared at him and letting go of Kassidy's hands answered them both. "Kassidy, remember when you thought of your blanket and it appeared?"

Kassidy's brow crunched together tighter. She seemed to be struggling with the impossibility of conjuring a feather blanket out of thin air and the reality of remembering the 'dream' and having the blanket now wrapped snuggly around her.

"I remember dreaming that happened."

"Kassidy, it wasn't a dream. The blanket is real and you brought it here. You are a path. There are things you can do that others can't."

"Yes, I'm quite a good teacher, but I've never had the 'gift' of three dimensional faxing."

"Not before, but you do now!"

Kassidy raised one eyebrow, "Wow, this is some dream within a dream, I'm having. Freud would love this! Probably means I'm insecure and need a super power to feel important!"

"That's not it!"

"Maybe if I just lie down and go back to sleep my alarm will go off and I can get up and go to school! Wait until Jeanine hears about this dream!"

"Jeanine?"

"School librarian. She's looking for a good idea to write a book." Kassidy walked back to the couch to curl up and sleep again."

"Kassidy, this is not book fodder—this is real!"

"That's what all my dreams that look like Clark Kent say." She yawned.

Luke rolled his eyes and sighed in exasperation. "Kassidy, do you dream in color?"

"Sometimes."

"Figures! OK, when you dream, do you dream in detail? Can you see things like wall color, wallpaper design, or textures . . . can you feel textures?"

"Yes, if I make myself concentrate on them."

"Ugh!" Luke threw up his hands in exasperation. "You are not dreaming!"

"Sure!" she started to feel sleepy again but then her eyes popped open wide! "But I never lay down to go back to sleep in a dream! Sometimes I want to, but never can seem to accomplish it!"

"Well, if it will help you believe—try sleeping for awhile. If you accomplish it, you'll know in the morning."

"OK," Kassidy's voice was uneasy. If this was a dream, it was disturbing. It was like being in a dream, within a dream that threatened yet another dream. How odd!

She slept again for a couple of hours. Mark was back asleep shortly too, but Luke couldn't quite turn his mind off. He remained awake, watching this beautiful woman sleep peacefully, knowing she was in for many surprises and hoping she'd awake ready to face them.

When she did finally wake up, she opened her eyes in the dim light seeping from a small basement window indicating early morning, to see Luke, watching her from a chair across the room. At first she just laid there while a troubled expression began to creep across her face. She stayed still, feeling the blanket wrapped snuggly around her, paying close attention to the texture of the couch, the way her ear was smashed against the armrest by the weight of her head resting on it. She noticed the colors of the room, Mark's soft snores and Luke's piercing eyes.

"You're still here and my alarm didn't go off!"

They were quiet for a while. Then Kassidy sat up. "This is real, isn't it?"

"Yes."

"You and your perfect face are real and we are really in Germany?!"

"Yes."

"What's going on?"

"First, why don't you get dressed?!"

She gave him a look that said, "Yeah, right, into what?"

"Think about the outfit you would like to wear . . . but not anything from the bag I packed because we don't know if the labbies have it yet, and concentrate on wanting it.

"Well, OK . . ." she rummaged through her closet in her mind, deciding what kind of outfit a person on the run would wear. Her favorite jeans, her periwinkle turtleneck sweater, socks, clean underwear and tennis shoes appeared in a neat little pile on the couch. She stood staring in shock at their appearance.

"I see it, but I can't believe it."

Mark had awaken and smiled at her. "It was tough for me too, but seeing isn't believing, believing is seeing!" he smiled. "Little quote from the movie 'The Santa Clause' . . . not sure what it means but I bet it applies . . . somehow!"

Kassidy smiled at him, took the clothes and went into the next room to dress. When she returned Luke had produced brotchen, cheese, lunchmeats, fruit and coffee.

"Wow, my favorite European breakfast!" exclaimed Kassidy. "Guess I'll have to forgive you for your breach of privacy into my underwear drawer. I can't remember ever being this hungry," she said as she dug in, making a brotchen sandwich and choosing a cluster of big green grapes.

"Thought you'd like it!

"Wait a minute," she paused mid bite, "Where did you get this?"

"I 'borrowed' it from a nearby bed and breakfast."

"You borrowed it?! You didn't pay for it?" Before Luke could register what she was up to she thought about the 40 Euros she had left over in her purse from her days living in Germany. They appeared in her hand. The disbelief registered again in her eyes but only for a minute this time. She handed them to Luke and told him to pay for the breakfast.

"Where did you get this?" Luke asked.

"I had it left over from when I lived here." Kassidy gave all her attention to the sandwich in her hand and began to devour it like she hadn't eaten in weeks. "I kept it in my purse for lack of a better place."

Luke glanced at Mark. "They know where to look, and now they know for sure that she's a path." Luke turned back to Kassidy. "From now on, ask me before you 'think' of something you need."

"What . . ."

"Mark needs to get back to his hospital before he is missed. Also, I need to get my jeep out of Laramie before they find it. I don't think they can trace it to me but I don't want to take chances. So I think we need to head back to Laramie very briefly. I think Kassidy is well enough to have her mind do the transporting while I do the navigating. We can drop Mark at his car, pick up my jeep and head to my place. But we need to find out if they have gotten to the cars before we pop in on them. We'll have to stop at my place first and check out the news."

"Wait, who are 'they'? Why are they searching for us? AND why do I have to 'clear' my thoughts with you?" Kassidy was still confused and becoming angry again.

Luke picked up her hands again and showed her what had happened to Regina with the labbies. He showed her the face of the guy who had taken Regina. *"You are no longer just a school teacher,"* he explained. *"You are one of a small minority. We call ourselves 'paths' because our minds are capable of incredible things. We acquired our talents when we were injured and needed brain surgery. The brain surgery somehow releases the telepathic powers and voila! The lab guys want to be able to reproduce that same effect in anyone, but they haven't figured out how to do that. They try to find paths to continue their research; however, they have eventually killed every one they have captured. The surgery we paths went through when we were initially injured is tricky enough, tampering with it is fatal."*

Kassidy's face had lost its color. *"How am I going to go back to my class?"* she thought.

"You aren't. At least, you aren't for a while. You can't return to Laramie, or your life until it's safe. I've been working on a plan to shut the labbies down. Until we take them out, completely out, we will never be safe." Actually, he hadn't come up with any solid ideas about how to take the labbies out, but he figured Kassidy needed a little hope about now not more worries. He figured this little white lie wouldn't hurt too much. He kept that thought buried in the back of his mind away from Kassidy's awareness . . . he hoped. He needn't have worried, she was already thinking of other more pressing things.

"I have to see my parents, to let them know I'm OK . . . I can't just leave them worrying! And, Kenny, I have to make sure Kenny is OK. He's going to be so messed up over this."

"No, Kassidy. We'll try to get news to your parents, but Kenny is definitely out. Your parents will be difficult enough. If the labbies get even a hint of your where-abouts, they'll come after you with a vengeance. Although your disappearance from your hospital bed only hours after major surgery probably tipped them off to your telepathic abilities, you can bet on the fact that they knew the contents of your purse. They know the Euros have gone missing. They know you are a path and they know you are in Europe. They will start looking in places you are familiar with from your past." Luke had spoken out loud to include Mark in the conversation. "Actually, Mark, you may be in danger also. We are going to have to come up with a plausible cover for you too!"

"I've been thinking about that. The last time I performed one of these surgeries was on you, then your parents had you moved from the hospital room. Well, at least I thought they had you moved. I was furious! I ranted and raved to no avail, of course. Why won't that work again? I can arrive at the hospital to check on my patient after a good rest, only to discover that my patient is missing. I throw a suitable fit about hick hospitals that can't seem to keep track of unconscious patients and then I head back to my practice leaving instructions for them to call me immediately when they find my patient. It gets me off the hook and keeps you out of it. Then all you have to do, Luke, is keep Kassidy hidden."

"What do you mean, 'keep Kassidy hidden!'? What am I supposed to do until you figure out how to shut these guys down? I'm not changing my life just because some stooges are jealous of . . . our . . . what did you call us? . . . . path . . . . abilities. I've got a life. I love my job. I don't want to change! You can't just kidnap me!" Kassidy's fit was stopped short as she looked into Luke's stubborn eyes. She saw no compromise there.

"You don't have a choice sweetheart." The way he used the term 'sweetheart' left no impression of endearment. The sarcasm dripped from it as Luke began to loose patience with Kassidy's inability to grasp the seriousness of the situation. "This is the way it has to be. Do you need to see what happened to Regina again?" Luke reached for her hand, but Kassidy pulled it away from him.

"*No.*" Kassidy didn't need to have that scene replayed again. She could still visualize it in her head. Regina had been on her stomach, the beautiful face, even in death, facing the side of the gurney with the back of her head opened and torn to pieces as if someone had been rummaging through her head just like Luke had rummaged through Kassidy's drawers.

As Luke looked into Kassidy's troubled eyes, even now deepening in color from a lighter hazel to a liquid exquisite green, he softened as he continued the conversation telepathically, *"I'm sorry, Kassidy. I wish it could be different, but until we nail these guys, I can't let you go back to work. At least they won't miss you for a while. They think you are in an intensive care unit somewhere. That will give us some time, though it won't be easy on you."* Luke wanted to comfort her, but there was nothing he could do. He knew that from having had to sever all his own ties. He knew what she was facing and that there was no comfort for it.

CHAPTER 7

A Change of Thought

After finishing their meal and cleaning up the area. The three gathered the big feather blanket, the hospital gown, and the left over breakfast and held hands for their trip home.

"Too bad we couldn't see some of Germany before we go," thought Kassidy.

"Yeah, that would have been nice." When Mark spoke, Kassidy and Luke nearly fell over.

"You heard that? You can understand what I'm thinking?" asked Kassidy.

"Yes! I can! *Can you understand what I'm thinking?"*

"Yes! Maybe it has to do with you touching us when we're touching! What do you think Luke?"

"I don't know. It's all new to me! I was never able to do any of this with out you, Kassidy."

Mark smiled widely, *"I like this! So Luke, remember the time we were in Rome and we picked up those two cuties in that little ice cream shop near the Pantheon? And yours turned out to be . . ."*

"Stop it, Mark, that is not funny!"

"OH, I think it's funny, tell . . . uh think more, Luke!" thought Kassidy, a very large smile crossing her lips.

"I think it is time for a change of thought." Luke began concentrating on his cabin in Mountain Meadows estates above Curt Gowdy State Park in Wyoming. As his mind settled into the living room, he began to feel the electrical energy pour through him and Kassidy and finally into Mark. Mark had begun his chanting ritual of "Oh my goodness, Oh no, oh no, oh, whoa!" They felt the rush and then they found themselves standing in the middle of Luke's living room.

Kassidy looked around the small living room. There was a wood burning stove in the corner with a comfortable couch along one wall under a picture window. The view was beautiful, overlooking rolling hills of prairie grass, shrubs and pine trees. Four deer with big ears pointing toward the cabin stood about ten yards from the front door. Their attention had been drawn to the cabin but when nothing moved, they continued their leisurely walk across the front yard.

Kassidy continued to look around the room. She noticed various pieces of art. Luke liked an artist by the name of Bev Doolittle. He had several of her prints, but Kassidy's favorite was a picture of an Indian with a wolf head dress on, sitting on a horse, overlooking a body of water. There was a rainbow circling away from the Indian's head to what at first looked like a rock in the water. But on closer reflection, she could see a wolf head formed out of the rocks and water hidden in the picture.

The kitchen opened up just off the living room. It had pine cupboards, modest but homey with an old oak table and four chairs off to one side. The floor was tile and nice, but also modest. The rest of the cabin consisted of one bed room, a closet sized bathroom with only a shower, no bath. The cabin had just struck out as far as Kassidy was concerned. She loved a good hot bath on a regular basis. No, actually she *needed* a good hot bath on a regular basis. Knowing that Luke was probably going to keep her prisoner, she hoped she could at least talk him into going somewhere with a bath tub . . . soon.

As soon as she wandered back to the living room to join the guys, she noticed one very important detail. No electrical media type stuff at all, no computer, no phone, and . . . . no TV. How were they going to check to see if their cars had been impounded?

Luke smiled, having heard her thoughts. *"Let me check out the perimeter and I'll show you a little secret I've been keeping."*

Mark was just getting around to asking the same question when he saw the looks pass between Luke and Kassidy. "I sure wish you guys would have these conversations out loud, that's rude! It's like speaking another language in front of a guest!"

"There's a secret room . . . . no secret rooms!" Kassidy, having gleaned that little morsel of information from Luke's mind, looked at Luke with unhidden admiration. Luke smiled and headed out to check the perimeter of the cabin. When he came back inside, Kassidy and Mark were snooping in the refrigerator looking for something cold to drink. They found a pitcher of unsweetened tea, a tub of butter, a bottle of Welch's grape juice, and a bottle of Ernest and Julio Gallo's White Zin.

"Well," Kassidy thought, *"if I can't have a bath, at least he has a bottle of my favorite wine."* She hated to admit that her taste in wine was so inexpensive, but the truth was the truth.

"I'm glad you like it. Bring the bottle, we'll have some downstairs."

"You have glasses?"

"Will you guys stop that? I can see the conversation on your faces, but I'm feeling a little left out! Oh, bring that bottle with you Kassidy. It isn't the best, but it will due until I can get you some of the good stuff," Mark said.

"Glasses are downstairs," Luke finished the conversation out loud for Mark's benefit. "Oh and she likes that kind of wine, it's her favorite! *Kassidy, don't worry about the bath, I have one downstairs. You can have a bath and drink your wine too!*" He smiled at her. It was more a smirk than a smile. He was wondering if he would be able to keep the mind connection while she was in the bath.

"Forget it. I'm not taking a bath with you anywhere near!"

"I promise you, I won't look!"

"Not taking any chances, too bad for you!"

"What are you too talking about now? I feel like a fifth wheel! If you guys don't knock it off, I'll have to blow this Popsicle stand and walk back to town!" Mark wasn't sure which was worse, being left out of the conversation, or just not having the ability to 'eavesdrop' himself. It had happened once in Germany, he was wondering just how that had worked. OH yes, the hand holding they thought. He wondered if he'd have to hold onto both of them to figure it out. Oh well, he'd look for opportunities and test out their theories . . . . especially when the facial expressions got going between them!

"Sorry, Mark, private conversation. Take a look at this." Luke opened a floor to ceiling cupboard to reveal shelves of stored food.

"Wow, that's a lot of food, Luke, but I'm still a little full from what ever meal that was that we just ate. I'm still not sure what time it is, or if I should be hungry," said Mark.

"Wait just a minute." Luke reached into the cupboard, under one of the shelves and flicked a little button that was disguised as part of a shelf support bracket. The cupboard swung open revealing a nearly invisible door. As a matter of fact, it was so well hidden that only someone who knew it was there was likely to find it. The whole thing still looked like just a very convenient food storage cupboard that swung out to allow the cook to see and get to food in the back of the storage unit. But Luke manipulated another "bracket" and a hidden door swung open. There were steps leading down into a basement and Luke gestured for the two of them to head down in front of him. As soon as all three were in the stairwell, Luke hit a switch on the wall and the entire door, shelves, and cupboard closed, hiding the entrance once more. A light came on in the stairwell at the same time and the three headed down the stairs.

Kassidy couldn't believe how far down they walked in the stairwell. It must have been about two stories down. The walls were off white with beautiful scenic works of art along them. The carpet on the steps was plush drowning out any sound from their decent. Finally, they came upon another door. Luke stepped up to the door and typed a combination into a small keyboard beside it and the door opened. Kassidy sucked in her breath as she looked into the spacious living room. It was beautiful!!! There was an entire wall dedicated to media, with a stereo, sound system, state of the art TV and surveillance monitors that kept track of anything moving or not moving around the immediate vicinity, in the air above, or within ten miles of the cabin. She wondered about the stereo system and all that sound, when the point of the secret basement was to hide out.

"*It's sound proof.*"

"So, why would you need such a nice stereo if you are trying to be quiet and hide out?" asked Mark, having missed yet another short conversation. He caught the look that passed between the two and surmised in an instant that the question had already been asked and answered.

"It's sound proof," said Kassidy.

"See, if you'd just include me in the conversation in the first place, you could save a lot of repeating yourselves!" retorted Mark with irritation clearly apparent in his reply.

The opposite wall was adorned with a picture window sized screen which displayed the same scene as one would see if they were looking out the big window in the upstairs living room. The deer had wandered off and were no where to be seen, but the view was beautiful even without them. It also allowed the inhabitants to keep an eye on the only way into the cabin by car. The length of the room was nearly fifty feet by thirty-five feet and contained a dining area with light oak table and chairs, a living area with an overstuffed high backed leather couch along the wall closest to the door from which they had entered, and two Lazy Boy recliners opposite the couch but facing toward both the couch and the flat screen TV taking up a good portion of the wall.

Upon seeing the wide screen TV on the wall, Mark deemed the accommodations "Acceptable!" and asked where the movie selection and the controls were.

"First we need to check and see what our 'friends' are up to." Luke picked up a control and began sifting through channels until he found a news channel finishing up a report on the disappearance of the heroine of Laramie, Kassidy Dover. Kassidy flinched at her new found nickname. Since the news channel was CNN, Luke figured that whatever they had missed would be replayed again in just a few minutes. Sure enough, only about ten minutes passed before they were back to the beginning of the incredible story of a heroine gone missing. The on-scene reporter rehashed all the clues to Miss Dover's abduction. She made a point of mentioning that Miss Dover's doctor had not yet been reached for comment and his whereabouts were also in question. Police were still looking for another person, a young man by the name of Paul

Thomas. They reported the incredible story of how he happened to be sitting in the parking lot, witnessed the shooting and managed to subdue the shooter. Fortunately, the little detail about Mr. Thomas calling in a brain surgeon had not made the evening news. The reporter concluded the news segment saying that foul play had not been ruled out and Miss Dover's very worried parents were pleading for their daughter's safe return. No mention was made of Luke's or Mark's car.

"Do you think it's safe to get the cars?" asked Mark.

"Well, I think we'll have to take a shot," said Luke. "At least they aren't looking for the owners of the cars yet . . . . as far as we know, but as soon as they get wind of that call I made to you on the principal's cell phone, they'll figure it all out. Of course, they could just be keeping it out of the news to sucker us in. I think we need to do a little recon first."

"Recon?" asked Kassidy.

"Both of you take hold; we'll go to the hospital again. We can concentrate on that clump of trees just outside the door in the front. We'll be able to see Mark's rental car and my jeep from there. But no one will be able to see us from inside it . . . unless they are looking for us there."

"If they know how 'paths' work wouldn't they be expecting us to arrive at the only point of camouflage in the area?' asked Mark.

"Where else could we go where we could see the cars without being seen?" asked Luke.

"How about the roof?" asked Kassidy. "Or the golf course next door. There are a lot of trees there and we could sneak a peek from somewhere over there. And we could be ready to zip out if we're seen."

"No, too far away. I've got it. The trash collection area is fenced in by a privacy fence. It's locked because of hazardous waste. We could peek through the slats and see both cars. Since it's locked, even if they spotted us, we'd have some time to get away." The others agreed though Luke caught Kassidy's thoughts, *Eeiuuww, the trash area? I liked the roof idea better,* right before Luke held out his hands to her.

"Hold on Mark." Kassidy took Luke's hands and Mark grabbed hold. By now Mark was getting used to the unusual sensation and beginning to enjoy the electricity flowing between Luke and Kassidy. His "Oh no, oh no, oh no" could now only be identified in his huge grin with his eyes squeezed shut. If Luke had not been mesmerized once again by the incredible green eyes looking into his and the electricity that seemed to light up every part of his body, he'd have had teasing fodder on Mark for the next ten years. When they arrived inside the trash collection area, Luke let go of one of Kassidy's hands. Was it his own reluctance or was it Kassidy's that kept their other hands locked together?

Mark let go and was already looking through the slats as Luke finally looked away from Kassidy and walked to the fence, still holding her hand. But his mind was not on what they were seeing. His entire concentration was centered on the lovely warm hand that he held. He wanted to reach over with his other hand and hold it between them. Well, that wasn't all he would like to do, but it would have been a nice start. He caught his thoughts, blushing as he wondered what Kassidy thought of all of that. He was finally able to focus on what they were seeing but he still did not let go of her hand.

There were men just outside the hospital door scanning the area. But they did not seem to have zeroed in on Mark's or Luke's cars. Luke and Kassidy both spoke at the same time, "They are watching the jeep. They haven't been able to trace the plates to the owner, but they are sure it belongs to the person who took Kassidy (me)."

"I thought you two couldn't read anyone else's thoughts!" Mark was feeling a little uneasy with the idea that his thoughts might be on display.

"We thought so too," said Luke. He was looking back at Kassidy again.

Kassidy was studying the two men who were trying to look inconspicuous as they kept an eye on the jeep. She looked to be in deep thought. She hadn't heard a word that Luke had thought about her. She was also concentrating almost entirely on the connection between her hand and the one that enveloped hers. It was warm and comforting. But there was more. The electricity seemed to become a part of every inch of her body. "*Get a hold of yourself!*" she thought. She was afraid to even look in Luke's direction. He was getting an 'ear' full now. How would she ever face him? She forced herself to concentrate on the two men at the door.

"Why can't I find out what else they know about us? All I'm picking up is how bored they are and how hot that last 'chick' was that just walked through the doors." Kassidy wondered out loud.

"I think they have to be thinking about what we hear." Luke was staring back at the men at the door, but he was also making himself think despite the electricity. He really should just let go of her hand, but he didn't. "Mark, what hotel are you checked into?"

"I'm just down the street. It was close to the college and the hospital. I thought that might be a good idea."

"Great! Are you still checked in do you think? Or will they have raided your room by now looking for you?"

"There's an easy way to find out. Take me to the hotel. I'll stroll in and see if there are any messages for me. The clerk should think about anything she knows and you guys can rescue me or leave depending. If she still has my room, and she should, I checked in for a week, she'll give me my messages with a smile. If the labbies have been there, she'll be thinking about that and you guys can swoop in and save me."

"What if the labbies are sitting in the lobby waiting for you?" asked Kassidy.

"Is there anyplace in the lobby to arrive and check out the area without being seen?"

"There is a little sitting area that is blocked from the desk clerk's view by a large fire place. There are trees and foliage in the sitting area that we could arrive behind. That way anyone in the sitting area wouldn't see us and we could make a hasty retreat." Mark was picturing the room as he spoke.

Luke and Kassidy took his hand, got the picture in their minds and in a couple of seconds they were there. Luckily, there was no one in the sitting room. Mark walked out from behind the trees, walked casually through the sitting room and peeked around the fire place. There were no waiting bad guys anywhere to be seen, so he walked up to the desk and asked for his messages.

The clerk, a neatly dressed woman of about fifty-five or sixty, silver hair pulled up into a severe bun with a face that, while kind, could not hide the ravages of the harsh Wyoming weather, smiled, "What room, sir?"

"Room 238, please."

"Your name."

"Dr. Mark Johns." Mark watched her tap her fingers rapidly over the computer keys. He wished he could see the screen. Her beautifully manicured fingers flew over the keys with precision and speed. He always wondered how women could type so fast with such long fingernails. He thought it looked a little uncomfortable. He smiled to himself as he pictured a secretary that was as fast at fixing the mistakes caused by her long nails as she was at typing them in the first place. Now he really wished he could see the page.

"Yes, Dr. Johns, you have several messages. Just a sec and I'll get them for you." She reached into a cubbie beneath the desk in front of her and produced a fist full of messages.

Mark wondered why she hadn't just looked in the cubbie in the first place rather than having to wait for confirmation from the computer . . . . what if the power went out, would she have to wait for it to come back on to see if anyone had mail? Maybe she was just checking to see if there was really a Dr. Mark Johns checked into a room. "Wow, thank you. I guess I have a little light reading to do!"

The clerk chuckled, "Anything else I can do for you?"

"No thank you." Mark turned and walked back into the sitting room opening the first message as he went. As he sat down in a plush Winchester style emerald green chair in front of the trees that Kassidy and Luke were still standing behind he asked, "Well, what was she thinking?"

"She thought you were quite attractive and was thinking of adding a message to your pile herself. I think her exact thoughts were 'hubba, hubba!' Maybe you should go back over there and ask her out to dinner." Kassidy was enjoying this far too much.

"I just might, she has very nicely manicured nails and can type like the wind. Just what every young man needs."

"Maybe you could replace Moneypenny and finally get on with your love life!" quipped Luke.

"Kindly stay out of my love life . . . and my office personnel choices, thank you!"

"What do your notes say?" asked Luke.

"They are mostly from the hospital. They are requesting my immediate presence at the hospital. It seems that my patient has gone missing. I better get right over there! Imagine a hospital that can't keep track of an unconscious woman just out of surgery. How long have we been gone anyway?"

"We've been gone about twelve hours."

"Won't they be suspicious about why they couldn't get a hold of you for an emergency?"

"Well, I'll tell them that I sleep very deeply. It's kind of true. A couple of times when I've been very tired and fallen asleep on the couch in my office, Moneypenny has had to throw water on me to wake me up. Of course, that was after *really* tough surgeries."

"Moneypenny?!" Kassidy's curiosity was piqued.

"I'll fill you in later," said Luke

Mark paused a minute as he read another message. "Uh oh, here's the one we were waiting for. This one is from the police. They want to talk to me about the disappearance of my patient. Surprise, surprise! You guys want to give me a lift back to the hospital. Time for my little temper tantrum. I gotta get back to my practice."

"It could be a trap. Mark, do you have your cell phone?" asked Luke.

"Yes, but it won't do me any good because your phone is in pieces. Remember your role as 'Rambo' at the school?"

"Oh, yeah. Kassidy, do you have a cell?"

"Sure, in my purse. You know . . . the one the labbies probably have now?"

"Shoot!" Luke ran his hands through his hair trying to think. "Now what? We could borrow one from Wal-Mart, but we'd have to get it programmed before we could use it. We don't have the time."

Kassidy was giving him a stern look, "Not to mention, that would be stealing! I think we can borrow my mom's phone without having to resort to crime. She hasn't really used it for a while. I can borrow it until we can replace ours. She lets me use it now and then for field trips when I need to stay in touch with other parents. If she looks for it, she'll just think I have it anyway and I can return it after we are finished with it."

"That works for me," said Luke.

Kassidy concentrated on the phone. It appeared in her hand. She gave the number to Mark.

"Memorize it, Mark. We can't afford for anyone else to get that number. And you don't know if you will have that little scrap of paper when you need to call."

"Good idea." It was an easy number and Mark had it pretty quickly. "OK, let's go."

They all took hands again. Just before they left, Kassidy asked, "So tell me about Moneypenny." By the time they reached the hospital, she had the story, from two different points of view.

They arrived just outside the hospital on the southern side of the building.

"You really should just go get her, if you love her. Life is too short to play it safe all the time," thought Kassidy before she released Mark's hand.

"Oh, not you too?!"

"Just think about it."

"OK, show time. Good luck Mark. Call us as soon as you can tonight. Will you head home after your tantrum, or will you be staying at the hotel?" Luke had dropped Kassidy's hand and was having to speak out loud to Mark. He spoke in a near whisper, just in case someone was around the corner.

"Depends on how it goes. I'll call you by 8:00 p.m. tonight. If you don't hear from me by then, come find me and bring the cavalry."

"Will do!"

CHAPTER 8

Really, Really Good Looking

Kassidy and Luke returned to Luke's cabin to await Mark's call. It was getting close to lunch time and Luke wondered what Kassidy would like to eat. He was looking through cupboards and in the refrigerator when it occurred to him that he couldn't "hear" her thoughts. That was odd. He'd been able to hear everything she'd thought since he met her. Why couldn't he hear her now? Where was she? He started toward the back of the underground house feeling just a little uneasy.

Kassidy had wandered to the back of the cabin, exploring the spacious underground hideout and the four bedrooms. She was more than just happy to see the deep oversized bath tub. It was beautiful! Of course, she would have thought that a steel gray wash tub, big enough to sit in would have looked great at this point. But this tub had style. It was sunken into the floor like a hot tub, but not as big. It had two steps walking down into it. As she looked around, she noticed that the bath tub was jetted like a hot tub and could be easily used as either a regular tub or a hot tub, though it was not suited for more than one person really. Two might be able to use it together, but they would have to be really good friends or more. She blushed to herself as she thought that thought. Normally, she could talk to herself like that, but since Luke now spent a lot of time in her head, those kinds of thoughts had gotten a little too embarrassing and she found herself beginning to stuff them into the back recesses of her mind.

Kassidy wandered out of the bathroom, trying to get the thoughts of a nice hot bath out of her head so she wouldn't be thinking them in front of Luke. If he had to hear everything that came into her head, at least she could make an effort at keeping personal stuff out of his line of thought. As she wandered back toward the living room she stopped and peeked into a room that was obviously Luke's. It contained a large queen sized bed. The bed sat in an oak frame in a European sleigh style. The sleigh bed was named for the head and the foot of the bed because it resembled the front and back of a sleigh. She had admired many European antiques while she was living there, but had never asked her dad for one. She knew from a friend's experience that furniture from Europe that is brought back to the dry climate of the prairies tended to dry out and crack. So her family had not brought back any large pieces of antique furniture. She had also never seen a sleigh bed made from such a light colored wood. She rather liked the light oak. It brightened the room as much as the style of the bed added charm. There was another oddity; the bed only had a fitted sheet over the mattress with a large feather quilt that was covered with a cotton material sort of like a large pillow case. *"Oh my goodness, Luke's been to Europe enough to acquire a love of the down blankets too!"* The furniture in the room matched the style and color of the bed. The dresser was also a beautiful light oak with a large mirror attached. There was another dresser, a chair and a couple of night tables with lamps on either side of the bed. The colors of the room were a dark forest green and off white.

She noticed another Bev Doolittle print on the wall and the closet that he had left open that morning was full of men's clothing. There was a little stool or something in the corner piled with clothes that must be between dirty and clean. She smiled because her father had the same type of stool in his bedroom, piled in the same fashion with the clothes that he deemed clean enough for another wear. Her mom was constantly refolding those things to at least make the pile look neat. Somehow this similarity between Luke and her father was comforting. She thought about wandering in and looking around, but she wasn't a snoop and even if she was, he'd know it as soon as he read her thoughts. Come to think of it she couldn't hear his thoughts at all right now. She wondered why that was. She had heard every thought in his head since the hospital and she couldn't hear anything right now. That didn't feel right. She suddenly felt very alone. After the last twenty hours or so, it was an odd feeling. She started toward the living room with concern rising in her chest and was almost running when she barreled right into Luke who had just made it to the hallway entrance himself.

"Luke where were you? *I couldn't hear you. I thought something had happened.*"

"*I couldn't hear you either.*"

"*That doesn't make any sense. We've been able to hear each other the whole day. What changed? I can hear you now. Why couldn't we hear each other a minute ago?*"

"*Where were you?*"

The pictures of where she'd been and what she'd been thinking flashed through her head. *"Damn,"* she thought, *"there went the thoughts about the bathtub."* She turned a very attractive shade of red of which Luke took full notice.

"You liked it! Luke said it like he'd just won a prize or swallowed the proverbial mouse. *I knew you would. I've never tried it with two people, but I've thought about it."*

"Never mind!"

"But I like this train of thought."

Kassidy made an effort to change the subject and moved on to the rest of her tour of the bedroom area. *Oh, you saw my bedroom too,"* Luke paused, *"You compared me to your dad?!"*

Now it was Kassidy's turn to smile. *"Yes, you remind me of him A LOT."*

Luke's brow crinkled up and that would have slowed the discussion until he caught her remembering the bed. His brows flew up, *"You liked the bed?"*

"Who wouldn't? It was beautiful. You've been to Europe?"

"Yes, you and I have the same taste in blankets," Luke smiled.

"Where did you find the beautiful sleigh bed in light oak?"

"I had to have it special ordered from a company in Colorado. Are you hungry? I'm starving."

"Yes, actually, I'm very hungry. What have you got?"

"Well, I'm very good at omelets. Also I have mastered a mean bowl of Top Ramen. I have some frozen pizza in the freezer, or some chicken strips."

"You don't cook much, do you?"

"You've found me out. I'm better with cars than pans."

"I'll take the omelet, but I better have a look at your supplies. If I'm staying for a while, I'd like to eat like normal people."

"What do you mean, 'normal people', I'm normal . . . for a single guy, living alone."

"OK, I'll give you that, but now you are not living alone; unless you would like to release me to go to my own home!"

"Hmmm, the kitchen is yours for the duration of your incarceration." Luke had begun to think about that remark about 'not living alone.' It had not occurred to him that he had made a big step in the very direction that he had been trying to avoid. He quickly stashed the thought in the back of his mind and began to think about omelets.

Luke started pulling things out of the fridge to add to the omelets. Kassidy seemed up for anything, green peppers, cheese, tomatoes, ham, and onions. By the time Luke had finished putting it all on the stove top grill, the omelet had become enough to feed four 'normal' guys. But the two of them polished off the thing along with some fried potatoes, orange juice, milk and even a little strawberry yogurt. Luke was impressed with her ability to keep up with him in the eating department on a day when he was exceptionally hungry.

"Oh, this is definitely not a normal meal for me," Kassidy assured him. *"I'm just wondering if I just ate myself out of half my wardrobe."*

"Well, I'm not normally this big of an eater either. Just every once in a while I seem to need a little extra."

"That's good, because at this rate, the two of us could eat as much as a family of four! Umm, you wouldn't happen to have any homemade chocolate chip cookies on hand, would you?"

"No, but I have some store bought cookies. Would you like some?"

"Sure, I'm not picky."

The two of them nearly polished off the cookies too. "Wow, I didn't know we had it in us," Kassidy said out loud. "It must be all the stress of the day."

They sat there in silence, just letting chit chat thoughts run through their minds. Then Luke remembered the earlier inability to hear Kassidy's thoughts and decided that they should investigate that further. Maybe something in the back rooms of the cabin had impeded their communication.

"There is only one way to find out," thought Kassidy. She got up, put her plate in the kitchen sink and began walking toward the back of the house. *"Can you hear me now?"*

"Yes."

"Good," she walked further back down the hall. *"Can you hear me now?"*

This little rendition of a Verizon commercial went on until the second that she couldn't hear him. There was a definite point at which one more step toward the back of the cabin interrupted the communication. Luke headed back to where she was, thinking that there had to be something there to interrupt the connection, only to discover that as soon as he took a step toward Kassidy, he could hear her again. They continued this little test until they determined that it wasn't *where* they were standing, but *how far* they were standing away from each other. They lost contact about 30 feet from each other.

"Why do we lose contact with each other in thirty feet, but from about one hundred yards away, we could listen to the two goons at the hospital?" What's up with that?" Kassidy voiced her last question out loud as if saying it out loud could help them figure it out.

"Hmm, what did we do different at the hospital?" asked Luke as he thought back through the hospital reconnaissance mission. As his thoughts traveled over the event, he remembered holding her hand. He hadn't thought about it then, it just seemed natural. Now as he thought back to the moment, he realized that he hadn't wanted to let go of her hand. The electricity was intoxicating when they touched. Even now, as he looked into those incredible green eyes, he was drawn to reach out and take her hand. He chuckled to himself as he thought about what Mark would have said: "The force is strong with this one." It *was* strong. Should he reach out and take her hand? Every time he touched her it seemed as though it was harder to let her go. He wanted to choose his own mate, not have one thrust upon him just because they were both paths. Surely, this incredible attraction would pass if he just fought it. Shoot! What would Kassidy think of him now? She had to have gotten that entire train of thought.

Kassidy stood there looking back into the deep blue eyes that seemed to be drawing her closer with each second. She was trying to concentrate on what they did differently at the hospital, but then she already knew. They had been holding hands. The memory of it was still as fresh as if it were happening now. Did he feel the same thing? Somehow, every time she started feeling this way, Luke acted like he didn't have a clue what she was thinking. He was also a lot better at hiding his thoughts about her than she was about hiding her thoughts about him. He was probably catching every word of this. But she wasn't picking up any of his thoughts.

Luke was the first to pull himself together and continue the conversation. "I think we heard those guys because we were touching. It worked with Mark too. As long as we're touching, we multiply our mind power. It makes sense, because we can't transport ourselves without touching. It takes two of us. So it's probably the same with mind reading. We have to be together to hear from more than thirty feet away. But we probably need to experiment with that to discover from just how far away we can listen. Also, there seems to be a disconnect on my part sometimes. I couldn't hear what ever it was you were just thinking and I missed some things at the hospital too."

"Wait, you couldn't hear me just a minute ago?"

"No."

"Not anything?"

"No. Could you?"

"Well, no. What was the last thing you heard?"

"You asked why we couldn't hear each other at more than thirty feet, but we can pick up what those guys are thinking from one hundred feet."

Relief crossed Kassidy's face as clearly as if she had said it. Luke smiled, he was very relieved too. She hadn't heard any of what had just gone on in his head. He thought it was the hand holding at first, but as he thought about it he began to believe that it was the distraction created in him merely by Kassidy's presence. If that was true, then she was having the same problem. He smiled at that thought. They were going to have to concentrate a lot harder to avoid distractions when necessary.

"Yes, we sure will." Kassidy agreed.

"I think we need to practice. We need to discover what we can and can not do before we end up in a situation that pushes us to our limits."

"Yes, but do you mind if we start tomorrow. I'm in need of a hot bath and now I know that as long as you are thirty feet away, I can take it by myself."

Kassidy noticed that another of those beautiful smiles crossed Luke's face. It sort of started on one side and spread to the other. *"Wow, he was handsome. No, he was perfect,"* she thought.

"Thank you! You're no slouch yourself. You should check out the mirror while you're in there. You may notice some changes."

Maybe she was getting used to accidentally thinking things that made Luke smile like that, but this time she didn't really mind that he knew she thought he was gorgeous.

"Oh, Kassidy, there is some bubble bath under the sink. There is shampoo and conditioner on the shelf beside the bath as well as a towel and wash cloth. There are extra toiletries in the second drawer down on the right hand side of the vanity. You can stay in the bedroom next to mine. I left you a T-shirt and a house coat on the bed. Your feather blanket is there also." Luke told her this as he walked back toward the living room. *"Kassidy, start your bath but don't get in just yet. I'll bring you a glass of wine to drink while you soak."*

"Thank you, that's sweet." She waited for him to reach the thirty foot mark before she dared to think about him. She couldn't wait to have her thoughts to herself. Of course she knew what she would be thinking about. It would be Luke of course. As she started the water in the bath she wanted to re-live that hospital recon mission in her head again. If just holding hands could send her flying, heaven forbid that he ever hug her. Wait, he had hugged her in Germany. The electricity hadn't been as intense then, she was sure of it. So what was happening? Was it intensifying because of the path powers or was it intensifying because she was more attracted to him now than before? Every time she closed her eyes now, she saw his face and those deep blue eyes. She could get so lost in them that she couldn't even hear what was going on around her. And then all she could think about was getting closer to him, resting her head on his shoulder, feeling his arms wrap around her again.

She was so engrossed in her thoughts that she missed his approach. She didn't know he was even close until he knocked on the door to the bathroom. That brought her out of her reverie quickly. For what seemed like the hundredth time since she met him she found herself looking into those beautiful eyes, and even without looking down at his mouth, she knew he was smiling again. He'd heard every word she had thought. He handed her a glass of wine, turned and left the room without saying or thinking anything except, *"Thank you, that's sweet."*

What was she thinking, thinking about him like that, and knowing he'd be back with a glass of wine? He probably thinks she's a doting idiot. How could she be so . . . so . . . stupid? It seemed that when he was around, she just did things like that. Oh, well, he'll be thinking about how to get her home sooner now. That would be nice. Her parents must be frantic. She would be happy to get back to her second graders too.

As she got up to get the towel, shampoo and conditioner, she caught her reflection in the mirror and took a good long look. She had changed. Completely changed! Her eyes had become greener than they had been. They were exactly the color she had tried to duplicate with colored contact lenses. She looked in the mirror to find the wound from the gunshot, but her hair had grown out over it now and it was completely healed. There were no signs or even traces of the wound any longer. Wow, Luke was right; she would have to stay away from school and her parents. How would she ever explain this without someone getting very suspicious? As she undressed for her bath, she also noticed that her muscle tone had increased and her tummy had slimmed down, leaving her with a nice little six-pack of abdominal muscles. Even her legs had acquired a better muscle tone; enviable for sure!!

Her hair had changed too. It had been thick and wavy, but now it appeared to be long and straight with a deep shine to it. Good heavens, it hadn't been washed since before the shooting, yet it looked, well, in need of a wash, but still not bad! And even her teeth were whiter and straighter. She could quit her job as a teacher and become a model . . . in a heartbeat! She wasn't sure if she should celebrate or panic. How long did she stand there? She didn't know, but she finally stepped into the hot bath with bubbles fluffing up all around her. This could change her life, she knew, but was it for the best or not? Her dad had always told her that beauty was only skin deep. What did this say about her belief that beauty was only skin deep, when the first thing her mind did after discovering its new powers was to fix up the old bod? Maybe she'd try to figure that out later and just enjoy being . . . oh, how did that movie say it? . . . The one with that Stiller guy? . . . Oh, yeah, "Really, really, good looking." She laughed out loud, slid deeper into the bath, listened for Luke and when she didn't 'hear' him, enjoyed the moment to daydream about him . . . just a little.

CHAPTER 9

House

After Luke and Kassidy left him, Mark turned to head into the hospital. He was a little nervous, but he decided to put on his best 'House' attitude, imitating the lead doctor on the TV series of the same name, and strolled through the front doors. He was looking a little rumpled after his speedy trip to Germany last night, so he stopped off in the staff room to pick up a fresh white doctor's coat for rounds. He straightened his hair and proceeded to the ICU. When he arrived at the nurse's station, he headed straight to Kassidy's room. When he obviously did not find her he stopped, turned to the poor soul on duty and began his act.

"Excuse me, but would you mind explaining to me why, when I got up to leave my hotel and come over here to check on my patient, I was bombarded by messages saying that you had LOST my patient? How in the world does an ICU unit lose an unconscious patient? Did she sleep walk? Do you have patient burglars? Was she kidnapped by aliens? Maybe she was just a figment of my imagination. I might have thought so except for all these messages!!!" He threw the messages at the poor young man behind the desk. "Please, explain this to me!"

"Uh, well . . ."

"UH? WELL? Oh, that explains it all! Thank you for your time, is there someone in charge around here that might know what's going on?"

"Uh, yeah, just a minute, doctor." The nurse picked up a phone and dialed an extension. "Hello, yes, he's here. Not happy, no! Thank you, sir. Yes, sir, I'd appreciate that." The nurse hung up and looked back at Mark. "The hospital administrator and the police are coming down to talk to you, Doctor. It will only be a minute. Would you like to wait in the waiting room?"

"No, I would not like to wait in the waiting room! Call him back and tell him I'll meet him in his office." Mark had decided ahead of time that where ever they asked him to wait, he'd choose somewhere else, just to be difficult. He sort of felt sorry for the nurse about now, but appearances were important.

"Yes, sir." The nurse dialed the number again and relayed the message. "They'll wait there for you, Doctor."

"Great! So where is his office?"

"Take the elevator down to the first floor, head toward the left and it's the third door on the right."

"Thank you! And if my patient wanders back, please, let me know!"

The nurse nodded but as soon as Mark turned away, he rolled his eyes and let out a frustrated sigh.

Mark stormed down to the administrator's office, picking up attitude steam as he went. He would have to play this to the hilt. His own life might just depend on it. And if they didn't believe his little tantrum and 'detained' him, it could cost Luke and Kassidy their lives too. He knew they would come after him. He couldn't afford to have that happen. He had reached the office and he paused outside the door. He dropped his head into his left hand to remove any tell tale sweat and to ready himself for his performance as his right hand reached for the door knob. He dropped his left hand to his side, gritted his teeth and yanked open the door without knocking.

"Sorry to burst in on you, but I assumed you'd be expecting me. Where the hell is my patient? She is not stable. She shouldn't have been moved and now I'm told she's completely missing. What kind of hospital are you running here? Can just anyone waltz in here and abscond with a patient?" He forced a look of utter shock on his face before he came up with his next scenario. "You're selling body parts on the black market, aren't you? Oh . . . no . . . tell me you aren't selling body parts! WHERE IS SHE?! Tell me NOW or I'll call in every law enforcement agency in the country until I find her!"

"Calm down Dr. Johns. We *are* the police and we are just as concerned by Miss Dover's disappearance as you are," said a heavy set dark haired policeman. He had a big bushy mustache that hung down over his bottom lip and reminded Dr. Johns of Kurt Russell's mustache in the movie Tombstone. He fit nicely in this smallish western town. All he needed was the wide brimmed hat and a long black coat, well and maybe a six-shooter.

There were four people in the room. The policeman who spoke first introduced himself as Officer Dana Forbes. He was a likable fellow and judging by his looks and his last name, Mark concluded that he was probably the son of the pastor of the Dover's church. Mark found it amusing that the father's job was teaching people to do what is right and the son's job was to enforce it. Officer Forbes seemed honest and sincere. He had stood when Mark entered the room and crossed toward him with one hand up in an effort to diffuse a difficult situation.

Officer Forbes was not alone. He had a partner with him. The partner had also stood as Mark entered the room but had not moved from in front of the low-back brown leather over-stuffed chair he had been sitting in. The hospital administrator was sitting in a swivel chair of the same brown leather behind his desk. The name plate on the door and also on the desk read Mr. Donald Boyd. He was a tall man that resembled Hoss from the old TV Show Bonanza. He was wearing a big belt buckle and a pair of western cut dark gray pants with a western style dress shirt and a nice leather vest. Mark had to take a glance around the room to try to find where Mr. Boyd had stashed his ten-gallon hat. Was it just being in the state of Wyoming that had Mark seeing old cowboys in the faces of the people around him, or was it the stress? Whatever it was, Mark needed to stop this and get on with the show.

The final person in the room introduced himself as Todd LeBeau. Ah, no resemblance to a cowboy here! Mr. LeBeau was tall. He had sandy, or maybe it would be better to describe it as dusty blond hair, about chin length, but he had pulled the front section of hair back into a ponytail leaving the sides behind the ears and back loose. He had blue-green eyes and Mark could just see an earring in one ear. It was a good sized blue stone in a silver setting. He looked athletic and lean in an egg-shell blue dress shirt, black pants and black tie with blue and turquoise stripes. He said he was with the Federal government looking into the disappearance of Miss Dover, as well as several other odd disappearances in hospitals of late. As he introduced himself, Mark noted that he never said which Federal agency he belonged to, or why they were checking into random disappearances.

"Dr. Johns, it's nice to finally meet you," said LeBeau.

Mark remembered this guy. He had seen him first in the hospital with Luke when Regina had disappeared and then again in the hallway just before he and Luke had taken Kassidy. Dr. Johns remembered the man all right, but not the scar stretching from under his jaw up into the hair line on the right side of his face. It was in the same place as the scar should have been on both Luke and Kassidy. But theirs were no longer visible. His was very prominent. "*How curious,*" Mark thought.

"Thank you. Now, can anyone in here tell me what is going on?" Mark was through with the pleasantries and was beginning to really get into this attitude role he was playing. He looked into the eyes of each person there and remembering the nasty, degrading way Dr. House looked at people he was trying to intimidate, Mark gave them his best imitation. "What, cat got your tongues? Come on people, I have a practice to get back to."

"Dr. Johns," LeBeau spoke first. "We were sort of hoping that you could shed some light on the situation. You were the last one seen leaving her room that evening."

Mark was relieved. If they saw him leaving the room, they were referring to the time when he moved Luke to the bed and left with the orderly. At least they weren't referring to the last time someone saw him *enter* the room.

"When exactly did she disappear?"

"Somewhere between 6:00 and 7:10 yesterday evening. You were the last one seen leaving her room after you moved her sleeping 'boyfriend' off a chair and onto the bed in the next room." LeBeau's eyebrow shot up accusingly and a nasty smirk crossed his face. If he had been a cat closing in on a mouse, he'd have been licking his lips about now.

Even though they were off track in their accusations, Mark wondered how he could have been so stupid. He hadn't thought about the orderly revealing that piece of information. He would have to be very careful or he would end up in an interrogation cubical at some unknown Federal agency at some unknown location for some unknown but probably very long time.

"You have to be kidding me. You think I had something to do with it? That young man was not her boyfriend; he was the guy who saved her life at the school. He was in the parking lot when the creep attacked her. He knocked the guy out and sent the kid that was with her in to call 911. He was just here checking on her, but it had been a big day for him too, so he fell asleep waiting for her to wake up. He's probably around somewhere, though. Have you talked to him?!"

"No, we have been unable to find him; however, we did talk to her parents who told us that he was waiting for you. He said that he was a friend of yours and that you two were meeting in Laramie to catch up on old times, since you had an engagement to speak at UW. We also know that he called you from the principal's cell phone to tell you to meet him at the hospital."

"Wow, that's interesting." Mark knew he had a look of shock on his face. He hadn't anticipated being caught quite so quickly. But he got an idea and let the shocked look on his face work for him as he tried to add a little 'Aha, that explains a lot' sort of a look to his face too. Then he put the idea into words, "I did get a call from a guy who asked me to meet with him during my stay in Laramie. He told me that he was a student at UW and was thinking of going into medicine and possibly surgery of some kind. He had originally asked me to meet him at the hospital during one of his lunch hours. I assumed that he worked here. But I never met up with him. He called that morning to tell me to meet him in the ER right then. He sounded arrogant and pushy. I thought about blowing him off, but I was curious. He sounded a bit like me. So I decided to meet him at the ER. But when I got to the hospital, they had just brought in a brain trauma and since that is my specialty, I offered my services. I never met the guy who called. He either never showed or I was too busy to notice . . . at least that's what I thought." Then Mark let another look cross his face. He closed his eyes and gritted his teeth as if he had just caught on to what LeBeau was suggesting. "Should I be getting a lawyer? It seems as though you are accusing *me* of something!"

"No, you don't need a lawyer; we are not accusing you of anything . . . yet. We are merely trying to discover the whereabouts of Miss Dover."

There was that cat and mouse look again. Mark was getting annoyed with it. He definitely didn't like this LeBeau guy. He was getting a little too close for comfort. Mark guessed that he better not use his cell phone anymore. He better turn it off as soon as he left this room, IF he left this room.

"So, do you have any legitimate leads?" asked Mark.

"You are pretty much it right now," said LeBeau.

Mark nearly let his guard down at that remark, but managed to keep his composure and his attitude. "Look, you Columbo-wannabe, I have absolutely no motive for taking a patient, whose life I had just saved, out of this hospital before she even had time to wake up after surgery. To move her without so much as an ambulance would most likely kill her. I have no reason to do that. If you think you have some sort of motive, bring it on! Otherwise, get your worthless butt up off that comfortable overstuffed, lovely chair and *find* her before she's chopped up into resalable body parts and finds herself walking around in about fourteen different people!!" Mark was glaring into LeBeau's squinted, angry eyes. They were nearly nose to nose and Mark held the glare, just long enough to convey the message that he had nothing to hide or to fear. Then he turned and walked back out of the room. He yelled over his shoulder as he left. "OH, and if you find my patient, please, give me a call at my hotel. I'm staying at the Holiday Inn for one more day; but you already know that don't you."

Mark was feeling mixed emotions as he left the hospital. He felt pretty good about his acting abilities, but then again, he didn't know for sure how they had been taken. Either they were rethinking their earlier assumptions, or they were thinking about when would be the best time to pick him up for further questioning. He was pretty sure he had the policemen believing him, maybe the hospital administrator also. But LeBeau was a tough one to read; a tough sell. And what was with that scar? Was he a path too? No, he couldn't be, or the scar would have healed and been completely gone . . . unless he liked it there. Luke had said that paths tend to fix the things about their own physical appearance and abilities that the mind didn't like. Luke didn't even know if it was completely a conscious effort . . . more unconscious he thought.

Mark remembered the cell phone and reached into his pocket to turn it off. He guessed he better get in his car, and head straight for Wal-Mart to buy a new one. He could call Luke and Kassidy on it. Then he would return to his hotel room and get some much needed sleep. Or maybe he would pretend to return to his hotel room and have Luke and Kassidy come and get him. That might be the better choice. No telling when they might decide to come after him. He could ask the desk to call him if anyone comes looking for him. Maybe that was too risky. Better just check in with them every so often instead.

CHAPTER 10

Follow the Leader

LeBeau was furious! How dare that doctor get in his face and make him look like a fool in front of these second rate hick town cops and that administrator who would rather be a cowboy. Dr. Johns was a smart one and a quick thinker, but LeBeau would keep an eye on him for sure. The doc knew something. At this point, LeBeau was pretty sure that he knew Kassidy Dover's hero and where she was. LeBeau would figure it out, or the good doctor would die while he was trying!

LeBeau already knew she was a path. The first thing the agency did after her disappearance was to secure her possessions. They had been aware of the disappearance of the forty euro's the minute they were gone. They had a team in the air and heading for Europe two hours later. Her parents had been grilled about everywhere they had lived or visited in Europe as well as places that Kassidy had particularly liked or felt comfortable in.

The parents had as many questions as they had answers. To their credit, they had thought to ask why agents would be looking in places familiar to Kassidy when she could not have left on her own. Someone had to have taken her and therefore would never have taken her anyplace that she would have felt at home, but instead to a destination of their choosing. That had been a tough one to cover, but LeBeau had just said that they were covering all the bases. Her father was particularly intelligent and hadn't believed a bit of that lie. LeBeau may have to take care of him later. The agency couldn't afford to have loose canons rolling around. There was too much at stake.

They were close to finding the link to the brain surgery and the telepathic abilities. LeBeau, himself, had been a guinea pig for their last experiment. They had learned so much from poor Regina. LeBeau had liked her. He could have even, possibly, loved her, given a little more time . . . . maybe. She was funny and incredibly beautiful and she seemed to like him and she was so trusting. She always saw the good in LeBeau. That was really what attracted him. No one had ever thought of him as a good person before. He nearly saved her, but they needed the information. *He* needed the information. He wanted to experience what she had so badly. He had hoped that she would survive the surgery, but it's a tricky surgery, taking a brain apart and putting it back together, and casualties happen.

The casualties are necessary. Just think of the advances that man could make if they had these abilities available world wide. We would no longer need vehicles for transportation. Pollution levels would drop off the chart. Any one could travel! You could go to your favorite place and spend the day. You would never have to board a plane again! Starvation could also drop off the charts. People could go where the food was and pick up a loaf of bread. There would be no shipping costs and no chance of humanitarian shipments being stolen by corrupt government militaries. The food could be in the hands of the very people who need it!

The possibilities were endless. There would be no more lying between governments because they would be able to read each others minds . . . at least when they were within twenty to thirty feet of each other. On that note, it was extremely important to understand just how much power paths had and what those powers could enable them to do. National security demanded that also. At this point, they didn't know if paths could just pop into a bank and take all the money, or play the market illegally, or what. They just didn't know and someone needed to find out before one of them tried it, if they hadn't already!

Those were the reasons for the agency; find out their strengths, their weaknesses and how to control them should the need arise. It also wouldn't hurt to know how many exist. Having American paths was one thing, but think about our enemies having them and a whole other ballgame would begin. Imagine a terrorist path. All that power would be his to use for unthinkable evil. No, the casualties had to happen to ensure the well being of the nation and the world.

LeBeau pushed a button on his watch and spoke into his sleeve, "Torgenson, you still got his car under surveillance?

"Yeah, I got it," came the reply.

"Great, have Donovan follow it."

"Will do! Anything else?'

"Call me if he heads out of town."

Mark didn't head out of town. Ron Donovan watched as he entered Wal-Mart. He followed discretely with some boredom as Mark walked leisurely through the food section and picked out some lunch meat, cheese, Kaiser Rolls and dill pickles. At the back of the food section, he stopped and made an abrupt turn. He almost ran right into Donovan, smiled and said, "Excuse me." Then he made a beeline for the bell peppers and chose four large ones. He meandered over to the apples and made a production of picking out the very best 10 or 12. Donovan lost count and patience and headed out to his car again. He'd wait out here for him; he obviously wasn't planning a big escape, just buying lunch.

Mark had known from the minute he left the hospital that he had a tail. He thought about trying to out run him, but decided against it because Laramie was such a small town that it would only take them minutes to find him again. Besides, where was he going to go? Instead he decided to try to trick him into believing that he had gone unnoticed. Mark led him to Wal-Mart, making sure to follow the speed limit so he didn't lose the turkey behind him. After he entered the store, he checked to see if the turkey tail was still following him. He saw him in one of those mirrors that hang in stores that allow workers to keep tabs on hard to watch areas that shoplifters hang out in. He then led him on a wild goose chase for groceries and waited for the tail to get bored and head back out. Then Mark walked briskly back to the electronics section and picked up a cell phone. He chose one of those pay up front phones. This one was a small 'brick' phone and he picked up another 400 minute card to put on it. That should keep him in touch for a while. Then if LeBeau's minions caught on to the new cell, he could just toss it and buy another one. Mark loved technology, especially cheap technology. Mark took his groceries and the phone to the check out stand and paid. Before he left the store he made sure that the phone was not visible inside the sack taking time to cover it with produce.

He decided he should stop and pick up a bottle of 'real' wine for Kassidy and pulled in at the liquor store down the street. Donovan kept his distance and watched from a parking lot across the street. Mark came out carrying a brown paper sack with a couple of wine bottles sticking out the top. He climbed in the car, seemingly without a clue that he was being tailed.

"The dope," thought Donovan. "A person could drive right up this guys butt and he wouldn't know he was being tailed!"

Mark was thinking similar thoughts about Donovan. "What a turkey! A guy could drive him all around this town, backwards and forwards, then lead him straight to the police station, have him arrested and this guy would still be unaware that he'd been made!"

Mark parked in the Holiday Inn parking lot, got out and headed up to his room, resisting the urge to turn and wave at the 'turkey tail' as he so lovingly called him. But if he did that, they would just trade him out with someone else who might be better at this game. So Mark kept his waves to himself and went inside. The minute he hit his room, he pulled out the cell and started the ten minute process to get it up and running. Ten minutes later, he was on the phone with Kassidy and Luke.

CHAPTER 11

Baby

After her bath, Kassidy put on the t-shirt Luke had left and then had fallen into bed. She had intended to stay awake and wait for Mark's call, but she was too sleepy to resist. She curled up under her blanket and was asleep before she knew it. It seemed like only minutes after her head hit the pillow that the phone was ringing. Kassidy registered it in her mind but couldn't quite get her motivation going to get up and hear the news, after all, she thought, the phone ringing was good news all by itself. As she drifted off into sleep her mind wandered back through the events of the last few hours. She lingered on the memory of his eyes again. What was it about them that just seemed to take her breath away? Why could she not seem to look away from them even in her dreams? As she gazed into the memory of them, they changed and became more vivid, more intense and then she saw worry in them. They were speaking to her . . . no . . . . he was speaking to her.

"Kassidy, we need to go get Mark. I'd just let you sleep, but I can't go get him by myself. I need you to wake up and come with me. Come on, baby, wake up." Luke was standing just outside her bedroom door.

"You called me baby," she thought. *"No one has ever called me baby. This must be a really great dream. Where are we going this time? How about Guam? I could use a little beach time."*

"Kassidy, we can go there later, but we have to go get Mark."

"Why do we have to take Mark? I'd rather just go with you."

Luke smiled, enjoying this conversation. He was going to love discussing it when she was fully awake, but now was not the time. He had gotten Mark into this mess and now he was going to have to get him out of it.

"Kassidy, open your eyes, please."

"Only if you call me baby again. I can be most compliant if you ask me the right way."

Now Luke was chuckling out loud. *"OK,"* he thought, *"I might as well make it really good."* He entered her room, crossed to her bed as he heard her reply.

"Yeah, do that; make it really good!"

Luke reached down, touched her wrist and ran his fingers lightly up her arm to her shoulder. He felt her shiver under the light touch. Then he knelt down on the floor beside her and took her head in his hands, moved as close to her lips as he could get without touching her and said out loud, "Baby, I need you to open your eyes, please, and look at me now."

Kassidy smiled and her eyes fluttered open. But her expression soon turned to mortification. "What are you doing in my bedroom? . . . your bedroom . . . that I happen to be sleeping . . . oh never mind that! What are you doing in here?"

"You told me to make it good and call you baby."

Kassidy pulled the feather blanket firmly around her exclaiming, "I would never say that! How could you say that I would say that?"

"Because you just did. Think about what you were dreaming, Kassidy."

"Oh, my goodness! I did! But I thought it was just a dream. That doesn't count! A person can't control their dreams!"

"Most people can't but you can. You told me so and I believe what you tell me, because you would never lie." He smiled widely.

She glared at him. It was easy to glare into those eyes when he was clearly enjoying her embarrassment. When was she going to learn how to control those thoughts and keep him out? "Out of my . . . your room! Now! Please."

"We have to hurry, Mark needs us to come and get him. He has a tail on him and can't leave the room. Actually, he called him a "turkey tail" because he was such a lame duck at following him. Mark made him in under twenty seconds. He said he could have driven him around town on a wild goose chase and the guy would never have figured it out!"

"Why didn't he call him a duck tail or a goose tail then?"

"Ha, we'll have to ask him. I'll wait in the living room. I can't wait to tell Mark that calling you baby can make you 'most compliant'."

Her shoe hit the door where his face had been a nano second after he had closed it. "YOU MAY *NOT* CALL ME 'BABY' EVER AGAIN!!!"

"We'll see about that, sweetheart."

When she heard him leave their thought reading range, she smiled to herself. She liked that he had called her 'baby'. And although some pretences had to be kept up with . . . like not letting him know she was already crazy about him, allowing him to know that she liked being called 'baby' didn't seem too risky. She jumped back into the only outfit she had with her and was in the living room in less than five minutes, including the time it took to brush out her hair.

"That was fast," Luke remarked.

"Don't be too impressed, I didn't have to decide what to wear!"

"Yeah, we're going to have to do something about that, but first, we better go get Mark."

"*Where is he?*"

"*He's in his hotel room.*"

"*We'll have to go to the lobby. We don't have a visual image of his room.*"

"*Feel like an experiment?*"

"*What kind of experiment?*"

"*We could try focusing on Mark and see if we could arrive near him.*"

"*We could end up on top of him . . . or inside him . . . eiww!*"

"*I don't think so. But if we do, we'll know not to do that again!*" Luke's eyes were positively twinkling as he laughed out loud.

Kassidy played along. "*OK, but if I end up seeing the insides of Mark, I'm telling him it was your idea, right before he falls over dead.*"

"*Fair enough. But just to be on the safe side, think about standing in front of Mark and not inside him.*"

Luke was smiling again. It was hard to concentrate while she looked into his eyes, so she closed her eyes and tried to imagine Mark . . . well, standing in front of Mark. But she kept seeing Luke. She looked into his blue eyes and ran her eyes down to his perfect mouth and that smile. "*Stop it,*" she thought to herself.

"*It's OK, you can linger there if you like, but you will have to explain to Mark why it took us so long to pick him up.*"

"*Damn!*" She hated it when she remembered too late that Luke might as well be standing in the middle of her brain hearing every single thought that passed through there. She decided to pay more attention to his thoughts; maybe that would help.

"*Are you ready yet?*" Luke looked a little exasperated.

"*Great, you hear thoughts of someone mesmerized by your face and I get exasperation!*"

"*I've been a path a little longer than you have; maybe it gives me an edge. Or maybe, you aren't looking deep enough!*"

Kassidy opened her eyes and looked at Luke again. His eyes were open and looking back at her. The electricity began to build and then she heard Luke telling her to think of Mark. Reluctantly, she did as she was asked and the next instant they were standing right in front of him . . . . blocking his view of the basket ball game he was watching on his TV.

"Nice to see you two. Do you mind?"

"Mind what? Asked Luke.

"Well, you make a better door than you do a window."

"What?"

"The game! You're blocking the game and the Lakers are beating the Celtics, but just by a hair!"

"Oh, sorry!" Luke apologized as he and Kassidy moved out of the way of the TV.

Without taking his eyes off the screen, Mark continued, "I'm impressed that you got here so fast when you said that Kassidy was in the bath."

"Well, she is very compliant if you call her 'baby'."

"Stop!" said Kassidy sternly.

"Baby, huh?!" beamed Mark, his eyes leaving the screen and twinkling at Kassidy.

"Really, Luke, stop it!"

"Yeah," Luke continued, "You want to try it out?"

"Luke! Stop it!" Kassidy was quickly loosing her patience with him.

"OK, Baby, I'm stopping, right now." Luke slid into the only chair in the room, put his legs up on the bed and crossed his ankles. He laced his fingers together over his head and rested his head back into them. His smile and laughter filled eyes were the icing on the cake. Kassidy thought about a large, lovely, very cold glass of ice water. It appeared in her hand and she sent the contents sailing across the room at Luke. It hit him mid stomach, drenching his shirt. The shock of the cold wiped the smile right off that beautiful face. It re-appeared on Kassidy's face as she slammed the glass down a little too loudly on the nearby table.

"Well, I can certainly see how calling her 'baby' makes her very compliant!" Mark erupted into loud laughter.

Luke stood up and would have scowled at Kassidy but she had begun to giggle at his startled expression. He couldn't be upset because he *had* deserved it . . . and . . . he loved it when she laughed. It made him want to do anything to make her laugh again. It was contagious; he began to laugh with them.

It was Mark that interrupted the chuckle fest. "You guys didn't happen to check on the turkey in the brown car downstairs did you?"

Luke responded first, "We didn't stop downstairs. We came right here."

"Yeah, uh, how *did* you do that? You guys have never been here before!"

"Well, we just concentrated on you and thought about standing right in front of you."

"I can see how that would work unless I happen to be leaning over the bow of a ship. In that case you would have found yourself falling into the water! You guys have got to be more careful! What if I had been at the Grand Canyon looking over one of those cliffs?" Mark shuddered at the thought.

"We sort of had an idea that you weren't looking over a cliff or leaning over the bow of a boat when you called and told us to pick you up in your room, but your point is taken and we'll be more careful," said Luke. "So what's the plan? Do you think it's safe to go back to your practice?"

"I don't know. I can't be sure that LeBeau bought my act. He may just be waiting to pick me up later."

"Maybe you better lay low at my house for a while."

"Yeah, let's go. Oh, wait, I have a surprise for you, Kassidy. Let me get it." Mark picked up the sacks with the wine and groceries in them and headed toward Kassidy as he hooked the plastic bags around his wrist. "I'll need to call Moneypenny and give her a heads up on when I might be back."

"No problem!"

They clasped hands, with the sacks between them and Luke concentrated on the safe house. There was that electricity again. As it became stronger and stronger Luke felt the now familiar urge to pull her into his arms and hold her close. He could imagine the feel of her hair brushing against his cheek as she leaned into him, his hands pressing on the small of her back. He could even smell the lilac in her hair.

"Now that is a much better thought than the exasperated one!" Kassidy thought back to him.

"It's just the electricity," thought Luke.

"How do you know?" asked Kassidy.

"Look at Mark!"

Kassidy looked over at Mark. The ecstasy on his face was totally readable, even if she hadn't been able to read his thoughts which were off the charts, enjoying the sensation. They both smiled as they found themselves standing in the downstairs living room of the cabin. Mark took a deep breath, let the air out slowly and let go of them. He headed to the kitchen to set the groceries down and find a cork screw and some glasses. He found the TV remote on his way and flipped on the TV to catch the end of the basketball game.

"So, what are we going to do about these guys? They're never going to let you guys go without a fight. I just met that guy named LeBeau. He was with the guy who took Regina. He was asking all kinds of questions about Kassidy's disappearance and he thinks I have something to do with it. I managed to walk out of there once, but I'm not sure I will ever be able to walk out again. That guy is a piece of work." Mark said, as he popped the cork of one of the bottles of wine and poured it into three glasses. He handed one to Kassidy and waited for her to taste it.

Kassidy took the glass with anticipation and took a sip. "Mmm, this is wonderful! It's fruity and sweet."

"Better than your Zin?" asked Mark as he handed the next glass to Luke.

"I don't know. I better drink a bit more before I make a decision."

"So really, is it better than my Zin?" asked Luke.

"No, but I'm not looking a gift wine in the cork!" Kassidy replied.

Mark missed the whole discussion as the Celtics hit a tying basket. "Ohhhh, no!!!" He was out of the conversation for the duration of the game.

Luke sat in an easy chair across from Mark and Kassidy curled up in the corner of the couch closest to him. "So how are we all going to get out of this mess? Mark needs to get back to his practice. He's already late by what . . . one day or two days?" asked Kassidy.

"One day. But it's going to be longer. I'm working on a plan, but we have to discover what we are capable of accomplishing before we get started. We don't even know how far we can push our talents." Luke took a sip of the wine and looked up at Kassidy.

"Well, we learned another one today. We can focus on a person and transport right to them, but as Mark pointed out, it's dangerous."

"We start tomorrow. We will push all our known talents to the limit and try to find out what we can and can not do. You better hit the sack."

"Soon as I finish this glass of wine. It kind of grows on you. I like it better with each sip."

"That's just because it has a high alcohol content and each drink gets you a little closer to not caring what it tastes like." Luke joked.

Kassidy laughed and took another sip.

Their conversation was interrupted by a loud whoop from the other easy chair. "They won, they won! Lakers are coming back!! They are now 1 and 2 in the NBA finals! Way to go Bryant!! You guys will have to do the victory dance for me though, since I'm getting all old and decrepit and the two of you are young and gorgeous!"

"I'm not so young, just gorgeous!" Luke teased back.

"You're not so young?" asked Kassidy. "What, you finally hit twenty-five or something?" she smirked.

"Well, actually, I hit forty-seven on April 24th this year. I'm older than Mark."

"Yeah, right!" said Kassidy.

"Really, he is!" piped in Mark, "I will turn forty-seven on July 17th."

"Oh, like I believe that!" said Kassidy. "I'm heading to bed before the rest of your wine hits your heads!" She got up from the couch and headed to the hallway. *"You two are such goof balls!"* she thought. *"I wonder if this line works on other women."*

"Actually, we've never tried it on other women because it's true Kassidy."

"Stop . . . please, I wasn't born yesterday!"

"Check out my memory, Kassidy."

"Maybe tomorrow, I'm bushed."

"Goodnight, baby." Luke said, just before he was distracted by something that Mark said.

Kassidy stopped in her tracks. *How could one little word completely light up her insides like this? Hmm, better hurry to the thirty foot line before Luke started listening to her thoughts again. It's been a long day and tomorrow, was probably going to be longer.* She walked on down the hall to her bedroom thinking about the last few sips in her wine glass, the school drama production last year, Kenny . . . . anything that she could stick in there besides Luke and his beautiful eyes . . . *damn* . . . her favorite flowers, favorite Chinese food, favorite pair of socks . . . . what would it be like to kiss him? *Damn,* she did it again. She listened for him, to see if he caught that one. What she saw in his thoughts was a clear picture of him pulling her into his arms and kissing her! She watched as he stopped, looked into her eyes and kissed her again. Her arms wrapped around his neck and pulled him closer.

Kassidy couldn't resist the temptation for a little payback. *"You can linger here if you like, but we have a big day ahead of us and you need your sleep,"* she told Luke. It was Kassidy's turn to giggle.

She heard a low sigh from Luke followed by, "What? What did I miss?" from Mark.

CHAPTER 12

As You Wish

The next morning, Luke got Kassidy and Mark up at 6:00 a.m. He was met with groans and complaints from both of them. "We need to get busy, or Mark will never get back to Moneypenny." Luke explained.

"Well, you and Kassidy can work on your stuff, but why am I up?"

"You are going to take notes, be our mind reading guinea pig and be around in case we try something that doesn't work so well."

"Shoot, what are you guys going to be doing? Jumping off cliffs?" Mark paused, "Never mind that . . . what do you mean, guinea pig?"

"We need to determine just how far away we can be and still hear your thoughts."

"No way, stay out of my mind!"

"Mark, do you want to see Moneypenny again? We need help from someone we can trust. You're it!"

"Why not just take a trip into town and try it out on the goons that are following me around?"

"Because, we need to know what we can do BEFORE we need to do it!"

Mark looked frustrated, but he seemed to be accepting the idea the longer he thought about it. "Fine, but keep to the surface thoughts please."

"We'll try, but we may need to know if we can see or hear deeper."

"If you get to that point, you can work on the neighbors!"

Luke thought about it, shrugged and said, "OK, that will work."

Kassidy got dressed in her only set of clothes, looked down at herself, wrinkled her nose and decided it was time to do something about the lack of wardrobe now! "Luke, I need fresh clothes, I'm going to hit my closet again. Is that OK?"

"Well, they probably already know that you are a path if they were paying attention to the euros you had stashed in your purse, so I guess it won't hurt. But before you put anything on, let's check it for bugs. They may try to track you that way."

"You really think they would try that?"

"It's what I would do," replied Luke matter of factly. "Go ahead and bring it here and we'll go through it before we start." Luke walked down to her room calling Mark to come and help them.

Kassidy concentrated on her favorite outfits, including some shorts, sweats, socks, underwear, sweatshirts, shoes, jeans and her favorite dress, (just in case). She also took some of her toiletries and her make up. *"Wow, was it ever going to feel good to wear some fresh clothes."*

"I should have found you something from my closet sooner. I'm sorry, I'm not used to having guests."

"Luke, how tall are you and what do you weigh?"

"6'3" and about 200 lbs. Why?"

"If you tell me I look like I could fit into your clothes . . . I'm going for one of those cliffs Mark was talking about and please, don't revive me this time!!"

Luke laughed out loud, took her hand and spun her around in front of him. *"I don't think you will be needing the cliffs anytime soon! Now, let's check this all out for bugs. Check the linings, the cuffs and the seams. Let me check your makeup and other toiletries. I've had some practice with those."*

"You've had practice with makeup?"

Luke rolled his eyes at her playfully. *"There are all kinds of things you don't know about me!"*

Mark knocked on the door to Kassidy's bedroom. "Its kind of quiet in there, are you guys occupied, or just having one of your private conversations?"

Luke responded first, "We're just checking out Kassidy's clothing for bugs. Come on in and help us out."

"Sure, I'll check out the ones she has on!" Mark made a beeline for Kassidy, put on his serious face and pretended he was about to body search her.

Kassidy played along, stretching her arms out straight to the sides at shoulder height. "Luke would like you to double check the pockets," she said as she returned his completely straight face. "Take your time; make sure you are very, very thorough."

"I think I will start with the collar of your shirt. I've heard it's best to search them with the lips . . . . harder to miss things that way." He wrapped his arms around Kassidy and nuzzled into her neck. She broke out in giggles and wiggled out of his arms. It was easy for Kassidy to play along with Mark. He always seemed to play along with the moment. For a brain surgeon, he didn't take life too seriously. She wondered about that. How could someone who very often held life and death in his rather large hands take life with so little seriousness? He always had a line from a movie, or a voice imitation to go along with the moment. He seemed to look for laughter rather than wait around for it to happen. Kassidy looked up at Luke and realized that he had been listening in.

Luke did not look amused. "May I remind you two that we need to find any bugs in this stuff BEFORE they can be traced?"

"Oh lighten up! We're helping!" Mark picked up a shirt and began working his fingers along the seams.

"Uh, shouldn't you be doing that with your lips?" asked Kassidy, erupting in yet another round of giggles.

"That only really works if there is a body still in the shirt . . . something about body heat, you know!" Mark leered back at Kassidy.

"OK, enough!" said Luke. "Just concentrate on checking for bugs, please."

Kassidy and Mark rolled their eyes at him but did as he asked. The conversation switched gears a couple of times before they finished with the clothes. No bugs having been found, Mark and Luke headed out to the kitchen to start breakfast as Kassidy pulled on shorts, a t-shirt, a sweat shirt with the Ramstein High School logo on it and a pair of tennis shoes. The sweat shirt with the logo had seen better times, but she loved it because under the high school logo it said 'Germany'. After all, how many Americans can claim graduation from a high school located in a foreign country? It had sparked the ignition of more than one unique conversation. Actually, there are more people who have graduated from American high schools abroad than you would think. Still, it was a cool novelty and she enjoyed the questions that arose from the reading of the logo.

The guys had whipped up some scrambled eggs, bacon and toast. Kassidy begged off, opting for her usual bagel and coffee. She was marveling at the fact that Luke had bagels when he looked up and answered her out loud so Mark would not be offended. "I picked them up from the store this morning. I heard you thinking about them when we mentioned making breakfast. Oh, and as for the next thought that I expect from that black and white mind of yours, I left a ten in their cashier's register and picked you up some cream cheese to go with it!"

Kassidy smiled and kissed him on the top of the head as she walked behind him to sit in the next chair.

"She kissed you! Over a bagel and cream cheese, she kissed you!!" Mark exclaimed.

"No, I didn't kiss him over the bagel and cream cheese. I kissed him because he paid for it! Now if he has my favorite coffee, I just might kiss him for that!"

Luke produced a small can of her favorite Hazelnut coffee from behind his back and a second later a carton of hazelnut creamer. "I left them another five in the register."

This time, Kassidy came around behind Luke, put her arms around him and leaned over his shoulder to kiss him on the cheek, but just as she got close, he turned his head and kissed her squarely on the lips. She dropped the coffee can in his lap, but Luke caught it and handed it back to her as she stood up, eyes locked on his face. That had totally surprised her. She wasn't sure, but she thought Luke was wrong about the attraction she felt for him. It wasn't just the electricity from teleporting. There was something more there. It was like she couldn't quite breathe when he was near . . . no it wasn't just his proximity, although that seemed to feed it too. It was . . . what was it? It was the way he looked at her, and talked to her. It was as if she were already his . . . . his what? She could no more figure out the thing than she could take her eyes from his. The kiss didn't *do* what ever was happening between them, it was a *result* of what ever was happening between them. She was sure of that. And whatever was going on, it was the most intense feeling she had ever experienced. How could this happen in a matter of days? Well, barely days . . . maybe it would be more appropriate to say hours at this point. Didn't these things take time? Maybe it was one of those love-at-first-sight things. Wow, did she just think the 'l' word? Well, damn, Luke was getting an ear full again! This was getting uncomfortable. She didn't even try to see what he was thinking; she was too embarrassed by her own musings.

Luke had not let his eyes wander from hers either. He listened in to her thoughts with curiosity at first, but then he began to deliberate over her attempt at explaining the pull they were both experiencing. Why had he kissed her? Why did he turn his head to feel her lips on his, when he was so completely sure that this attraction would dissipate with time, if he could just ignore it? He looked at her now. She was beautiful. Her eyes simmered with emotions just beneath the surface. Her hair hung down around her face, a deep shine revealing red and gold highlights. One small lock had escaped the main body and hung loosely over one incredible green eye. He knew from her recent hug that she smelled of lilacs and her skin was soft and smooth. She was funny and good to the bone . . . almost to a fault. She couldn't stand injustice or deceit. She was always concerned with the well being of others. She was sweetness and beauty all in one package. So why resist? He resisted because this attraction was not their choice. It had been pushed on them like they were some kind of science experiment. Luke refused to be a science experiment. He would resist with everything he was. But there was no reason that they couldn't be friends. Besides, she needed protection and he was it. He needed her mind. They would find a way to help each other and then she could go back to being the teacher that all the children adored and he would go back to . . . what ever it was he did. She must understand his thoughts; she was still looking into his eyes. He was waiting for some sign that she had gotten all of that when they were interrupted.

"Let's see, this is where I say, 'Get a room!'" exclaimed Mark. He was beginning to really miss Moneypenny and remembered that he was going to give her a call today and check on things. After all, he needed to let the hospital know that he was going to be later getting back than anticipated. "I have to call Moneypenny," he stated. No one was listening. He dialed and waited for her to pick up. As he looked over at Luke and Kassidy, he saw Luke take her hand and pull her down into the chair beside him. He stood, crossed to the cupboard, retrieved a mug, mentally filled it with the hot hazelnut liquid that Kassidy loved and placed the mug in front of her along with the creamer and a spoon. Kassidy's eyes never left him. Mark just smiled as Moneypenny answered the phone.

"Good morning, this is your most creative tax deducting patient!" he said into the receiver of the phone using a slightly higher voice with a bit of an old southern accent to disguise himself, just in case there were others listening in.

"Mr. Bond! Good to hear from you, sir. I can't wait to hear about your latest deduction." Moneypenny responded in the same professional, but familiar, voice she used for regular patients. "Your appointment was for yesterday. We missed you! Would you like to reschedule?"

As soon as she answered, Mark was glad he had disguised his voice. "Well, my schedule has filled up; it could be a month before I could make it in."

"That's all right sir, you can give us a call at that time to reschedule."

"Goodness, if you have many patients like me, you might as well talk that doctor of yours into a paid month long vacation yourself!"

"Thank you, I'll do that!" she laughed uneasily. "It would probably be a good thing; we could have the place thoroughly cleaned before Dr. Johns got back from his speaking engagement!"

Mark knew at once that she was telling him that they were being bugged. He thought quickly about how to tell her what she needed to know without telling those who might be listening.

"I'd heard he'd been delayed, I guess you'll be working hard to cancel his appointments and cover his butt with a leave of absence, huh?! The hospital administrator isn't going to like that, sure would hate to be in your shoes. At least the hospital has that other surgeon . . . what's his name? Oh, yeah, Dr. Charles Williams. Good thing you can always call him in. That guy is a workaholic anyway. Give him some good relaxing tunes in the background and that guy can work all day and all night, too! He'll love the extra time in the OR. Still scheduling could get tricky, especially with it being so important that you get it done right away. You'll probably go home so tired tonight you wouldn't want to go out with an old geezer patient like me, would you?"

Moneypenny caught on quickly. She was a little ticked off at the order to reschedule all his appointments in one day. She wasn't sure how she was going to get a tall order like that done. She also knew he was using the invitation merely as cover. He knew she never, ever dated patients, so she jumped on the other avenue he had given her. "I'm afraid that I just might prefer a quiet night at home, but I'm flattered you would ask."

"Well, ok, I guess I'll see you when I see you, then. I'll be sure to drop in or give you a call to reschedule as soon as I can."

"Thank you Mr. Bond, I hope we see you soon!" As Moneypenny hung up, Mark looked up to see both Kassidy and Luke staring at him.

"So what's up?" asked Luke.

Mark began explaining that the office had been bugged and that he thought Moneypenny was in danger. He replayed the conversation to them suggesting that they go get Moneypenny tonight and bring her here.

Luke wasn't convinced that having Moneypenny just disappear was the best option. "What if we have Moneypenny take a nice vacation in a tropical place? We could check in on her and they would never get suspicious. We don't want to endanger her anymore than she already is. We could have her go with a friend. Does she have a friend you would trust to stay close to her? Maybe a big guy that could protect her?" Luke was baiting Mark but didn't anticipate that Mark would respond quite so quickly or loudly.

"She isn't going to go to the tropics with some big guy . . . . unless it's me!" Mark responded, standing on the last part to emphasize his point. He even surprised himself with his fervor.

"Ok, how about a girl friend?"

"She might be able to get her sister to go with her. She's a teacher and just finished the year. I'm sure she would never turn down a trip to the tropics, especially a free trip to the tropics."

"Great, let's get her out of there as soon as possible. We'll pop in on her tonight and have her book the tickets on line. I'll have to get some money from my account. Do you think Moneypenny has enough in reserve to make it look like she's picking up the bill?" Luke was calculating how much he would have to get to cover the two tickets, meals and a hotel for a month. He didn't want any of the money being traced back to him. That would just make matter's worse.

"I'm sure she does. She's pretty frugal with money. It's one of her more endearing qualities."

"Wait, you have that kind of money available right now?" Kassidy was impressed but skeptical. "And even if you do, why don't you and I just take them someplace. That way the bad guys wouldn't even know where they went?"

"We want them to know they left on vacation so that everything is on the up and up. We don't want the two of them implemented in this thing. It's got to look innocent."

"But they need to be safe. If the lab boys know where they are, they will use them to get to us. They could be in danger even if it all looks innocent," said Mark.

"So, maybe," Kassidy thought out loud, "we should have them fly to Hawaii and we meet them someplace there and whisk them away to somewhere else. The lab boys know they went to Hawaii, arrived there safely, but they don't know where they are staying. It would buy us some time and if we run over time, they are still safely out of harm's way."

"That's pretty good! What do you think, Mark?"

"I think I can live with that. Where are we going to stash them?" Luke rested his chin in the palm of his hand and leaned on the table as he thought. "Hmm . . . we could bring them here," he said as he drummed his fingers on the side of his face.

"Wouldn't that look silly," Kassidy said, "they go to Hawaii but never acquire a tan. Besides, why would they agree to coming to Wyoming when they have tickets to Hawaii?" When both guys looked up at her she sighed, "Sorry, just thinking like a girl going on a dream vacation."

"OK . . . . I know a place and just the couple to watch over them, but we better give Rick and Sophia Dasher a quick visit, Kassidy. You want to come with us, Mark?"

"Where are we going, someplace warm, or someplace cold?"

"An uninhabited tropical island."

"I'm in."

"Oh, that sounds perfect!" agreed Kassidy.

Kassidy finished off her coffee, stuffed the last rather large bite of bagel in her mouth, wiped her hands and reached out to take Luke's hands. Mark joined them and Luke visualized Rick and Sophia's place. The electricity built again. It was stronger this time than the last. Luke wondered about it as he and Kassidy inevitably pulled each other closer. Luke pulled her hand up close to his chest and held her there. Kassidy was still chewing the bagel and had a cute little bump in one cheek where the majority of the remaining bite still remained. She was close enough for him to smell the lilac in her hair. He breathed in and then rested his cheek against her head.

"*Intoxifying,*" thought Luke.

"*Thank you,*" Kassidy smiled up at him, mouth closed; little bump still evident.

Luke looked down into her green eyes, "*Like a drug to a junkie, you're becoming too hard to resist.*"

"*So don't resist.*" She finally swallowed the bagel.

"*It's just the telepathic side effects, Kassidy. It's not real.*"

"*Oh, please!*" thought Mark, "*What happened to 'if you love her, go get her!?'*"

"Stay out of this or I'm leaving you home next time," rebuked Luke.

Luke concentrated on the Dasher's place and they found themselves standing on the front deck of their house. It was a large deck with flowers in planters in each corner. There was a table with four chairs around it shaded by an awning that was attached to the little house. The awning was white and navy blue striped with little scallops along the edge. The table and matching chairs were white and the cushions in the chairs matched the awning. The flower pots were navy blue also with red, white and blue petunias overflowing from the top. The house was painted white and lace curtains hung from the two front windows. The door was navy blue and the entire effect was delightful. Kassidy looked around astounded by the view. They were on a hillside over looking a small lagoon. The foliage was green everywhere she looked. There was a small beach with two sun chairs under a large umbrella. A little trail led down to the beach. It was a cobble stoned trail with a foot high stone wall along each side.

"It's like a dream house in a dream location! It's beautiful, Luke." remarked Kassidy.

Luke started to knock on the door when it suddenly opened. They were looking straight into the barrel of a gun. Because of the brightness of the day the person behind the gun was not visible in the shade of the doorway. Kassidy's reaction was subtle but intense. She never screamed but she began to shake uncontrollably. She was looking at the wrong end of another gun; the second one in a matter of days. As she stared down the barrel, she seemed to lose her balance, or her concept of what was up and what was down. Had she stopped breathing? Why did this keep happening to her? She was just a second grade school teacher! That was her last coherent thought. The bright colors around her dimmed and became black and white fuzz. She felt her body struggling to maintain its upright position but ultimately losing. Then there was nothing.

What Luke noticed first was that her thoughts shut off completely. They just stopped. They were enjoying the scenery, thinking about how peaceful the lovely setting was; then he picked up confusion then they stopped, as if she had just ceased to be. He chanced a quick glance at her and noticed that her skin was pale and her eyes were wide and staring at the gun. She began to shake and loose balance. He caught her before she hit the ground and was yelling at the man as he gently laid her on the deck.

"Rick, it's me, Luke, put the gun down!" Luke didn't even look up to see what the man with the gun was doing. Every part of his attention was focused on Kassidy. But Mark watched as the barrel was lowered and a tall incredibly good looking man of about twenty-five or twenty-six stepped out into the sunshine and knelt beside Luke. He was about as tall as Luke but not quite. His hair was cut fairly short but had grown out just enough to reveal a light brown color with golden streaks in it. The man had sage green eyes, a strong jaw line and a little light brown goatee that gave him a scruffy but handsomely casual look. With his shorts and baggy Hawaiian shirt with deck shoes and no socks ensemble, Mark expected him to start his first sentence with the word 'dude'.

"Holy smoke, I almost shot you! I couldn't tell who it was by the thoughts going on. The girl saved you with the comment about the dream house when she said your name, but I had to be sure. Next time, come thinking something like 'Hi Rick, it's me, Luke!' That ought to keep you from getting killed and me from having a heart attack! So what brings you here and who is this lovely lady? I recognize the doctor, but I'm sorry, I can't remember the name." He directed the last line to Mark.

"This is Kassidy and Mark. Mark, this is Rick. Kassidy became a path a few days ago. Someone shot her! I don't think she was ready to look into the barrel of another gun."

"Kassidy! Come on, baby, wake up, it's all right."

"What happened? Where am I?"

"We're at my friends Rick and Sophia's house. They didn't know who was at the door, and since they don't get many visitors, they had to play it safe. But everything is all right now."

Kassidy's eyes fluttered open. She was still shaking but Mark and Luke helped her into a nearby chair.

"Well, I'll be! You're the heroine of Laramie! Awesome!"

There was the beach 'dude' word that Mark had been waiting for. He smiled to himself. It fit!

"Some heroin!" Kassidy laughed shakily. "This time I black out at the mere sight of a gun. I couldn't even *see* your eyes! I'll never forget the last guy's eyes. And I made no effort at all to disarm you. What a wuss!"

"Ah, but this time you didn't have a little person to protect. This time you were not the only thing between him and death. It makes a difference. Haven't you ever heard the saying, don't get between a mother bear and her cub? It makes perfect sense to me. Sorry I scared you, but we were a little shook up ourselves. We usually don't get visitors unless we bring them here ourselves." He paused looking at Kassidy, then continued. "You know you're all over the news, but they aren't mentioning that you are up and walking around so quickly after major brain surgery." He looked over at Mark. "Did you do the surgery?"

"Yes, that was me!"

"Nice job! So, Luke, you found yourself a mate. You're lucky, she's a pretty one!"

"I'm not his mate!" Kassidy blushed. "I'm just with him until its safe to go home."

Rick stared right at Luke. "You haven't told her about the telepath process yet, have you, Luke?"

"What telepath process?" asked Kassidy. She was also looking directly at Luke.

Luke looked first at Rick and then at Kassidy. He took a deep breath and let it out slowly. "He thinks we don't have a choice, Kassidy. He thinks that paths are called or drawn to someone and they don't have a choice about who they choose as a mate. But I don't believe that. I am of the opinion that if we ignore the telepathic tendencies, they will eventually decrease in intensity and we will be able to choose on our own," Luke explained.

"Oh, that explains a lot," said Kassidy. At least she understood where he was coming from now. She stopped thinking and concentrated on the scenery, the temperature, which was perfect, or on this new gentleman.

Rick was laughing, "So, has the intensity been decreasing yet?" He laughed again and waved off the response that Luke was about to shoot back and motioned for the other two to sit at the table. "Would you like a drink? We have anything you want." He chuckled again. Before anyone could respond an ice cold glass of lemon aid, Coke, and Mountain Dew sat in front of Kassidy, Luke and Mark respectively.

"Wow, that was fast!" thought Kassidy.

"I've been a path for a while, I've been practicing," answered Rick.

"You heard that?" asked Kassidy.

"Oh, Sophia and I have discovered a lot of tricks that you'll be interested in. We've been practicing, as I said. We made a little discovery." He spoke out loud now for Mark's benefit. He had seen the 'here we go again' look on his face and assumed that Mark had some experience in loosing track of conversations that he couldn't hear. He shook his head and ran his fingers through his short hair. "I'm ashamed to say it took us quite some time to discover it. We should have figured it out sooner, but we always tried to stay out of each other's minds. Then something happened that changed that. I'll explain it all to you sometime."

"Where is Sophia?" asked Luke.

"She'll be along in just a minute. When I heard you coming, I sent her to our safe house. But she knows it's you, Luke. She'll be along as soon as she catches the cat again. The cat doesn't like teleflight!"

"Teleflight! That's a good name for it," piped in Mark.

"Wait, don't you two have to be together to accomplish teleflight?" asked Luke.

"No. Have you ever read Genesis? 'A man leaves his father and mother and is joined to his wife, and the two are united into one.' It is the same, well more so, with the path mind. The two minds become one mind. When that happens, you will be capable of doing all kinds of things that you never thought possible alone. Instead of having only the strength of one mind, you will have the strength of both minds. The two minds compliment and augment each other. The two of you can increase your talents exponentially. But you have to allow it. You have to accept the gift. Embrace it! Until you do, you will never become the creatures you were created to be. Make no mistake; you were created for a purpose."

"We were created for a purpose!? Who are you kidding? We're just trying to stay ahead of the lab boys long enough to figure out how to bring them down and live in peace. Then Kassidy can get on with her life and I can begin mine again."

Kassidy had not been prepared for that statement. Well, she should have been, but she hadn't. It took her by surprise and she caught her breath.

Her thoughts might have betrayed her, but Sophia made her entrance at that moment. She was radiantly beautiful. Her skin was a natural olive brown. Her eyes were light blue contrasting nicely with her skin and setting off her face in an exotic look which fit perfectly in the tropical surroundings. Her hair was dark brown, long and straight with a few wispy bangs over her forehead. She had an easy smile that showed off very white straight teeth. Her figure was perfect and she wore jean shorts and a loose fitting bright pink t-shirt that only enhanced the beauty within. She was carrying a Siamese cat who made it very clear that he was ready to be down on his own four feet.

"Patience, Suki, there you go kitty, no more teleflight today." Sophia let the cat down and went straight to Luke. He was in the process of standing but hadn't quite made it all the way up before she was hugging him. "Luke, I was wondering when we would see you again." She kissed him on each cheek before she continued. "What nonsense are you talking about? You want to resist your mate? What do you think; someone BETTER will come along? Please!!!"

Kassidy stood, "Sophia, Rick, it's very nice to meet you but, you guys obviously have things to catch up on, so if you'll excuse me, I think I'll just wander down and check out the beach." She smiled uncomfortably and turned to walk to the beach. Her mind was whirling, but she kept it on light topics like how beautiful the trail to the beach was and wondering if the water was as warm and refreshing as it looked. She also kept count of her foot steps as she went. As soon as she hit thirty steps away from the others, she let her thoughts run wild.

"So, he was feeling the same things she was feeling, but he was resisting. Why was he doing that? The feelings he provoked in her anytime he was within the thirty feet just seemed to increase over time and they never left her, even when she was away from him, like now. Of course, they hadn't been very far away from each other since that day in the hospital, but she had been enjoying the interchange between them. It *was* like a drug . . . . no more like oxygen. It was as though every breath she took belonged to him. Without him, there would be no point in breathing. Well, there it was again, she was hooked but for some reason he was not. If it were true, what the Dasher's said, that the feelings would increase until their minds became one and she had already surrendered, she was in trouble if he continued to resist. How had she missed this? She could read his mind; why had this not registered before now? But then she had been so caught up in her own thoughts and how embarrassing it was that he could hear everything she thought, that she had made it a point not to listen to his. She didn't want to know what kind of a twit he thought she was. Now she knew what he thought. And now she knew that she was hopelessly lost and in love with him and he would not return that love. So what should she do?"

"Don't do anything, he'll come around, I guarantee it." Kassidy heard Sophia's voice and jumped as she instinctively looked around. She could see Sophia's back. She wasn't even looking at her.

"How are you doing that? I have to be looking at someone and I have to be touching Luke to hear anyone else's thoughts. Oh, crap, is Luke listening? Can he hear me too?"

"Relax, he can't hear a thing. Rick could hear, but he is listening to Luke and not paying attention. I was worried about you, forgive me for intruding. Luke will not be able to resist much longer. He will come around. Just be patient."

"Yeah, uh thanks." Kassidy just wanted time by herself with no one in her head. *"Sophia, please don't take offense, but just how far away do I need to be from you and Rick, not to be over-heard? I just need some time alone with no one in my head. Please say you understand."*

"Of course, don't worry, you are fine where you are, I'll stay out of your head and I'll make sure Rick does too."

"Really?" Kassidy wasn't so sure.

"I promise, but if you are really uncomfortable, walk down the beach toward the rocks. There is a little cave down there and we can't hear anything while you are in the cave. There is something about the rocks that interrupts the brain waves. I go there when I need to get away from Rick's mind."

"Thank you, Sophia, you are sweet."

"No problem. Bye!"

Kassidy found the cave easily and walked inside. Sophia had left a lounging beach chair inside and Kassidy sat down and watched the waves role in and out just outside the entrance. Then everything hit her at once. Here she was on a tropical island out in the middle of who knows where. She couldn't get back home without the touch of a man that she found increasingly irresistible and who was doing everything in his power to resist her. But he was failing just often enough to confuse her. What about the kiss this morning? She had meant to give him a peck on the cheek for the coffee. *He* had kissed *her*! Why was he doing this to her? She wished she could just leave him here and go back to work. She missed the kids, she missed her friends and she missed her classroom. Who was teaching for her she wondered. There were only a couple of days left of school before summer break in Laramie anyway. How was Kenny? She also missed her mom and dad and her church family.

This was all just getting a little too complicated. And people kept sticking guns in her face! And how long was that going to go on? What was next? If things kept on as they were, they were going to have to face the lab boys soon enough. Would that mean more guns? She thought she might be able to face that . . . maybe. But Luke, what was she going to do about that? Was she going to be forever in love with him, and what if his idea of resisting worked? What if he found someone else? The tears began to fall and Kassidy feared they would not stop for quite a while. How had her life gotten so out of control?

As Kassidy walked down the trail toward the beach Rick turned and watched her walk for a moment and then asked, "Luke, why is Kassidy counting her foot steps as she walks to the beach?"

Mark answered before Luke could figure it out himself. "She's making sure she is outside of Luke's thought zone."

"She's what?!" replied Luke a little too loudly.

"She doesn't want you to listen in to her thoughts, so she is making sure she is far enough away from you that you can't hear what she is thinking." Mark clarified as if he were talking to a small child.

"Why would she do that? I'm not listening. We have work to do. We need to finish our business and head back home and start working!"

"Yeah, well, let's see, why would she need to get away from you. It's not like she's getting mixed signals or anything . . . is it?" The sarcasm was thick enough to cut.

"What mixed signals?"

"Well, let's see, you kissed her this morning, called her intoxicating and I'd be willing to bet that after she fainted and while you were holding her and talking to her mind . . . which I know you were, so don't deny it . . . you probably were calling her by some term of endearment . . . . like 'baby'?! Then when she is fully awake again but still a bit shaky, you finally explain to her that you are not interested really; that it is just a symptom of the telepathic things that are happening to you both. Then you explain that you are determined to turn her loose and get on with your life so you can choose someone else. Did I leave anything out?"

"Wow, Mark, how did you know about him calling her 'baby'?" chuckled Rick.

"That is his pet name for her," replied Mark. Out of respect for Kassidy, he did not finish saying what he was thinking, 'and it melts her like butter on a very warm day.' But Rick heard it anyway and smiled.

"What I don't get," Mark continued, "is how you can look at that beautiful girl, know exactly how she feels about you at any given time and delude yourself into thinking that you will ever be happy with anyone else. I know you feel the same way about her, but you are kicking up such a stink about not having chosen her yourself you just might lose her. But if you had just met her that day, no strings attached, who's to say that you wouldn't have fallen in love with her on your own? Think about that Luke!"

"Well, we'll never know that, will we?!" Luke was getting angry now. "Mark, this is not the time, or place for this conversation. We need to do what we came here to do and leave. Kassidy and I need to practice." Even as he said it, he was wishing he could leave the table and go find out what it was she was thinking that she didn't want him to know. It was irritating! He liked knowing what was going on in her head, but up until now, he hadn't really thought about how this might be affecting Kassidy, but rather about how it was all affecting him. Of course, he had been thinking all of this before. She had been looking right at him. She couldn't have missed it. Still, he'd been dipping his feet in and trying the water but never committing to an entire swim, and that had been OK for him but what had it been doing to her? And now suddenly, he cared about what it was doing to her. Damn! When did that happen? He didn't want to hurt her. As a matter of fact, he wasn't sure *he* could stand it if he did hurt her. There he was again, thinking of himself and how it was all going to affect him.

Luke knew he couldn't just let her go. She needed protection, and he needed her mind to stop these labbies from harming any more paths. But the more time the two of them spent together the more difficult it was to remain two separate people. If Luke gave in to that magnetism; that attraction, which seemed such an inadequate word to describe what he was feeling, would he resent it later? Would he eventually take that resentment out on Kassidy? When he thought of that, he always pulled back away from her. It had to be his choice! Not the choice of some force out there. It had to be his. That was the only way he could be the mate she needed.

"Practice what?" Sophia's question brought Luke out of his reverie and back into the conversation. Sophia seemed to have just come in on the conversation even though she had been sitting there the whole time.

Rick answered her, "They need to practice their talents, and determine what they are capable of doing. *Where has your mind been, love?*" He caught up on the entire conversation between Sophia and Kassidy in a couple of seconds and returned the favor with his conversations of the last few minutes. *"Don't worry,"* thought Rick, *"he'll come around. You did!"*

"Yes, but look at you, you're gorgeous, charming, you have an irresistible smile and your hands, my favorite part, by the way, are incredible! Who could resist?" she smoldered as she looked into his hazel eyes. They always looked greener when she listed his assets for him.

"Well, Luke isn't without his 'assets'! Look at him! He's rather 'cute'! Doesn't have my hands though," Rick teased, raising his eyebrows and smiling back at her.

"Sorry sweetheart, I only have eyes for you!" Sophia said without even looking away from Rick. *"Besides, it's not Kassidy that needs to come around. It's Luke."*

"Don't worry. Kassidy is already working her magic on him. He just can't see it yet. But he can't get her off his mind either. He keeps telling himself that he just wants to protect her, but he wouldn't make it three minutes without her."

The whole exchange had only taken a few seconds. Luke and Mark were finishing their bickering about Kassidy when Rick broke into the conversation.

"So what do you need us to do?" he asked.

"We need to get Mark's secretary out of danger. We're going to go see her tonight. We are going to stage a vacation for her and her sister in Hawaii. But as soon as they get off the plane, we're going to meet them at an out-of-the-way restaurant and bring them here . . . if it's all right. The labbies will know they got off the plane but will not know where they are staying. We hope to buy ourselves a little time, while they search Hawaii for the women. If we can't take the labbies down in a month, we will at least have Mon . . . uh Lisa and her sister out of danger. This was the only place we could think of that would allow the women some "vacation" in the sun that the labbies don't know about. We thought about Luke's place, but they would not be able to leave the cabin much at all; too close to civilization. What do you think?"

Sophia was quick to respond, "That would be wonderful! Girl talk again! I can't wait!"

"Girl talk!!!" Rick groaned. "I guess that would be all right. But don't kid yourself, the labbies will have someone waiting to tail them from the airport. You need to take them off the plane during flight. Can you fix on a person, not a place, to transport to yet?"

"Actually, we did manage that the other night," said Luke, glancing over at Mark.

"Good, tell them just to take a carry-on and after the plane is in the air to put the carry-on in their laps. You guys fix on them and think about arriving in the galley near them. That way you may only startle a couple of people instead of the entire plane. If you plan a late night flight, most of the passengers would be sleeping anyway.

"Wait a minute," interrupted Mark. "Isn't that just a little dangerous? What if they miss the galley and land on the outside of the plane? What if they land on top of someone?! Anything could happen. It's too dangerous!"

"Don't worry, Mark, we've never landed on someone that we didn't intend to land on. Remember, we are telepaths, we can 'see' the place before we actually land. I'm not sure we are even totally aware of what we're doing, but we're doing it anyway. It's like walking, you see the area in front of you and you miss obstacles, even when you don't realize you are doing it."

"Yes, but people have been known to trip once in a while!"

Rick couldn't argue with that. "Point taken! Be careful when you land in the plane. Then get to the ladies, enhance the memories of the flight attendants and the people sitting around them and bring them back here. Can you enhance a thought in someone's mind yet?"

"Can we what?"

"Replace a thought. Take their thought and add to it so that you change it. For example, when you arrive in the galley and a flight attendant sees you appear, can you add to the thought that she saw you come from the seating area."

"You can do that?"

"Well, it takes some practice, maybe I better go with you."

"Wait, won't it be more difficult with four people arriving in the galley than only two?" asked Luke.

"Well, I wasn't planning on taking the women. I was thinking that you and I would do it."

"I can't teleport without Kassidy. Speaking of which, how do you and Sophia do that?"

"I don't have time to explain it or teach it, especially if you insist on resisting Kassidy, so you will have to depend on Sophia and me to accomplish it. I would go without you, but I need someone who knows the two women we are abducting."

"There's a problem. I don't know what the two women look like. Only Mark knows."

"So, I'll go instead of you!" said Mark. "You can take me, can't you, Rick?"

"Sure!" Rick drummed his hands palm down on the table and concluded, "I guess it's all settled."

"Wait," said Mark suddenly, "You are asking two women who are going on vacation for up to a month to only bring a carry-on? They'll never be able to accomplish that! That would only hold their make up and a bikini . . . maybe!"

"I think I would resent that remark . . . . if it weren't the truth!" Sophia admitted with a teasing scowl at Mark.

"I know women!" Mark defended.

"Yeah, that is why you haven't dated the one woman who pulls all your heart strings," quipped Luke sarcastically.

Rick stared at the two as if he were going to enter into the banter but thought better of it when he caught his wife's expression. "Well, just have Luke and Kassidy pick up their luggage and bring it here ahead of them. Oh, and I think we should still take them to a restaurant in an out-of-the-way place in Hawaii and let them use a charge card to pay for the food after the plane lands. That way the labbies will just think they missed them somehow, but that they obviously arrived. As a matter of fact, we may want to do that periodically throughout their stay."

"Good idea!" replied Luke. "Well, I guess we better get going. We have some work to do before we can get started on a real plan to put the labbies out of business."

"Let me know when you come up with your plan, I think I can rally a little help and I can give you some short cuts to the learning curve you and Kassidy are on," said Rick as the four of them stood. They shook hands and Luke hugged Sophia good bye.

As Luke looked toward the beach where Kassidy should have been, he noticed she was not there. He looked back at Sophia, "Do you happen to know where Kassidy may have wandered off to?"

"Just head down to the beach and walk toward the rocks, I think you'll find her somewhere around there. Mark, I'm curious about the operation you performed on Kassidy, could I ask you a few questions while Luke goes and finds her?"

"Sure!" Mark knew she was detaining him while Luke and Kassidy worked something out so he played along. "See you in a few, Luke."

"That was subtle," thought Luke but he was happy for the time to go talk to Kassidy by himself.

"Thanks," chirped Sophia.

"I was being sarcastic."

"I know!"

Luke headed down to the beach admiring the incredible view. It might be nice to switch his place of residence from Wyoming to the tropics. But he thought he might get bored with perfect weather every day. Maybe he should think about a second home. He could come to the tropics when it was windy and nasty in Wyoming and head back when the snow was piling up. He liked a good snow storm in the winter.

When he reached the beach his thoughts turned to Kassidy just as abruptly as his body had turned to the rocks. He noticed a little cave at the base of them and as he got closer he saw Kassidy sitting inside, her knees pulled up to her chest with her arms wrapped around them. Why was she sitting in the cave when the weather was so nice out here? He was within twenty feet of her when he noticed that he wasn't picking up her thoughts.

"Kassidy?"

She didn't answer. She didn't even look up at him. She was watching the waves and hadn't noticed him yet. That was odd. Why couldn't she hear him? Wow, she must really be angry with him. He started to pick up speed as he approached and the movement finally caught her attention.

She turned her back on him and tried to wipe the tears off her cheek and look presentable before he reached her. "Clear your thoughts," she said to herself over and over again. "Sunny day, beautiful weather, I wish I had brought my swim suit and some sun block." She kept up the parade of simple thoughts, but then she noticed that she couldn't hear Luke's thoughts either. Maybe the cave would allow her a little cover even when he got to her. That question was answered when she felt his hand on her shoulder. She caught her breath again. One touch and she melted every time! He sat down on the lounge beside her and didn't say anything. She guessed that he was trying to talk to her mentally, but he'd figure out that she couldn't hear him in a minute and Kassidy needed every second to try to get herself under control.

Sure enough, Luke finally spoke to her. "I can't hear you. What's wrong, Kassidy?" Was that panic in his voice? "Did you find a way to shut me out? That's . . . that's good, you're resisting!" But he didn't sound all that happy about it.

"I'm not resisting! But I would appreciate if you would not touch me unless absolutely necessary. I'm obviously having more trouble with that than you are."

Luke doubted that but moved his hand off of her shoulder anyway. He scooted around the chair so he could see her profile, but she looked away. "What's going on, Kassidy? Why can't I talk to you telepathically? Are you angry with me? Is it anger that allows you to tune me out? I've never seen you like this."

"Well, you never have had the opportunity to see me like this. After all we have only known each other for a few days, haven't we? You don't really know me at all. I'm not angry with you. I think I finally understand you perfectly. I just have to figure out what to do now."

"What do you mean? We have a plan; we worked it all out with Rick. We can leave now and go start our practicing."

"Well, that's what I'm talking about, Luke. I really can't be around you any more. You *are* like a drug. The more I'm around you the more I want to be around you and I'm afraid that if I stay with you, I will find that I can't live without you. You, on the other hand, are working very hard to keep your distance from me and you resent having a mate chosen for you by some unknown force. I can understand that but I can't stick around and watch it happen. You're stronger than I am. This isn't going to work for me. So, let's go home and you can work on getting rid of labbies and I'll go . . . ."

"You'll go where, Kassidy?" Anger surfaced with each word. He couldn't let her go! She'd get herself killed! "There is no place to go. You can't hide from these guys by yourself." The anger in his voice was replaced with what sounded like panic again.

"You did. You have stayed away from them for, what, ten years? If you can do it, so can I. I just need a few tips."

"No, I won't let you go." Luke almost yelled that response but his next was softer, more reasonable. "I can't do this without you. I need you!"

"Well," Kassidy tried unsuccessfully to hide the sadness in her voice but it cracked as she finished, "when you decide that you *want* me more than you need me, let me know. Until then, I can't stay with you." Kassidy rose from the chair and started to walk out of the cave. It hadn't occurred to her yet that she didn't have anywhere to go. She needed him to get off this little island. She'd have had to turn around and come back eventually, but then Luke stood too, caught her hand and pulled her back into his arms.

"Kassidy, it's very important that you stay. If we can take these guys out, then all paths can live peaceful and relatively normal lives. Don't you want that? Wouldn't it be nice to go back to your teaching job? Wouldn't it be nice not to have to run to stay just a step ahead of them? You can't leave me now."

Being in his arms made her want to agree to everything he suggested. It was warm in his embrace. He felt strong and . . . . delightful. When he held her like this, she wanted to rest her head on his chest and stay there enjoying the peace, the comfort, the security and the need. Tears began to fall as she felt the first stirrings of the now familiar electricity building between them, how could he resist that? Was it only Kassidy feeling that? She wanted to look up into his eyes, but she was afraid of what she might find there. Still, she had to know, she had to see the distance in his eyes. It was the only way for her to fight the feeling, seeing it in his eyes would definitely help her let go. Slowly, she raised her eyes to meet his.

Luke had not anticipated the emotions he would have to deal with by taking Kassidy into his arms. As soon as he had her there, all he wanted to do was keep her there, protecting her and enjoying that warmth and . . . . and . . .

peace. He felt peaceful holding her! That was a unique revelation. He hadn't felt peaceful in years. What was she thinking right now? At least she wasn't pulling away from him . . . yet. He was missing the privilege of reading her every thought. What was she thinking now? Had she figured out how to resist him; because if he faced the truth, he hadn't figured out how to resist her? Every time he was near her, he was less inclined to let her out of his sight, let alone out of his touch.

All this talk about resisting and he was losing that battle so very quickly. Funny, when she was in his arms, he just didn't care about all that. He only wanted her. HE WANTED HER!! Maybe Mark and Rick were right. Maybe he should just let go and accept. He looked down at Kassidy and when he saw her looking at him, with all the questions in her eyes, it was more than he could bear. He leaned his head down and touched his lips to hers. Her lips were soft and warm and inviting. She didn't pull away as he should have expected. She gave him the privilege of this first real kiss. He felt sensations erupt all through his body. One touch of his lips and he couldn't seem to stop. This time he would not get away with a fun little peck on the lips like this morning. This time he was lost in the kiss.

Kassidy had not been ready for this response. What was he doing? He was making it incredibly more difficult for her to make the choice she knew she was going to have to make. But she couldn't resist him. The first touch moved through her body like a lightning bolt. She thought she might sink right into the sand as the control she thought she had over her knees suddenly vanished. But Luke didn't let go and Kassidy slid her hands up his chest and around his neck. She retuned his kiss, pressing herself closer to him.

Luke responded in kind, pulling Kassidy tightly against him. He deepened the kiss, touching his tongue to her lips and tasting the sweetness for which he longed. He didn't want the moment to end, ever. Clearly, he was going to have to rethink this whole choosing thing. That was the last thing he remembered thinking before he gave himself over to the sensations he was feeling and provoking. When Kassidy opened her mouth to his, he couldn't stop the moan in his chest from escaping. He moved his hand up behind her neck and stroked the soft underside of her jaw with his thumb.

When ever he thought about this moment later, he would wonder if they would have been there still if they hadn't heard Mark calling for them. Luke pulled back to look up when Mark called but never quite got the whole 'look' thing in before he was kissing her again. Just once more, before the moment was broken. No, maybe just twice more. Kassidy's eyes didn't even bother to open between kisses. She just waited for the next one as if she, too, was prolonging the moment. "Mark and his bad timing," Luke whispered between kisses.

"Mmmm, ignore him and kiss me again, please."

"As you wish," Luke found himself stealing a line out of the "Princess Bride", a movie he had seen many years ago, as he rejoiced over her invitation. Then he kissed her one last time. This one contained the decision that he was so reluctant to make. She would be his from now on. And just as importantly, he would be hers. No more fighting it. Luke gave his heart and his mind to Kassidy. He had been foolish. He hoped that she could be convinced to stay, but he still couldn't read her thoughts. She was somehow resisting him and his thoughts, and he was going to have to work hard to correct that decision. *Kassidy, stay with me, I want you too."*

Kassidy did not respond to his thought. But she hadn't pulled away from the kiss either. That was at least something, Luke thought.

"Is this how you resist the force, Luke?" Mark hollered from just outside the cave in his best Darth Vadar voice. He was laughing to himself. "She has you now."

"Yes, she does." Luke whispered in her ear.

"Luke, please don't tease me. If you want me, you have me. If not, please let me go now before it's too late." Kassidy was whispering back. She could feel the tears building again either way.

Luke didn't hesitate even for a moment before answering. "I want you. I've wanted you all along, from the first moment I saw you dive at that gunman . . . no, even before that, but I had been resisting the pull of the path life for so long that I just couldn't stop. Don't leave me Kassidy. Let me back into your thoughts. Stop resisting me. I don't deserve it, but I'm begging you."

Kassidy's eyes brimmed over with tears. He wanted her! She rested her forehead against his chest as the tears rolled down her cheeks and his words soaked into her heart.

The two had not moved an inch and Mark was beginning to get a little impatient. Still, he held his tongue and sat down in the warm sand pulled off his shoes and socks and turned his attention to the rhythm of the waves and watched the water roll up the beach to just touch his toes and then roll back. He couldn't wait to sit here with Moneypenny. Maybe he would have to take his own advice, begin calling her Lisa and quit resisting the 'force' himself. After all, even though everyone around him was defying age, he, himself, wasn't getting any younger.

Kassidy reluctantly pulled away from Luke, took his hand and led him out of the cave. As soon as they hit sunlight, Luke heard her reply. *"As you wish."*

CHAPTER 13

Spaghetti Noodles

By the time the three made it back to Luke's cabin, it was lunch time. Kassidy conjured up her favorite meal of chicken pot pie. She was enjoying thinking up her favorite recipes without all the hands-on work. She noticed that all the teleflight tended to increase the appetite quite a bit. She didn't mind as long as it didn't increase the waist line. The three of them sat at the kitchen table enjoying the pie, fruit salad and tall glasses of iced tea. Mark kept up the conversation. He didn't require quite as much food as Kassidy and Luke so his mouth was the most frequently void of food and able to converse more freely. He didn't mind as long as the other two didn't slip into many non-verbal conversations.

Luke and Kassidy were sitting across from Mark appearing to hang on every word, even making comments every once in a while. But under the table, Luke slid one hand over Kassidy's knee wrapping it down under her leg and lifted it over his leg. Kassidy had just taken a bite and the sudden intake of air in response caused her to choke on the bite momentarily.

As Luke tried to help her out by pulling her closer to pat roughly on her back, he only increased the problem.

"You . . . are . . . not . . . helping . . ." she choked out.

Mark had stood up and started around the table but stopped when he heard her speak and sat back down.

"What are you doing, Mark? Get over here and help her!" barked Luke.

"She'll be fine, if you will just let her work it out." Mark calmly took another bite as he kept his eyes on Kassidy.

"She's choking!" a frustrated Luke pointed out.

"Yes, but she can talk, and she is breathing. Let her body do its job, Luke. She'll be fine in a minute. Am I right, Kassidy? Just nod 'yes' or 'no'."

Kassidy continued to cough but nodded 'yes', to Luke's relief.

"Next time, wait for her to swallow before you touch her, timing is everything!" Mark said with all seriousness. But as he looked down at his plate and scooped up his next bite the smirk on his face was obvious.

After the meal had been cleaned up, the three headed outside for the long awaited practice. Mark found a comfortable lawn chair and a brought out a book from Luke's stash. He got comfortable and told the two to head on out and listen in on his thoughts at will. He would be reading and thought they might enjoy the story too. It had been an idea that Sophia had given him just before they left when she was supposed to be asking questions about Kassidy's operation. She had told him that in the beginning of her and Rick's relationship, if she wanted to bore him out of *her* mind, she would read a romance novel. He usually only stayed for the first chapter before he couldn't stand all the unbelievably mushy stuff. It usually allowed her a couple of hours of personal time.

Mark didn't really need them to stay out of his mind, but he didn't want them digging up things he'd rather keep to himself. Aside from the personal stuff, there was some patient confidentiality to keep in mind . . . . or rather OUT of mind. So a book seemed the perfect cover . . . no pun intended he thought to himself.

Kassidy and Luke started off walking beside each other, hand in hand. They were listening to Mark's book as they went. Luke had some ulterior motives as he chose the direction of their hike. He wanted to make it to a place called Flat Rock. It wasn't too far from his cabin, maybe about two miles hiking distance. It rose above a small creek with an old beaver dam in the middle of it. There were lots of deer in the area and other wild life like turkeys, and fox. The wild life was one of the reasons that Luke loved it up here.

"Do you think we'll see some of the deer and turkeys today?" Kassidy had been listening in on his thoughts.

"Probably, but don't be looking too deep into my thoughts. I want you to experience Flat Rock for yourself, not through my mind."

"Too late! But I'm sure it's more beautiful in person than in your memory!"

"I can see surprising you on birthdays is going to be difficult."

"I expect so." Kassidy laughed. She loved that he used the plural of birthday, it reminded her that he was planning to keep her around.

"Around and very close!" Luke responded.

It was beautiful out. The weather was in the lower seventies and the wind was not blowing. That was unusual for spring time in Wyoming. The hills were green and scattered with wild flowers. The green was not the dark green of a well manicured lawn, but more of a darker shade of sage. The spring had brought several late snows and some good rain showers that had produced the beautiful colors.

"Well, we can still hear Mark's book," said Kassidy.

"Yeah, I should have found him one I haven't already read."

"So don't concentrate on it, just tune in every once in a while."

"The only thing that comes to mind if I do that is the cave."

Kassidy caught her breath as she saw very clearly what crossed Luke's mind. *"Yeah, I have the same problem."*

The two started up an incline, stepping over small rocks and jumping on top of and down off of larger boulders. It was becoming more and more uneven. They had to let go of each other's hand to walk single file. Kassidy was thinking that it might be easier to just telefly to Flat Rock.

"What would be the fun in that?"

"Well, let's see, you would have to hold my hand and then the electricity would build and we just might find ourselves in another embrace. Besides it's more fun to lose my breath because of you than because of these huge rocks."

"You argue a great case, but I would still like to know the exact range of our 'hearing' abilities."

"OK, how about we telefly to Flat Rock and if we can't hear him, we'll hike back until we can."

Luke didn't need any more convincing. He turned around, pulled Kassidy into his arms again, pictured Flat Rock in his mind and kissed her. He had wanted to do that since they walked out of the cave but there was no relief in the kiss, only more longing, more need.

Kassidy was not surprised that she had talked him into the teleflight, but his swiftness in acting on it surprised her and the kiss sent her soaring. She didn't even feel them touch down on Flat Rock. Did she breathe? She didn't care. If she died right here, right now at least it would be in his arms.

"Hmmm, you're thinking of dieing while I kiss you. I'm not sure that is a good thing."

Kassidy chuckled. *"Shall we get back to work?"*

"What work?" He kissed her again.

"Luke, we need to check on Mark's book, remember?"

"First things first!" Luke took her hands from his shoulders, spun her around so her arms were crossed in front of her with Luke still holding her hands. He pulled her back into his chest and whispered in her ear. "Is it better than my memory?"

The view was incredible. They could see for miles. There were several cabins in view, though Kassidy could barely see Luke's. The closest one was a log cabin with a forest green roof that Luke told her belonged to the Scott's. They were an older couple with a large family and when they all got together on holidays there were sometimes as many as five or six dogs there and over thirty people. They got a little loud sometimes with all the dogs and kids and big kid toys, like a four wheeler they had for a while. But they were a very friendly group.

Clarence and Ila had owned the cabin since they built it in the 80's and the two were pillars of the little community. Everyone called him Scotty and it was said that he never met a stranger. That was because he treated everyone like a friend and was capable of getting an entire life story out of anyone within the time span of a TV commercial. He and Ila were totally trustworthy. *"If you ever need anything and I'm not around, you can count on them. They would take you in, feed you and they would never tell anyone you were there if you asked them to keep it a secret. Of course if you don't ask them to keep it a secret, Scotty will assume that it is fair game for any conversation."* Luke really liked Scotty and chuckled as he thought about the way the man loved to talk and the way Ila always corrected inaccurate facts. They were a team.

"Well, Mark has made some progress in the book." Kassidy could just make out the lawn chair on the deck and had zeroed in on his thought waves. They were easy to hear even from this distance. *"That's amazing! Let's try listening without touching, Luke."*

Luke let go of her and stepped back. *"We can still hear him!"*

"Maybe we are still too close to each other; I can still feel the electricity bouncing off you."

Luke walked a short distance away toward the trees. *"I can still feel you and hear him."*

Kassidy glanced toward the log cabin with the green roof and saw a person waving at them. The person was very far away, but she could still make out the obvious attempt to get their attention. *"Look over there, Luke. What do you suppose he wants?"*

Luke came back to stand beside her and both of them heard him at the same time.

"Oh, he just noticed we were up here and was trying to say hello!"

"I wonder if we can communicate with Rick and Sophia?"

"Oh, I doubt it. They are . . . well, do we really know where they are?" asked Kassidy.

"No, but it's worth a try."

The two concentrated on Rick and Sophia. They called to them but couldn't hear a thing. Kassidy was in the middle of one last try when Luke stepped up behind her and pulled her back into his chest again and wrapped his arms around her. At that moment both of them heard Sophia respond. *"What was that? I only caught the last part of your question?"* It was Sophia's voice but they could hear Rick asking the same question of them.

"We just wanted to know if we could hear you from here!" Kassidy was so excited she nearly jumped up and hit Luke in the jaw with her head. He dodged his head to the side just in time. *"Oh, I'm sorry!"*

A confused Rick replied, *"Oh don't be sorry, we were hoping you guys would figure out how to keep in touch like this. But we didn't expect it so soon. It definitely takes two paths touching at first. It works especially well with mind mates. Not as well with two unconnected paths."*

"No, I was saying sorry to Luke, I almost beaned his jaw!"

"Do you know how to stop this connection when you want to?" asked Rick. *"You don't want to be broadcasting every thought you have to us."*

"Wow, good point. Do we know how to do that, Luke."

"Well, I guess we could let go of each other."

"Hmm, well, that does work, but what if you like touching each other at times when you would rather Sophia and I not be listening in?"

"That might be a good thing to know." Luke was trying hard not to think of situations that he would rather they not be privy to.

"OK, what you are doing right now is projecting your thoughts out. Pull them in. Think about bringing those thoughts back home. It's like sucking up a long spaghetti noodle only you do it with your mind and not your mouth."

It took them a couple of tries, but once they got the hang of it the connections broke. They practiced a few more times until Rick begged off to return to sleep. Apparently it was very early morning where they were. They said their good byes and broke the connection.

"So what's next?" asked Kassidy. She turned around and looked into those blue eyes again.

Luke pulled her to him and leaned in to kiss her again. Kassidy thought that if she were a cat, she'd be purring. Instead, she moaned as he kissed her deeper. She felt like singing, except that would require her lips and they were happily busy right now. So she picked her favorite song and let the lyrics and the tune play through her head. The song seemed to get louder when Luke began to pick it up and join in.

Their bliss didn't last long. They both heard Rick very clearly at the same time. The frustration in his voice was mixed with amusement as he reminded them, *"Remember the spaghetti noodle? Mind practicing that a little harder?"*

"Sorry!" Luke and Kassidy reigned in their thoughts again. Luke smiled down at Kassidy. *"Guess we better practice a little more before we try that again."*

CHAPTER 14

Rooster Feathers

It was about 6:00 in the evening when Kassidy and Luke arrived once more on the deck of the cabin. They had taken time to try separating by greater and greater distances to see how far away from each other they could be and still hear Mark. They discovered that they could be about one hundred yards away from each other and still hear Mark from any distance where they could still see him. However, they could hear each other even when they were up to one hundred and fifty yards apart. This was a huge change from the original thirty foot distance that they had experienced before. The only change between then and now that they could think of was Luke's choice to choose Kassidy and the closeness in their relationship that had ensued. If so, thought Luke, as their relationship grew, so would their hearing range.

They also worked on trying to control projecting thoughts. Could they keep each other out of their heads? It was a lot harder to keep a thought from each other. Luke was much more successful than Kassidy. Blocking thoughts was hard work. If you wanted to keep a certain thought from another path, you had to keep it out of your thought line. Of course, if they really wanted to know something, Luke thought they could still get to it, if they delved deeply enough. He tried it on Kassidy.

"Kassidy, block your mind and think of your most embarrassing moment. I'll try to figure out what it is."

Kassidy did as he asked but held up a finger telling him to wait just a moment. She had to choose between several events that could make it into the embarrassment hall of fame. Once she had one, Kassidy stuffed the memory in the back of her mind and thought happy thoughts. She thought about the view from Flat Rock, about her favorite pet while she was growing up, but the best block she came up with was naming the kids from her second grade class in alphabetical order first and then by birth date order next. She was blocking very well until she got stumped about midway through the birth date list. She looked up at Luke for just a second and he caught the embarrassing moment.

Actually, he caught all three of the embarrassing moments that she had originally thought up. He saw her locked in a bathroom stall at a McDonald's in Germany while three maintenance guys who only spoke German worked to get her out, walking smack into a stop sign just as a car load of school friends drove by, and the time she swatted her best friend, who happened to be a boy, on his rear end before class one morning only to discover when he turned around that it wasn't him! His personal favorite was the swat on the stranger's behind . . . but then he hadn't ever been in a girl's bathroom stall, with Larry, Curly and Moe speaking German while trying to get him out, now, had he? She had to laugh with him . . . though she wished he hadn't gotten that much amusement out of any of the situations.

Kassidy made Luke do the same, hoping to discover a few of his most embarrassing moments. But he was much better at blocking her than she had been. She worked on him all the way back to the cabin, but to no avail.

"How do you do that?"

"Maybe it's because guys can compartmentalize things in their brains better than women. You know, we can have our whole world falling apart at home, but still manage to do our job. Women tend to think about it all at once. They can't keep it separate."

"Hmmm. Maybe." Kassidy hated to agree with that statement, but she had experienced the whole not being able to keep it separate thing first hand. She'd have to practice.

As they walked hand in hand up to the cabin, Mark was happy to see them. It had been a long time since he had sat in one place and read a book for an entire afternoon. Though it had been kind of fun, he was beginning to feel a little stiff . . . and hungry. He was also anxious to get to Moneypenny. The sooner he got her out of danger, the happier he would be.

Luke acquired funds from his account via "telebanking" as he put it. Which Kassidy made him put right back, because he had left no paper trail for the accountants of the bank. Luke couldn't believe that she was going to make him go to his actual bank and get the money. Since his bank was in a country where the current time was 3:00 a.m. they would have to depend on Moneypenny's accounts and pay her back the next day. "What are you thinking? We have the power to give her the money right now and you are insisting on this ridiculous plan!" Luke's frustration was not hidden from Kassidy as he voiced his opinion loudly.

"It's not a ridiculous plan!" she shouted right back at him. "It is the good and right thing to do. Now if you can make the paper trail for the accountants at the bank telepathically, go right ahead. But I will not be party to anything that even LOOKS like deceit!"

"OK, How about I write them a note. Will that help?"

"As long as they know how much money should be missing from which account, I'm fine with it. I just don't want some poor clerk trying to explain to his boss what happened to a couple thousand dollars."

"You are a goody-two-shoes, you know that?" he teased as his anger dissipated with the adoption of a solution. "I will have to do it after they open, but I think I can slip it into someone's drawer. Everything all right, now?"

"Yes, thank you."

Moneypenny was already pretty shaken up about a car she noticed following her home that afternoon and the fact that the car was parked down the street. It hadn't moved since she had unlocked her door. She had figured that they were probably after Mark, since he had gone to such pains to disguise his voice and talk in code on the phone. Not to mention the fact that someone had bugged the office. It had been a fluke that she had discovered that. It was that stupid little desk lamp that Mark had bought her for Christmas one year. If he hadn't given it to her, she'd have put the thing in a garage sale by now. The lamp shade was attached to the stand in such a way that you had to take out two screws from under it and then unscrew the light bulb, but before you replaced the light bulb you would have to take off the lamp shade to remove it. And the darn thing went through light bulbs like college students used to go through white-out . . . before computers, of course. Any little bump to the lamp and the bulb was blown.

The lamp was on two days ago when a couple of investigators came into the office looking for Mark. They had asked her for his card. She motioned to the stack she kept in a little rack on her desk, but it was empty. That was odd because she always filled it up in the evening before she left work and they had come early in the morning. There should have been plenty. She had to go over to the storage closet and get a new stack. She had her back to them for about a minute at the most. When she came back to the desk she handed them a card and refilled the little rack. After the gentlemen left, she noticed the lamp was out again.

She would have just left it, but since Mark was due back in the office, she thought she should make sure it was working. As she was unscrewing the two screws, she noticed a little black square thing attached to the bottom of the lamp. She had turned this lamp over so many times; she knew the little thing was not part of the original equipment. It was stuck fast to the lamp so it hadn't just slipped under it. This had been placed there. That explained why the lamp had quit when she hadn't even touched it. The two men must have put it there. She still may have had her doubts, except that she already knew the woman that Mark had operated on was missing and since they hadn't been able to locate Mark, he was a suspect in her disappearance.

Moneypenny trusted Mark more than anyone in the world. She knew he would have nothing to do with the disappearance unless there was more to the story than the press was allowed to print. So she waited to hear from him. It nearly killed her; she was so worried about him. She tried his cell phone number but it was either turned off or out of range. She had left messages on his home phone but no one picked up. She had even driven by his house a couple of times. Again, he was no where to be found. When he had finally called in, she nearly fell off her chair. It took her only a couple of seconds to pick up on his comment about the investments. They had been part of their last conversation. But once she knew it was him, she did everything possible to tip him off without tipping off those who were listening in.

So she had stayed at home even with the mysterious car sitting just across the street and down a couple of houses. She didn't know how Mark was going to avoid being seen, but now he knew they were being bugged, so hopefully, he'd come in the back way. But she never suspected that he would not need either door. The little group's sudden appearance did not leave much time for the confusion of the moment to wear off before Moneypenny defended herself. She picked up the nearest item she could swing and hurled it at the voices in the middle of her living room. The tallest of the three caught the lamp, and then she saw Mark. Relief and shock hit at the same time. She fell into his arms and began to cry.

After Moneypenny calmed down, it took the three of them about two hours to explain the whole teleflight thing, how paths work, that Luke was indeed not dead and that Kassidy was really the teacher from Laramie that took the bullet to the head. But it only took them minutes to convince her that she, too, was in danger and that they needed to get her out of the continental United States for a while. It helped that Mark was totally serious about paying her for the entire time she was gone and she was sold on the plan when she heard that she could bring her sister, and enjoy a paid vacation in the tropics.

Mark assured her that the teleflight necessary to get her and her sister from the plane would be "a hoot." He also guaranteed that she would enjoy the remote island they were headed to better than Hawaii. Well, except that her sister wouldn't have any eligible male company to flirt with.

"What about me?" she asked, "Will I have any eligible male company to flirt with?"

"You, Lisa, will have me!" Mark responded tentatively.

"You never call me Lisa, what's with that?"

"I should have been calling you Lisa all along. From now on, you will hear it a lot more frequently." Mark smiled sweetly at her.

"What if I like the name Moneypenny?"

"Moneypenny never gets her man." He explained.

"Then you better call me Lisa."

"OK," interrupted Luke, "Enough mushy stuff already, we need to purchase plane tickets."

Lisa called her sister, Sandy, to see if she wanted to head to Hawaii. She thought she better keep all the vacation plans a secret until she could talk to her face to face. There was the chance that her sister might freak out a bit, but Sandy was pretty open to weird stuff. After all, she had dated some pretty weird stuff in the past few years. Her sister jumped at the chance to go to Hawaii for a month and didn't even balk at the thought of flying out that very night. Lisa told her she just wanted to get away and didn't want to waste any time on plans. She just wanted to be spontaneous. She thought sure that her sister would see through that little lie. Lisa had always been the planner, but perhaps Sandy just didn't want to squelch the moment. So Lisa went on line and bought two tickets for Hawaii on the red-eye flight and told her sister to meet her at her house in an hour. Her sister pointed out that it would be faster for the two to meet at the airport, but Lisa convinced her to just come to the house as soon as she could.

An hour later, Sandy stood on the porch with two over-stuffed suitcases and a large carry-on. When Lisa let her in, she gave her the short version of what was really happening, told her to leave her bags with Luke and Kassidy and only take the carry-on. Sandy was in the middle of a protest when Luke, Kassidy, and Mark picked up her and Lisa's bags and disappeared from the room. She didn't even have time to come to her senses before Lisa was pushing her out the door and into the car. They had to rush, but they made their plane. It wasn't until they were in the air that Sandy came out of her stupor.

"What in the heck was that!?" The volume of her comment caught the attention of the flight attendant who was near them handing out drinks and pretzels.

"Ma'am, may I help you?" She asked in her sweetest flight attendant voice.

"No thank you, she was talking to me." Lisa returned the sweet smile and turned to look into the wide freaked out eyes of her sister. Lisa leaned in close to Sandy and whispered, "Sandy, you've got to trust me and stay quiet. I don't know who is listening and I can't afford for anyone to over hear what I need to tell you. So please save it for a later moment. I promise I will make it all clear after we're on the ground. Please, trust me."

"Oh my goodness, weirdness has seeped from my previous relationships and into my family!" Sandy's eyes had lost the freaked out look and had taken on a look of curiosity. "Can't you give me a little hint?"

The flight attendant stopped at their row and asked what they wanted to drink.

"We'll have two glasses of white wine, please," replied Lisa.

"You are having wine? You never have wine! What's the celebration?" If Lisa thought her sister was curious before, she now thought that Sandy was about to explode with anticipation of this explanation. If Sandy only knew that Lisa was just nervous about the moment when Mark would arrive in flight to take them the rest of the way to Hawaii, *she* might have been ordering something a little stronger than wine.

Lisa hoped for some clarity herself before she had to fulfill the promise to make it all clear to Sandy. She seemed to be missing some information, but she knew that Mark would never have given her a month off without a very good reason. She had always suspected that vacations were limited not because he needed her doing her job, but more because he just liked having her around. Since she liked being around him too, she never complained, even when there wasn't much work to do. She was a very efficient secretary, but that was mostly because she loved working for him. She had understood for a long time that Mark was daring in the operating room, but a total chicken in relationships. But after his conversation tonight, she was hoping the chicken was growing some rooster feathers.

CHAPTER 15

Da Big Kahuna

The plane was almost into the landing pattern before Mark approached Lisa's seat from behind and whispered that she and Sandy should head for the bathrooms at the back of the plane. The two of them left their seats and followed him back toward the small compartment of the plane that contained the back bathrooms. Lisa noted that no one seemed to notice except for one flight attendant who stood in the back of the plane talking to another gentleman. Mark, Lisa and Sandy approached the man and the flight attendant. The flight attendant turned and walked away with an unconcerned expression on her face and went about her business. Mark then introduced the women to Rick who had been conversing with the flight attendant.

"Did you augment her memory?" Mark asked.

"Yes, she now remembers us walking back from the isle, but she told us to hurry in the bathroom because we will be landing soon."

The two men took Lisa and Sandy's hands. Rick connected with Sophia, who was waiting for them at a little restaurant not far from the airport. The electricity built until Lisa thought she just might be squealing like a school girl and the next thing they knew, they were standing just outside of a restaurant called Da Big Kahuna's.

"Well, Kassidy told us this was an outstanding little restaurant, even though it is very small and out of the way, but I guess she forgot what time we would be arriving. It doesn't open for another three hours," giggled Sophia. "We'll have to come back."

"Well, I guess we could go to my favorite little out-of-the-way place for breakfast," suggested Rick. He smiled broadly. Everyone take hold. They all clasped hands again and in an instant, Lisa and Sandy beheld a large deck with a blue and white striped awning, pots of red, white and blue flowers and a view that was to die for.

Luke and Kassidy were already there, relaxing in a couple of chairs, drinking some fruity concoction, and holding hands like a couple of teenagers.

"Welcome to our little out-of-the-way home," said Sophia. "What would you like for breakfast?"

The group enjoyed a lovely breakfast together of fruit, flavored yogurts, granola and coffee. Afterwards, Sophia led them inside the house. It was spacious and beautiful. The living room was brightly lit with sky lights, a hard wood floor reflecting light from its glossy planks, and a fireplace in the center of the wall directly across from the door. One side of the room had floor to ceiling windows over looking another patio and a little lagoon down the hillside. There were trees and vines surrounding the patio and Kassidy thought that the windows might be very difficult to see from the lagoon due to all the foliage.

The room was furnished very tastefully with a fluffy couch with bright tropical flowers on it, and matching chairs and loveseats. One wall contained an over sized flat screen, high definition TV. The TV being a total necessity explained Rick, because you couldn't have the perfect out-of-the-way home without a place to watch some serious football! Across from the windows was a hallway leading to the bedrooms. The Dashers had family and friends come often and there were rooms to accommodate everyone. Each room had a different color and all the colors had a delightful tropical feel to them. Lisa and Sandy's rooms shared a bathroom. Their luggage had already been delivered to the right rooms and they were encouraged to relax and change into something more comfortable. Mark would also be staying with the Dashers and he had been given a room on the opposite side of the hall. Kassidy and Luke had made a little side trip to his house and Luke had picked up some of his things. They had also been delivered to his room much to his delight.

"You didn't forget my swimming suit or my sun block did you?" he asked.

"Absolutely not!" smiled Luke "How could you woo that wonderful woman without a swim suit in the tropics?"

Everyone changed into their suits, slathered on sun block and headed down to the beach. Not surprisingly, they discovered that the two beach chairs that were down there the first time they had visited had been increased by five.

Luke had not given up on the training time with Kassidy and insisted on practicing keeping their thoughts to themselves. They would push it as far as they could, carrying on a conversation with each other telepathically and deliberately ask Rick if he had heard any of that, while at the same time pulling the thoughts in to themselves. Sometimes, Rick would reply, but as the morning wore on, Luke and Kassidy had gotten so good at it, that they could even risk short kisses without including their friends.

Guarding her thoughts, Kassidy suggested that they try to sneak up on Rick and Sophia with a couple of buckets of sea water and douse them from behind. It would be tricky enough to get the buckets behind them without them realizing what was going on, but it would be even trickier keeping their thoughts from giving them away. Luke thought this was a good test of their abilities. So the mission was decided upon and preparations were made. The two concentrated on sand buckets from a store in Hawaii and left some money for them at Kassidy's insistence.

"We could always give them back after we complete our mission!" exclaimed Luke.

"That would not be right," complained Kassidy. "What kid would buy a used sand bucket if he could have a new one?"

"We'd clean them out so no one would know they were used," protested Luke, but he gave up when he realized that Kassidy was much more stubborn on this issue than he was.

Buckets in hand, the two progressed down the beach as if to build a sand castle. They filled the buckets, poured the sea water on a pile of sand not far from where Sophia and Rick were sunning themselves on beach lounges. Luke and Kassidy worked hard for a while, practicing keeping their plans to themselves as they fine tuned the mission logistics. It wasn't long before they had help with the sand castle. Mark joined them claiming to have the steady hands of a surgeon for the difficult details of the castle. Lisa chimed in that he may have the steady hands, but she, being the best secretary around for miles, had the plans for the details he would be working on. Sandy concurred that Lisa probably had the plans, since that was what she was known for in their family, but that being a teacher, Sandy, herself would be the best at overseeing the production of those plans.

Luke just winked at Kassidy and the two headed to the water to replenish the buckets. Kassidy was in front of Luke by a couple of steps and as the two reached the water's edge, Luke put his stealth thoughts into action and snuck up behind her. She never heard it coming and in the next few seconds, he had picked her up carried her about three feet out into water that was just about as deep and deposited her into an oncoming wave. He was laughing at his own cleverness when he felt something grab his ankle and pull it right out from under him. He went down with a splash. The two came up sputtering and laughing at each other. They had to chase after the buckets which were free floating a little way away from them. Luke was a bit further out than Kassidy in hot pursuit of the escaping buckets and was surprised by another wave coming in. He nearly fell and went under again, but Kassidy grabbed him and leveraged herself to help keep him standing.

"I guess I owe you one," he laughed as he regained his footing.

"I guess you do!" she confirmed.

"When would you like me to pay up?" he teased as he ran his fingers up her back and over her shoulder. He didn't stop his hand until he had a hold of her chin and was pulling her closer to his lips. He kissed her just as another wave hit and took them both back into the surf.

"You are dangerous," Kassidy sputtered as they struggled to their feet again.

"I'm dangerous!? You should have seen that one coming, you were facing that way," Luke was laughing so hard he couldn't seem to get his footing.

"You were distracting me."

"I was doing my best," Luke finally had his footing and helped Kassidy up.

"Hmm, then I'd say you are pretty good at it. Just be careful when you are distracting me. I'd like to live through the distraction to the part when you have my undivided attention and visa versa."

Luke caught his breath at that thought, "I promise not to start anything I can't finish properly."

They retrieved their buckets, filled them with water and headed back to the sandy construction site. No one noticed as they marched right by and walked up behind Sophia and Rick. The two were just commenting to each other that Kassidy and Luke were getting much better at keeping their thoughts under wraps when the cool water from the sea poured unceremoniously over their heads. Kassidy and Luke were mid celebration dance when the ice cold water from the cooler sitting beside Rick was suddenly sent sailing in their direction.

"Aahhhh, revenge is sweet!" yelled Rick as Sophia erupted in gales of laughter.

The shock of the cold water only lasted a couple of minutes in the heat of the morning and amid laughter and recollections of the looks on each others faces, the four sat back down on their chairs to dry off in the sun.

"What do you say, we head back to Hawaii and pick up some pizza for lunch?" asked Kassidy. "I'm wishing for a lovely 'everything but da kitchen sink' pizza from Da Big Kahuna's."

"Sounds delicious to me . . . as long as that doesn't include anchovies," said Luke.

"No anchovies, but lots of great shredded pork and veggies!"

"We need to take Lisa and use her credit card to leave a trail."

Rick added that they should take Sandy too, so that if descriptions are made, there would be two blond women, not a blond and a brunette. He also pointed out that the four should not be seen as a group, but instead as two separate groups. The two women should only order enough for two women. Kassidy and Luke could order for everyone, but only use cash.

Though Luke had already come to a similar conclusion he only replied with, "Of course! Good thinking." He kept the part about 'what do you take me for, Rick?' to himself just to practice. *"This mind reading . . . or rather mind leaking thing was becoming more and more easily controlled,"* thought Luke.

"Don't get too cocky sweetheart. I can still hear you!" and as Luke looked over at Kassidy, he saw a rather large smile cross her face.

"I am no longer trying to keep you *out, though."* He raised his eyebrows back at her.

"I hope that is more difficult for you than keeping Rick and Sophia out."

"When we come back maybe I'll practice that." Luke teased.

"You can try! But you realize that I will use every weapon I have to distract you."

"Hmmm, maybe we should work on this before we go!"

"Later, I can't work on an empty stomach."

The pizza turned out to be everything Kassidy had said it would be. Lisa and Sandy were still talking about the little hole-in-the-wall place in the middle of an industrial area. It was a little green and white building that looked more like a beach shack with surf boards on the walls and four or five tables for eating than it looked like a restaurant. But the food was top notch. Kassidy told them that they would have to go back and try the BBQ pork sandwiches next.

After lunch, Luke led Kassidy up a little path to the top of the hill behind the house. They walked for about thirty minutes before they reached the summit. From this point, a good portion of the island could be seen. But Luke had not brought her up for the view. He had not been satisfied with the short kisses and electrically charged banter they had shared all morning. He had insisted that they continue their 'training' up here a little distance away from the ever present minds of his friends.

Though Kassidy knew his thoughts, she still wasn't sure what took her breath away first, the view of the incredible aquamarine blue that started out the color of the light sand and changed to turquoise and blue with the deepening of the water as it stretched out into the ocean that surrounded them as far as the eye could see or the look in Luke's eyes as he pulled her into his arms. He didn't kiss her at first, just looked at her face as if he were memorizing it. His eyes were the deepest blue, his mouth slightly open; his hair was ruffled in the warm breeze. Kassidy didn't wait for him; she stretched up on her tiptoes and kissed him lightly on his lips. He didn't respond at first. He just let her brush lightly against him but his eyes never left hers. They smoldered, like the pinpointed spot beneath a child's magnifying glass on a hot, sunny day. She could see the smoke there, just before ignition to flames. When she rose up for a second sweet taste, he met her half way. The kiss didn't linger long on the light sweetness like the kisses they had been enjoying all morning, but progressed almost immediately to an intensity that Kassidy had longed for.

As Luke's mouth moved on hers, she pressed into him; she just couldn't seem to get close enough. Her hands moved slowly up his chest. She paid attention to every detail this time. The smoothness of his muscles, how they tensed as she progressed up to his shoulders. Her hands slid into his hair and pulled him closer, tighter into the kiss. She nearly giggled as she thought that if she pulled him any closer, she'd be standing behind him. She felt him chuckle at that thought with her. But the laughter didn't last long. The emotional intensity increased too quickly. Now she could feel him inside her mind, or were they in his mind? She lost the distinction between their two minds. No longer could she tell if a thought belonged to Luke or to her. Was it her request that he slowed the assault on her lips, broke the kiss to look into her eyes. It didn't matter. She could feel everything he was thinking of, or was she thinking of it?

Their minds wrapped around each other. They saw every thought, every memory. They saw the good, the bad, and the ugly. But they also saw the beautiful. Kassidy was nearly overwhelmed by Luke's intelligence and the information he had stored in his memory. And, oh my goodness, he really was forty-seven! She also noted that he had been alone for too long. He had never realized just how alone until Kassidy had come into his life and filled up that void. He really did want her; he wanted her for his very own, and when she felt how he loved her, her own heart overflowed with hope and love for him as well. Though she wished to stay in that spot, there were other thoughts and memories pressing in. He was quite the entrepreneur and very, very wealthy. He was also very protective of her. He would be hard pressed to let her out of his sight until he had taken care of the present threat. He had also been working hard at discovering a way to take out the labbies without involving Kassidy. How had he managed to keep that from her? There was so much information that Kassidy could not take it all in. Since it took years for Luke to accumulate all this information, it would take Kassidy a lifetime to see it all.

Luke was most impressed by Kassidy's compassion for others and a deep faith fostered and nurtured by the church family she missed so much. She loved and missed her immediate family even more than her church family. She was worried sick about Kenny. He realized that he was going to have to work out a way to get word to her family though he couldn't do anything about Kenny just yet. As Luke saw deeper into Kassidy's mind he felt the love she had for him developing at an incredible rate. That pleased him beyond measure. He lingered once more on the scene at the school when Kassidy had first been whisked into his life. He couldn't believe the fear she had overcome to protect the child.

The thoughts continued to flow from one to the other. As their minds melded together and became one mind, the present came back into view. They didn't know how long they had been standing there, looking into each other's eyes. They still held each other tightly. Kassidy's hands were still intertwined in Luke's hair and Luke's arms were still holding her by the small of her back. Their faces only inches apart were beginning to draw closer again. They hardly noticed the surrounding area, or that the sky was beginning to darken. The sun was low on the horizon and a spectacular sunset was displaying its colors proclaiming the glory of the One who created it. Luke and Kassidy missed the whole thing.

CHAPTER 16

The Next Move

LeBeau seemed to spend most of his time in a fit of anger over the incompetence of the men under his command. Donovan and Torgenson had lost Dr. Johns. Somehow the doctor had managed to get past them during the night. When he hadn't emerged from the hotel by nine, the morning after his little charade at the hospital, LeBeau had given orders to apprehend him for further questioning. But as LeBeau had suspected, he was gone.

The desk clerks on duty remembered him coming in last night, but no one had seen him this morning. Questioning the rest of the staff also proved to be fruitless. No one had seen him leave.

Where was he? How had he gotten away? Did paths have more abilities than originally believed? He knew they could teleport things, could they teleport people? That would explain a lot. That could explain how Miss Dover left a hospital most likely unconscious without being seen and why she had needed the forty Euro. Perhaps they had teleported her to Europe. But there had been no sign of her there. They had checked all the places her family had said were favorite haunts of hers, but no one had seen or heard from her. Since the forty Euros had disappeared, there had been nothing to suggest that she was still in Europe . . . . if she ever had been.

So the logical next step was to watch the people she and the good doctor were closest to. LeBeau had put a couple of guys on the secretary, but they had lost her and her sister after the plane took off. The women didn't exit the plane. He knew that for sure. There was no way to lose them when he had people inside. But they were missing . . . except for a receipt for pizza at some little hole-in-the-wall place on Oahu. There had been an order placed by two women who were identified as the secretary and her sister, but nothing since, and they had not discovered where they might be staying.

Since it is a little odd that they would pay cash for a hotel, but use a credit card for a meal, LeBeau's theory that paths could teleport people was beginning to hold water. After all, it was not much of a stretch from teleporting things to teleporting people. That had to be it. It would also explain how the French couple had made it out of the agency's facility. We find them and apprehend them and they slip through our fingers. Teleportation would definitely explain a lot. If that were the case, how do we stop it once we have them?

As LeBeau sat in his office reviewing field reports, he glanced around to find his cup of coffee. He had left his coffee somewhere in the room . . . . there it was, on the window sill where he had set it when he closed the blinds on the windows beside his desk. He concentrated on the cup and it began to move down the window sill toward him. It took him a minute or two but the cup was finally within reaching distance. He picked it up and looked at it as if some answer could be found there to explain why he could move stuff from one place to another, but couldn't pick it up telepathically to transport it. He also had to be able to see the item to make it move. Unlike the paths, he could not concentrate on something and have it appear. The experiments with Regina had given them hope, but when they tried it on him, it had proven to be only a shadow of what he knew paths could do. She had said that she could read the mind of the man she had been visiting in the hospital. This had surprised them; they had been tracking her at the time, never suspecting that she would lead them to another path. She had just figured out the mind reading thing when they picked her up. There had been something about him that had drawn her to him. It was then that the agency had figured out that they had made a mistake. The man was also a path.

They rushed back to the hospital, but the man, a Luke Matthews, had already been transferred. Other paths had moved him, LeBeau was sure of that. There were no forwarding records, and they didn't find him again until he came back to his old life and friends. It had taken them some time to recognize him, he had come back changed. He was about fifteen years younger looking. That was a new revelation. Now they knew that Paths could alter their appearance. They tried to catch him, but he was always one step ahead of them. Then he was killed in a very tragic car accident. LeBeau often wondered if Matthews could read minds and that was how he had always managed to elude them.

LeBeau had acquired a very small ability in mind reading. He could sometimes tell if someone was lying or telling the truth, but he couldn't hear their thoughts. While having a built in polygraph was handy, it was not always reliable. He hadn't been sure if Dr. Johns had been telling the truth. He rather suspected that there were hints of truth in his story and that was what had confused his internal lie detector. He kept hoping that if he worked on it hard enough his abilities would grow, but the growth had been slow and the practice tedious.

Regina had no evidence of a scar from her surgery, yet LeBeau still had a very visible scar running from just under his jaw all the way up through his hair line to the top of his skull. Though paths seemed to look younger and stay that way, he was clearly aging. It was aggravating. How had they come so close and yet missed it by so much? He took a drink of his coffee and let the warm liquid slide down his throat. It was a little cool in the office. It was always a little too cool in the summer time. They could never seem to get the air conditioning right. It was great to have it, but why did it always have to be around sixty degrees? Why couldn't anyone ever seem to get it to stay around seventy degrees? It was probably the same guys in charge of the temperature in the office as had been in charge of his surgery; always close to the mark but never really hitting it. He laughed sarcastically to himself.

"Back to the problems at hand," he thought. What is our next move? We'll have to keep watch over the Dovers. Their daughter is bound to try to contact them. We'll keep people in Hawaii; the women may still turn up. But once they do, how do we detain them if indeed Kassidy and whoever she's with can teleport people? For that matter, could there be more than one path helping her?

The jeep belonging to the stranger who had saved her had been traced back through several smoke screens only to discover a dead end. It supposedly belonged to some guy named Jerry Bennett. Unfortunately, Jerry Bennett turned out to be a dog trainer in Connecticut who had never owned a Jeep Cherokee in his life. He was also about sixty years old and looked every minute of it which meant he was either, extremely happy with his leathery wrinkled skin and sagging body, or he wasn't a Path. So the real owner was very smart, but had made a grave mistake. He had left prints in the jeep. They had not found a match yet but they would keep looking. They would find him. They always found their man.

A thought occurred to him then. He had spent enough time in Wyoming. Maybe it was time to head for Hawaii himself. It was the next best lead they had. He decided to book a flight and go check things out. He set down the cup of coffee and buzzed his secretary. "Get me a ticket on the next flight out to Honolulu. Oh, and also book me a hotel for a couple of weeks. Thanks." Maybe he'd feel better if he checked everything out himself. At least the weather would be better than Laramie had been. Who ever heard of snow in June, for crying out loud?!

Chapter 17

Willpower

The sun went down with Luke and Kassidy still standing on the hill top locked in each other's arms. It had been a warm, wonderful day and neither was willing to see it end.

"Hmm, check out those stars!" Luke was tilting his head up, taking in the beautiful night sky.

"They're so bright. I've never seen a night sky look quite this incredible!"

"There is no light pollution. It makes it easier to see them."

"No, that's not it. Well, that's true, of course, but that isn't what makes this night sky so incredible. It's the company that is sharing it with me."

The two sat down on a large boulder nearby. Luke took Kassidy's hand and laced his fingers through hers. They didn't talk for a while, each lost in the thoughts and memories they had just shared.

"Luke, couldn't we just move here with the Dashers, forget about the rest of the world and the labbies and live happily ever after?" She knew the answer even before he thought it, but the day had been so carefree and relaxing that she couldn't face what might lie ahead just yet.

"I would like that a lot," said Luke, *"but what would we do with Mark and Lisa and Sandy? Mark is an incredibly talented brain surgeon. We are both here because of him. He needs to get back to his practice. The only way to make sure that happens is to get rid of the threat to our lives and his. But I promise you that one day, we will live the life you are dreaming of. But I think you would not be happy for long without your teaching position. You love those kids too much."*

"Yeah, but it's not just the kids, it's the creativity that it takes to find fun ways to teach some of the boring stuff that they need to know. There is something about taking a boring old lesson and making it so much fun that the kids can't help but remember what you need them to know. Oh, and I have not attained my goal yet."

"Your goal . . . I think I saw that in your thoughts . . . it was funny . . . your sister in law laughs when you mention it. I can't remember what it was."

"The goal is to have such a fun classroom environment that my students are sad when they are made to have a snow day."

Luke was laughing by the time she finished the thought. *"Good luck with that one!"*

"Well, you gotta aim high! That's what makes it so fun. Well, that and those chance meetings in the grocery store when you hear a little voice saying, 'Mommy, look! It's Miss Dover! Hi, Miss Dover!' And those random run-by huggings! I love that part."

"I may be able to help you out there." Luke wrapped his arms around her and hugged her close. He nuzzled into her neck, kissing just under her jaw and working his way to her lips.

Kassidy spoke between kisses. *"That's nice . . . but most . . . of my students . . . don't take the affection quite . . . that far!"*

"Most?" He paused and added out loud in a high pitched kid's voice, "Miss Dover, you are my very favorite teacher!" He kissed her on her neck again. "You want to come home and live with me?" He batted his eyes for effect.

Kassidy played along with Luke, adopting a slightly Southern accent. "Well, young man, I'm not sure that would be wise. What are your intentions?"

Luke suddenly got very serious. His voice dropped back into the low register and picked up a husky tone. His words caught in his throat, "Kassidy, you know my intentions." He pulled her up with him onto their feet and pulled her once more into his arms. His hands moved up and down her back as he stood there just as they had begun, with him looking into her eyes memorizing each detail of her face. Reluctantly he thought, *"We should get back to the beach house and say our good byes and go home."*

"It's too soon. I'd like tonight to go on for just a little longer . . . say just fifty years or so. Then I'll go home with you without a fight . . . maybe!"

"There is a song about that. The guy asks his girl to stay with him for a thousand years and then . . . if it don't work out, then you can tell me goodbye" Luke sang the last part. *"That's the only line I can remember."*

"I'd take a thousand years!"

"And I'd give them to you, but you have to sleep sometime so we better head home."

They thought of the deck and found themselves in the middle of a rowdy group of friends. Mark was sitting as close to Lisa as two deck chairs could get and was laughing with everyone else at something that Rick had said. Luke noticed that he had a strangle hold on Lisa's hand. He smiled at his closest friend.

They had sliced up a large watermelon and had evidently been having spitting wars to see how far they could shoot the seeds out of their mouths. It was hard to say who was winning, they were all giggling and both Rick and Mark were claiming to be the proud shooter of the seed farthest away.

"Where have you guys been?" asked Mark. "You're missing the Watermelon Seed Spitting Olympics!"

"How could we have been so remiss!" joked Luke. "And there we were, just being bored out of our minds looking at the incredible starry sky up on the hill, alone, just the two of us! Really, Kassidy, how will we ever live with the regret that we'll share forever at not having been here for the very first annual Dasher Island Watermelon Seed Spitting Olympics?"

"I guess we'll just have to make sure we don't miss it next year, dear!"

Rick made an effort to take a sneak peek into what they had been up to by trying to read Luke or Kassidy's mind, but they had mastered the spaghetti noodle trick and didn't give away a clue. Sophia picked up on what he was doing and kicked him under the table. When he looked at her in pain, she gave him the 'knock it off' look and he just shrugged his shoulders with a 'boys will be boys' sort of look.

"We'll see you guys tomorrow. We're going to go home and get some rest. Rick, tomorrow, we should start working on a plan. I have some ideas, but I could use a sounding board and some advice."

"Sure, but how about if I get a hold of some of our friends? We could use all the help we can get. They may also have some ideas."

"As long as you trust them, the more the merrier!"

"Great! What time do you want to meet?"

"Not too early, it's been a long day," Kassidy added. She was thinking of the early morning wake up that had lead to nearly an all nighter, followed by the long sunny fun filled day today.

"How about we meet here at noon for lunch?" asked Sophia.

"Sounds great! See you all then." Luke looked back at Kassidy; the two concentrated on the cabin and were gone.

By the time they made it back to the cabin he was kissing her again. She was so distracted by the warmth of his body pressing against hers and the way his lips seemed to fit perfectly with hers that she was stunned for a moment when he broke the kiss, let her go and began turning on all the media equipment along the wall. He was checking the perimeter and making sure no one had been there. He checked all the rooms and headed over to the little keypad by the door they had first entered on the first day she had come to the cabin. He punched in a number and the panel slid open, he took the stairs two at a time and crept quietly through the hidden food cabinet. Kassidy followed him up the stairs and through the cabin as he checked it out.

"What are you looking for?" asked Kassidy.

"I just had the feeling that I shouldn't take this feeling of safety too casually. We need to be careful. As a matter of fact, we should start making our meals up here so this place looks lived in and not like a façade. That's the only way the basement will be safe if they find the cabin. If they think this is where we live they won't be looking for any hidden compartments."

"You're making me nervous." Kassidy stated the obvious. Luke could see the fear in her face.

"Don't worry. They won't catch us off guard. I'm just trying to be cautious. I have all kinds of little detection devices around here." He touched her hand and shared the information with her mentally. It took only a couple of minutes to show her what would probably have taken thirty minutes verbally. He could feel her tension release as she saw the protection surrounding the little cabin. "Does that make you feel better?"

"Much! Thank you." As Kassidy relaxed again, the length of the day began to catch up to her. She was definitely ready for bed.

"You need some sleep, baby." Luke stated the obvious.

Kassidy caught her breath for the umpteenth time today. What was it about that word that melted her every time Luke said it! *"Yeah, well, if you want any sleep, you might want to choose your words just a little bit more carefully."* She stood up on her tiptoes and kissed him sweetly on the lips.

Luke smiled, returned the kiss then turned her around and led her back down the passage way. He locked the food storage door behind them and the secret panel at the bottom of the stairs. He continued down the hallway, turning on lights in front of them and turning off the lights behind them. When he got to the door of Kassidy's room, he stopped, and turned to face her. "My Lady, your room!" Luke bowed as he opened her door and turned on her light.

The light-hearted way he brought her to her room nearly distracted her from the way he had called her 'baby' but not quite. She reached out and wrapped her hand around his neck, pulling him closer to her. She pulled his hand off the door knob and wrapped it around her waist. *"If you are going to use the word 'baby' to refer to me, you are going to have to suffer the consequences."* She kissed his chin; that being the only part of his face she could reach without standing on her tiptoes again.

"Kassidy, as much as I would like to suffer the consequences of my actions, you need your sleep." He kissed her on her forehead, disentangled her arms from his neck and waist and reluctantly, very reluctantly, sent her into her room. *"Damn, that was difficult. She is so perfect, so lovely. Maybe I should rethink this decision."*

"I heard that. Go to bed, you are just as tired as I am! See you in the morning."

"Good night, ba . . ."

"Watch it Luke!"

"Sorry . . . good night, Kassidy."

Luke left her door and headed down the hall to his room. He slipped in, got ready for bed and should have been asleep before his head hit the pillow. But his thoughts were filled with Kassidy. He had to work extra hard to keep from sharing them with her. If he had known she was doing the same thing, he might not have worried so much. He wanted her right here with him. The distance from this room to the next seemed too far.

Luke sighed. She was proving to be a great distraction from things that needed doing. Like fighting bad guys! How was he going to concentrate on keeping her safe when he couldn't concentrate on anything but kissing her lately? That was going to have to change, or Luke was going to make a mistake that could be costly to them both. If he messed things up and anything happened to Kassidy . . . . or Mark, Lisa or Sandy how would he live with himself? Tomorrow he would concentrate. If he could just get a plan formalized and implemented, he could discipline himself long enough to take care of things. Once they were safe, there would be plenty of time to spend with Kassidy. There would be his whole life to give to her. But for now, he was going to have to concentrate on saving that life, not intertwining with it. He was going to need a lot of willpower.

Kassidy had difficulty getting to sleep that night also. She couldn't believe that she had tried to tempt Luke into coming to bed with her. She was mortified! Where was her faith in God? There she was perfectly willing to ignore His teachings and go against everything she believed in just because a man she'd only known for a few days had called her 'baby'. Well, it was more than that. She loved him, that was for sure, but things were moving so fast! When he was kissing her, she just didn't care about anything except Luke. And when he called her 'baby' she lost all reason altogether!

This was going to have to change. She was not going to get sucked into anything that would not please God and giving in to Luke before she was married wasn't going to happen. It went against her moral beliefs. So, the question was, how was she going to slow things down? She'd have to try to keep her distance just a bit. If she just wasn't as easily kissed, maybe she could resist him. Luke was going to have to stop calling her 'baby' or she was going to have to overcome the effect it had on her. She wasn't sure how she was going to do that. Surprisingly, she was sure that if anyone else called her that, it would have no effect at all. So why could Luke get anything he wanted with just that one word?

She said her prayers, asking for a little extra help, and decided that tomorrow she would concentrate on anything other than Luke. She would get to know Sophia, Lisa and Sandy. Well, she'd get to know Lisa if Mark had been able to pry himself away from her yet. She smiled as she remembered how close he had been sitting to her and how tightly he had been holding her hand. It was as if he thought she might somehow get away from him on that little itty bitty island.

As Kassidy finally closed her eyes and drifted off to sleep, her mind wandered back to what was becoming her mind's home page, Luke. Well, so much for willpower, she thought and slipped into a deep sleep.

CHAPTER 18

Friends and Foes

Kassidy and Luke had breakfast in the upper cabin the next morning, each trying not to provoke the other's attention, and left the dirty dishes as evidence that the cabin was in use. Kassidy also quickly dusted the sparse furniture and the pictures on the walls. Luke rumpled the bed sheets and quickly re-made the bed so it would appear slept in and quickly made. Kassidy also used the upstairs bathroom to brush her hair and teeth and did a quick wipe down to remove any tell tale dust. After they had taken a short walk in the cool morning air, they were ready to leave for the Dasher's.

When they arrived at the beach house shortly before noon, their fists were clenched and their bodies tense from resisting the natural pull of the teleflight. They let go of each other's hands quickly and glanced around for their friends. There were quite a few more people there than they had expected. Rick was talking with a couple who were speaking very fast French. Kassidy had taken French in high school and a couple of years in college, but it had been a few years and she didn't think she could even remember how to ask them where the bathroom was. But Rick was conversing with them easily. There was also a German couple and a couple from a country Kassidy couldn't identify by listening to the language. There was also a couple speaking English and Spanish to each other. The gentleman would ask something in Spanish and the woman was answering him in English.

While Kassidy was fascinated, Luke was frustrated. How were they going to coordinate if they couldn't speak each other's languages? And just as importantly, why would international paths care about the agency in the United States? . . . . unless the agency . . . the labbies, were world wide! As that realization hit Luke, his fear for all of them increased ten fold. How would they stop them all? Would they ever be free to live normal lives?

Rick finally looked up from his French conversation and smiled at Luke. "Luke, I'd like you to meet Andre and Cecil. They are from France, obviously. Would you mind speaking with them, while I greet our other guests?"

"Well, that would be wonderful Rick, but I don't speak a lick of French."

"Just sit and listen for a minute and concentrate on the language. I think you're in for a pleasant surprise."

While Luke had been conversing with Rick, Kassidy had been listening to the French, trying to remember some of what she had learned. The more she concentrated, the easier it became. At first it was only a few words, but in a very short time, she was picking up whole sentences. When Cecil asked her husband if he knew where the bathroom was, Kassidy found herself telling her where she could find it in perfect French.

Luke stood looking at Kassidy in amazement. "*I didn't know you spoke French! How did I miss that last night? All you had left in your memory was a few key phrases left from college.*"

"*Luke, I don't know how I can do this, but I can understand everything they are saying. Maybe learning a language is like riding a bike, once you learn you never forget!*"

"*But Kassidy, you spoke it perfectly, without so much as even a slight accent!*"

"*I don't know how I did it, but it sure is fun!*"

"*Kassidy, ask Andre if the labbies are at work in France also.*"

Andre had been listening in since Kassidy and Luke had not been blocking their thoughts. He answered Luke in perfect English. "Yes, your agency has been after paths in France as well as Germany, Poland, England and Russia. I think the couple across from me said they were from Japan." He also did not have any trace of an accent. "We are here to coordinate our efforts to stop them completely. We believe that the American agency is the only one privy to paths. Well that's what we think anyway! If we can stop them here, before it spreads to other countries, we will be safe to live normal lives again. However, we are going to have to keep very close tabs on present and future paths. We will have to develop a set of rules and regulations to keep ourselves from drawing attention to our kind again. But, first things first. Let's take care of the agency."

"Are you American?" asked a confused Luke.

Andre smiled, "No, I was born and raised in France but I picked up English from Rick when we first met a few years ago. Actually, your mate picked up French from Cecil and me. If you listen while I speak it to you, you will be able to access my language memory and pick it up also." Andre began speaking in French and before ten minutes had passed, Luke was answering him in French also.

As the paths all began to get to know each other, the deck began to sound like a fundamentalist prayer meeting with everyone speaking in tongues. They were asking and answering in two or three different languages at a time.

"I sure wish I'd had this talent when I lived in Europe and Japan!" exclaimed Kassidy. "I had dreamed about being able to converse with my neighbors without the struggle to translate and use sign language. This is so fun!"

"Yes and very useful. How many languages do you think LeBeau can speak? We could really confound him, especially if we start using several languages at a time. Or we could learn an obscure language that would be difficult for them to translate! I think we've stumbled on something here!"

"You mentioned LeBeau, have you met him?" asked Andre.

"I've met him briefly, but my friend, Mark, has spent a little more time with him," answered Luke.

"We should watch out for him especially. Did you notice his scar?"

"Yes, we did!"

Andre looked grave as he continued, "LeBeau has had some experimental surgery. After the labbies got hold of a woman path, they dissected her and tried the surgery on LeBeau. He did not benefit quite as much as he had hoped, but beware around him. I don't know how many talents he now has, but I did see him close the blinds in his office once without getting out of his chair. He had to look at the blinds and he wasn't very fast, but he is probably practicing. And who knows what else he is capable of doing."

"You've been in his office?" Luke's interest was peaked.

"Yes, unfortunately."

"How did you manage to get away? I think I knew the woman path that you were talking about. She never made it out alive."

"Rick and Sophia heard about my accident and when I disappeared from the hospital, they came after me. As a matter of fact, the labbies had picked up Cecil at the same time. She was with me when I woke up after surgery. They took us both to the facility and locked us in separate rooms, but they didn't know that we could communicate even if we *were* in different rooms. We kept in close communication, but things were getting pretty precarious. They X-rayed us and did MRIs, ran a battery of tests, but the next step was so secret they weren't even sharing it with us. I was getting pretty worried because there was no other test they could do that wasn't invasive. So when Rick arrived outside my door dressed as a doctor but with the ability to talk to me within minutes in my own language without moving his lips, I decided to trust him. I gave him a visual of Cecil's room, we picked her up and he transported us out of the facility to here. Then he and Sophia began educating us about the path life. Cecil had been a path a little longer but she was as surprised as I was about teleflight capabilities. The ability to acquire languages has been the most fun. We like to go to tourist hot spots and learn the languages and help them order food, or ask for things. It's a hoot. We've made a few very close friends from several countries around the world."

Sophia served a delightful lunch of assorted salads. She had really knocked herself out with a seafood salad, green salad, two different pasta salads and a potato salad. She set out all kinds of dressings and toppings for the green salad and a large bowl of homemade breads. Of course, she did explain that the homemade breads were not quite made at home. Luke glanced at Kassidy, hoping she wouldn't ask the question she always asked him. "How did you pay for this?" But Kassidy was enjoying her conversation with the Japanese couple so much that she wasn't even thinking about how paths acquire food.

After lunch, the group began their planning meeting in earnest. They all retired into the main living room and left the deck to Mark, Lisa, and Sandy. Sandy was planning a lazy day down by the beach with a good book. Mark and Lisa were already planning a hike to the top of the 'mountain' behind the beach house. It wasn't really a mountain. It was more like an over grown hill. But they were planning a nice dinner picnic to check out the stars as Kassidy and Luke had done the night before.

Inside the plans were beginning to form. "First, I think we should try to determine just what our enemy knows about us and what we know about them." Uri, the gentleman from Germany suggested. "For instance, they know that we can teleport things, do they know we can teleport people?"

"I don't think they know that for sure yet, but they probably are close to discovering it. After all, we have teleported many times right out from under their noses," replied Luke.

"Maybe we should assume that they do know that, just to be safe," added another of the group.

"Do you think they have caught on to mind reading?"

"We must also assume they know about that because they have experimented on that monster, LeBeau. We know he has limited talents, but we don't know if he can read minds. If he can, he surely knows *we* can."

"I don't think he can read minds though," said Luke thoughtfully, "because he would never have let Mark leave the hospital the second time if he had." Luke relayed the hospital visit that Mark had made after Kassidy had disappeared. He showed them telepathically from what he had gleaned from Mark's memory that night.

After that, the meeting got a little quieter as members of the little group began telepathically reviewing any contacts they had had with the labbies either personally or from friends and family. The information began to fall into place piece by piece.

The labbies stretched out their hands world wide, but they were based in the United States. The facility was underground. The paths weren't sure where it was located, because they had always found it by centering their concentration on a missing path that had been taken there. That little piece of information probably had not been part of the labbies information or they would have been working diligently to interrupt telepathy in the building.

"Rick discovered a computer lab when we were looking for Regina. Her tele-signal was too weak to telefly right to her. We got within a few hundred feet and then had to start physically looking for her. The computer system is the most advanced he's ever seen." Sophia added. "Rick, show it to them."

Rick mentally shot the images to them from what he could remember. The computer lab was set up in a large room with computers along three of its walls. It seemed to be the mind of the facility. Rick did not stay long to see what information was being processed there, but he was most intrigued that the room had not been locked up more securely. It was in a secure hall, but they were dealing with telepaths after all. Why would they risk one wondering into the room? No one had even looked up from their work when Rick had poked his head in. What was with that?

The group agreed that it was strange, but perhaps the labbies had never had an escape or a security breech before Rick, Sophia, and Luke had gone looking for Regina. They all searched through their memories and telepathically asked friends if anyone had been in the facility before that particular date. The room fell silent as their thoughts and minds wandered to outside friends and paths. Luke noticed that you could see exactly when a path stopped communicating and came 'back' to the meeting. Their eyes would shift their focus from far away back to their surroundings.

It appeared that Rick and Sophia were the oldest and most experienced paths there. They had been first to discover how to teleport together and later individually. None of the others had tried teleporting separately. Rick explained that they had discovered the ability during a fight when Sophia had decided that she was leaving the island. Rick had pointed out that she would have to stay because he wasn't going to take her. Sophia was stomping out the door and Rick grabbed hold of her and she thought of her mother's house. He saw her thought and let go to stop the teleportation just as the electricity started up but he was a second too slow and she was gone without him. He thought he was going to be exiled on the island forever because he couldn't touch her and they had no other means at the time to leave. She reached her mother's house and panicked because he wasn't there. For three days they anguished over each other. But then they each got a little sentimental and were longing for the same place, a special place they had gone on their honeymoon. It was at the top of the Eiffel Tower.

Sophia had wanted to see the top on their honeymoon, but didn't want to wait in the lines and then look out over Paris with a thousand other tourists. So they had waited for the Tower to close and then teleported to the top and spent a wonderful evening with a little picnic at the top of Paris. It had been a very romantic evening and they were both longing for the moment at the same time in their misery. Their minds found each other and they were teleported to that spot.

Since then, they have been able to teleport each other in a sort of sling shot method. Then they would just have a rendezvous point and time already in their minds for the return. During emergencies when the two get separated accidentally, they know to just think of the Eiffel Tower and they will eventually end up together again.

Rick suggested that the couples try it a little closer to each other so they wouldn't end up stranded somewhere for three days while they learned the technique. "Oh, and by the way, we now have a small yacht in a secluded part of the harbor that can be manned by one person . . . just in case!"

"Can the yacht be seen from the ocean?" asked one of the guests.

"No, it's a very small harbor and the entrance is only wide enough for a small boat to navigate. Sophia and I searched quite a few islands before we found this one. We wanted a place that passersby would not normally stop to investigate. The island is so small that no one usually bothers with it. We've only had unexpected guests one time in ten years and we augmented their memories and thoughts of the place so that they can't really find it again, and they don't remember that we were here."

"How does that work? Augmenting memories and thoughts, I mean?" asked Satoro, the gentleman from Japan.

"It's sort of like shooting an image to you guys, only I fake the image and change details. So the person gets a picture or memory that is customized for them. Keep in mind that the image can't be something that the person's mind would absolutely know could not be true. So if you shoot an image to them, for example, that they have really met Bugs Bunny, their mind will not accept that and you may be jeopardizing our secrecy with that kind of thing as well as making the receiver quite ill. I have never actually tried that, but I did try augmenting a thought to a pilot telling him that his plane wouldn't fly because it was the wrong color. He just shook his head like he had a bad taste in his mouth, turned a little green like he was going to throw up and I changed the image. He immediately felt better and got in the plane and flew away. So I don't think it's a wise idea to play around with that one if you don't have to. When you practice, though . . . and you should, so that you are able to do it right if you need to, only change small insignificant details. For example, you might suggest to them that their totally plain looking wife is very sexy, or that the outfit they are wearing really does make them look fat and they should probably change. Then watch and see what they do. They should react immediately. If they look sick though, change the image back quickly."

As the meeting progressed, many ideas were suggested on how to take the facility completely out of commission. It was suggested that they blow it up, but Kassidy threw a fit. "Think of all the innocent people there who think they are working for the better good of society! You can't kill them just because a few lunatics are trying to kill us. There has to be a better way. Besides, they would just rebuild. It wouldn't really stop them."

The group also suggested eliminating the thugs that were running the operation, but Kassidy was no more comfortable with that plan. It was also pointed out that if you take out one thug another just fills his place. It had to be a plan that completely destroyed all the information about paths and redirected the people who had been working on the project. It was finally decided that they needed to dump the information in the computer lab, fill it with something else, like AIDS research and augment the memories of the employees there so that they think they are really working on AIDS research. The real trick was that there were so many people working on the project in that huge facility, that it would take quite a few paths to augment everyone's mind at the same time. If they missed someone, they would try to cover them as soon as possible but it could also jeopardize the entire plan. If they messed anything up, the whole thing could start again.

They needed to get all the lab operatives identified and covered at the same time. Then they would have to destroy the path information electronically keeping the computers up and running, up load data bases from another research facility and then augment the minds all at once.

Each of the couples had a part of the plan. Rick and Sophia would begin gathering paths using every connection they could find, starting with the people already in the room. Satoro and his wife would do a little research to discover the best AIDS research facility in the world at this time and find a way into their data bases. He knew a few computer gurus in Japan and thought he could persuade them to divulge that information either willingly or not.

Luke, Kassidy, Uri and his wife, Ute, would head up investigations into the lab operatives to discover how many were really out there and who they were. The other couples would begin tailing operatives in their countries and countries nearby. They would report back to Luke and Uri. They thought they could start with LeBeau and his men. Maybe they could 'pick' their brains for information leading to other labbies.

Andre volunteered to find a way to disrupt all the computers and dump the path information. He had met a Russian tourist to France when they found themselves both in the same French restaurant. The Russian was having difficulty ordering dinner for his family in French and Andre listened in on his Russian until he could converse easily and was able to assist the man. Andre and Cecil joined them for dinner and the two families had struck up a friendship. Since that time, they had visited each other at least once or twice a year. Demetri was a computer geek for the Russian government. If there was something that they needed done to a computer, he was probably their man. The difficulty would be in the fact that Demetri spoke nothing but Russian, so there would have to be a translator with him as he worked on the American computers. Fortunately, they now had a network of excellent translators. Also, Demetri was totally unaware of Andre's Path abilities. That could get tricky. It was suggested and agreed that they could temporarily let him in on their secret and then augment his memory after he was finished.

Tomas Garcia and his wife Deborah, the Spanish/English speaking couple would be working on a new Path constitution, so to speak. They would draw up regulations for Paths that would help to keep Paths safe from detection after they cleaned up this mess with the agency. It was going to be a big task because they would have to start monitoring brain trauma patients just like the agency had been doing. They would have to find them and protect them from detection until they could be trained to control their abilities.

"Perhaps we should keep the information that the agency has already gathered to use for our benefit," suggested Kassidy.

"Not a bad idea," agreed Uri.

The next step would be to convince all Paths to go along with the Path laws. Otherwise, all the work they were about to do would be for nothing.

"I think we can convince the present Paths," said Luke. "After all, most have been living in hiding for quite some time. If they are honest with themselves, they would probably enjoy the freedom to lead relatively normal lives. It will be new Paths that may rock the boat a bit. We'll have to devise a plan to convince them to use their abilities wisely."

"We can always show them telepathically what it was like before we took out the agency. That should convince them," said Cecil. "I know that if I saw what they had been doing to Andre and me, I'd change my ways!"

"Then that is where we'll start when the time comes," said Tomas. "At least we are united and we now have a plan. Let's pray for its success."

The meeting broke up and each of the participants said their farewells, thanked Sophia for the excellent lunch and disappeared from the living room. Luke and Kassidy stuck around to visit a little longer to formulate their plans with Uri and Ute.

"I guess we need to find our old friend, LeBeau," said Luke.

"Yes, I believe that is a good place to start," agreed Uri.

"Where do you think we will find him?" asked Kassidy.

"I think we should find Mark and get a good feel for LeBeau and what he looks like again. Then maybe if we all search for him together, we might be able to 'feel' where he is. We've never done that before, but it's worth a try."

"Mark and Lisa should be on top of the hill by now," said Kassidy, "Shall we join them?"

Luke smiled as he remembered the hill top. A little shiver of excitement shot through his body as he thought of their evening together. He avoided looking up at Kassidy; he had to keep his focus.

Since Uri and Ute had never been to the top of the hill, nor were familiar enough with Mark to telefly to his position, the four held hands together. Luke pictured the hilltop and the four found themselves standing beside Mark and Lisa, overlooking an incredible view of the entire island.

Mark and Lisa jumped and Lisa screamed!

"Luke! You could have given us both a coronary! Couldn't you guys knock, or something?!" the startled Mark complained . . . loudly! "We need some kind of a fore warning. Please."

"Sorry, Mark. We weren't thinking. I'll let you know first, next time. We just need your help for a minute."

"OK, what's up?" He was more interested in getting them to leave soon than in helping, but if that was the only way to get his hilltop back, then so be it!

It didn't take them long to brief Mark on what they needed. He was more than happy to help out. The four held hands again with Mark joining in. He thought about the day he went back to the hospital and in only a matter of minutes, the four had reviewed the entire confrontation with LeBeau. When they all let go, Mark returned his attentions to Lisa. He sat down beside her, kissed her on her shoulder which was bare except for a thin spaghetti strap. She handed him a glass of white wine and whispered something in his ear. He smiled stood back up and wandered back over to Luke.

"Luke, would you guys mind looking for your villain somewhere else? It's the first time Lisa and I have been alone since we got here."

Luke smiled broadly at his good friend. "We're already gone!" Luke asked the others to please join him down on the deck and the four were gone in a second. When they arrived on the deck they all took chairs around the table.

"OK, lets try just holding hands and concentrating on LeBeau's image," suggested Luke. "I don't know if it will work, but it's worth a try."

The four took hands and began to concentrate on LeBeau's face. The intent had been to find him but not to telefly to him, but the four found themselves in the lobby of a large hotel.

"Wow, that didn't work the way we thought it would," said Luke.

The lobby was decorated in a tropical motif with exotic flowers. The staff was easily identifiable in their white slacks and Hawaiian style shirts of blue with white flowers. They had arrived right in front of the desk and to their surprise, LeBeau was checking in. Before the desk clerk could exclaim over their sudden appearance, Uri managed to augment his memory to include their walking in through the door. Kassidy had caught the expressions of another couple who had been standing a short distance from them and had also seen them make their surprise appearance. She quickly 'reminded' them that they had seen the four step out of a cab and enter the building.

Once their entrance was covered, they hurried for a place out of view of the desk clerk and their enemy, who thankfully was not facing them. They found a secluded area with lovely flowered love seats looking out over the hotel atrium. The atrium was actually down a floor; the love seats looking down into it. In the center of the atrium was a large fountain shooting water in three different directions. The bottom of the fountain was scattered with coins and plants grew from four pots placed in strategic spots so as to miss being directly in the path of falling water. Standing above the tallest water spout was a Hawaiian dancer carved of stone. The beautiful statue stood on a pedestal, hands extended mid-dance in a most graceful and peaceful stance, with her lovely face looking up toward the top of the building.

Kassidy would have loved to just sit and enjoy the scenery for a moment, but the danger of having LeBeau so close to them was more than a little unnerving. The little group was concentrating on him, keeping him in sight while trying to stay out of his sight. They were listening to his thoughts. Since his thoughts were all on checking in and taking a shower right now, they weren't learning very much.

"*Maybe if we hold hands, we can see deeper into his mind,*" thought Kassidy.

Luke took her hand and the two concentrated together. They weren't getting very far until Ute took hold of Kassidy's free hand. Uri must have taken hold of Ute's free hand because all of the sudden, LeBeau's mind was opened wide. The four could access nearly anything they wished to know about him.

"He's here looking for Lisa and Sandy. He thinks they have been teleported off the island, but this is the last lead they had, so he's here to investigate on his own. He is also taking a bit of a vacation while he's here. He plans on hiking up Diamond Head and doing a little snorkeling in his off time. If the women are still here, perhaps he will run into them. He is working with five other operatives here in Hawaii."

The four could clearly see the faces of the other operatives and where they had been stationed. One was staking out Waimea Falls State Park. There was another at the Polynesian Culture Center. Another was working out of a hotel suite doing computer surveillance on boat tours and other attractions looking for reservations being booked by the two women. Another, very handsome, operative was staking out Waikiki Beach in hopes of catching them sunning themselves on one of the most famous beaches in the world. The final operative was concentrating on the other Hawaiian Islands in hopes of picking up their trail there. Kassidy wrote down each operative's name and where they were stationed on a little notepad she had reacquired from her house.

The four of them began picking LeBeau's mind for the names and faces of other operatives. *"Bless his heart,"* thought Kassidy, *"He's a wealth of information!"* She had no sooner thought this thought than LeBeau surprised them all by turning around and looking straight back at them at that very moment! He knew they were there! He was yelling at someone and running right for them, his gun already in his hand.

"Luke Matthews!"

Before he got half way across the lobby, Luke had pictured the beach house deck and the four of them found themselves once again transported to safety.

Luke had a tight hold on Kassidy when they arrived. He had expected the sight of the gun being pointed at her once again to upset her and he was prepared to catch her before she had time to even think about fainting. But he was surprised when he looked into those gorgeous green eyes and found no fear at all. Still, he couldn't help himself when he asked her, *"Baby, are you all right?"*

"I'm fine; you were wonderful!" she smiled up at him, *"But please don't call me baby in the midst of other people after a teleflight which is always intense, but even more so when it is preceded by such a close call! I don't have that much willpower in my reserve!"* Her eyes were locked to his. She was struggling with her emotions and if he didn't let go very soon, she would give in no matter who was watching.

Luke heard all of that and smiled, despite his efforts at controlling himself. He gave in to his desires; after all, they were in a safe place. It was probably the safest place on the planet for them right now, so giving in just a little couldn't hurt, right? He kissed her. He had intended to keep it short and sweet, but he hadn't intended for all the passion of the entire day of restraint to be unleashed. He pulled out of the kiss, looked into her eyes and took her to the other side of the island. There was a small inlet there that he had noticed when they had been up on the hill. They were completely alone and safe. Luke kissed her harder, demanding her response. He picked her up and carried her to a little grassy knoll in the shade of the encroaching jungle surrounding them.

"Damn!" Kassidy thought as she kissed him back with just as much passion. *"It really isn't working! I'm going to have to do better!"* she thought as she struggled to regain her senses.

"What's not working? I think you are doing fine. If you do any better, I'll never be able to concentrate on anything again except your lips."

Kassidy began to laugh. *"I've been trying to not kiss you today, to keep my distance from you. I seem to be stepping over many of the lines that I have had drawn for myself for years. I have never had trouble staying on my side of the lines before. But then you call me 'baby' and suddenly, I am having trouble remembering why the lines were drawn in the first place."*

"OK, I know we're good at languages, but I think I will do better if you can explain that in simple English. And why were you trying not to kiss me today?" Luke didn't even pause what he was doing as he asked her to explain again. He just left her lips and kissed down her throat. He leaned her back down into the grass and kissed the base of her neck and across her collar bone. He traced the tracks of his kisses with his fingers, sending Kassidy into another dimension.

Her breath caught for only a second before a moan of pleasure escaped her lips. She was losing the battle quickly.

Luke, hearing her moan, felt a jolt of electricity spiral through his body lighting up every nerve. He pulled her closer, as he plunged his hand into her hair. He returned to her lips kissing them and probing deeper, holding the base of her head at the back of her neck as if he thought she might be thinking of breaking the kiss.

Kassidy couldn't help but respond. Her arms were around his neck, pulling him closer. Every touch seemed to bind her more to him. She was his, how could she deny that? She had given herself to him mentally, why should she resist giving herself to him physically? Then she heard her father's voice, just as he had always said it, "Love is a commitment first and an action second. The commitment is not complete without the spiritual consent of God through marriage."

Before Kassidy could register the thought and act on it, Luke was already untangling himself from her arms. He lay back in the grass beside her; the two of them staring up at the palm trees swaying in the wind above them trying to catch their breath. *"Wow, was that your father's voice?"*

Kassidy just nodded.

"I'm sorry, Kassidy, I didn't understand at first. It's been hard for me to resist too, but we can wait. I won't press you and I promise not to whisk you off to romantic places and try to sweep you off your feet . . . literally, until I have made it my right to do so."

"Luke, how are we going to do that? I was ready to give up right now! It's not like we can run off and tell our parents that we'd like to get married, could they help us book the church. We are stuck until this whole business with the agency is over. How are we going to make it, when every time we make a teleflight, or hold hands

to augment our mental power we are drawn closer with less control than the last time?"

"Well we'll just . . . . . . Kassidy, did you really . . . are you . . . does every touch really bind you more to me?"

"Yes, I'm yours, Luke . . . forever. I have been since you first showed up in my head and helped me with that black fight thingy. I haven't stopped thinking about you for even a minute . . . though I have made some efforts at distracting myself. Deluding myself, I should say."

"Well, then, we do have a problem, because I'm going to be touching you a lot more than usual." When Kassidy started to protest he continued, *"But I will not call you 'Baby' again until you request it and I will try very hard to limit my kisses to quick, less . . . intimate ones until we are finished with this mess."*

"OK, and I will try not to respond so quickly, if you forget. I will also try very hard to keep my kisses less intimate also."

"Agreed, but Kassidy, please remember what I really want is . . . well . . . just don't ever doubt how I feel about you. You belong to me whether we are married or not."

Now it was Kassidy's turn to smile. She leaned over him and kissed him quickly.

"Aaugh!" Luke growled out loud. "This is going to be difficult!" He took her hand and the two returned to the deck of the beach house.

They were a little sheepish about having left in such a hurry leaving Uri and Ute so abruptly, but apparently Uri and Ute had left for home at almost the exact time that Luke and Kassidy had disappeared. Neither couple had so much as looked around before disappearing again.

"So what the heck happened to you guys?!" asked Rick.

"You looked like you were going to devour each other!" smirked Mark.

"We nearly did! I think Kassidy has a few bites missing!"

"No," Kassidy made like she was checking to be sure all the pieces were still there, "no, I'm all here!"

They all sat down at the little table and Luke filled them in on the event with LeBeau. "He could hear us! He turned around before we were in his mind more than two minutes. He also got a good look at all of us. He recognized me, I heard him think my name right before we left. I guess I can retrieve my Jeep now . . . since they know whose it is."

"Something's been nagging at me." Kassidy looked up at Rick and Mark. "If we don't know where the agency is, and the only way we have gotten in is if they have a path in custody, how are we going to get in and take care of the computers?"

"I can zero in on the place. I've been there enough times to remember the rooms. I don't think that will be a problem," said Rick.

"OK, but how do we distract the computer guys long enough to get them out of the way to down load the Path information and up load the Aids information.?" asked Luke.

"Relax!" Rick handed them a couple of ice cold drinks from a cooler next to the door. "We'll think of something. Right now, we need to begin up loading the information you stole from LeBeau's head into our computer. We'll keep adding each piece and maybe something will come to us." Rick took Kassidy inside to the computer and she typed in the information on the five operatives and LeBeau.

"We need to keep LeBeau under surveillance." Luke said when Rick stepped back onto the porch. "But we will have to be very careful not to push into his mind again. Otherwise, we may give away important information ourselves."

"Yes, and we need to start really monitoring head trauma accidents. I wonder if we could tap into the agency's computers and see what they see. If we could manage that, we could get to new paths before they could. They have to drive or fly for hours to get to new ones, but we could telefly there in minutes . . . . or seconds. We could keep them from revealing themselves or just get them out of harms way completely."

"What do you say about having a peek at the lab tonight? We could go in at about 3:00 a.m. They will probably have a limited staff around then. We could 'remind' them of a staff meeting they are all required to attend at the other end of the building." Luke was ready to get the show on the road.

"I'm up for it," replied Rick.

"I'd like to go with you both." Mark commented. "I'd like to check out their facilities. I might be able to learn something that might help us later."

"Mark, are you sure? You would have to stay very close to one of us. You don't have a way out if you get caught."

"Sure I do! You guys would come back for me. So if we get separated, I'll just hide out and wait for you."

"We better get Andre here for this. He'll need to see it to . . . do you think he could pick up Demetri?"

"Maybe, I'll get in touch with him."

"Ok, it's set then. We'll meet here on the deck at 2:50 a.m. and head to the agency."

"What?" Kassidy had just stepped through the door. "Where are we going?"

"You and I are going to keep an eye on LeBeau." Luke evaded the question having no intention of taking Kassidy with them that night. He switched thoughts in his mind also so she wouldn't pick up the deception. "But just listen to his thoughts. He didn't notice us until we probed his mind. We'll try listening to the thoughts of those around him. Rick, would you mind letting Uri and Ute know what we're up to? See if they caught any international information from LeBeau, we were all kind of listening to different things. No wonder he heard us; with four people in his brain, it had to get noisy!"

"How are we going to find him without risking turning up in the same room again?"

"I think we'll do it the old fashioned way! We'll telefly to the hotel lobby and pick the brains of the staff. Someone may know where he went. We just won't let the staff *know* we're picking their brains."

"Sounds like fun!" Kassidy smiled. "Let's get this show on the road. The sooner we nail these guys the better!" Kassidy was standing and had grabbed Luke's hands and was pulling him to his feet.

"You're not in a hurry are you?" Luke asked innocently.

"Big hurry. Let's go now!" Kassidy told Luke but to everyone else she shrugged and said out loud. "No, no hurry, just ready to get started."

"I'm thinking that I'm not going to get much rest until we get these guys," thought Luke.

"Maybe not then either!"

The others on the deck never saw the smile on Luke's face, but Kassidy did!

CHAPTER 19

Stake Outs, Daiquiris and Uncontrolled Fantasies

It was late afternoon when the too snuggled up together in a love seat in the lobby of LeBeau's hotel. They picked a seat in a corner partially obscured by a large fish tank full of exotic, beautiful fish and coral. They began 'listening' to the staff. At first the thoughts were about check-ins, tips, check-outs, and room service. There was one desk clerk whose mind kept drifting into reruns of a book she was reading. Kassidy made note of the title, *Twilight*, because the parts the girl kept thinking about were quite . . . interesting. Who would have thought that a romance between a girl and a vampire could entertain a mind for an entire shift of work even without the book being present?

Luke had caught a bit of the desk clerk's thoughts. "Yuck! Do girls really like that kind of stuff? There's so much kissing and lovey dovey stuff in there . . . not enough action."

"How do you know there is not enough action? She isn't thinking of the action parts . . . only the sweet parts."

"Sweet parts? Kassidy, guys aren't really like that."

"Not at all? Don't you ever think of me that way?"

"What way? Like you have to be babysat all the time?"

"No . . . . well, yes . . . Don't you ever feel like you want to protect me, keep me close to you? Kiss me passionately with reckless abandon?" Her eyebrows shot up and a mischievous smile spread across her face.

"Well, maybe, but reading about it and doing it are two entirely different things. Guys don't like to read about it! And guys in romance novels are always a figment of a woman's perspective. They aren't real. The woman always makes him too perfect!"

"Yeah, you're right about that. They are always way more understanding, thoughtful, and romantic than the real McCoy."

"You saying that I'm not understanding, thoughtful, and romantic?"

"Present company excepted, of course!" Kassidy giggled.

"I'll show you romantic . . . but not right now. We're on the job. Quit distracting me with this romance novel . . . . stuff."

"Promise?"

"Promise, what?"

"To show me romantic!"

He leaned over and kissed her lightly on the nose. "I promise."

"Hmm, you're off to a rough start!"

Entertaining though the desk clerk's thoughts were, Kassidy and Luke finally hit pay dirt. LeBeau had called the front desk asking for the operating hours of Diamond Head for the next day. He was also interested in renting some snorkeling equipment for a day at Hanauma Bay. That was interesting. He really was doing a little vacationing as he worked. Kassidy took notes on the times they had given him.

A short time later, Luke thought that they had probably hit a dead end for the day when he listened in on a request for room service by LeBeau, but Kassidy talked him into waiting for just a bit, just in case anyone else showed up. She didn't know who she thought would show up at LeBeau's hotel room, but she thought it odd that he would order room service when he could eat at any of a dozen close restaurants over-looking the beach where he could sample great food and sit in beautiful weather, watching a breath-taking sunset and bikini clad beach bunnies. It just didn't feel right for a single man to eat in a hotel room in Hawaii.

Luke could see her point and the two sat and waited. Luke was holding Kassidy's hand and stroking her arm as they waited. Kassidy thought she could really enjoy stake outs if this was par for the course. Too bad they didn't have a couple of strawberry daiquiris . . . oh wait, they could have. Kassidy produced two of the delicious concoctions, topped with whip cream and a cherry, on the table in front of them; reached out picked one up and handed it to Luke.

"So, how did you pay for this?" Luke reversed the tables on her teasingly.

"I make these at home. I already had the fixin's in my freezer."

"Fixin's?" Luke chuckled.

"Are you poking fun at my choice of words?" Kassidy gave him her best indignant face.

"Absolutely!" Luke laughed out loud.

"Laugh if you like, but taste it, I make a mean daiquiri!"

"Kassidy, we really shouldn't drink these. We need to keep our wits about us."

"Wits, schmits!" said Kassidy. "Don't worry, if you lose control I won't take advantage of you . . . much!"

"Kassidy, may I remind you that the boogie man is just a couple floors above us!"

"That's why these are non-alcoholic. Also they taste better without the rum!"

Luke took a drink. *"Mmmmm!"* Luke was impressed. *"I have had the honor and the pleasure of touring your mind and yet I keep finding little things about you that I find quite surprising. How delightful!"*

"Well sweetheart, it took me 26 years to store up all that stuff and you have only been in there, what . . . a couple of weeks? Besides, most of what's up there even I have forgotten. You may be in for quite a few surprises!"

The two sat quietly, listening to the thoughts of passers-by and enjoying their drinks and just sitting together. All of the sudden Kassidy tensed up. Luke looked at the gentleman who had caught her attention. He could hear the thoughts just as clearly as if the guy had been shouting them.

"Damn that LeBeau! It was his fault they got away, but we're all paying for it like we personally let them saunter out the door. He is using this as his own little vacation, while the rest of us are busting our butts looking for people who are not even on the island . . . or on any of the islands for that matter! I would bet next year's pay that they're long gone by now. We have the best operatives in the country . . . maybe the world. If the two ladies were here . . . or the four spies . . . paths . . . whatever they were, we'd have found them. Now I wonder what he wants us to do! Hang out in ladies' rooms, just in case they gotta go pee?!" the man laughed bitterly to himself and stepped into the elevator.

Luke set down his drink, jumped up and ran to the elevator, watching to see where it stopped. He hadn't seen if the elevator was empty for sure, but he thought so. Kassidy set her drink down and followed him.

"Where did it stop?"

"Top floor, let's go!" Luke got into the next elevator pulling Kassidy along with him. *"No sense in having to alter people's perception of reality if we don't need to!"*

"Luke, what are we going to do? Hang around the hallway?"

"Yep!"

When they reached the top floor, they held hands and began to 'listen' as they passed each door. There was difficulty listening through the doors. When they couldn't see someone, it was more difficult to zero in on thoughts. Then they passed LeBeau's room. He was projecting his thoughts so loudly, it was quite easy to pick up his half of the conversation. Luke and Kassidy were pleasantly surprised.

"Remember not to probe . . . just passively listen." Luke reminded Kassidy.

There was no place to listen and remain out of sight, so the two were on high alert standing beside the door, holding hands and looking like a couple of sweethearts having a hard time saying good night to each other. LeBeau was laughing at something. Then he answered the question posed by the guest in his room that had caused the laughter, "Of course they are not on the island! But they did come here to see what I was up to. Why else would they have been found in the same hotel as me? They were using that little trick of theirs to find out what I know. I'm not sure what they learned, but what I learned was that they will be back. They are fighting back. It's the only explanation. They will keep coming back until they think they know enough. All you have to do now is tail me! When you see them, take them. But you will have to be very careful. They are becoming more powerful. They will hear you coming. If you want to take them into custody, you will have to tranquilize them! Set up a sniper ahead of time. What ever you do, do not shoot them in the head or neck. Aim for their torso. I will be going to Diamond Head tomorrow. Have your guy set up before they open. I am not sure how far away they can be and still hear thoughts, but I doubt it is more than fifty feet. Also, I'm fairly certain that they can not listen in if they can not see their target so keep an eye on people who are interested in watching me."

"How do you know that?"

"Why would they have all been looking straight at me in the lobby if they could hear my thoughts without seeing me?"

"Good point!"

"Still, be ready for anything. See you tomorrow."

Luke and Kassidy thought about the beach house and were gone before the room door opened.

"Well, I guess, we're finished tailing LeBeau!" said Kassidy as soon as the two had landed on the deck.

"Maybe," said Luke thoughtfully.

"No maybes about it! We can't safely tail LeBeau. We'll have to expand and tail his tails!" Kassidy was not going to be shot again, even if it was only a tranquilizer gun this time. And she would not risk losing Luke for any information.

"That's not a bad idea. Tailing the tails!"

"What's going on?" Luke had not noticed Uri and Ute until Uri spoke.

"LeBeau is going to be touring, to try to get us to tail him. He will have snipers set up to shoot tranquilizers at any recognized path that comes near him. Kassidy just suggested that we stop tailing him and start tailing his tails."

"Hmm," thought Uri, "maybe what we need are paths that LeBeau has not seen."

"That won't help," said Kassidy. "He obviously has some talent at knowing when we are picking his brains."

"But he didn't know we were listening tonight." Luke reminded her. "The trick seems to be in just waiting for him to think about something, instead of actually probing around in his brain looking for information."

"If that is the case, then we might as well not even get near him. He would probably be thinking about the scenery, or wondering if his guys had us in their sights yet. None of that would gain us anything. We need to know names of other operatives. If LeBeau is the only one that they have tried the surgery on, we have a good chance of picking the brains of his tails. They would never know we were doing it. Only LeBeau has been able to sense us."

Ute entered the conversation then. "I agree with Kassidy. Why endanger ourselves for minimal gain. Let's go after the little guys and let the big one enjoy his little holiday."

"OK, let's find out when Diamond Head opens and we'll be there before the snipers get there. We'll watch them set up and pick a safe place to listen to their thoughts," said Uri.

"I think they open at 9:00 a.m. At least that is what the desk clerk told LeBeau when he called down asking about it. We should be there around 7:30, I think," said Luke.

"Where do you think would be a good place to listen from?" asked Ute.

"There may be a tall building not too far away from there. Maybe we could set up on a roof with some lawn chairs, pretending to be sunbathers. We could perhaps see both of our targets," suggested Ute.

"No, there aren't any tall buildings near there. We could possibly hide out in a souvenir shop. Except that the sniper will probably be targeting that area." Kassidy was thinking out loud again, rubbing her hand over her cheek as she thought.

"Maybe we should go even earlier, to find a good spot before anyone else gets there," said Luke.

"That sounds like a good plan. We could meet here at 7:00 a.m. on the dot and head over together. When we are finished with the sniper, we could check out the guy on the beach and pick his brains. Then you two can take on the Polynesian Cultural Center guy. It will probably take all of us to listen in on the guy in the hotel room, since we can't see him," added Uri.

Luke reminded them not to forget about the guy at Waimea Falls Park. "Which ever team finishes with their guy first can pick up the Waimea guy. If we miss him tomorrow, we'll get him the next day.

"Well, I'm for heading home. We are already a little confused about what time it actually is!" complained Uri. "We better get some sleep before tomorrow morning your time."

"Thanks, Uri . . . Ute. We appreciate your commitment," Kassidy told them sincerely.

"No problem, it is in our best interest also!" Ute assured her. She took Uri's hand and they were gone.

Kassidy looked wearily at Luke. "You ready to head home?"

"Just a minute, Sweetheart. Let me tell Mark good night." Luke was thinking very hard about telling Mark goodnight to cover his real intentions.

He didn't want Kassidy to become suspicious about where he would be going tonight. He was going to make sure that she did not come with them.

As soon as he had walked into the house, he met Rick. He struggled to block his thoughts as he and Rick discussed their plans for the night. Rick would bring Mark and Andre to the cabin to pick up Luke. Then they would all head to the lab boys' computer room.

"Do you think Andre and Demetri can cover their tracks well enough to stand up to computer gurus who might be looking for a breach in security?" Luke asked.

"Andre says that Demetri is the best in the business."

"Let's hope so."

They would try to keep the whole event to less than an hour. Sophia would have to be in on it, because she had to be awake to help Rick teleport. But Cecil, Kassidy, and Lisa could remain oblivious until it was over. Luke said his good byes, returned to Kassidy and cleared his mind of the plan by thinking only about kissing her. That he didn't give in to the thought right then was impressive to say the least.

"You want to stop that?!"

"Stop what?"

"You are thinking about kissing me and it is not a very quick, sweet kiss, it's a very . . ." Kassidy sighed and looked at him. *"You are not helping matters! Stop, please."*

"We never said we couldn't THINK about what we promised not to do!" Luke looked innocently back at her.

"Thinking about it only tortures each other and you are torturing me. Stop! Luke!"

Luke's innocent look had become a combination of seductive mischief.

"Stop!" Kassidy stopped thinking, started speaking and was raising her voice at him more and more with each time she had said 'stop'.

Luke took her hand and paused in his thoughts long enough to think of the cabin and the two found themselves once again in the hideout under the quaint little cabin in the hills above Granite Lake. As soon as they arrived he returned his thoughts to kissing her, even as he dropped her hands. He was smiling as he looked down into her face. His thoughts did not stray from the kiss as he turned on the surveillance equipment and checked the cabin perimeter. He didn't check the upstairs, but decided to trust his alarm system. He turned back to Kassidy then and continued the train of thought.

"Well, two can play at this game!" Kassidy was now smiling back at him. "Never underestimate the power of a woman to imagine romantic situations." She pictured herself running her hands up his chest. She wrapped her hands around his neck and kissed him at the base of his neck. As she stood on her tip

toes, she proceeded up his neck to his jaw. She pulled his head down to hers and began kissing him as she had at the little inlet on the island. Her hand slid down his neck to his collar and slid under the collar to his shoulder.

Kassidy was totally enjoying herself, but the real Luke whose own thoughts had been over-powered by hers, stepped forward and took her in his arms. He leaned down and kissed her softly at first, and then pulling her hands up to his face, he kissed each palm and worked his way up her arms as he wrapped each of them around his neck. When his lips found hers again, he had lost what little control he seemed to have possessed to that point. His breathing was uneven and rapid. His kisses were soft but persuasive. Luke wrapped his arms around her tightly and lifted her off her feet. He began walking toward the bedrooms.

Kassidy thought her heart was going to pound right out of her chest. He was so warm and inviting. His kisses were melting every bit of the resolve she had been building and nurturing. She felt like she had started a wildfire with no hope of putting it out. Maybe there would have been hope but there was certainly no *wish* to put it out. She wanted to stay locked in his arms forever. When they made it to her room, Luke held her tightly to him using one arm and the wall. With the other arm he turned the knob on her door and opened it. He didn't stop kissing her the entire time. She could feel his breath mingling with hers as she opened her mouth to his. He kissed her thoroughly, delighting in every touch.

Unaware they had even made it to a door; Kassidy was lost in his embrace. She wrapped herself more tightly around Luke. She was clinging to him, one hand playing in his hair, the other draped over his back exploring the tensed muscles that were holding her off the floor. Her breathing matched his in its choppy quickness. A moan escaped her lips as Luke kissed her neck and then allowed her to slide down his body until she was once again standing on her own two feet.

Finally realizing where they were standing, she slid her hands back down his chest and found his hands. She looked up into his eyes. They were smoldering. They must have reflected hers, she thought. She turned to her doorway and pulled Luke after her. But he stopped before he crossed the threshold.

"I can't go in there, Kassidy."

"Why?"

"You know why. You are not yet completely mine. I can't . . ."

"What was all that . . . that . . . all that kissing about, then?" Kassidy's disappointment was clear.

"That was an extreme loss of control! Obviously, I should never think what I want to do, before I am in a position to follow through. Thinking about it will only bring it to fruition. I'm so sorry, Kassidy. I promised you that I would be more

careful and I . . . I wasn't. I won't do it again. It was wrong to tempt you . . . us . . . both that way."

"Luke you are killing me. Besides, it took two to play that game."

"You would never have played if I hadn't been messing with you."

"Luke . . ." Kassidy started to reason, no, to plead with him, but his fingers touched her lips.

"Kassidy, don't. Let's get this right. Remember commitment first and then the action."

"I'm beginning to hate that saying!"

"Yes, but later you will be glad we waited."

"Mmmm." She wasn't sure she believed that, but there was no point in arguing with Luke about it. She stepped back out of her room and wrapped her arms back around him as his closed around her in response. She looked up into his face. Her eyes explored every inch of that beautiful face. She reached up and brushed a strand of hair from his eyes. When her eyes met his again, the heat of the moment had left his and all she saw was love. It was an ocean of love, falling over her in warm powerful waves and for the moment, it was enough. She smiled up into those eyes that were now her life, reluctantly let go of his waist, slid out of his arms and turned to enter her bedroom.

'I love you, Luke.' She thought as he closed her door and headed to his own room.

"I love you, too." She heard him say, and then she heard his footsteps as he headed to his own room.

Kassidy changed into her pajamas and climbed into bed. She was tired, but her thoughts were too full to sleep. She tried to relax and turn off her mind, but finally decided that this was one of those times when only a nice hot bath was going to do the trick. She hoped that Luke was already asleep. She would have checked his thoughts, but when she remembered how his thoughts had aroused her earlier, she thought better of it and tried to think of other things.

As she drew her bath she wondered how her parents were doing. She needed to go see them. They had to be suffering greatly because of her disappearance. She had also come to the conclusion that if LeBeau had even a hint that they knew anything, he would go after them. She thought about calling them from a cell phone, or even better, a pay phone. She could just tell them she was OK and not to worry. But she knew that any contact she made would bring LeBeau right back to them. If not LeBeau, then someone else from the agency would show up. As long as she was making no contact, her parents would remain in some semblance of safety. Then Kassidy got an idea. She wondered if she could augment their thoughts just enough for them to know she was all right . . . to relieve their anxiety, but not enough to give them any information that LeBeau could use against them or the paths. She could do the same for Kenny, for that matter. She would definitely ask Rick or Sophia about it tomorrow. Little did she know that the events of the night to come would cause that thought to be completely forgotten.

The hot water began to do its duty and Kassidy could feel her muscles relaxing. She was beginning to feel drowsy, so she washed her hair, rinsed it well, squeezed the water out of it and stood up. She grabbed a towel and wrapped it around her as she stepped out of the bath. She hurriedly dried off and headed back to a very inviting bed. This time she was asleep in a matter of minutes. She slept so well, that she never heard the visitors to the cabin at 3:00 a.m. She didn't wake even when Luke, against his better judgment, stole into her room and kissed her on the forehead. Moments later, he had joined his friends in the living room, and they were gone.

CHAPTER 20

Surprise, Surprise, Surprise

The group turned out to include Demetri who was still having some trouble adjusting to the whole teleflight thing. He kept holding his breath and tightening every muscle in his body. That would not have been so bad, but he had his hand on Andre's shoulder and every teleflight had produced large hand shaped bruises. Andre finally had to suggest that Demetri hold another's shoulder.

"Sorry, my friend," came Demetri's sheepish apology.

The five men arrived just outside the agency's computer lab. As expected the hall way was empty at this time in the morning and there were only two men working in the lab itself. Rick telepathically 'suggested' to the two men that the phone had just rung. One of them picked it up but as per Rick's second suggestion, he never heard the dial tone. Instead the young man 'heard' an order to come to the conference room and wait there for the director to come in and brief them on some new policies. Rick pushed the young man further, suggesting that the request was urgent, and reminding them that they should wait there until the director arrived.

The man receiving the 'phone' call relayed the message to the other man and the two exited the room heading down the hall sending the five invaders scrambling for cover. Luke and Mark had hidden around the corner from the lab and now found themselves right in the two men's path. They quickly began checking doors and hid in the first unlocked room they discovered. The room was dark, and the two closed the door and listened behind it until they heard the labbies walk past them and open and close a door at the end of the hall. Luke peeked out to see if the coast was clear just as Mark turned on the light.

"Be careful! Someone could see that!" whispered Luke.

"Look at this!" said Mark who was looking into the room with his back to Luke.

They had stumbled upon a room that was filled with lab jackets of every size as well as scrubs, and various other hospital attire. The two quickly donned a couple of lab jackets and borrowed three others for Rick, Andre, and Demetri.

They might as well look the part incase anyone comes by! They turned off the light and hurried down the corridor back to the computer lab.

Rick, Andre and Demetri were already checking out the lab, looking for a way to hack into their system and down load information. They paused for only a moment as they each put on a lab coat and then went right back to work. Andre's fingers were flying over the keys as Demetri gave commands. Andre was translating everything from English to Russian as fast as if everything was already in Russian and he was just reading. The two were a magnificent team. While Andre and Demetri were hacking into the data base and setting up connections to Rick's computer on the island, Rick was downloading information onto disks just incase they ran out of time before the hacking was completed. Luke was keeping a look-out for the two labbies. There was always the chance that someone would see them heading to the conference room and send them back . . . or maybe, however unlikely at 3:00 in the morning, the conference room could already be in use. The confusion that would cause would not last long before someone was sent to investigate.

Mark was checking doors throughout the corridor, exploring the area, looking for any kind of information that might help the cause. One door opened easily. He went in to find a generic looking little office. It had paper supplies and other office equipment. As he was backing out of the room something caught his eye. One of the envelopes from a stack near the door was left sticking out of the box it shared with 200 other envelopes. He pulled the envelope out and looked closely at the return address. It read, "Arizona Cancer Research Facility, P.O. Box 21387, Tucson, AZ. That was interesting. The cover for this place was already a cancer research center. That would make things easier.

He took the envelope, closed the door and walked to the end of the hall. He turned a corner and had made it about three quarters of the way down the hall when he came to a door that was locked, but he could see a young man through a window. The young man had brown scruffy looking hair and very light skin. From the looks of it he was around 5'10 to 6' tall and in good physical shape. He was lying in a hospital bed and there was an IV attached to his arm. He appeared to be sleeping but all of the sudden, he opened his eyes, turned his head looking straight at Mark. His eyes were a golden brown and there was anger and hatred in those eyes like Mark had never seen before. Mark also noticed the trace of a wound, mostly healed but extending from just under his right jaw, up into his hair line.

"Luke, come here! Hurry!" Mark yelled.

"Quiet!" Luke whispered loudly as he ran around the corner toward Mark, "You'll bring the whole place down on us!"

"Hurry!" said Mark more quietly but just as urgently.

Luke ran down the hall and was at his side in seconds. When he looked into the room the angry eyes turned on him. The young man pulled out his IV and ran straight at the window, hitting it with both hands extended, but the window didn't even crack. The man had hit it with his palms flat, and the effort had clearly stung. He pulled his hands back, rubbing them, but he never took his eyes off of Mark and Luke. He appeared to be only about 18 or 19 years old.

"Can you talk to him?" asked Mark.

"I can try. I don't know if it will work without Kassidy here. Maybe he's close enough to me, though." Luke put his hand on the window and threw his thoughts to the young man. "*Who are you? Why are you here?*"

The man's eyes flew open in complete astonishment. His answer was barely audible through the glass but Mark thought he detected a bit of an English accent. "You obviously work here, I'm sure you already know the answer to that question!" He looked directly into Luke's eyes. "What kind of games are we playing now? And how can I hear what you are saying when you are not even moving your mouth?"

"*I don't work here. I broke in. I'm a path . . . telepath . . . like you.*"

"Really!" came his sarcastic reply. "You're club uniforms betray that lie!"

"*Oh, just props!*" assured Luke. "*I see your scar, I had one too. I'll explain all this soon, but if you would like to leave this facility, we have to move fast. You are going to have to trust us. My name is Luke Matthews, this is my friend Mark Johns.*" Luke was frantic to give enough information to gain trust but to limit time lost in conversation and explanations.

The young man laughed, "I'm Jonas Carter . . . . uh, I guess I have to trust anyone with the names Luke Matthews and Mark Johns, no bad guys would admit to those names! And anything that gets me out of here as soon as possible is worth the risk."

"*We have others with us. I have to get the other paths to get you out of there. I can't do it by myself! Wait here for just a minute!*"

"Where would I go? The door is locked!" Now Jonas knew for sure they had to be good guys, because bad guys would be better organized and smarter!

"*I heard that! Be nice or I'll leave you there!*" Luke was chuckling despite the insult as he dropped his hand and turned toward the lab. He ran back down the hall and called to Rick. He relayed the information telepathically. Rick nodded and then his gaze drifted off into the distance as he talked to Sophia. As soon as his face refocused on the computer in front of him, Luke knew he had finished his conversation with her.

"*Just a minute, let me finish this disk.*" Rick punched a couple more buttons and then followed Luke down the hall to Jonas' room. The computer continued to hum finishing its job as they left it.

Rick came to a stop beside Mark and peered into the window. He greeted Jonas and then his gaze became distant and in the next instant he was inside the room with Jonas.

Jonas nearly fell over at Rick's sudden appearance. Rick caught him before he fell and then Jonas felt the electricity build around them. It was so intense that he didn't even notice at first when he found himself, somehow, impossibly outside the room! His eyes were as big as saucers. And then they all heard it at the same time! An alarm began to sound.

"Hmm, new security system!" Rick stated the obvious. "Guess we better hurry boys!"

The four of them turned and ran down the hall, as they turned the corner heading toward the computer lab there were three men in security uniforms running down the hall toward them. They had their guns raised and the first shot came so close to Luke that it put a hole in his borrowed lab jacket. The shot startled Luke and although he did not allow a sound to escape from his mouth, a telepathic shout radiated from him. All of them heard it including Mark who had taken hold of Luke's arm in preparation of a hasty teleflight, but instead the four reversed direction and ran back to the turn in the hall. They also all heard Luke's groan.

Kassidy's blissful sleep was abruptly interrupted as she distinctly heard Luke shout. She was out of her bed and running down the hall before she was fully awake. She threw open his door and ran to his bed. She sailed over the sleigh styled bedstead only to discover a completely empty bed. Panic shot through her as tangibly as the bullet had sailed though Luke's lab jacket.

"Luke!" she screamed, "Where are you?"

There was no audible response as Kassidy's hands began to shake, but she did 'hear' a groan.

As soon as they rounded the corner, Mark was talking. "Luke, where did they hit you, buddy? Are you all right? We gotta get out of here, Luke's been hit!" Mark was frisking Luke, trying to find the bullet hole and wondering how Luke was able to stand so easily, when Rick grabbed his shoulder and he found himself and the others standing on the other side of a locked door.

Luke grabbed his friend's arms to stop the frisking and looked him in the eye. "I'm not shot! It's just a scratch! I'm fine! I do have a new air conditioning system in this lab coat though," he said as he held up the coat and stuck his finger through the new bullet hole.

"You scared me to death!" yelled Mark.

"SHHHH! It scared me too!" whispered Luke.

Mark whispered back, "So, what was the groan about?"

"Apparently, it also scared Kassidy and now she is going to be really ticked off."

When he peered into the semi darkness, lit only by small bluish lights in glass cases, Mark realized they were in another lab . . . this one had been used for dissections and still displayed various sections of human brains in the cases.

Jonas was confused about their destination. He was sure they had intended to leave the facility. Why were they now locked in yet another room and this time with . . . body parts . . . . on display? "Why don't we just get out of here?" he asked making no attempt at being quiet or patient.

"You can just think what you need to know, we'll hear you but the bad guys won't. To answer your question, we can't leave just yet because we still have people in the computer lab. We need to give them a bit more time, before we get back to them and telefly out of here," Luke responded. *"As long as these goons are chasing us, our lab imposters will be safe."*

"Yeah, maybe . . . maybe they have enough people in this facility to check out more than just the guys outside my room!" quipped Jonas.

"Yeah, but maybe we can talk to more people than just you without moving our lips." Luke matched Jonas' sarcasm. Luke's attention seemed to drift and then he let out a sigh of relief. *"They're fine! The security guys ran right past them!"*

Mark was still looking around.

Luke followed his gaze. Oh, no! He knew this room. This had been the room they had found Regina in!

Rick, hearing his thoughts, shot back to him, *"It was the only room besides the lab that I could remember well enough to telefly us into."*

"It's OK. Sorry, it just caught me off guard. How far do you think we are from the computer lab?"

"Who's Regina?"

"Pipe down kid. We'll explain it all later, right now we have to think."

Mark whispered in response to the exasperated look on Jonas' face, "Don't worry, Jonas, I never know what's going on either . . . you get used to it!"

"I thought we weren't supposed to talk out loud." Jonas whispered to Mark.

"I don't have a choice. I'm not a path. Which explains why I never know what's going on. I have to wait for someone to finally speak up!" Mark whispered back with a frustrated look on his face.

Jonas listened in on the conversations shooting back and forth between Luke and Rick and then shared the information with Mark in quiet whispers. "Well, they just said something about Andre and Demetri being all right. No one has discovered them yet. Security ran right past them and is in the process of checking all the rooms in the wing. Demetri has successfully hacked into the main frame and they are waiting for the down load that Rick started, to finish. Then they will be ready to go."

Kassidy was frantic. She raced down the hall toward the living room calling for Luke. He hadn't answered telepathically . . . . as a matter of fact; he hadn't been in her head for a while. That was a funny feeling. He was always mentally close by. But he was not there now! She had heard that shout. It was a shout of fear. She was sure of that. She hit the living room at a dead run looking for him everywhere. He wasn't in the downstairs apartment. She ran to the secret passage, but he had never told her the combination. She began putting in combinations that she thought might mean something to him. But nothing worked.

"Wait a minute!" she told to herself. *"You have to calm down, think. You've seen the code in his mind. What was it?"* Kassidy began to calm her thoughts and think through the things she had learned from Luke the night they had been on the hilltop on the island. She began to hum a tune as she thought. Humming always seemed to help her concentrate. The closer she got to remembering, the louder the song became in her head and the closer Luke felt. She was looking into his mind, concentrating on the information that had been stored there. She remembered how the information had soared through her mind that night and sang louder. She knew it had to be there. It was just difficult sifting through so much information. She probed deeper, the song returning to the chorus over and over again in her head. *"What is the combination?* She sang the question to the tune.

"Why do you need the combination? What's going on Kassidy?" Luke had heard the song as soon as she had started humming, and the question was as clear as if she were standing right beside him.

His thought startled her! *"Luke?"*

"Yes, ba . . . Kassidy." Now it was Luke's turn to feel a little panic. Why would Kassidy need to leave the living quarters for the upstairs? Was someone there? *"What is going on there? Are you in trouble?"*

"No, I'm not in trouble!" Relief flooded Kassidy's mind. She felt her shoulders relax at the sound of his voice in her head. She slid down the wall and curled up at the foot of it. Suddenly the relief was replaced with anger. *"You are in trouble. Where are you?"*

"Uh . . . I'm at the agency with Rick, Mark, Andre, and Demetri. We're not in trouble at the moment. Everything is OK. We're just . . ."

"Oh, they may not be in trouble, but you are in big trouble! Why didn't you tell me you were going? Why didn't you take me? I thought we were a team! You scared me! I thought . . . never mind what I thought!" Kassidy was beginning to lose all

her bravado, anger was being replaced with . . . well, she wasn't sure what this emotion was. She sounded as if she might cry at any moment.

"Kassidy, I'll be home in a few minutes. As soon as we finish with the computers and drop off Andre, Demetri, and Jonas, Rick will drop me off. Don't worry, and don't panic. Everyone is OK. I'll explain everything then."

"You are in deep trouble!" chuckled Rick. *"Glad it's you and not me! I told you to tell her."*

"She'd have wanted to come!"

"Sure she would, but you could have talked her out of it. I talked Sophia out of it."

"You talked Sophia out of it?"

"He bribed me!" Sophia's voice filled Luke's head.

"He bribed you?"

"Yes, he owes me an hour long back rub! I'm a sucker for a good back rub."

"Ahhh! I see! Who is in charge at your house, Rick?"

"Sophia, of course!"

"Good answer, dear! Now hurry up and finish and get home to me, please. Remember that I am a party of two . . . I don't like this home alone stuff!"

"Yes, love!"

Luke was thinking about that comment about a party of two. His head tipped to the side and his brows furrowed as he thought about her comment. Something was bugging him. Then he had it. He turned to Jonas. *"Hey, kid, did you come here alone, or was someone with you?"*

"That's a stupid question. Of course, I didn't come here alone! Some guys brought me here. They took me right out of my hospital room. Brought me here and locked me in that room. They've been doing tests since I got here. They haven't let my family come to visit and they didn't let me out of that room for anything! I haven't even been able to make a phone call!"

"No, I meant was there a girl with you; someone who could talk to you like we do."

"No, no one was with me."

"Are you sure?"

"I think I'd remember if I had a girl with me that could read my mind! Wow, wouldn't that be a nightmare! It'd be kinda fun to read her mind though . . . no more," Jonas made the tone of his thought high imitating a woman's, *"you should know what you did to hurt my feelings!"* He dropped his tone again. *"I really would know what I did!"*

Rick and Luke both snorted. Then Luke returned to his original thought.

"That's odd that you were alone."

"Why is that odd?"

"Because there are always two paths. One is always drawn to the other's crossroads!"

Luke was getting a bad feeling about that. What if they had picked up Jonas' mate before she even made contact with him? What if there was another path in here? They had found Jonas, what if there were *a lot* more than one?

"Jonas, have you heard anyone else at all talk to you like this?"

"No, you were the first."

"He might not have picked up on it without having made contact with his path mate. You didn't until Sophia and I, together, talked to you." Rick had joined in the conversation.

The five heard a commotion outside the room. People were rushing down the hall and someone was barking orders. "Check all the rooms. They could still be here!" They heard the key in the lock as the four clasped hands and concentrated on the computer lab. They were there in an instant. Jonas was elated over the electrical power of the process of teleflight. He couldn't seem to wipe the smile off his face as they landed.

"That is a ruddy hoot, now isn't it?!" His upper class English accent had almost slipped into a cockney accent with all the excitement.

"Shhhh!" said Andre. He had been keeping a watch out since he and Demetri had finished their part. It was important that no one realize that they had been in the lab. "Rick, you might want to augment the lab boys' minds again and tell them they've had their meeting and now they need to get back to work."

"Good idea!" Rick set to work on that just as the disk he'd started, before they had found Jonas, popped out of the computer.

Demetri grabbed the disk and joined the circle of men. Just before Rick teleported them out, Luke stopped them. "Why don't we try to talk to any paths that might be in this building? If we are all holding hands, we may be able to find them even if they don't have a mate yet.'

"It's worth a try," agreed Rick.

"Please hurry," said Andre. I don't want to become a guinea pig in this place.

Andre, Rick and Luke broke from the rest of the group and clasped hands. Luke reached out and pulled Jonas in with them.

"We can use all the help we can get."

Rick threw his thoughts out to the building. The sound in Andre's, Luke's and Jonas' heads was quite loud and they flinched a bit. They waited and let their minds wander out through the building. There it was! It was just a faint response but it was urgent.

"Help, us!"

"Where are you? How many are there of you?" Rick asked.

"I don't know where we are. They have kept my husband and I locked up in separate rooms and they keep us pretty drugged up. I'm due for another injection soon. I won't be able to talk coherently if they get here before you do. You have to find us. We aren't going to last long like this and then who will take care of him? He's so little and he doesn't understand what is going on."

A second voice then joined the conversation. This one was loud and cheerful. *"Hi, I'm Dewick Twinder. Mama sayed dat we can go ousside twater! Are we going ousside wight now?"*

You could have heard a pin drop in the computer lab at that moment. Every voice and every thought fell completely silent. A toddler telepath!!! Everyone looked at Rick. They all wondered if he had ever encountered a telepath that wasn't an adult. But the look on his face assured them that he was just as surprised as they were.

Mark knew something big had happened but no one was talking. They were just standing there looking dumbfounded. "Hey, guys, we gotta get out of here. What's going on? Did you find another one? Let's get them and get going already!!"

"Let's go and let's do it very quickly! If she is about to get another dose, we may run into the labbies while we're picking them up, so be prepared. We'll explain everything later to the rest of you but we have to go. Hold on!"

The six men joined hands and Rick got a mental picture of the room from the woman they had just been talking to. They were there in an instant. The woman was nearly unconscious on a bed in the corner of the room while a little guy of about two or three sat on the floor playing with matchbox cars.

Luke picked up the smiling boy while Andre scooped up the woman. Luke was talking to the child, reassuring him that they would be going outside for sure, but first they had to find his daddy. That brought a screech of what could only be described as pure joy from the depths of the boys lungs as well as a resounding, very loud telepathic echo of the same emotion that Luke was sure every telepath within the country must have heard. And fortunately for them, it woke a very groggy daddy.

"Derrick? Are you OK? What's going on, spud?"

"Daddy! We comin' to get you and go ousside!"

Luke cut in then, *"Sir, we're telepaths just like you. We're coming to get you but we have to act fast. As soon as we leave this room an alarm will probably . . . most definitely go off. We need to find you quickly to get out of here. Show me your room. Can you open your eyes?"*

"They are coming now. I can hear them. Just get out of here with my wife and son, please. Leave me and get them out!"

"Well, see we're like the Musketeers. 'All for one and one for all'. Open your eyes!"

At that moment Luke got a clear picture of the room, the group gathered close and arrived just as the door was being unlocked. The technician with the dose of sleepiness for the man stood in shock as the alarm began to sound, indicating that the woman and the boy had left their room. Before he could gather his wits about him Luke was 'reminding' him that his first duty was to check on the woman and the child in the other room. This time it didn't work. Luke had forgotten to erase the crowd of people in the room from the technicians mind. The technician began to look a little green. He just stood there looking like he was going to throw up.

Rick reached down to grab hold of the man lying helpless in his bed and the group was gone before the technician could find a trash can in which to barf.

CHAPTER 21

Secrets Revealed

The group arrived on Rick's deck. They took the nearly unconscious couple into one of Rick's guest rooms to sleep off the rest of the drugs they had been given. Sophia assured the woman that she would keep a close eye on Derrick. The couple had to trust them. Neither of them was coherent enough to watch him themselves. Sophia managed to get a jelly sandwich down the little guy. He was so excited to be outside and was more interested in going down to the beach to play in the sand than in eating. It was about 5:30 in the morning when Rick and Sophia managed to drop Andre and Demetri back at their homes and sent Luke back to the cabin. Mark headed back to his room with a little stop off to check on Lisa.

When Luke arrived in the cabin living room, Kassidy was still sitting in a little ball with her knees pulled up to her chin.

"That was more than a couple of minutes!"

"Hi, B . . . Sweetheart. Sorry I woke you!"

"Yeah, you will be! How did you keep that little escapade to yourself?! More importantly, why would you keep it from me? What if something happened to you?" Kassidy couldn't have been yelling louder at him if she had been speaking out loud. Then her expression changed to worry. *"Wait, something did happen to you! What made you scream like that?"* Kassidy got up from the floor and began checking him over. She was turning him around and running her hands over him as if she might find a piece missing.

He rolled his eyes and growled at her, "I didn't scream!" Luke looked indignant, "Kassidy, I'm fine!"

She didn't hear him; she had found the hole in the lab jacket. She wasn't sure if steam would start pouring out of her ears, or tears down her cheeks as she also saw the blood. It was still bleeding and Kassidy quickly began pulling his lab jacket off and then started on the buttons on his shirt. Luke caught her hands on about the third button and looked down into her eyes.

"Kassidy, I'm fine! It's just a scratch."

"Let me see it," her voice sounded shaky.

"Kassidy . . ."

"Shirt. Off. Now!" she demanded.

"You just want a reason to get my shirt off," Luke teased trying to lighten the moment.

"Actually, I could think of a lot of reasons to get your shirt off and none of them include getting you shot. Now come on, off with it!"

"Really," Luke, still playing with her, continued, "Name one!"

"All right, I need my lawn mowed and it's a very hot day. You could mow it; I could watch. Do you want another?"

"Mmmhmmm." Luke was smiling.

"I could take you swimming . . . . of course, you would need a lot of sun block. I would be sure to help you with that part." Now Kassidy was smiling. "See, no guns . . . no pain . . ."

"Really . . . no pain! How big *is* that lawn?"

"Not nearly big enough!" Kassidy reluctantly teased him back. "Now, quit distracting me and get that shirt off, please."

Luke took his shirt off while Kassidy dug through the cabinet for the first aid kit. When she turned around to face him, Luke was facing her but twisting down to look at the injury. She had known he was well built with muscles and a nice six pack. She remembered from the time they spent on the beach, but seeing his chest without the cover of even a t-shirt took her breath away again.

"Absolutely perfect!"

She had Luke's attention immediately. *"Ha, you* did *just want to get my shirt off!"*

"No, but it certainly is a nice fringe benefit." Kassidy crossed to him and took him by the hand. She led him to the coach and made him lie down and put his arm over his head so she could get at his injury. She cleaned it with peroxide first.

"OW! What are you doing? I didn't know torture was one of your talents!"

"Quiet! And hold still. *You big baby!*"

"You just called me 'baby'!"

"I called you 'a big baby', there's a difference!"

"Hmmm. I don't know! First you make me strip, then you lay me down on the couch and next you call me 'baby'. I'm beginning to see a pattern here." He caught her by her collar and pulled her down for a kiss.

Kassidy pulled away from him. "Luke, first things first. You are going to bleed all over the couch if you don't let me finish." She shook her head at him. *"Besides, when I come after you, you won't have to stretch the truth quite so much to make your case."*

"Try me!"

"No."

"Please."

"No."

"Why not?"

"You know why not. If I turned my full feminine charms on you, you would cave like a bumped soufflé."

"You have quite a lot of confidence, my dear."

"Hold still, I'm almost finished."

The wound was a little deeper than Luke had first thought, but by the time Kassidy had cleaned it up and put a bandage over it, the healing had already begun. She leaned over until her face was only an inch away from his and surprised Luke completely when she slapped his stomach playfully, looked up into his eyes and said, "This is promised to me. You *will* take better care of it in the future! AND I will be included in all your future adventures. You will not keep me in the dark again . . . even if I am sleeping!"

Luke wrapped his arms round her, pulled her on top of him, hugging her tightly as he leaned his head into her neck and whispered into her ear. "I'm sorry. I didn't mean to worry you. I just wanted *you* home safe. I thought you would be still sleeping when I got back." He kissed her on the cheek in an effort to maintain their agreement, but as she started to disentangle herself from him, he pulled her closer and kissed her warmly and tenderly on the lips. Kassidy, feeling her resolve slipping, tried to pull away again.

"Don't make me use my secret weapon." Luke whispered. "Kiss me."

"You have a secret weapon?" Kassidy found it difficult to breathe let alone talk.

"Oh, yeah!" he nodded his head, holding on to her as she made another attempt at getting up.

"What weapon would that be?"

"You don't want me to say it, you'd lose control. So just kiss me; then I'll let you go."

"Luke, you promised." Kassidy whispered.

"I promised not to take what is not yet mine and I won't."

Kassidy looked into his too blue eyes. They were smiling in anticipation. Any resistance she had to that point melted with the tension in her muscles. She relaxed into his chest, leaned forward and kissed him. Her hands slid up that perfect chest, around his shoulders and into his hair. She moved her lips over his, kissing the upper lip and then his lower lip. It wasn't long before her attentions wandered to his jaw and down his throat.

Oh my goodness, how she wanted him!

Luke moaned as he listened in on her thoughts. Kassidy heard him saying her name. It was like adding lighter fluid to a smoldering fire. Her hands left his hair and explored the muscles in his shoulders and then his chest.

"Kassidy, stop. Baby, you have to stop." Luke was breathing hard and grasping for her hands.

"Mmm, you called me 'baby'." Kassidy returned to his lips. She kissed him again, as her entire body lit up like Tim the Toolman's house at Christmas.

Luke caught her hands and rolled her into the couch. He pushed himself up on one elbow putting a little space between them. He was waiting for his breathing to return to normal before he spoke or moved. Kassidy's disappointment was tangible.

Luke took a deep breath, let it out and looked down at Kassidy. "Cave like a bumped soufflé?"

"Give me another minute. Just one minute." Her eyes locked on his.

"I can't."

"Chicken"

"We have to get ready to go."

"Go where?"

"We're spying today, remember?"

"You were up half the night. You are not going, you are sleeping. Ute and Uri and I can handle the spying today."

"No."

"Look at you! You're tired. You need some sleep. It's too easy to make a mistake when you are tired."

"OK, I'll stay home and sleep but you will stay with me."

"Luke, that doesn't solve anything. We need to get this finished."

"We will. Tomorrow. Today, we catch up on our rest."

"Luke!"

"Too late, I already told Uri." Luke had interrupted Uri's evening meal to telepathically tell him that *Kassidy* had had a long night and they would not be able to make it today. Uri said he and Ute would keep an eye on things for them. He had heard about the raid on the facility from Rick.

"Kassidy, make sure Luke gets some rest too!" chuckled Uri.

Luke pulled away from Kassidy, stood up reluctantly and headed for the kitchen. "Would you like a cup of coffee?"

"Silly question. If not *you*, of course, I want some coffee, but mostly I want the whole story. What were you guys up to?" Kassidy, having been reminded of the whole reason she was up this early, settled into one of the kitchen chairs sitting on one foot while the other dangled to the floor and waited for Luke's story.

Luke relayed the whole adventure in a few short telepathic moments. Kassidy's eyes got bigger and bigger as the story played out.

"Oh, my goodness, Luke! A baby? You guys found a baby path?" Kassidy could see every detail of the little guy in Luke's memory. He was a fairly tall toddler, with large brown eyes and dark hair. When he smiled two deep dimples revealed themselves on his chubby cheeks. He seemed to replace all his L's with 'tw' when he spoke. So when he had said his name was Twinder, he had actually meant Linder. He also had a cute habit of replacing all his 'r' sounds with the 'w' sound. The whole encounter made Kassidy smile. It seemed to take her mind off the fact that Luke had been shot.

"So, when are we going to go meet them? Where are they going to live until we get this mess all sorted out? Sophia and Rick have to be running out of room. Especially if they have to keep Jonas too! We have extra rooms here. Are you thinking of bringing someone here?"

"Well, I hadn't thought of that, but we may have to. I sort of hate to give up the privacy, but I guess we can't leave everything up to Rick and Sophia."

"It might help to keep us honest too." Kassidy smiled up at him as the memory of the last few minutes reverberated though her body.

"Yeah" replied Luke a little less than enthusiastically as he caught the memory Kassidy was replaying in her mind.

A thought crossed her mind and Kassidy suddenly changed the subject. "Luke, something happened while you were gone. I tried to get up the secret passage to look for you and I couldn't remember the combination. What if you hadn't come back? How would I have gotten out of here? I need you to put that combination somewhere so I can look at it if I forget it when I'm . . . ." she was at a loss for words to describe the panic she had felt.

"Emotionally handicapped?" Luke offered.

"Yeah, good way to put it!"

"OK, but I don't want you to use that exit if I suddenly disappear. They might find it. It would be safer to use the back door."

"You have a back door?"

"Follow me, please," Luke took her hand and led her to the bathroom between his room and hers. He walked over to the shower, opened the door and stepped in. Without closing the shower door he turned the cold water knob to the left. Kassidy tried to step back to avoid the cold shot of water that she knew would be cascading down on them, but Luke chuckled and pulled her closer to himself. She was happy to discover that the water didn't come, but the back wall of the shower stall opened out into a dark passage way. Luke flipped a switch on the wall and the passage lit up. There was a box of flashlights on the floor beside the door but other than that the only thing she could see was tunnel.

"This tunnel is a mile long. There should be plenty of time for you to make it to the other entrance before the lights would go out if they are dependent on battery power. Right now they are using electricity from the cabin, but if that were shut off, they would run on battery power for forty-five minutes. After that you would need a flashlight." He pointed to the box as he spoke.

"At the other end of the tunnel," he continued, "there is a one car garage with a jeep in it. The keys are under a rock behind the back passenger side tire. The garage door opens when you push the remote inside the jeep. There is no road leading to the garage, but if you turn left as soon as you exit the garage, you will hit a dirt road on University of Wyoming land about fifteen yards away. Follow the road to the right and it will lead you back to town. Don't forget to close the garage door after you exit. It is camouflaged and you may want to come back to it. So keep it hidden. The jeep is registered to some guy who lives in Montana. You should be safe driving it."

Kassidy's jaw was hanging open. *"How do you do that?"*

"What?"

"Keep these things from me! Why can't I do that?"

"Kassidy, this was all in my head when we were on the mountain at Rick's, it probably just didn't seem important to you at the time, so you didn't look at it very closely. I'm sure there are things you have in there that I will not remember seeing when we finally get to hang out on your turf."

"Maybe." Kassidy didn't look convinced. *"Show me how it closes and let's go have some of that coffee you mentioned."*

"Kassidy, don't forget to leave the shower door open when you need to use this. There are two things that have to happen for this door to open. You must have your full weight on the shower floor and the shower door has to be open. If either of those things are not right, you will just get cold water. To close it from the tunnel side, just push the door closed and flip on the lights. The door will lock into place. To close it from this side, just turn the cold water off while the shower door is open and you are standing on the shower floor."

Luke closed the secret door and the two exited the shower and headed back to the kitchen.

"Don't worry! I'll keep it to myself." Luke had that teasing sort of smirk on his face.

"Keep what to yourself?"

"That we've been in the shower together!"

"Ha, Ha!" Kassidy was walking beside him and flipped her foot up behind her, crossed it over her own body and kicked Luke in the behind.

"Hey, watch it! You might hurt something important!" he teased back.

Kassidy returned to her place at the table and Luke brought a hot cup of coffee over to her. As he set it in front of her, she noticed how tired his eyes looked. She took a drink of the coffee, thinking that she appreciated how he remembered to mix in the flavored creamer. She smiled up at him.

"You need some sleep." She stated the obvious. Damn! She sure wanted to get this whole mess behind them. She felt like every minute they were doing something else was delaying what she wanted most. She wanted her family and her job back, but mostly she wanted to be able to get on with a normal life with Luke. Kassidy thought fleetingly about allowing Luke to drift off to sleep and then sneaking out to meet Ute and Uri. She hadn't even gotten to the part about how she was going to go, without Luke's help. It was only a half thought . . . just drifted through her mind. She hadn't really decided to go through with it, hadn't even considered it a serious thought, but Luke caught it mid drift.

"No!!"

The 'no' caught her off guard, since it really hadn't been a serious thought anyway. *"Don't worry. I'm not going anywhere."*

"I know. You will be with me!" He looked down at her coffee. *"You might as well finish that. You aren't going anywhere."*

Kassidy set her mug down. Luke was looking at her like a lion waiting to pounce on its prey. "Well, I guess I'll go take a shower and get dressed then." She stood and walked around the table toward the bathroom.

"Come with me." He took her hand.

Then she caught his thoughts. She looked incredulously at him. *"No way!"* Kassidy tried to pull her hand out of his, but he held tight. *"I'm not going to bed with you. You need sleep, not distraction and we've already been over this. Don't you remember the part about commitment before action?"*

Luke started toward his bedroom. *"No action, just sleep."*

"That will make for a restful sleep . . . NOT!"

"Restful or not, it will have to do."

"Luke, I promise not to go without you."

"No promises necessary." He made no move to release her hand. He pulled her down the hall. *"You need sleep too."*

"You can't be serious. Luke, remember the couch."

"I'm trying *not* to remember the couch, thank you! Kassidy, I couldn't stand it if you left without me. What if you needed me and I couldn't get to you? LeBeau is a sneaky son of a gun. You may not go chasing anywhere near him without me."

"I hope you are listening to yourself. What do you think you did this morning? Look, I promised you I wouldn't leave you, so there is no reason for you to take me in that room with you. You go ahead and get some sleep. I'll do some laundry or something."

"Sorry, Kassidy, I wouldn't be able to sleep a wink without knowing where you are."

"You always know where I am! You're in my head, remember? The only reason you have to have it this way is because you can't trust yourself, so you assume you can't trust me."

"You don't want to sleep with me?" Luke was trying to distract her, but Kassidy wasn't falling for it.

"Oh, yeah, I want to sleep with you, but you are not going to change the subject, Luke. You can't trust me because *you* know I can't trust you! You figure if you did it, then so will I. That is not fair!"

"You *do* want to sleep with me!" Luke was smiling.

"I think I made that abundantly clear on the couch, quit trying to change the subject."

"I don't think we were anywhere near the assumption that you wanted to *sleep* with me on the couch."

"Stop changing the subject, Luke! Admit that you don't trust me!"

Luke sighed audibly. "Sweetheart, I just listened in when you thought about doing the very thing you are saying you would never do."

"Well, just because the bird flew over the tree doesn't mean I'm going to let him make a nest in it!"

"What? . . . Never mind. No more argument. You need sleep and so do I." They had reached his room and Luke dragged her in and closed the door. "Kassidy, I'm a light sleeper. You move off this bed and I'll know it."

"Fine!! Is this how it's always going to be?" She was yelling and becoming a little hysterical.

"What, you sleeping in my bed? I sure hope so. But I hope you aren't always as ticked off about it."

"Luke, I'm not ticked off about sleeping in your bed!! I'm ticked off that you don't trust me when I promise not to do something!" Kassidy was not sure if she was more hurt or angry at this little development. But it didn't matter because tears were threatening regardless. She turned her back to him.

Luke grabbed her around her waist and pulled her into the bed with him. He threw his feather blanket over them both and pulled her back into his stomach, tucked one arm under his head and wrapped the other around Kassidy. She stiffened.

Luke sighed. He wasn't sure why he had insisted she come with him. He trusted her with his life. He was a little over protective, but he didn't want her in here just because he was afraid she would leave. He believed her when she said she wouldn't leave. He just *wanted* her here. He was still pondering that when he felt her inhale raggedly with a sniff.

"*Kassidy?*"

"*Stay out of my mind.*" Her thought cracked just like her voice would have if she'd spoken out loud. She was trying to block him out of her mind, but it wasn't working. It never seemed to work very well. He usually figured out what was going on.

"*You're crying?*" Luke's irritation at himself crept into his thoughts.

Damn she was wrong, he didn't usually know, he always knew. "I said, stay out of my mind!" Kassidy yelled in response.

"*Kassidy, I'll stay out of your mind, if you'll take a closer look at mine.*"

"*What?*"

"*It's not that I don't trust you . . . I . . . well, I am a little over protective, I suppose. But it's more than that. Kassidy . . . I just want you here. That's all. I won't try anything. I won't even know if you get up after I go to sleep, because, I lied, I sleep like a bump on a log. You could throw a party in here and I'd probably sleep right through it. I will even . . . let you go . . . right now if that's what you want. But I hope you will stay.*" She felt his thumb stroking her rib as he spoke.

"*How do you do that?*" Kassidy rolled over to face him as she asked.

"*How do I do what?*" Luke wiped a tear from her beautiful green eyes.

"*How do you keep all that stuff from me? Why is everything I think laid bare in my mind to you, but you can have all those thoughts and never reveal them to me? I might as well not even be able to read your mind . . . because mostly what I get is only what you want to show me.*"

"*I don't get everything you think. Some of it you hide quite well.*"

"*Like what?*"

"*Like when you were down on the beach in the cave at Sophia and Rick's house. You didn't let me in on anything there. I didn't know from minute to minute whether you were going to stay with me or leave. I couldn't hear anything you were thinking. It was like . . . well . . . it was horrible. I hope you never do that to me again.*"

"*I didn't do it to you.*"

"*Yes, you did and you made me realize that every thought between us was a gift.*"

"*Well, the gift was from Sophia. I wasn't doing it.*"

Luke stared at her in confusion.

When he didn't comment, Kassidy explained it to him. "*Sophia told me that if I wanted to be truly alone with my thoughts I should go in the cave. There is something in the rocks that disrupts telepathic abilities. I couldn't hear any of your thoughts either.*"

"*You're kidding me!*"

"No"

Luke thought about that for a few minutes. Kassidy closed her eyes, began to forgive him and was definitely enjoying having him so close. Her muscles began to relax and she found herself drifting off to sleep. She was more tired than she had thought. Or maybe it was just the security of Luke's arm wrapped around her. Luke rolled onto his back pulling her arm across his chest. Kassidy's head was pulled onto his shoulder and within minutes, he heard her shallow even breathing as she slept. Luke, however, had too much food for thought to fall asleep just yet.

If there was something in that cave that disrupted telepathic abilities, they needed to know what it was and just how many telepathic abilities it affected. What if LeBeau got his hands on that kind of thing? He would use it putting the paths at a definite disadvantage and a whole lot more danger. Luke and Rick would have to check out that cave . . . tonight. That decided, Luke rolled his head to the side, catching a whiff of the lilacs in Kassidy's hair and drifted off to sleep himself.

Chapter 22

A Ray of Light in His Darkness

His snipers were in place. He was sure the paths would come. They were curious. They needed information. He would take his time. A leisurely walk up Diamond Head would be a pleasant way to trap paths. It was a beautiful day . . . of course, nearly every day was beautiful in Hawaii. The worst weather recorded in the last ten years was during President Clinton's week long trip here in '96 or '97. He couldn't remember the year exactly. He just remembered torrential rains that kept the leader of the free world off the golf courses. It rained the entire week he was here. Some of the areas even reported some minor flooding. LeBeau had laughed and laughed over that. If he believed in God, he would have thought it was a direct indication of God's opinion of Clinton's presidency. Hawaii experienced perfect weather 98% of the time and Clinton shows up during a typhoon! Well, it wasn't really a typhoon, perhaps God was only a little miffed at him. LeBeau never really liked Clinton. He thought he was too weak. He embarrassed the country because he couldn't keep his hands to himself. LeBeau could never be that weak. He would never allow a woman to bring him down or stand in his way.

LeBeau took his time walking past a couple of souvenir booths that had been set up in front of the entrance to Diamond Head. One of the booths sold flash lights under a large sign that stated that the hiker may need one as the trail led through a couple of very dark tunnels. LeBeau threw down his money and took one of the little red flash lights with him. He glanced at the T-shirts with the slogan 'I survived Diamond Head' printed in bright orange letters with a picture of the volcano on the front. Somehow, he could never quite picture himself in a T-shirt. It just didn't fit his personality. He felt he was as casual as he could get in his polo shirt and khaki slacks. He had been known to wear shorts on occasion . . . to the beach. But he felt most comfortable in slacks.

He passed the last booth which sold cold drinks and headed up the path. As he reached a landing leading into a tunnel, LeBeau turned around to survey the area. He was checking on his snipers and also trying to detect any paths that might be in the area. He could feel them sometimes, he thought, like an intuition. But he wasn't getting anything right at this moment. He could just make out one of his guys in a very large tree. He didn't think anyone else could have seen him, if they didn't know he was there. His second sniper had gone out on his own. LeBeau didn't know where he was and he couldn't see him. It was just as well. If a path was in the area, the less LeBeau knew the better. But just to be on the safe side, he should probably keep his thoughts on the scenery. To that end he started making mental comments about the other tourists that were around him. There was a young couple standing at the entrance to the tunnel. The young man was leaning toward the girl who was obviously angry with him. He was reassuring her that he had never been up Diamond Head with anyone else before. "Liar," thought LeBeau. The couple slipped into the dark of the tunnel and disappeared.

He flipped on his flash light and entered the tunnel. The little light barely gave him enough illumination to see the floor immediately in front of him, but he was glad he had bought it. It was pitch black in the tunnel. He noticed the volcanic rock that surrounded him. It was rough on his hands as he moved them along the wall. As he looked up to examine a particularly large rock jutting out of the wall, his foot caught on a bump in the floor and LeBeau went sprawling. Unfortunately, there were no other tourists close enough for him to use their light to see. The little flash light had hit the ground and gone out and LeBeau found himself in total darkness. He wasn't panicked because he could always feel his way out of the tunnel, but he was annoyed at the stupidity of the whole thing. He had torn his pant leg and his knee was throbbing a bit.

At least he would be able to get his flashlight back. He concentrated on the thing, trying to pull it to him. For some reason, he was having trouble 'feeling' the flashlight's presence as he concentrated on it. Usually, he would 'feel' the item as his mind touched it and moved it closer to him. He couldn't 'feel' it, no matter how hard he tried. He also should be able to hear it scooting across the floor. Nothing! What was this? His frustration peeked when a tourist approached him with a flash light in hand. The man was nice enough, asking if LeBeau was all right and helping him find his little flash light, but LeBeau was aggravated at the man's ability to sneak up on him. He had not 'felt' him approaching. He hadn't known the man was there until he saw the light. That was unusual. Were the effects of the operation wearing off? He had felt someone approaching him in the dinning room this morning. He had known it was Gaff even before the man had spoken. He had also known that the young man at the entrance to this tunnel had lied to his girlfriend when he told her this was his first time up Diamond Head. LeBeau concluded that what ever was happening to him, it had just started.

LeBeau progressed slowly through the rest of the tunnel into the bright, hot sunshine, the light blinding him momentarily after the darkness from within. As soon as he left the tunnel, he could 'feel' again. There was the same young couple and sure enough, LeBeau could feel the lies drifting silkily off the young man's tongue. Someone should warn that young lady. Someone should . . . but not LeBeau. He was more interested in what had happened in the tunnel. He stepped back in. He couldn't tell if the young man was telling the truth or not. As soon as he stepped out, it was quite clear again.

A thought began to form in LeBeau's head. What was in the tunnel walls that disrupted his path powers? What if the agency were to employ that very substance? Could they gain an advantage over the paths? A wicked smile began to form on his lips. He stepped back into the tunnel and withdrew his pocket knife. He hammered on the rock wall until he chipped off a piece and stuck it in his pocket. He decided that this was more important than catching his paths at the moment and turned to make his way back down through the tunnel. He took out his little flashlight. It took some fiddling to get the thing to work again, but once he got it turned on, he headed back down though the darkness. He tried to be a little more careful this time watching for rough parts in the flooring.

As soon as he stepped out into the sunshine again, he 'felt' Gaff's presence.

"What's wrong?" he said before Gaff even had a chance to step out of a shadow near the entrance.

"We've had a little problem at the agency."

LeBeau's facial muscles tightened. His eyes grew hard. He turned to face Gaff. "What *little* problem?"

"Well, they tell me that Jonas Carter disappeared last night as well as the Linder family."

"WHAT?!! We lost the whole family? How did they know they were there?"

"We don't know sir. But we think they may have been in the computer lab. The two techs that were on duty said they got a call about 3:00 a.m. to meet in the conference room immediately for a very important briefing. They were told to wait for the director to come and brief them. The director said he never called them and never showed up, but the two techs swear up and down that he came and briefed them. When asked what he briefed them about, neither could remember."

"The alarm on Jonas' room went off at 3:27 a.m. Security responded immediately and saw Luke Matthews, Dr. Johns, Carter and an unidentified man in the hallway in front of Carter's room. They ran and security fired on them. They thought they hit one when they found blood on the floor where the group ran around a corner. By the time security got to the corner, they were gone. Security called for a sweep of the building. During the search they heard movement and voices from the dissection lab, but when they opened the door, there was no one in the room."

"The lab techs were sent back to the lab at 3:56 a.m. They arrived there around 4:00 a.m. At 4:01 a.m. the alarm sounded from Mrs. Linder's room. At 4:02 the nurse on duty for the Linder's entered Mr. Linder's room to administer his sedative and saw six men, one of them carrying Mrs. Linder and one carrying the child. He was told that he needed to check Mrs. Linder's room. It didn't make sense to him but his mind seemed to be arguing with itself and then he got severely ill. He saw one of the men reach out and touch Mr. Linder and then they were gone. The nurse proceeded to throw up for the rest of the night. At least he was still sick when they called."

"I suspected as much. They can teleport themselves and others. That's going to make the game more interesting. But how did they know the others were there? They weren't even close to each other. We kept them all at least 30 feet away from each other. They can't read minds outside of 30 feet . . . . that we know of. Get a missing person's report going on the child. Make sure you run a picture with the silly chipmunk hat on. He loves that hat. He'll be sure to have it on, if he's out and about. We may have lost him for good, but you never know. They may get sloppy."

"Oh, and get some security in the lab, find out if they messed with anything. They may be bugging us." LeBeau started to walk on down the path leaving a stunned Gaff behind him. "Aren't you coming?" he asked as he continued walking.

"Uh, yes . . . sir." Gaff thought LeBeau, who was known for his temper, had handled that particular bit of nasty news quite well. This morning when Gaff and LaFave had been drawing straws to see who would be the unlucky one to have to tell him, Gaff, being the said 'unlucky one', thought surely that with news like that he'd be looking for a job by noon. He wasn't going to look a gift horse in the mouth though, and he was definitely going to get lost for a while. He didn't want to be around when the news finally sank in.

"Oh, Gaff, I have another job for you."

"Uh-oh", thought Gaff, "here it comes. I'll be sent to work in the morgue or something just as grisly."

Picking up on Gaff's feelings of foreboding, LeBeau laughed. "Don't worry." LeBeau took something out of his pocket and handed it to Gaff. "I just need you to take this sample to our labs and find out exactly what is in it. Get on a flight as soon as possible. That sample is very important. Don't lose it! Tell me as soon as you know anything."

Gaff might have stood there with his mouth hanging open in shock for quite a while if LeBeau hadn't looked up at him and finally returned to his usual character. "Do you need a note from your mommy for this field trip? GET GOING!!"

Gaff was gone in a heartbeat. LeBeau watched him sprint down the sidewalk; then turned to catch the eye of his sniper. He motioned for him to come down and follow. The second sniper would return to the hotel when he saw LeBeau leave.

Despite the loss of the baby, LeBeau's mood was buoyant. He'd found a weapon.

CHAPTER 23

The New Guy

Kassidy woke first. She lay still, watching him sleep for a few minutes. Then she slid quietly out of bed, gathered up his laundry from the corner of the room, and headed for her own room. She gathered her laundry also and headed for the washing machine at the end of the hall. She separated the clothes into like colors and put in the first load.

She headed back to the bath room and took a shower, pausing as she reached for her usual shampoo, choosing the peach scented shampoo instead. She wondered where it had come from. It wasn't a brand she normally used, but maybe Luke used it. No, he never smelled like peaches. It couldn't be his, could it? Maybe she'd ask him later. She brushed her teeth and blow dried her hair. After she got dressed, she headed for the kitchen to make some breakfast. She grabbed the cups of cold coffee off the table and heated them in the microwave. She took them both down the hall and peeked into Luke's room. He had rolled over since she left, but he seemed to be still snoozing. She brought the coffee into the room and set it down on the night stand beside him. She turned to leave, but she didn't get far.

"Come back," Luke's voice was groggy.

"Sorry I woke you." Kassidy slid onto the bed beside him.

Luke flopped his arm across her lap almost hitting her coffee cup. Kassidy recovered quickly and set the mug down on the night stand on her side of the bed.

"Sorry."

"Are you going to wake up, or did you just need some sleeping company again."

"I'm getting there. I'm just enjoying being here with you"

Kassidy slid down beside him and wiggled her way under his arm and snuggled up closer to him.

Luke let out a little groan . . . or was it a moan? *"You smell good!"*

"Luke, we have to get going. We have bad guys to catch . . . remember?"

"What time is it?"

"It's two o'clock in the afternoon."

There was another groan. *"We're going to be all turned around. I never sleep in like this."*

"Well, you really didn't sleep in. You just caught up."

"Doesn't matter. It still works the same way. We won't be able to sleep tonight so we'll stay up too late and then sleep in too long and on and on until we are completely turned around."

"Well, if we keep doing that sooner or later we'll be back on the right time zone again!"

Luke laughed out loud and finally opened his eyes to look into hers. *"How did you sleep?"*

"I don't know. I was unconscious the whole time! How about you?"

"I slept very well, even though I was conscious . . . of you . . . the whole time."

"Except when I slipped out to shower and start the laundry. You were out like a light."

"No, I was listening in."

"Not while I showered . . . . !!!!"

"Uh, no . . . not while you showered. But thank you for choosing the peach scented shampoo." He chuckled to himself.

"Luke Matthews, look at me and tell me you didn't do what I think you did." Kassidy was speaking out loud to him now and quite loudly.

Luke laughed harder.

"Listen to me, sweetheart, and I'm using that term loosely. I am never taking another shower or bath until we're married if you don't look me in the eye and tell me that you weren't in my head when I was in the shower and you didn't augment my thoughts!"

"You'd never make it. You like your baths too much!" Luke was in an all out full gale fit of laughter.

"Don't try me! After a couple of days you wouldn't feel such great desire for much snuggling." That seemed to sober him up a bit.

"Fair enough," Luke caught his breath, "all I did was put the peach shampoo in there just after you started the water. I stayed out of your mind until you left the bathroom. Truly! Though the temptation was great . . . . nearly unbearable. I think I deserve a reward for my restraint."

Kassidy scrutinized his face and dug into his mind checking to see if he was telling the truth. When she was convinced he was, she leaned over and kissed him. It was a quick kiss and she was out of his reach and headed for the door before his protest got past his lips. "Hey, come back here. I didn't get to reciprocate there."

"That was a reward, not an invitation!" Kassidy paused at the door. *"Luke, what was wrong with my Lilac shampoo? You didn't like it?"*

"Actually, I love it, but I'm also very fond of peaches."

"Oh, I like them too. Now, get up and go shower, we need to get going. I'm in a hurry to meet the new guy."

Luke sat up then and threw his feet over the bed. He was after Kassidy in a shot. He caught up with her in the hallway. *"You want to meet who?"*

Kassidy turned to look at him with a faux, sweet, innocent look on her face. *"The new guy. I want to go meet him. Hurry up! You're wasting time!"* She turned to retreat down the hall, and now it was her turn to giggle.

Luke was already delving into her thoughts and erupted in laughter once again when he caught the picture in her head of a two year old toddler with huge dimples.

Kassidy and Luke didn't make their appearance on the deck of the beach house until around 4:00 p.m. The little Linder family was just returning from the beach, all smiles. Derrick was hanging from their hands, his dad on one side and his mother on the other. Every other step they would swing him in the air between them. He erupted in giggles; saying "Again!" each time they set him back on his feet.

When the couple made it to the deck, Anthony and Teresa Linder looked up at Kassidy and Luke. Teresa recognized Luke immediately. "Thank you so much for saving us. We will be in your debt for ever! I was so afraid for Derrick especially."

"No problem. How did they get you three? How did they miss the two of you before umm . . . before the little guy came along? I'm assuming that you weren't all three in a serious car wreck or something sustaining serious head injuries where a miracle happened and all of you were saved by brain surgery at the same time."

They laughed. "No, that isn't quite how it happened," said Teresa. "But let me introduce my husband. This is Anthony. He is a professor of geology at a university in Mexico. He was injured in a boating accident five years ago. Then four years ago, he was drawn to my house. There was a wind storm and a tree was pulled from the ground. I was inside the house that it hit when it fell. We were married within a couple of months after my operation and we had Derrick the following year. We never displayed our 'talents' because we were afraid it would scare people. Goodness knows, it scared us at first.

We managed to keep it a secret until Derrick came along. He is too little to understand that his abilities are strange to others. We covered it up as best we could, but obviously, someone figured it out. The guys from that facility came to our house and took us at night. I'm sure none of our friends have any idea what happened to us. Anthony and I have been sedated and kept apart since that night. They didn't want us to be able to get away using our talents. Derrick can't telefly yet. So, as long as Anthony and I were sedated, they had us. They would still have us if you hadn't come along when you did."

While Anthony, Teresa and Luke talked, Kassidy was getting to know Derrick. She was so good with children, thought Luke as watched her. She listened intently to what ever important story Derrick was relaying. Kassidy asked him about things he liked to do. Derrick began telling her about his house and his toys. He stopped suddenly and said, "But I, I, I, don twike dat bad guy. He a bewy bad guy. He taked my daddy away fwom mommy and me. He maked mommy seepy. Den mommy don play. I don twike dat bad guy!"

Kassidy smiled at him and assured him that the bad guy couldn't get him or his mommy or daddy here. They were safe and could play and play.

"Das good, cuz I don twike dat guy."

Jonas made his first appearance on the deck just then. "*Hi,*" he thought. He was really getting into the fact that almost everyone here could hear each other without opening their mouths. He looked down at Kassidy then and forgot all about his new talents. "Wow, who is the beautiful lady, Luke?"

"This is Kassidy Dover, Jonas. Kassidy, this is Jonas Carter."

"Hi, it's nice to meet you, Jonas. Nice accent!" Kassidy stood and shook his hand. "Thanks, but you're the ones with the accent!"

"I never thought of it that way." Kassidy's smile lit her face and then got serious. "Luke said they found you at the facility."

"Yes, thank heavens. Not a nice place to spend your time."

Jonas could not seem to take his eyes off of Kassidy. She was gorgeous! He had never seen such beautiful green eyes in his life. He thought maybe he could stare into them forever.

"Thank you!" Kassidy was blushing having heard every thought.

Jonas blushed. He'd forgotten that his thoughts were easy pickings.

"*Down boy,*" Luke stepped between them and ushered Kassidy into the house to look for Mark and Rick. "*She's mine!*" he threw back at him as they left the porch.

"*We'll see!*" Jonas shot back at him.

"He needs a crossroads to be drawn to," Luke whispered to Kassidy.

"That could be a while. How long did you say it took you?" asked Kassidy.

"Ugh! I'd rather not think about Jonas without a mate for that length of time."

Kassidy just giggled. "You afraid of a little competition?"

"Bring it on . . . I have a secret weapon!"

Kassidy let that comment slide as another thought occurred to her. She stopped Luke just as they entered the house. "Luke, was there a path with Jonas?"

"Not that we have discovered."

"I thought there was always another path."

"So did we. We thought his mate might be in the facility. That's how we found the Linder's. We were checking for anyone that might have been brought in with him. We are going to check the computer lab to see what information the labbies have in their computers. We just haven't had the time yet. If you think about it though, I guess that there can't always be a path at every crossroads. Sometimes you'd have to have an odd number of them."

Mark and Lisa were in the living room sharing a bottle of wine. "Hey, you two! Care for a glass of REAL wine?"

"Ooo, I'd like a glass." Kassidy was already heading for the china cabinet. She took out a glass and headed back over to Mark and Lisa. She held it out and Mark poured her a glass. It was a very sweet Riesling. "Mmm. Would you like a taste, Luke?"

"No thank you, sweetheart. You go ahead."

"Sweetheart? What happened to 'baby'?" Mark couldn't help himself; he got to tease them both with one line!

"Shhh! You'll give away my secret weapon!" Luke decided to sidestep that rub and let Kassidy field it.

"Remember what happened the last time someone teased me about that particular term of endearment?" she reminded him, producing an ice cold glass of water again.

Mark raised his eyebrows and made a motion as if he were zipping his lips.

"That's better." She drank the water and sat down beside Lisa and the two were deep in conversation in no time.

"Mark, have you seen Rick?"

"No, why not just tele-look for him?"

"Well, his house is so full, I didn't want to disturb him if he needed time away from everyone. Kassidy and I were going to see if he wanted to send some people home with us. We have a couple of spare rooms. That's what I built them for anyway . . . just in case other paths needed a place to stay until they got on their feet."

"You might want to take the Linder's with you. They are struggling to keep an eye on that little guy here. He loves the beach and the water. If you aren't watching him closely, he heads down there by himself."

"I'd like that better than taking Jonas. Too many hormones racing around in that one!"

"He liked Kassidy, did he?" Mark was already laughing.

"Oh, yeah!"

"Are you afraid of a little competition?"

"No, I have a secret weapon!"

Both men laughed and the women looked up to see what the joke was but both men slapped on their innocent looks and replied, "What?"

Rick and Sophia came into the living room. They had been somewhere in the back of the house. Sophia was looking a little tired. She had not had much sleep, having taken the time to watch little Derrick while the Linder's recovered. Rick was trying to talk her into heading to bed early.

"It's too early for bed. It'll mess me up. I'll be on the wrong time schedule then. I can make it a couple more hours and then it will be all right to head to bed."

"Kassidy and I will take some of your guests off your hands. I have a couple of rooms open at the cabin."

"That would be great. You should probably take the Linders."

"Yeah, that's what Mark was saying too. He loves water, huh?!"

"Oh, yeah!" Sophia sat down wearily. Kassidy poured her a glass of wine and handed it to her. "Thanks!"

"Sorry you've had to work so hard! I should have come to help you." Kassidy was feeling a little guilty about the long rest she and Luke had when Sophia had been up since three in the morning.

"Oh, it wasn't much work. I just watched the little guy. Everyone else took care of themselves. I think I brought in food once . . . for Mark, Lisa and Sandra, but that was no problem. They are easily pleased." She smiled at Mark and Lisa affectionately.

"Where is Sandra?" asked Kassidy.

"She's into another book. That woman is a book-aholic!" Mark didn't look too unhappy about that. "She knocks down one every day or so. Good thing Sophia has a great library."

"I don't have a great library . . . . Honolulu has a great library. However, if we keep Sandra here much longer, at the rate she is reading, we may have to find a library she hasn't read! She says she loves teaching and likes to read historical biographies so that she has something new to share with the kids in her class. She even takes notes on some books."

Luke changed the subject abruptly. "Sophia, what can you tell me about that cave you sent Kassidy to the first time we came."

"What do you want to know?" Sophia looked confused.

Luke looked over at Rick and then back at Sophia. "Why can't we hear each other's thoughts in the cave?"

"I don't really know. Something in the cave disrupts our telepathic abilities."

"What kind of rock do you think it is?" probed Luke.

"It's volcanic rock. Why are you so interested?" asked Rick.

"I just think we should know all about it. If our telepathic abilities don't work in there, we need to know why. What if LeBeau got hold of that kind of information? He would have a way to keep us when he catches us. We wouldn't be able to hear each other. If we can't hear each other, how would we telefly out? We wouldn't be able to access the power of joined minds. And guess where he was yesterday. He was in Hawaii . . . . land of volcanic rock!"

"Oh no!" Kassidy had been listening to everything Luke had said and now was looking a little pale.

"What's wrong?" Luke was on his feet.

"LeBeau was going to Diamond Head today!"

"Don't worry, Kassidy, the cave has no effect on us when we are on top of it, only when we are in it. He could walk all over Diamond Head and never experience the loss of what ever powers he has." Rick reassured her.

"You don't understand . . . . there are tunnels leading to the summit of Diamond Head! He had to go through tunnels! He could already know this!"

"Did Uri and Ute follow his tails today?"

"Yes, they stopped by earlier to tell us that he only went about half way up and then turned around and called off his shooters. Uri said that a man named Gaff went to find him and tell him about the disappearance of the Linders and Jonas. He met LeBeau as he was coming back down, before he had even reached the top! The man was positively afraid of LeBeau. But surprisingly he didn't take the news too badly. He just gave Gaff a . . . rock . . . . to . . . analyze." Rick's voice trailed off as the realization of what had happened shook them all.

"We have to find out all we can about that cave!" Luke didn't have to say it; they were all thinking the same thing. As a group they set down their glasses and headed out the door.

The Linders and Jonas were still on the deck. Probably too much confinement in the last few days had inspired a wish to be outside as much as possible. Luke was not surprised to find them still there. As he looked over at Anthony a thought occurred to him.

"Anthony, what did you say you were a professor of?" there was an idea forming behind his eyes that hadn't been there a minute ago.

"I'm a professor of geology." There was only confusion in Anthony's eyes as he answered. He wondered why that would suddenly be so important that everyone had come out of the house.

"We need you to come down to the beach with us, please."

"Of, course, but what is this about?"

"We think LeBeau has discovered something that could put us in a lot more danger, if we're caught."

Everyone headed down the little brick lined path to the beach. They turned left at the bottom and headed toward the cave. Kassidy ran a bit to catch up to Luke and slid her hand into his. He smiled down at her and the twinkle was back in his eyes. Both Kassidy and Luke were remembering the last time they had been here. They were also blocking those thoughts from their companions. Only Mark, watching them as Luke, without breaking his stride, took her hand and wrapped it around his waist as his arm slid around hers, seemed to know what they were thinking about at the moment.

CHAPTER 24

Poor, lucky Luke!

As soon as they entered the cave, every telepath felt the difference. But only one voiced it.

"Hey, where is eberbody?" Derrick, who had never known a day without other thoughts in his head, had a difficult time understanding. "It too quiet hewe, mommy. I don twike it hewe." He was pulling his mother back toward the entrance to the cave. "OUSSIDE! OUSSIDE, pweeze! Mommy, pweeze!"

She hurriedly left with the panicked little Derrick and the cave sank back into silence for the moment. But the moment didn't last long.

Jonas was first to comment. "Wow, I can't hear a thing anyone's thinking." He seemed to be concentrating on Kassidy as he spoke. He had been trying to figure out why he had been shut out of what ever thoughts were filling her head on the beach. It had been like hitting a brick wall. Then she had skipped ahead and caught up with Luke. Jonas hadn't liked that much. He guessed she was going to be more of a challenge than he had anticipated. Girls had always been pretty easy for him. He was, as he liked to think, ruggedly handsome with a set of abs to match. He was a very serious athlete and an important part of his college swim team. The university he attended in England had produced more than one Olympic contender over the years. That was his goal. That was why he chose that college. He worked hard to get the things he wanted and he was usually successful. And what he wanted right now was the girl with the beautiful green eyes.

"It's the cave. It blocks telepathic abilities somehow," said Luke. 'What we need to know is what does it; the rock, the shape, the sand, or what?

"Well, I think we can rule out the sand because we don't lose abilities when we are on the sand or in the surf. When we're underwater, there is sand all around us in small particles, of course. We have never lost abilities under the water." Rick surmised.

"It can't be the shape either," Kassidy said almost to herself. Then a little louder to the rest of the group she finished her thought, "The tunnels at Diamond Head are not shaped anything like this."

"Anthony, is there any way you could run some tests on the rock to see if there is something in it other than just volcanic rock, like a mineral or something?" asked Luke.

"I could if I could get to my lab. I don't have any equipment here. I wouldn't have any place to put it if I brought it here telepathically. We could maybe sneak into the lab. I doubt anyone would be expecting us to show up in the middle of the night."

"We better do it quickly . . . tonight. If they figure this out before we do, they may think to stake out your lab." Luke was thinking it through as he talked. "We should check out the building before we telefly into the lab. We need to know if they have it under surveillance, just to be on the safe side. After all, they know you are at large and they want you back."

"I'll get some samples from around the cave to take with us. I'll need a chisel and hammer." Anthony was concentrating on something and then an 'Aha moment' look crossed his face. "Guess I can't get them from inside here!" He and the others headed toward the open side of the cave and made their way out into the sunshine.

Luke still had his arm around Kassidy's waist and held her back for just a moment after the others left. He pulled her around in front of him, reached up and took her chin in his hand. He pulled her chin up and kissed her lightly on the lips. He looked down into those clear green eyes and tried to read what she was thinking just from the look on her face. She still smelled like peaches. Luke leaned down to kiss her again but someone near the entrance cleared his throat impatiently.

"Excuse me! I can come back later!" a very amused Anthony stood in the entrance of the cave.

"No, it's OK," said Kassidy dragging her gaze away from Luke. She pulled away from Luke's embrace with some effort. He was not ready to let go and was quite willing to let Anthony come back later. She took hold of one of Luke's hands and began to tow him to the entrance. His disappointment was so palpable that she was sure that even without path powers; Anthony could read the frustration on Luke's face.

"We'll meet you on the deck," Luke said briskly.

As soon as the two exited Anthony began to chuckle. He remembered the first two months after he had met his Teresa. It was blissful torture. She was living with her parents again because her house had been demolished in the storm. That had kept them very honest. They'd have gotten married sooner, but her parents insisted on a wedding with all the trimmings. Two months was the bare minimum her mother allowed before the wedding. She said she needed time to plan and make arrangements. Anthony liked his in-laws. Teresa's mother was so much like Teresa that he could no sooner have denied her the joy of a big wedding than he could have denied the attraction he felt for Teresa. So they had waited. It was excruciating and incredibly wonderful all at the same time. Poor, lucky Luke!

Jonas had been waiting for the two to exit the cave. He watched as they stepped into the sun-warmed sand and headed back toward the house. He was pleased to note the expression on Luke's face. Clearly, she had ticked him off. He looked positively . . . well, positively dejected! Jonas' spirits soared. He felt like dancing. True, they were still holding hands, but something had definitely not gone Luke's way in the cave. That was just the wedge between them that Jonas thought he could work with. Ah, the battle begins!

Luke stopped mid beach. A smile returned to his face. Kassidy stopped with him. *"What did you stop for?"* she wondered. She was trying to read his thoughts, but he was blocking them from her. That was interesting. Why would he do that? She would have felt uneasy but the smile on his face let her know he was all right. Luke spoke softly to her.

"Block your thoughts from everyone but me and I'll tell you."

"OK, what's up?" Now her curiosity was peaked.

"Listen to Jonas' thoughts right now. He thinks you and I have been fighting or that you stopped me short in the cave." Luke wrinkled his brow and stared down at her. *"Of course, you did stop me short in the cave."* Luke was back to looking frustrated again.

"No, I didn't stop you forever, I just delayed you. There's a difference."

"I like that difference . . . I think!"

"Shall we give him something to help him keep his feet on the ground?"

"I was thinking we should mess with him. I could attack you unmercifully right here in the sand, running my hands through your hair and kissing you with wanton abandon and you could jump up, slap me and run for the house!" Luke was looking lecherously down at her.

"It won't work, sweetheart."

"Why not?"

"Because if you throw me in the sand, run your fingers through my hair and kiss me with wanton abandon, I will never be able to slap you. More likely, I would return the favor! Then where would we be?"

"We'd be in the sand and very happy . . . until someone threw cold water on us and chastised us for such behavior in front of a toddler." They both peaked down the beach toward the water where Derrick and his mother were throwing seashells into the surf.

"Well, it was a fun fantasy for a moment there."

"I have a better idea."

"What did you have in mind?"

"You can see *what I have in mind."* Kassidy let go of his hand and wrapped her arms around his neck. She stood on her tip toes and leaned into him. She kissed him sweetly on the lips. Then she just looked at him with all the love she felt radiating from those crystal clear green eyes. Luke would have followed her anywhere and he did . . . all the way up to the deck.

That sweet moment was devastating to Jonas. He saw in that moment what he had somehow missed every time he had looked at the two of them together. She was totally, completely, whole-heartedly lost to, besotted with, and intoxicated by Luke. Of course, in his own defense, he had only seen them together about three times including when he met her. So, he could see how he had missed it. Still it was discouraging. She was so beautiful!!! Oh, well, there would be other fish in the sea. There always were!

"You realize," teased Luke, *"You have just ruined my fun for the next couple of weeks. It would have been fun to watch him work his manly wiles on you."*

"No, it would have been a pain to watch him work his manly wiles on me. But it might have been fun to watch you squirm a bit while I let him."

"While you let him . . . what?"

"Work his manly wiles on me."

"He'd have never gotten close enough for you to fully discover any manly wiles he might have."

"That's my point!"

CHAPTER 25

Dimples

It only took a few minutes for Anthony to gather his samples. He brought them up to the deck and set them on the table. Then he took a seat across from Luke and Kassidy and produced a cold drink. He was sweaty and dirty from chipping away samples from the walls of the cave. Teresa and Derrick were not far behind him. When they reached the deck they sat beside Anthony. He handed Teresa a glass of cold tea and produced a glass of milk for Derrick. Throughout the entire time, his eyes maintained the air of amusement every time he caught Kassidy's or Luke's eyes.

As the sun began to set, most of the paths that Rick had originally recruited began to arrive with news. They all sat around the deck on chairs, on the railing or on the floor. The plan was taking shape with each new piece of news. During Kassidy's and Luke's nap, Uri and Ute had managed to track down over twenty field operatives for the agency. They had picked up another path couple to help out and with the four of them and Kassidy and Luke, Uri thought they could get definite numbers within a few days.

Andre and Cecil had been working with the computers and had learned a lot about what the agency knew about paths. They were happy to announce that their knowledge was not that great. They believed that paths could read minds within twenty to thirty feet of their 'mark', that they could teleport items, (which was what had tipped them off to paths in the first place), and that they could telefly. Teleflight was their most recent entry into their computer information system. They had also made a connection between teleflight and the necessity of two paths working together. That explained why they separated paths in the facility. They were trying to keep them at least 30 feet apart. There was no evidence that they knew the true extent of the mind reading capabilities of a fully matured telepath.

Most of what they knew had been gleaned from their experiment on LeBeau. His powers were much more limited than the normal paths. He can't telefly or read minds, however he is very sensitive to people around him. He can tell if they are telling the truth or lying, but he can't tell what they are thinking.

199

He knows when someone is near, even if he can't see them or hear them yet and he can guess their mood, though he probably wouldn't know what caused the mood just from telepathy. He could also move objects telepathically, but he couldn't pick them up or produce them like paths do. His mind just wasn't' strong enough.

Andre concluded his report on LeBeau by telling them that LeBeau's greatest strength and also the most lethal to paths was his greed. He wanted what they had and would stop at nothing to get it. He was ruthless and cared nothing for his subjects. He had proven that over and over again. The files they had hacked into at the agency revealed more than just Regina's death. There had been several paths who had died at his hands. And it was *his* hands . . . . he was, as the files revealed, the director, manager, and founder of the agency.

Andre had one more thing to share with the group. The tests they had run on Derrick were highly encrypted. He hadn't been able to get to those yet, but what he had discovered was that they had run many more tests on him than on any other path. He had discovered this detail through a back door of sorts. Instead of looking in Derrick's file which had been unattainable to date, he had been looking through nursing work orders and discovered the requests for the tests. So although there was no information on what they had discovered yet, they did know where they had been looking. They were studying his DNA. They were also looking at Anthony's and Teresa's DNA.

"My guess," explained Andre "is that they are comparing the two, trying to figure out what changed between parent and child that would allow the child to have the talents of the parents without the accident that normally precedes it."

"You think they are trying to figure out how to duplicate his DNA in someone else?" one of the guests asked.

"We won't know until I can get into Derrick's files, but I think it's safe to say that if LeBeau's behavior holds true, that is exactly what they are after. He's been trying to duplicate it all along. This is just a different avenue he is exploring."

A silence fell over the group. It lasted for a good two minutes before Rick finally moved them forward by asking for the next report. Mark raised his hand. I'd like to show you all something that may make our job a little easier. He was hoping that his little surprise might lighten the mood a bit. He stood from the railing where he had been sitting and reached into his back pocket. He pulled out a white piece of paper.

"When we were visiting the agency the other night, I discovered a little storage room full of this stationary." He held it up for them to see. "Notice the return address. Arizona Cancer Research Facility, Tucson, AZ!"

"They already have a cover for the facility! We don't have to invent the whole thing!" Rick was already across the deck and patting Mark on the back.

There was a groan from the deck amid all the cheers. Rick looked around and saw Satoro with his head in his hands. "I just finished persuading the director of an AIDS Research Facility in Africa to allow me to down load his information into the computers at your agency! It took me two days to convince him that the more we share information the closer we could get to a cure!"

"Don't worry, Satoro, now you know what arguments to use on the next guy!"

"Well, I doubt they will work on the next guy because the AIDS epidemic is so huge in Africa that they need all the help they can get, but the cancer research gurus may want to keep any up coming breakthroughs to themselves; money being a big factor there. They will want the glory and the money from any cures."

"Maybe we can sneak in a back door. Sort of borrow the information without them knowing. It would be underhanded, but it would get the bad guys off our tails and it might even help society . . . if LeBeau remains as diligent they may come up with a cure more quickly."

"Yea, but lets hope LeBeau doesn't decide that research is going too slowly and they ought to open up a few patients to see what the problem is!" snorted Jonas sarcastically.

"We'll just have to watch and see how he takes the augmentation," replied Rick. "If he turns green and throws up when we're finished, we'll have to think of a new plan for him."

"OK, but can we let him throw up for a while first?" Teresa surprised every one with her comment. She had been the quietest of the group but she had been thinking about all the tests they had inflicted on her little Derrick and the thought tumbled out of her mouth before she even had a chance to think it. The group was silent only for a couple of seconds, stunned not by the comment but by the source. Then as if on cue the entire deck exploded in laughter.

When the laughter died down Mark started it all again when he made the observation that if LeBeau stayed true to his course, he would probably have the cancer artificially put in his own body so they could try out their cures on him!

"We can only hope!" concluded Anthony.

Rick took over the meeting again by telling the others about the cave and the possibility that LeBeau had discovered the anomaly. He told them about the planned trip to Anthony's college lab. He finished by warning them to be very aware of their surroundings because if LeBeau figured out how to use this weapon against them, things could get very dangerous.

"If everyone can reassemble here in five days, we will report what we know and plan our final attack. If everything goes well, maybe we can get this wrapped up in two to three weeks. Wouldn't that be nice?" Rick sounded hopeful and the optimism seemed to spread through the group like syrup over a stack of pancakes.

Tomas spoke up before anyone could leave. "I have one more thing to ask of the group. Deborah and I are working on a . . . sort of . . . constitution for paths. We need your input. If you have anything you think is important to add, please let us know."

Kassidy spoke up immediately, "We need to stress that paths need to pay for the things they 'borrow'. No more producing without paying someone for it!" She looked directly at Luke as she finished.

Luke looked back innocently as if he were saying, "What?!"

Tomas nodded, "OK. It might be hard to enforce that, but we can include it. Also, I would like to know if there was any information about current path identification in the computers at the agency. We need to start our own data base and begin tracking new paths so we can get to them first."

"I'm pretty good with computer data bases." Jonas had his hand up now. "I don't really have an official job here, so I have lots of time, if someone has a computer I can use."

"Luke, you have a pretty good computer at your place. Is it OK if Jonas goes with you and the Linders tonight? He could work out of your house and Andre would still have my computer for his work on the computer lab at the agency."

Luke was about to let out an auditable groan when Kassidy spoke up. "That would be great! The more the merrier! *Luke, relax, it'll be fine!*" She sent that last thought only to him. She was getting pretty good at keeping her thoughts away from other paths, but she still wasn't good at hiding them from Luke. *"Must be the close connection,"* she thought to herself. Luke didn't comment on the last thought, just reached over and took her hand.

Rick closed the meeting and everyone said their farewells and headed to their homes. Luke and Kassidy collected their guests and the six left for the cabin. When they arrived, Anthony and Luke sat down to plan their trip to the lab while Kassidy gave Teresa and Jonas a tour of the cabin. She led them each to the rooms they would be using while they were here. She showed them the guest bathroom at the end of the hall and pointed out the toiletries and towels.

She also took the time to show them the exit through the bathroom that she and Luke shared. She didn't want them stuck here by accident in the event of an emergency. After all, she and Luke would be gone to the lab for a while this evening and they would be the only ones here.

When they finished the tour, Kassidy led them back to the living room. She made them a large dinner of chicken tetrazzini, tossed salad, fresh sliced peaches, and chocolate cake for dinner. Teleflight continued to have the side effect of creating quite an appetite. Kassidy figured that it must take a lot of energy because despite the increased appetite, she hadn't put on a pound of extra weight.

After dinner Luke asked Kassidy to leave the dishes for a bit and come upstairs with him to make the cabin look lived in again. The two made their way up the stairs and entered once again through the food closet. Once it was closed they worked their way around the cabin, dusting and using the sinks. Kassidy added some food to the refrigerator. She put some of the left over chicken tetrazzini in it, just to make it look more used.

Luke was working in the bedroom when Kassidy caught a thought that he was deliberating over. When she heard it she knew he'd let something slip that he hadn't intended for her to hear. Anger was already in full swing by the time she made it back to the bedroom where she caught him rumpling the bed covers, rolling from one side to the other. It would have been funny if she wasn't quite so teed off.

"Why are you having such a hard time telling me? Just spit it out! You are planning on going without me?! Again!" Kassidy was so angry that the tears were already spilling down her cheeks. But her voice was nearly a whisper. "What were you going to do? Sneak out again?"

Luke sat up with a start and threw his legs over the side of the bed. "Kassidy, no, I wasn't going to sneak out. I was going to tell you. That's why I came up here. I wanted to talk to you alone, without everyone around, but I didn't know how to tell you."

Kassidy turned to stalk out of the room. Luke caught her in the hallway. His arms were around her in a minute. She struggled to free herself but he held her tight. She wanted him to catch her. She wanted his arms around her, but she was so mad at him that she didn't want *him* to know that. Too late. She couldn't seem to keep anything to herself.

"It's OK, baby. Your thoughts are safe with me, even if you don't want me to know them."

He called her 'baby' again. It took her breath away as surely as when he kissed her. What was it about that word? It was just a stupid word and it wasn't that great of a word after all. You would think that it would take a much better word . . . like . . . like . . . oh, like what? And why, oh, why did it have this affect on her every stinkin' time?

"Every stinkin' time?" He turned her around in his arms to face him.

"You know it has this affect on me! Why do you keep using it?"

"Because it has this affect on you and I don't want you to be angry with me."

"Luke Matthews! That is not fair! Besides, it's not working! I'm still mad." Kassidy made another attempt at loosening his hold on her to no avail. *"And I have every right to be mad at you."*

"You do. But hear me out before you say 'no', please." Luke leaned his head down to look into her eyes. She was avoiding his eyes trying to hold onto her resolve but suddenly her head snapped up.

"Before I say 'no'? Does this mean I have a choice?"

"Yes, if you still want to go, I'll take you with me."

"OK, baby, talk!" Kassidy crossed her arms between them, leaning as far back as she could with his arms wrapped so tightly around her waist and watched his reaction closely.

"Did you just call me 'baby'?" Luke's eyebrows shot up.

"Yeah, any effect on you?" She searched his features looking for any hint of weakness.

"Sorry, I liked it, but that's my secret weapon, not yours."

"Give me time, I'll find mine . . . now talk!"

Luke ushered her to the couch, pulled her down onto his lap. He ignored her stiffness and pulled her close to his chest. She didn't resist but she didn't relax either he noticed. *"Stubborn!"* he grimaced.

"Pot calling the kettle black!" she retorted. *"Talk!"*

"OK, here's the thing, Kassidy. I don't want you with us because I don't want to be distracted if anything goes wrong. When we were running down the hall in the facility with people shooting at us, I was so glad that you weren't there. See . . . I worried about Mark and Rick and even Jonas while we were high-tailing it down that hall . . . but if you had been there, I'd have been frantic trying to keep you out of the line of fire. No one thinks well when they are in a panic and we didn't have time for anyone to be playing hero in a panic . . . we just needed to run! I love you too much to put either of us in that position."

"That's sweet, honey, but I'm not buying it." Again, Kassidy watched him for any sign that 'honey' might be his Achilles' heel.

"Try again!" He smiled broadly. *"I would also like someone to be here with Teresa and Derrick. This is all new to her. She can't go because we can't take Derrick, obviously. She needs you here!"*

"Darling, Jonas is here. She doesn't need me. He'll be here working on the data base. Nice try though." 'Darling' seemed weak, but you never know until you try.

"Darling is not even close . . . makes me feel old!"

"Hmmm. Could be my defense against the dark side of Luke! Call him 'darling' just to remind him he's almost twice my age." The corners of Kassidy's mouth began to turn up into a smile.

"Go on ahead then, baby." Luke emphasized the word 'baby' his white teeth gleaming as he smiled even wider than before.

He had knocked the breath out of her again. She closed her eyes to fight the ripples of excitement that coursed through her. What a combination . . . the smile and the stupid word. She struggled for composure as pictures of kissing him flooded her mind and her senses. She became acutely aware of his arms wrapped around her, his chest where the side of her body touched it.

Luke was hearing every thought and seeing every picture that moved across her mind's eye. He slid her off of his lap to sit beside him and un-wrapped his arms from around her. Wow, that had backfired. He needed to keep his wits about him for this conversation.

Luke's sudden retreat confused Kassidy. *"What's wrong?"* She looked up at his profile. He wasn't looking at her. He was blocking thoughts! Kassidy suddenly knew what he was thinking without 'listening' to a word. *"You were losing your advantage! I found it! I found my secret weapon! I should have recognized it earlier! The same thing happened before! I just missed it."* She thought she might laugh out loud, but Luke wasn't listening.

When he finally did look back at Kassidy, she was staring at him with a grin bigger than he had ever seen on her face before. She didn't just look like the cat that got the mouse; she looked like the cat that got the *last* mouse! As she watched him she bit her lower lip in pure joy.

"What?" Luke asked innocently.

"It's not a word . . . it's visual! And I call myself a teacher! I should have known. I should have figured it out sooner! Some people are audio centered, some are kinesthetically centered and some . . . are . . . visually centered. You, my love, are very visual!"

"I don't understand a word you are saying!"

"Let me demonstrate!" Kassidy took his hand and thought back to their first kiss in the cave; the one that had been interrupted by Mark. She let the images linger in her mind, her senses filled with the memory of his hands tightening around her back. She replayed the mingling of their breath between kisses. Her breath caught once again with the picture of his blue, blue eyes gazing into her green ones.

Luke was all over her in a mere flash of a moment. His arms were around her again. He pulled her down into the back of the couch, his body between her and the rest of the room. He was kissing her hard. He had too much weight on her and she was having trouble breathing.

"Luke, I . . . . can't . . . . breathe!" she squeaked out between kisses.

He pulled away from her just long enough to roll her on top of him. His hands caught her face and he pulled her lips back to his own. He was gentler this time taking his time moving and molding his lips to hers. When her mouth opened to his, he lost all control again. He couldn't think clearly, all he knew was how much he needed her, right now, right here.

Minutes . . . no seconds. She had seconds to stop this before it would be too late. Wow, when she found a secret weapon . . . . she *really* found a secret weapon! Unfortunately, she could never use it again. Well, not until they were married. It was way too powerful!

"*Luke.*" Kassidy was pushing away from him. She had both hands on his chest and was trying to sit back up again.

"No!" Luke moaned. His arms tightened around her.

"*LUKE!! Honey, I'm sorry. This time was my mistake. I'll keep my secret weapon to myself. I'll never use it again . . . well, at least not until you marry me.*"

"*Kassidy, you can't . . . .*" anger and frustration were clearly present on his face. He looked at her for what seemed like forever. Then his expression became hard and unyielding. "You are not going tonight! There is no way I can concentrate on anything with you present!"

"Luke, you can't mean that! You're just upset . . . ."

"Yes, I'm upset! You are too distracting. You are not going!"

"Luke, be reasonable!"

"I'm being very reasonable. If I take you, I could jeopardize the whole mission if we get interrupted by labbies. I would only be able to concentrate on you. We need to get Anthony in and out of there without losing him or the information he can get for us. If you are there, I'll be concentrating on you, not on our job. You are not going!"

"You said it was my choice, that you would take me if I wanted to go. I'm going!"

"NO!!" His face was set and very angry. Kassidy knew she had lost, again! He would not budge tonight.

Luke left the couch in a hurry heading back to the secret passage way. Kassidy was stuck in the same spot. She couldn't move. The tears began to fall faster than she could wipe them away. She pulled her legs up to her chest and wrapped her arms around them stuffing her face between her knees and her chest. She was so angry with him! And he had never been this angry with her before. She didn't want to go back downstairs to face all those people. She just wanted to go to her room. She wondered if she could just run up and catch his hand long enough to do that slingshot thing that Rick and Sophia had discovered. She could just think of her room and be gone before Luke knew she was there.

Suddenly he was back, standing over her. "Kassidy . . . ." He took a deep breath, not sure what to say, and let the air out slowly. "Hold my hand and I'll get you to your room."

Kassidy reached out a reluctant hand and he took it, holding it with both of his. She pictured the room in her mind.

"*Wrong room!*"

"*What?*" her head snapped up to look at him.

Luke pictured his room.

"*Luke, that would not be wise.*"

"*Just stay there until I'm back. If you fall asleep, I'll move you to your room when I get home.*"

She let him take her there. He hugged her and kissed her on the top of her head. Peaches! He inhaled deeply. He let her go and went back out to the living room. Anthony and Luke left for the lab with a little help from Teresa. She and Anthony were pretty good at that sling shot trick. As soon as they were gone, Teresa came down to knock on Kassidy's door. Kassidy heard her from Luke's room. She dried her tears and peeked out of his room.

"Hi, Teresa, do you need me?"

"I just wanted to know if you wanted to take a walk with Derrick and me. He wants to go outside. He would live out there if I'd let him."

"Sure, just let me get my jacket. Do you and Derrick need one?"

"No, we got ours from home a little bit ago. But thanks."

Kassidy walked with Teresa down the hall. When they got to the living room, they found Jonas already at work on the computer. Derrick was standing by the secret entrance, jacket on and smile in place.

"Ousside now mommy?"

"You bet!"

Kassidy punched in the code, which she could remember quite well now for some reason. They hiked up the stairs and out the food closet and to the front door. There was still a little daylight left and Kassidy suggested they walk down the road a little ways.

The air was perfect; not too cool and not to warm. Derrick skipped along in front of the two women. Well, it was really more of a gallop than a skip. He was dressed in jeans and a T-shirt sporting Winnie the Pooh on the front and a little pair of tennis shoes with a picture of Scooby Doo on each side. He had a blue jean jacket on with Mickey Mouse on the pocket and the whole Disney gang on the back. His hat was orange and looked like Chip, from Chip and Dale, with two little chipmunk ears sticking out of the top and two little chipmunk eyes right in front. He was a cartoon from head to toe.

Kassidy had to smile as she watched him. Children were such a delight. That's why she loved teaching so much . . . . well one of the reasons. Kids were a hoot and they all had so much potential, even the ones from rough backgrounds. Actually, some of the ones with rough backgrounds came out better than the ones who have it all. She wondered about this little guy. He had had it rough. But he seemed to be handling it very well. She liked him, especially the way he replaced his l's with tw's.

Sophia was right; it was nice being with another woman and sharing some girl talk. The women visited about a lot of things but when it grew silent, Teresa finally asked Kassidy why she seemed so sad.

"Oh, I just really ticked Luke off before he left. I've never seen him so upset."

"Oh, Kassidy, I'm so sorry. What happened? Do you want to talk about it?"

Maybe it was the sweetness of her disposition, or the real sincerity in her voice, but Kassidy couldn't hold back the tears any longer. They started to fall in torrents. She had to wait for a moment as they walked along to be able to speak coherently.

"There is just so much . . . tension . . . between us. We have no way to release it and there is no real end in sight right now. I know that Rick said we might be able to put this to rest in a couple of weeks, but we don't really know that. Every thing is so uncertain. Then I touch him, and I struggle to just keep thinking . . . you know? Then he's so protective that he keeps me out of everything. That just makes me want to push harder, which doesn't work with Luke. That probably doesn't make any sense at all, does it?"

"Actually, it makes all the sense in the world. Kassidy, I'm not sure but I think the bond between a path and their mate is much stronger than between normal people. We can be a part of the innermost parts of that other person. We know what they are thinking . . . the good and the bad. I think it makes it harder to do what is right, especially with two of you wanting the same thing but waiting for the right moment. But don't fret. Just remember that with women the frustration comes out in tears, but for men it comes out in anger. But he won't stay angry long. He will realize what's causing it too. Just don't take it personally. Take it as the ultimate compliment . . . . he loves you so much it's killing him!" She smiled, then giggled as she wrapped her arms around Kassidy in a brief hug.

"Thanks for listening."

"Thanks for sharing. I feel a little like a fifth wheel around here. Everyone is doing something for the cause and I'm just being a mother."

"Yeah, the mother of the very first ever telepath baby! He's wonderful, by the way."

"Thanks, I'm pretty partial to him!"

"How do you think it happened?"

"What?"

"How do you think Derrick got his abilities?"

"Oh, my opinion is that his father and I gave them to him. We had been wondering about children and how it might be difficult for them to grow up with telepathic parents when they might not be able to do the same things. We both wanted our child to be just like us. I think, we mentally programmed him to be a path. Just like we can change our eye color and return our bodies to a young healthy state, we also gave our son his abilities. I don't know for sure, but I think that if a path couple did not want their children to have these abilities, they would not have them. But it's just a theory. But I think some of it is proven in his dimples."

"His dimples?"

"Yes, there is no one on either side of the family that has dimples. But I was always partial to dimples. His are quite distinct!"

"Good theory!"

As they turned the corner and walked down the hill a cabin came into sight. It was an ordinary kind of a cabin, with brown wood siding and a large covered front porch. The front porch had a couple of chairs sitting on it and a man was sitting in one of the chairs smoking a pipe. He had on an old pair of jeans and a blue T-shirt. He was wearing a pair of scuffed up work boots and a cap with some sort of logo on it that Kassidy couldn't read from where they walked. She waved at the man as they passed.

He didn't seem interested in them at first. He didn't even bother to wave back. Kassidy wished briefly that Luke was there. She could easily read the man's mind then. She supposed that she could just reach over and touch Teresa to get the same results, but then she laughed silently to herself. Look how dependent she was becoming on her telepathic abilities! She supposed she could afford to let an eccentric old man retain his privacy.

All of the sudden he stood up and walked all the way down to where they were walking on the road. He seemed interested in the boy.

"Howdy!" He croaked with a gruff voice.

"Hello," both Kassidy and Teresa responded, just a little taken aback.

"That's an awfully cute little guy you have there. About how old is he?"

"He's two and a half," replied Teresa.

The man turned his questions to Derrick then. "Well, son, who do you have on your head?"

"Dats Tip!" Derrick slapped his hand on top of his hat. At first Derrick seemed to enjoy the attention. "An I got Pooh on my sirt! See!?" He pointed to his T-Shirt.

"I do see! How nice is that?!"

"Dats weal nice!" Derrick smiled and his dimples made him irresistible. Kassidy thought the man might scoop him up and hug the stuffin' out of him right there.

At that same moment, Derrick stiffened up, turned away from the man abruptly and ran for his mommy. Startled, Teresa scooped him up. He buried his head in her shoulder and both she and Kassidy heard his thoughts, "*I don't twike dat guy, mommy. I wanna go home.*"

"*It's Ok, sweetie, you are safe here. He's not like the other bad guys. Mommy's got you. We're OK.*"

The man's smile seemed to get wider as he watched Derrick sprint to his mommy. Then he abruptly stood up straight and said, "Well, you guys have a nice walk. I better get inside and see about supper."

"Bye." Kassidy waited until the man was inside before she continued, "That was a little weird!"

"Yeah, I guess it's going to take Derrick a while to get over the agency!"

"Yeah, is he all right?"

"He'll be fine, I'm sure."

"Ready to turn around?"

"Yeah, it's about time to get Derrick ready for bed."

The man hustled straight in to his phone. He dialed three numbers and began talking as soon as someone picked up on the other end.

CHAPTER 26

Company Coming

Mr. LeBeau, sir, this is Torgenson, we have them. An old man sighted the kid in an area above Curt Gowdy State park in Wyoming. He saw the kid and two women walking down a road by his house. The two women match the descriptions of Teresa Linder and Kassidy Dover. There is only one other cabin up that road. It belongs to a guy named . . . uh . . ." he looked down at some notes he had made, "yeah, here it is . . . Joseph Davidson. Ring any bells?"

"No, but that doesn't mean anything. OK, get our guys up there. Keep the police out of this. Pretend you're FBI and you have jurisdiction because they crossed state lines with a kidnapped kid. Oh, and be careful. Tranquilize first, ask questions later."

"Yes, sir!"

LeBeau was on the phone again as soon as he hung up with Torgenson. He told the front desk to check him out and called the airport to catch the next plane out to Arizona. He wanted to be there when they brought them all in. He was hoping that they would get the Linders, Kassidy *and* Luke. That would make the year worth it. He made a third call before he left the room.

"Gaff, what do you have on the rock I gave you?"

"Well, sir, it's a rock. There is nothing special about it. It is just volcanic rock."

"Can you get your hands on more of it?"

"Well, yes, I'm sure we can. What for?"

"See if our lab guys can grind it up into dust and get it into some kind of spray or liquid paint. I need a lot of it. We need to cover the roof of the facility with it as soon as possible."

"Uh . . . really? May I ask what for?"

"UHHH . . . YEAH, REALLY! It has unique properties. It interrupts telepathic abilities. We are going to have company at the facility soon, so get it sprayed on the roof!"

"Yes, sir!"

CHAPTER 27

Crossroads

Kassidy and Teresa headed back down the long stair case behind the food storage unit and Teresa took Derrick to the back bedroom to get him into bed. Kassidy went into the kitchen to get the dishes done and put away. She noticed that Jonas was still working on the computer.

"How's it going, Jonas?" When he didn't answer, Kassidy turned to look at him. He was sitting there in a sort of daze. He wasn't even blinking. "Jonas? Are you all right?" She walked over to him but before she got to him he fell sideways out of the chair and hit the floor. He wasn't moving, just staring into space.

Kassidy ran to him and checked his breathing. He was still breathing. He still had a heart beat. His eyes were wide open, staring at nothing and he was as white as a sheet.

"Jonas! Jonas! Can you hear me?" Kassidy put his head in her lap. *"Jonas, can you hear me? Jonas, what's happening?"*

"Kassidy?"

"Yes."

"I don't know what's happening. I see . . . I see . . ."

"I can see what you are seeing. Where is this place?"

"I think it's the school at the American Military Base in Lakenheath. I've been here before . . . well, not on the track field like now. I used to have swim meets against these guys. I came here once or twice a year to compete when I was in high school. I feel like I need to be here. Something is going to happen here and I need to be here. I have to get here soon. I need to be here today, I think!"

"I don't see anyone."

"Not yet, but wait. There, over by the stands, do you see them?" Students began to emerge onto the field. They were trickling in. It looked like a high school track team getting ready for a practice. *"This has happened before. I keep seeing this place. I see it in my dreams almost every night. But this is the first time I've seen it when I was awake . . . at least I was awake. I don't know that I still am. What do you suppose is happening to me?"*

"Well, I'm not totally sure, but if I had to guess, I'd say we're looking at a crossroads." Kassidy looked down at the young man in her lap. His eyes were beginning to blink again.

Jonas' eyes began to focus on the present. He noticed his head was in Kassidy's lap. "Uh, thanks!" He sat up too fast and nearly fell back over. Kassidy caught his arm and helped him into a sitting position. "I think I'm all right. I have to go though. I have to get to Lakenheath tonight."

"Tonight?"

"Please, I have to get to Lakenheath, now." Jonas appeared to be in a panic over the need to leave. He was pacing the floor. "Kassidy, can you take me to Lakenheath? Please, I have to go now!"

"I can't get you there without Luke, but I can ask Rick and see what he can arrange. Take my hand, I need help to talk to them because they are so far away."

"Please! Hurry!"

"Rick, I need help. Jonas needs a lift to Lakenheath . . . I think it's a crossroad . . . He needs to go now!"

"Wow, no kidding? That was fast! It was a couple of years before Sophia met me. Sophia and I will be right there. She wants to come too! Should we bring Mark?"

"Couldn't hurt!"

Within ten minutes, the three were in the cabin hide out. Jonas had broken out into a cold sweat and was about to jump out of his skin. He was pacing the kitchen floor at a speed that was probably too fast for such a confined area. As soon as Mark, Rick and Sophia arrived, he had their hands and was showing them the track field. They were gone again in an instant.

Kassidy was suddenly alone in the living room. It seemed overly quiet with everyone gone. She stared at the big faux picture window that showed the view from the front of the house. It looked lovely tonight. She thought she might just like to head on up and sit on the front porch for a while. She punched in the code again, and turned off the lights as she hiked her way up the stairs for the third time tonight. When she reached the top, she triggered the release button and entered the kitchen. She turned and closed the secret passage, flipped on the kitchen light and then walked briskly to the front door. She opened the door and stepped out into the cool night air. It felt good. She couldn't believe she felt that way. She had always hated the Wyoming weather. It had always seemed just a shade too cool for her taste. But tonight it felt quite good.

She sat down in the lawn chair that Mark had used that first day she went hiking with Luke. It seemed like an eternity ago. She was thinking about their teleflight up to flat rock.

"Kassidy, are you awake or dreaming about flat rock?"

"Luke? Where are you?"

"We're still here. We made it into the lab and Anthony is working on his tests. We thought we should check in. How is everything there?"

"Well, Jonas just left to go to Lakenheath American High School in England. He was being very powerfully drawn there. Rick and Sophia and Mark took him."

"No kidding?! That's wonderful news . . . it'll keep him out of our hair!"

"Don't be that way, Luke. He has been working on the computer since you guys left. He's been behaving himself quite well."

Luke's thoughts caught on the part about 'behaving well' and he felt the guilt of his own behavior earlier in the evening. *"Mmmm. Kassidy . . . I . . ."* Luke was trying to figure out how to apologize when he was interrupted by Kassidy.

"That's funny, I just saw something in the trees. Something reflected some light. Do you think it's a deer? You know how the eyes reflect light?" Kassidy stood up to look more closely.

Although Kassidy could not hear them from the deck, alarms began to sound downstairs.

"Kassidy, where are you?"

"On the deck of the cabin."

"Go back inside, Kassidy" Luke had a bad feeling about this. *"Did you hear me?"* There was worry in his voice. The worry increased exponentially when Teresa began speaking excitedly in Spanish to her husband.

"What's going on . . . ow!! . . ." Kassidy felt the sting just as she turned to go back inside. She wondered what kind of elephant sized bug would hurt like that. She had just enough time to see the dart that had stuck into her shoulder, pull it out and call out. *"Luke!!!"* Then she was out. Her body fell limply to the deck.

Luke felt a panic surge through him. He had been holding on to Anthony's shoulder to help with telecommunications. When he lost Kassidy's thought, he gripped down with such force that Anthony flinched.

"Ahh, Luke, that won't help. Lighten up on the shoulder and talk to Teresa."

"Sorry!" Luke concentrated on Teresa, *"Teresa, what did you say?"*

"Alarms, there are alarms going off!"

"Where are you?"

"I'm in the bedroom with Derrick."

"Go out to the living room right now! Look at the big screen in the living room that shows the view out the front window. Hurry, Kassidy's in trouble!"

Teresa ran to the living room. She hunted around for the lights and when she found them she flipped the switch. *"How do I shut off the alarms, Luke?"*

She looked at the screen and saw men bending over something on the porch. She screamed when she saw them pick up Kassidy and put her on a gurney. *"Luke can you see what I'm seeing?"*

"Yes, don't leave the cabin for anything. Don't go upstairs! You should be OK where you are. We'll be home in a minute! Flip the yellow switch between the main monitor and the window. It'll turn off the alarms." As soon as the alarms turned off, Teresa heard Derrick.

"Mommy! MOMMY! It's da bad guys. I can heaw dem mommy." Derrick's last 'mommy' was more like a shriek than a word.

Teresa ran to her son and picked him up. She held him closely and tried to calm him. He began crying loudly. *Dey comin, mommy! I wan daddy!*

"Daddy's coming, sweetheart. It's going to be OK, they don't know how to find us. It will be all right. Shh! Shh! Everything's all right."

Teresa heard footsteps running down the hall toward them. *"Anthony?"* She hoped it was Anthony. She prayed it was Anthony. It had to be Anthony.

"We're here Teresa!"

"Thank you God!" she ran to the hallway, straight into Anthony's arms. He held his family tightly, kissing them with relief. Derrick seemed to calm down a bit in his presence, but fear still gripped the little guy and tears streamed down his little face as he sobbed into his daddy's shirt. Teresa looked around him down the hall. *"Where is Luke?"*

"Front room."

When the Linders made it to the living room, Luke was checking surveillance tapes and watching the men search the upper cabin. They hadn't found anything to lead them down into the hide out. He watched as they put Kassidy in a van. How did he let this happen? How had they found the cabin? His life was being put in the van and the doors were closing. He had to get to her fast. The van would be the best place to ambush. He had seen the inside.

"No, Luke, the van is heavily guarded and there are people inside with tranquilizers. You won't have her help because she is unconscious! If you hop in there, you may not be in a position to help her. We can get into the facility the same way you got in to help us. We will find her, but we have to be smart."

Luke had never known this kind of anguish before. She was everything to him. She was the reason he got up in the morning; the reason he lived and breathed. She was what made fighting back worth while. He thought that leaving her here at the cabin would enable him to concentrate on something other than needing her and wanting her. How was he ever going to concentrate on anything now? He should never have left her alone. He should have listened to her. He had been so angry with her for pushing him out of control tonight. But it was just as much his fault. Then he had left her before they had really made up.

The guilt and depression seemed like a black hole. He just kept falling deeper and deeper into it. As he watched them drive away with all of his hopes in the back of that van, Luke was barely able to think. His jaw was clenching, and his hands were balled up into fists. He was screaming for her in his mind, *"Kassidy, wake up! Kassidy, can you hear me? Baby, you have to wake up!"*

"You will have to wait for the drugs to wear off, Luke. She can't respond."

"I talked to her when she was unconscious after her operation." He reasoned. Why wasn't she responding?

"But you were probably touching her. You are not touching her now. Try again every fifteen minutes for about a half hour. Then every ten minutes after that. Perhaps we will get lucky and catch her before they dose her again."

"She talked to me from a different room while she was unconscious in the hospital."

"But at that time, she wasn't completely full of tranquilizers. She was coming out from under the anesthetics. She is under with a full dose right now. You'll have to wait for it to wear off, Luke."

CHAPTER 28

The Cliff

LeBeau was frustrated again! They only got the girl! What happened to the Linders? He was sure they were there somewhere. Torgenson had assured them that they had checked every part of the cabin, but there was no one there but Kassidy. LeBeau sent them back again. There must be something there. Maybe they missed a secret passage to somewhere. Of course, Torgenson had a good point. "Why would they need a secret passage to somewhere when they could teleport at the drop of a hat?" It made sense, but there just had to be something. Why would she be there alone? He knew that it took two to teleport, so why would they leave her in an exposed position by herself? That's why they had to go back and tear the place apart. They had to find it . . . what ever it is. He was sure that the baby and Mrs. Linder had to be there somewhere.

As soon as his plane landed, he would catch one to Wyoming. He had to 'feel' the place for himself to determine whether or not they were there. He would know. He would be able to feel their presence. He was sure of it. Damn! He wished he had that teleporting skill. Soon, he thought.

He took a couple of sleeping pills and finally drifted off to sleep. It was a good way to spend the time on a plane. It made the trip less of a bother. He hated flying, it took too much time, and he could never get comfortable without the little pills. But they were wonderful pills. He was asleep within 20 minutes.

His dreams were troubled. He was standing at the foot of a large rock formation. He was looking up, but there was really nothing to see. It was just a large rock formation. Nothing was particularly interesting about it, except that it was very tall. As he turned around to walk away, he noticed the trees and shrubs surrounding the area. It was a remote area. He wondered where his car was. He took a step away from the rock but was immediately drawn back. He couldn't seem to leave it, or stop gazing at it.

"Curious." He thought to himself. He tried to leave again. But each time he tried, he ended up turning around and walking back to the rock. He did notice a trail leading from the rock out to some unknown area. But he couldn't make his feet go there. He began to break out into a cool sweat. Why couldn't he leave? Then the ground began to shake, or was he just dizzy? He heard someone calling him.

"Sir, the plane has landed. Are you awake?"

LeBeau blinked his eyes open. He was disoriented for a bit. He half expected to see the large rock formation right in front of him as he opened his eyes, but here he was in the now empty plane and it had landed in Arizona.

"Oh, thank you, sorry, I must have been more tired than I thought!" LeBeau wiped sweat from his forehead, still feeling a bit dizzy.

"No problem, sir, glad you got some rest!" The pretty flight attendant smiled.

LeBeau gathered his things and walked quickly down the isle. He lost no time from the gate to baggage claim. He picked up his luggage which was already making its way around and around the carousel. He walked straight out of baggage claim to the ticket counters to book the next flight to Wyoming.

CHAPTER 29

Missing

Luke sat in shock, not sure what to do. He just knew that he needed to talk to Rick and Mark as soon as possible. He had to get to the facility before they started working on Kassidy. They had to save her. He couldn't live without her. No, it was worse than that. He couldn't even exist without her. To live is to enjoy life, to laugh and to love. To exist is just to breath in and out and he didn't think he could even do that without her.

Anthony put his hand on Luke's shoulder. "Come on, man! You have to pull yourself together. Kassidy needs you. She needs all of you!!!"

Luke couldn't speak, but he nodded his head in agreement. He began pacing then; back and fourth in the living room. His head down, one hand on his hip and the other rubbing his chin. He was thinking fast and hard. What would LeBeau do first? How did he find the cabin? Did he know others were here?

Derrick had calmed down a little more, but couldn't stop talking about the bad guys. He could still 'hear' them. They had not left the cabin upstairs yet. Anthony turned on the TV to try and find some cartoons to distract him. As he was flipping through channels, he heard Derrick's name. He had just passed a news channel and he quickly flipped back. He caught a news bulletin about a missing family. It was his family! He watched as their smiling faces flashed on the screen. The news reported them missing from a relatives house in Arizona. It was asking for any information regarding the whereabouts of the Linders. Luke had stopped his pacing when he heard their names on the TV. He was looking over Anthony's shoulder. The little orange hat of Chip from Chip and Dale sat glaringly on the TV Derrick's head. Under it the beautiful dimples were plain to see. Identifying him would be as easy as getting him to smile.

"*Teresa, were you out of the cabin at any time tonight?*" Anthony asked nervously.

"*Yes, Kassidy and I took Derrick for a walk down the road a ways.*"

"*Did you see anyone?*"

"Yes, we saw this odd older gentleman sitting on the porch of the next cabin down. He didn't pay us much mind . . . didn't even bother to wave, until he saw Derrick. He took a liking to him and even came down to the road to talk then. Asked Derrick all about his hat and his clothes. Then he abruptly turned around and headed back inside. It was odd."

"That explains how they found the cabin. But they were expecting to find all of us. This place isn't safe. We need to leave and head to the beach house." The prospect of leaving without Kassidy was making him sick to his stomach. Had it been fifteen minutes? Luke placed his hand on Anthony's shoulder. "Kassidy, can you hear me? Come on, honey, wake up!" There was still no response. Luke turned his thoughts to Rick. "Rick, Sophia! I need your help! LeBeau's got Kassidy. They found the cabin. We need to go get her."

"Luke, I'm so sorry. Don't worry just yet. You know they run a lot of tests before the big show. Kassidy is going to be fine. We'll be able to get her out in time. But Luke, we can't come just yet. Jonas has been called to a crossroads. It hasn't happened yet, but he's very peaceful in this particular spot. So I guess we'll need to wait for it. I don't want to leave them unguarded."

"OK, just come as soon as the new one is stable. I'll ask Uri and Andre if I need something. I'm taking the Linder's back to your place. We aren't safe here. Don't let anyone come to the cabin right now. I can keep an eye on things here with your computer at the beach house. Guess we'll soon find out how well I hid the secret passage."

CHAPTER 30

The Daredevil

Rick looked over at Sophia. She had been listening to the entire conversation and was visibly shaken. He reached out and put his arm around her. He pulled her tight to his side and whispered in her ear not to worry. "We'll get to her in time. Everything is almost in place. Everyone is working over time to pull it together." Rick was hopeful for good reason. They had a plan. It was coming together. He felt confident that they would be out of this mess within a couple of weeks. But he was worried about Kassidy. It only took about a week of LeBeau's 'research' to kill a path. They needed to move up the time line. Could they get everything done soon enough? Suddenly he wasn't as sure. He shifted on the bleacher where they were sitting.

Jonas looked over at the worried couple. "Hey, you guys don't need to stay. The doctor and I could make sure she's Ok and then I can teleport with her. Right?!"

"We better stay, it's too risky."

Jonas thought for a moment. "It will be a HER not a HIM, right?!"

Rick laughed, "Worried, are you?"

Jonas didn't laugh back. His eyes were glued to Rick, worry etched in them.

"Don't worry, kid. It's always one guy and one girl. It's never been a guy and another guy. I think you're safe."

"Well, yeah, but there has never been a path baby before either . . . . and . . . and you said that there is always a path drawn to each crossroads, yet here I am . . . I hit my crossroads and no beautiful woman was standing over my bed! Seems to me that things are changing!"

"Maybe," Rick had to admit the kid had some good points, "I'm sure the two of you will be very happy regardless. The path connection is very strong and very intense." If Rick had not had his arms resting on his knees with his hands clasped in front of his mouth, Jonas might have seen the smirk on his face and laughed along with him. As it was, it just made Jonas that much more nervous.

"Great! Doc, if it's a guy, you don't have to try so hard . . . OK?!"

The track team entered the field at that moment. The four sitting on the bleachers, turned their heads at the same time to watch them begin their practice.

"How does a person get a life threatening head injury in track anyway?" asked Jonas. "I'm probably going to be hopelessly in love with a klutz for the rest of my life!"

"My best guess is that you should look for someone doing pole vaulting or high jump." Mark suggested.

"Great . . . do girls even do pole vaulting?" now Jonas had stood and was looking down at the high jump and pole vaulting areas. "I'm going down there to get a closer look." He jogged easily down the steps to the field. Fortunately, he had been wearing shorts and a t-shirt and running shoes at the beach house and he hadn't changed at the cabin. So he was dressed to fit in with the other students on the field. As he hit the bottom of the stairs, he noticed a tall slim girl with very long dark hair pulled back in a pony tail. She was talking animatedly with another girl. With each part of the story she was telling, her big blue eyes would widen with excitement. Her hands moved faster than her lips creating a very animated story.

Jonas hoped it wasn't her. *She'll talk my head off. I'll never have another moment's peace from the time she wakes in the morning until she conks out at night.* She was cute though. She had long legs and a beautiful smile. She was walking toward him and as she got within a couple of feet she looked up and smiled. She only paused in her story telling for a second though and was talking again, even before she got to where Jonas was standing.

"So he dared me to try it. I said I'd do it! But now I'm scared crapless." The girl was saying to her friend.

That got Jonas' attention and he started to follow the two girls. He wished he could listen to her thoughts, but he needed another path to do that. He'd have to stay close enough to find out what some wanker had challenged her to do that scared her. *Probably wanted something he shouldn't!* Jonas hoped she was smart enough not to do what ever it was.

"So what are you going to do?" the girl's friend asked.

"I'm going to do it, of course! It's either that or put up with his crap until we graduate next year!"

"*Great!*" thought Jonas, "*We have a winner here. She deserves the guy.*"

"Oh that's brilliant . . . would you jump off the proverbial bridge, too?"

"Only if he did it first . . . and survived . . . twice!" the girls giggled and picked up their pace. They jogged across the field.

Jonas would have to jog to keep up with them; he decided he'd heard enough. He continued at his pace to the pole vault area. He glanced back at the two girls who were practicing the triple jump. Pony tail girl was pretty good at it. He watched her practice a few times and then looked back at the pole vault area.

A tall lanky looking guy with dark hair and the peach fuzz shadow of a mustache beginning was taking his first practice run with a pole. He punched the pole down into the ground, and swung his body easily up into the air. He arched his back over the cross bar and landed effortlessly on the pads below. He jumped up and yelled at someone called Jennie behind Jonas.

"It's your turn, Jennie! I warmed up the pole for you! The cross bar is on the lowest notch. Should be a piece of cake for a jumper like you!"

Jonas turned to see who he was talking to and sucked in a surprised breath when he saw the pony tail girl heading toward them; determination written all over her face.

"If you can do it, it can't be that hard!" she teased him.

Jonas couldn't help himself; he could feel the whole accident coming on. He spoke up. "Uh, have you ever done this before? It could be dangerous!"

Jennie looked surprised that he would talk to her. He could tell, she was trying to place from where she might know him, but drawing a blank.

"Don't worry," she smiled that beautiful smile at him. "If that thing can make it over, so can I." She pointed in the direction of the boy with the pole when she said, "thing".

Jonas would have smiled back but he knew somehow, that this was going to be it. This was the accident waiting to happen. He turned to look at the others on the bleachers. *"Rick, if you're listening to me . . . this is probably it. This girl has no idea how to pole vault. She's doing it on a dare."*

"Gotcha, we're coming!" Even before he turned around, the three had stood and were headed their way. Jonas noticed that Mark now had what looked like a doctor's case in his hand.

"Good thinking about the doctor's case!" Jonas thought.

"Thanks, but it was Mark's idea," replied Rick.

"How's he going to explain it though?"

"Not sure yet, any ideas?"

"Uh, I just happened to be in the area . . . walking across the track field . . . on an American Military Facility . . . without clearance . . . with my doctor's bag on me? Honesty! They'll never see it coming!" Jonas' sarcasm was deep enough to wade through.

"You're a lot of help. Be quiet and pay attention, your future seems to be getting ready to fly!"

As Jonas turned around to watch Jennie, he saw that tall, dark and stupid had his arms around her showing her how to grip the pole. He was explaining something using one arm to point at the crossbar. He was leaning in as close to her ear as he could. If he got any closer, Jennie might be missing an ear before she even took off. Jonas didn't think he liked this guy's attitude and was gritting his teeth, when Jennie reached up and grabbed the guy by his hair and pulled him away from her ear.

"Back off a bit, Aaron! I still need that ear!"

Jonas smiled, *"She's got pluck, that one!"*

Jonas was glad when the wanker finally let go of her and backed off. Jennie was concentrating on the place where she would plant the pole. She gave a nervous look to her friend who was standing off to one side. She took a deep breath and started her run.

Jonas was shifting from one foot to the other. He found himself hoping she would make it. Heck this probably wasn't the one. She would be landing in soft pads. She'd be alright.

Jennie planted the pole in the ground. She swung her body up toward the cross bar. But she didn't quite have the momentum to keep her moving forward. As her feet started to cross the top, her forward motion slowed to a stop and she started to fall backwards. She still might have been ok, except her heals caught on the bar. The backward motion held the bar in place just long enough to keep her from being able to swing her feet back under her before she landed.

Jonas saw the problem and ran to try and catch her. But he made an error in judgment, expecting her to fall straight down. Jennie fell backward still clutching the pole. Had she let go, she may have been all right, she'd have fallen on flat ground and quite possibly right on top of Jonas. Because she still clutched the pole, she fell in an ark backward at an angle. She landed at the edge of the field, her body landing in damp grass, but her head hit solidly on a concrete curb that ran around the perimeter of the field.

Jonas and the wanker were standing over her in a second. She didn't look good. There was a lot of blood and she wasn't moving.

"Jennie! Jennie!" The wanker was panicking. He reached down to shake her but Jonas caught his arm and pushed him away.

Mark was running across the last couple of yards to reach her. He was there in an instant and was checking her vitals and yelling orders at the same time. "Someone call 911!" he ordered.

Jennie's friend was digging though her backpack and pulled out her cell phone. She was shaking so hard that she had to start over twice, before Jonas pulled the phone from her hands and placed the call himself.

"They're coming!" he told Mark.

"We have to get out of here right after they get here. Find out from the friend where they will take her, Jonas." Rick was thinking ahead trying to figure out how to avoid questions.

Jonas sat down beside Jennie's friend and handed her cell phone back. "Are you OK?" he asked her quietly.

"Yes, just worried. She's my best friend!" A tear slipped down her cheek.

"She'll be OK, uh . . ." Jonas raised his eye brows as he looked at the girl and paused for a name.

"Jenn." The girl filled in.

"No, I know her name, I was wondering what your name was."

"It's Jenn. There's usually a little confusion when people first meet us. But she's Jennie and I'm Jenn. She's been my best friend since we both moved here two years ago."

"Oh. Well, she'll be OK, Jenn. That guy working on her is actually a renowned surgeon. He'll take good care of her."

"Not too much information, please, Jonas!" Rick was looking sternly down at him.

"Sorry," He responded and then turned back to the girl, "Do you know what hospital they will take her to?"

Jenn nodded and told them where they would take her. She even gave them directions. Fortunately, she never thought to ask who they were or why they were there.

Mark looked up at Rick and caught his eye, *"You listening to me?"*

Rick nodded.

"Do you think you can augment a doctor's memory enough to get me on the surgical team?"

Rick raised one eyebrow, and whispered, "Maybe."

"Try, please."

Rick nodded. He wrapped his arm around Sophia who had come up behind them and was standing beside him.

It didn't take too long for the ambulance to arrive. By this time the coach and the principal were hovering over her. Mark, Rick, and Sophia were trying to blend into the back ground. Rick had to physically grab hold of Jonas to get him to move.

"Who did the first aid?" asked the principal.

That was it, Rick gathered them and they were gone. They arrived just outside the base gate and Jonas told them what he could remember from being in the area for competitions. He pictured the building he thought was the American hospital based on his memory and Jenn's directions and the little group teleported to that place. Luckily it turned out to be the hospital and the group entered through the front door. Mark led them through the corridors following signs to the surgical unit. When they arrived, Jonas and Sophia took seats in the waiting room. Mark got he and Rick past the first obstacle bluffing his way past the ER crew. They had arrived before the ambulance and Mark told them he was a visiting surgeon. Rick augmented as they went, causing the people around them to believe that the driver's license that Mark was producing was really a military I.D.

By the time the ambulance arrived, Mark was accepted as one of the team. The surgery began as Jonas settled in for a long wait.

Rick told Jonas that he and Sophia were going to check in on Luke and that they would be back. "As soon as you can get to her, hold her hand and try talking to her, even if she's still unconscious. Once you make contact, try to teleport her and Mark back to the beach house with you. If you aren't back there in ten hours, we'll come check on you. We should have asked Mark to give us a ball park on the operation."

"A ball park?" Jonas looked confused.

"I guess they don't use that one in England," Rick mused, "it just means I wish he had told us about how long the operation would take."

"Oh."

"We'll see you soon Jonas. Oh, and stay away from people that ask questions. Just tell them you were watching practice and you wanted to make sure she was all right. Don't give them your name. They are probably still looking for you here."

"OK."

"See you soon."

Jonas smiled and waved his fingers at them, "Thanks!" he said, and they were gone.

CHAPTER 31

Silence

Luke and the Linders left for the beach house. The sick feeling in Luke's stomach was not improving. It matched the anxiety he was feeling in every nerve of his body. Every fifteen minutes he'd chase down Anthony, grab hold of his shoulder and call out to Kassidy. There had been nothing . . . no answer. It was maddening. Luke had paced the living room, the deck and half the beach before Rick and Sophia showed up.

"Luke, where are you?" Rick called out to him.

"Beach. Where are you?"

"We're on the deck. Come on up."

"Be there in a minute."

When Luke made it to the deck he told them the whole story. He left out the argument the two had had in the upper cabin, of course, but he couldn't fool Rick. He recognized the anguish on Luke's face and knew there was more to the story. He'd seen it on his own face more than once. But he left the subject untouched.

"We could just telefly in tonight and get her out," suggested Rick. Then a thought occurred to him. "Luke, what did you guys find out about the rocks from the cave?"

"I don't know how far Anthony got in his work before we had to go."

Anthony had been listening in on the conversation and appeared on the deck at just that moment.

"I had done enough work to discover that it was just volcanic rock. There was nothing exceptional about it at all. It's the rock itself that does it. I can't explain it without a lot of further study. If LeBeau has been running the same tests, he probably already knows that it's just rock. We need to consider how he would use this knowledge."

"I know what I'd do. I'd find a way to cover parts of that facility with the volcanic rock so that Kassidy would not be able to use her talents and no one would be able to talk to her." Rick had already been thinking along these lines since they had made their trip to the cave.

227

"How do you think he would do that?" asked Luke. "It would take a lot of rock."

"Yeah, but if there is a way, LeBeau will think of it."

"If he does that could we still get into the facility?"

"Yes, I think. But we probably couldn't get back out. We'd need to find the real exit and get past security."

"Has anyone tried teleflight from inside the cave? Maybe it only interrupts the thoughts. As long as both parties are thinking of teleflight to the same place, maybe it would still work. We need to try it."

"Good idea, Anthony. No time like the present."

"We should try teleflight into the cave also."

The three men stood, put their hands on each other's shoulders and thought of the inside of the cave. They made it as far as the entrance. They hit hard against the rock over the entrance and fell eight feet landing in the soft sand just in front of the cave opening.

"Ahhh, that hurt!" Anthony was rubbing a twisted ankle.

All three men were groaning. "OK, it's safe to say that we will not be able to get inside the facility if LeBeau gets the rock on it.

Luke reached out and grabbed Rick to check on Kassidy. *"Kassidy, are you awake? Come on, baby, you have to wake up!"* There was still no answer. Luke let out a furious groan. "We have to go now! We can't wait until he has that stuff already on! We won't be able to get to her."

"Wait, we need to try teleflight out of the cave. We need to know if we can get back out if we are thinking of the same place." Rick's logic made sense, but no one was relishing a smack into the inside wall, if they failed. Still they had to try. They reluctantly stood and hobbled into the cave; each rubbing the spots that had hit the rock the hardest on their first attempt.

"OK, let's just try for landing in the sand outside the cave," suggested Luke. The men all concentrated on the sand outside the cave, but nothing happened. They didn't even feel the electricity build with their effort. "I guess that answers that question." They dropped their arms and walked toward the mouth of the cave.

"Let's go see what we can find out on their computer system. They may have maintenance information in there. Perhaps we can find out what they've been up to," suggested Rick.

"NO!! I need to get in there. I need to go now! Rick . . . I . . . please!" What had started out as a yell ended in a whisper.

"We still have time, Luke. Think rationally! Let's go check the computer."

Luke wasn't happy with the decision, but he respected his friend's opinion enough to listen. The three limped back up to the deck, rubbing out sore spots as they went.

Kassidy was beginning to wake up from the drug induced sleep. She didn't move yet, her head felt like it was splitting in two at first, but as she regained consciousness the pain began to dissipate. She didn't even try to think before she was calling for him. *"Luke. Luke!"* There was no reply, but she heard voices nearby.

"Hey, you're back. I was told you were heading to Wyoming."

"I was but then it occurred to me that once we took Miss Dover, any one else would have escaped to more private accommodations. They won't be there, so why waste the time. Did you finish the volcanic spray?"

"Yes, sir. But we only had enough for this room. We are making more now. We think we may have enough for the entire roof by next week.

"That's not fast enough! Get more people on it if you have to. We need it applied to the roof now! They'll come after her and we need to make sure that they don't find her! Secure this door. I want an armed guard on the door at all times. Make sure they are armed with tranquilizers not bullets! We want them all alive. Let me know when she's awake. I want to start on the tests as soon as possible."

Terror swept through Kassidy then. She remembered the dart from her shoulder. She knew she must be in the facility. She tried to look like she was still unconscious. Maybe they wouldn't start anything until she woke up. She was thinking furiously. So, they had sprayed the room with volcanic rock. She knew what that meant. She would not be able to talk to Luke. Tears threatened to spoil her charade. Her thoughts were racing. Had she remembered to close off the food closet? She couldn't remember. Had she compromised the whole hideout? Were Teresa and Derrick here too? No, she thought, they couldn't be or they would be in this room too. Only one room had the volcanic covering. They would never risk losing the baby again by having him in a regular room. They had learned that lesson. She was glad that they only had her so far. She must have closed the passage way! That was at least a little consolation.

Now how was she going to get out of here? She cracked her eyes just enough to see where she was. Oh no, she recognized this room, or at least one like it. Regina had been in a room like this. She had seen it in Luke's memory. She felt her heart rate race. That was when the man in the white coat entered her room.

"Well, Miss Dover, I see you are waking from your beauty sleep! That's good! You of all people don't really need more beauty sleep." the man was looking at a machine that was attached by a wire to Kassidy's chest. It betrayed an increase in her heart rate. He came over to her and unceremoniously opened one of her eyes with his thumb and forefinger and shined a light into it briefly. Then he did the same with the other eye. "You have very beautiful eyes!" The man turned to someone else in the room, "Tell Mr. LeBeau that she's awake, please!"

The mention of LeBeau caused another sharp increase in her heart rate. "Calm down, Miss Dover, we aren't going to hurt you. We just need to run some tests. We would like to understand your abilities."

Kassidy opened her eyes and found her voice. "You don't want to understand them, you want to duplicate them. And you don't care how many of us you kill to do it, so skip the pleasantries; they don't fit with your profession."

"My profession is science. I see no reason why we can't be pleasant."

"Your profession is kidnapping and murder!"

"Oh, come now. Aren't you being a little melodramatic?"

"I don't think so, I saw what you did to Regina."

"Regina? I don't recall a Regina."

"She was a 'guest' here about ten years ago."

"How could you know that, you didn't even get your talents until last May."

"I saw it in the mind of someone who was here! You dissected her! You are not fit to share the planet with the rest of civilization. You are truly the scum of the earth!"

"Well, hopefully, it won't end that way for you. We have learned a lot in the last ten years. I think we can keep you alive." The man smiled.

If Kassidy had not known the kind of enemy that faced her, she might have fallen for that smile, but she knew better.

LeBeau entered the room then. She was surprised by his appearance. She had never seen him up close and facing her. She had only seen him angry and glaring in Mark's memory and as a blur from the hotel experience. Quiet and in control of his temper, as he was now, he was nearly handsome. His hair was stylishly long and sandy blond. He was athletically built and very tall. If it weren't for the scar on the right side of his face, he could have been a model. Kassidy grimaced as she looked at the scar. She would have had one like that except for the fact that paths healed so well.

Kassidy wasn't sure where all her bravado was coming from, but she started in on LeBeau almost the second he stepped into the room.

"You having trouble using your stolen talents to heal that horrible scar on your face?'

LeBeau smiled a wicked smile, destroying the earlier handsome impression. "Spirited aren't you?! Don't worry, when we are finished with you, I should be able to correct that little short coming. You, however, might want to be a little more pleasant. You are not in a position to taunt your hosts."

"Bite me!!!" It was all she could think of at the time. She supposed it was a little juvenile, but she was under a lot of stress after all.

LeBeau leaned into her face, "I just might!!"

He turned to the guy in the lab coat then. He was about to say something when he noticed the lab coat guy's eyes fly open. Before he could turn to see what was happening behind him, he heard a clatter and felt a needle stick into his neck. He turned in response and hit Kassidy across the face sending her flying out of the bed and into the wall. She was out cold again. LeBeau noticed that an IV stand lay on the floor and he was amused that the tube leading from the IV bottle lead straight to his neck. She had stuck him with the only weapon she could find; the IV needle.

How interesting! She had known that she would not subdue him. This was a total act of defiance! She had not really hurt him much. The needle was long enough to cause pain, but not do much damage. Too bad he had reacted without thinking. Now they would have to wait until she was conscious again to start the good stuff. Oh well, they could get some of the little tests done, the ones that didn't require a fully awake human to do. But since he didn't enjoy needles that much, he would have to restrain her now.

"Get her back in bed, hook up a new IV and strap her down. We can't have her using us as pin cushions in the future. Go ahead and start with the blood work."

"Yes, sir!"

"So what's it say?" Luke was pacing the room as Andre was pouring through files in the lab's computer system. Andre had come as soon as Luke could get a hold of him and tell him about Kassidy. Cecil was with Sophia, but they weren't too far away just in case the guys needed to get somewhere quickly.

"They are bringing in more people to work on some maintenance . . . . bingo . . . it's roof maintenance. They are just getting started. They haven't gotten very far."

"I have to go now! I can get in and out before they get finished!"

"Yeah, I think that would be a good idea. But how are we going to arm you?"

"Arm me?"

"You can't just go barging in there. They are going to know you are coming. They will be expecting you!"

"Rick, I don't own a gun, I've never even shot one!"

"You live in Wyoming . . . . and you've never shot a gun?!"

"I think you may be confusing your states. Wyoming is not like Texas or California! We're . . . more civilized!"

"Yeah, right!" Rick rolled his eyes. Well, you need to be prepared. They will try to drop you with a tranquilizer and use you as a guinea pig too!"

"Not if they think I'm one of them. We still have the lab coats. Don't we?"

"Luke, by now, they all know what you look like. We can't risk both you and Kassidy being in there." Rick had begun pacing along side Luke.

"I think I should be the one to go." Andre stood and walked toward the two men.

"I could get in; no one has seen me since my brief incarceration. Well, except the one guy who we met briefly in Anthony's room, but I think he had too many people in front of him to remember me."

"No one is going without me. She's mine, she's my responsibility. I can't just stay here and wait." Luke stopped pacing to make his point and the other two gentlemen stopped with him.

"Luke, you could jeopardize the whole thing. As soon as they see you, it's over!" Rick reasoned.

"I'm going. I'll stay behind Andre, and let him do the talking, but I'm going!"

"What if you both get caught? We need Andre's computer skills." Rick had a bad feeling about this whole rescue thing. He was sure that time had run out for tele-rescues from the agency.

"How about I go get Demetri and bring him here. Then you will have a computer genius way more qualified than me here. If anything delays us, you guys just go ahead with the plan . . . . but do it quickly. I like my brains where they are."

"Go get him," Luke's voice filled with more hope than he'd displayed since Kassidy's kidnapping.

"Don't you think you should ask Cecil? She has a pretty big steak in Andre's decision." Rick was still grasping at straws.

"She already gave me permission. She would want someone with me if the shoe was on the other foot and she was in there. So she told me to do what I could to help. I'll get Cecil and we'll go get Demetri. Luke, don't go anywhere until we get back. It'll only take a few minutes."

"Ten, you have ten minutes, Andre. I can't wait any longer!"

"Sheesh, you two gotta get married or something. You're a basket case!" Andre's effort at lightening the mood fell flat.

"Are you telling me you wouldn't be if it were Cecil?" Luke didn't even look up at Andre. He already knew the answer to that one.

"Sorry, Luke, I just . . . I'll be right back!"

Luke took another shot at reaching Kassidy. He laid his hand on Rick and called out to her again. There was, of course, still no answer, only Luke's anguished look.

Kassidy felt the pain before she even knew she was conscious. The whole right side of her face hurt. When she did regain consciousness, it took her a minute to place her surroundings again and remember what had happened. Oh, yeah, she had stabbed that monster and he had hit her. As she rolled off the bed, she had hit the same side of her face against the wall. She wondered what her face looked like. *"Vanity, thy name is Kassidy!"* she thought. She knew one eye was nearly swelled shut. She could barely see out of it. She was also having some trouble breathing through her nose. She suspected that it was broken. The other eye wasn't as badly affected and she could see pretty well out of it. She wouldn't be able to use her abilities to speed up healing, but maybe she could use it to her advantage. She might be able to slow down the testing pace if they thought her injuries might affect the outcome.

She tried to move, but discovered that she was strapped to the bed. Well, she should have expected that. There were needle sticks in her arm. Looks like they had gotten the obligatory blood work done, as well as who knows what else. It didn't take long for her thoughts to turn to Luke. She missed him. She missed his thoughts tripping through her mind all the time. She even missed trying to hide hers from him. She knew it wouldn't work but she called out to him anyway. *"Luke, Luke, can you hear me? I love you."* Now where did the tears come from? She was still alive and there was still hope. She knew he would come for her. Why worry? Her breath caught in a sob as she answered her own question. She worried because if he did come for her, he might be stuck here too. She couldn't let that happen. But how could she stop it?

There were foot steps coming down the hall. Then there were voices. Though she had only heard LeBeau's voice once, she was pretty sure it was him. Something about the authority with which the person was talking gave him away.

"So we're ready for the next step?"

"Yes, sir. As soon as she wakes up, we can start. I just want to make sure she is all right after the beating you gave her. We can't take any chances that something is injured before we start."

"I only hit her once. It was the wall that did most of the damage." LeBeau chuckled as he continued. "You make it sound as though I had taken a whip to her or something." LeBeau did not feel remorseful about hitting her, only that his experiments were delayed.

"Yes, sir." The man seemed cool but irritated.

"Developing a conscience Dr. Brannen?"

"No, just irritated that we couldn't start on her yesterday."

They had wanted to start yesterday! Kassidy wondered how long she had been out. She wondered what day it was. She thought she better look like she was still asleep. She needed to buy Luke some time. He would get here . . . . he just needed time. She tried to be brave and confident, but time was running out.

Kassidy wasn't sure what had caught her attention in the hallway, maybe it was the opening of her door. No, that wasn't it. It was the sudden cessation of the conversation between the monster and the 'doctor'. Kassidy chanced a peek out of a mostly closed eye. What she saw floored her.

LeBeau had stopped dead in his tracks. His face looked vacant, as if he had just stepped out of his body for a minute and left it standing in the hallway. The doctor was still holding the door open for him, but when he didn't enter, the doctor looked back at him.

"Sir, are you all right? Mr. LeBeau?"

LeBeau began to move, his face looking up toward the ceiling. He broke out into a cold sweat. Then he crumpled to the ground. He wasn't moving and his face became very pale.

The doctor began calling for help. The only one in the hallway at the time was the guard at Kassidy's door. So the doctor sent him for help.

"I have orders not to leave this door unguarded." The guard complained.

"Your orders have been rescinded. Go get help!"

"With all due respect, sir, you do not have the authority to rescind my orders. Only the man lying on the floor in front of you has that authority."

"Go get help, you moron!"

"No, sir!"

"Fine, help me get him onto a gurney. There's one in her room. Get it, please!"

The guard came into the room and rolled a gurney out to the hallway. The two men lifted LeBeau onto the gurney and rolled him into the room with Kassidy. As soon as his head passed through the door it was as if the man were released from some alien force. He was back!

"What am I doing on this gurney?" Though confused, LeBeau had not lost his attitude and began shouting at the guard, "What are you doing in here? Get to your post!! You are not to leave your post!"

"Sir, I needed him! You were too heavy to lift by myself."

"What happened? Why did you have to lift me?"

"Sir, you went totally white, you broke out into a sweat, you stopped walking forward and then you dropped to the floor."

LeBeau looked as if he might be sick as he remembered what had happened. "It was nothing. We have work to do. Check her and see if she's still asleep or just trying to fool us again!"

"But Mr. LeBeau, you . . ."

"Check her now! I'm fine! I'll be right back. I just need a little air." LeBeau swung his legs over the gurney and headed for the door, but as soon as he hit the hallway again, he also hit the floor again.

The doctor was hovering over him again. This time, he told the guard to watch him, that he would be right back. He was going for help. But he was interrupted mid sentence.

"You can't help him. I know what's going on." Kassidy had spoken without much emotion in her voice, but she stopped the doctor mid step.

Doctor Brannen put his foot back down and turned to look at her. "What did you say?"

"I know what's wrong with him." She repeated.

"How would you know?"

"I've seen it before in another path."

"Mr. LeBeau is not a path, or what ever you call yourselves. The experiment failed with him."

"Not entirely! And he is reacting to a path reality right now. You can't help him, only another path can help him. Let me up and I'll help him."

"I can't do that. You can't come out of that room."

"Well, I'm not sure what will happen to him then. I've never seen it get this far without intervention. You better drag him in here. It's the only place in the hospital where path abilities are interrupted. He needs them to be interrupted badly."

The doctor thought about that for a minute but when LeBeau started yelling something about needing to go and having to be at the rock, the doctor grabbed him by the arms and dragged him into Kassidy's room.

As soon as his body crossed the threshold, he began to regain consciousness. He didn't recover as quickly this time, however.

"Oh, he's bad! How long has this been going on?" Kassidy asked the doctor.

"I have no idea."

LeBeau opened his eyes then and sat up looking at Kassidy.

"What am I doing back in her room?"

"Mr. Monster," began Kassidy, "How long have you been having the visions?"

"What visions?" LeBeau asked just a little too innocently. "And please refer to me as Mr. LeBeau."

"Not likely." Kassidy paused, "I'm not sure where you were just now, but I bet you were thinking of a specific spot that you see in your dreams over and over. You've been ignoring it, but now it is happening even when you are awake. You feel an over whelming urge to be at that particular place. Am I close, Mr. Monster?"

"If Mr. LeBeau is so difficult, just call me 'sir'. So what if you are close? How do you know about it?"

Kassidy pointed to herself with her finger only since her hands were still bound to her bed. "Path, remember? You better stay in here. You will pass out again every time you walk out of this room." She wasn't really sure about that, but given his last attempt at leaving, she felt it was a safe bet.

LeBeau sat there on the floor looking at Kassidy. He seemed to be trying to decide whether to trust her or not. Still in indecision, he decided to ask. "Why should I trust you?"

"Good question. Who else do you have to trust? Is there anyone else here who is a path that you could trust, with your life? Because that is what you are playing with, Mr. Monster . . . . sir." Kassidy didn't really know that for sure either, but anything to gain the advantage.

LeBeau pulled himself off the ground, using the foot of the gurney he had been on earlier. He seemed shaky on his feet and did not let go of the gurney just yet. His eyes betrayed nothing, but Kassidy was sure that he indeed had no one to trust in this place or anywhere. She would have enjoyed the cat and mouse game, if she could have gotten past the fear of him that gripped her every time she was within hearing range of him. Even now her hands were shaking. She was almost thankful for the cuffs that held them securely to the cart. At least the shaking was minimized by being tied down.

"What are you talking about?" he asked her suspiciously.

"Let me out of this room where I can call my friends and we'll take you to that place, where ever it is."

"I reiterate, why should I trust you?"

"Because if you don't, something bad is going to happen. Do you know the place you are being called to?"

"I am not being called anywhere."

"Yes, you are. You were lying on the floor out there saying, 'I need to go, I have to get to the rock.' What rock do you need to get to, Mr. Monster?"

LeBeau shot an angry glance at Dr. Brannen. "You left her door open?"

"Chill out Monster! He was on his way out to help you and even if he hadn't been, everyone within this wing probably heard you! But time is running out. The rock won't wait forever and you need to get there . . . soon!"

LeBeau made a decision. "Forget it. I'll take my chances with my own misplaced dreams. Start the work on Miss Dover now."

"Have it your way you murdering monster, but you better stay in this room. Otherwise the pain may get to be more than that scarred head of yours can handle. It's probably only visions, falls and sweat right now, but you can't deny your destiny much longer."

Some of the color seemed to evacuate LeBeau's face. He turned to exit the room once more. He was determined to make it out of sight of Kassidy before he allowed the vision to take over, if it actually did. But he didn't make it two steps out of the door before he dropped once more.

"You should just leave him lying out there. The man's a head ache looking for a place to happen. If you drag him in here again, he'll just yell at you. He doesn't understand what's happening and you can't help him . . . unless you want to shoot him up with some sleep inducing drug . . . but he'll still dream the dream and torture himself. Let me go, it's his only hope."

"I can't, that would get me fired or worse."

"Yeah, you're probably right, might as well let the boss die. Then you can all go free."

"You think he'll die?"

Kassidy thought she had him. Maybe just a nudge in the right direction. "You remember that kid you guys had in here . . . ah, Jason, no John . . . . uh? Hmmm . . . oh, yeah, Jonas?"

"Yes."

"We got him out of here, but he was already seeing the vision. He fell flat on the kitchen floor yesterday night. We were too late. He was young and didn't know what the visions were. He'd been ignoring them for a while. He started screaming something about a field he was supposed to get to. When help arrived, he was gone, but not before the pain." Whew! She had become a colossal liar lately. Well, it wasn't quite a lie. She didn't actually say he was dead . . . just gone! Ok, the pain part was a lie. Thank heavens no one here was a path but the preoccupied Monster on the floor.

Kassidy heard the guard just at the same time as the foot steps coming down the hall. "Stop, where you are and identify yourselves."

Dr. Brannen, who was now leaning over LeBeau, turned to look back at Kassidy. He never saw the kick to the head coming. One minute he was looking into the bruised liquid green eyes and the next minute everything was black.

CHAPTER 32

The Rescue

It took Andre more than fifteen minutes to bring Demetri back. "The man was in his pajamas, Luke!" He tried to explain.

Rick had been close to blows with Luke, trying to keep him there for the last five minutes. The only thing that stopped Luke was that he needed someone to send him to the agency. He couldn't do it alone and Rick had promised that if Luke rearranged anything on his face, he would not be the one to help him. Luke had refrained under protest.

To distract him, Rick had produced the lab coats from the agency and a small hand gun. "You may need this. I borrowed it from a gun store. Here are some extra rounds. Please bring it back, because I haven't paid for it and Kassidy would have my neck if I couldn't return it."

"Rick, I don't even know how to use this thing. Let alone load it!"

Rick showed him how to load and shoot it, taking him outside to the deck to shoot one round off. Rick pointed to a nearby coconut tree. He pointed to a coconut and shot. The coconut dropped to the ground spilling its milk across a three foot area.

"Where did you learn to shoot like that?"

"I was in the Marines! I did 30 years in the Marines; long enough to learn to shoot!" He let Luke take a shot at a second coconut. He missed by a mile. Rick laughed. "Don't worry, just aim at the torso. If you miss, it will at least make them cautious and buy you some time!"

"Thanks, I feel so much better." Luke said sarcastically.

When Andre, Demetri, and Cecil arrived, Rick thanked Demetri for coming and shook Andre and Luke's hands. "Good luck, you two. If you aren't back in an hour, we'll assume the worst and put the plan in motion, ready or not. Put on the lab coats gentlemen. Now, Andre, get this man out of here and reunited with his woman before he has an aneurysm and drops dead before our eyes!"

"Ok, but you may want to put the plan in motion now anyway. They are starting on that roof and we need to be able to augment everyone in the agency's mind at once. We won't be able to do that if they get that stuff on. We could be right back at the drawing board."

Rick thought about that for only a second. "Yeah, I had sort of been thinking the same thing, but I'm not sure we're ready."

"We have to be." Demetri had already sat down at the computer, installed his own translating software and was clicking away at the keys. What he read made his eyes pop open almost audibly. He blurted out his findings in Russian but everyone in the room understood every word he said. "They have enough of that stuff made to cover a fourth of the roof. It will only be hours before they get it applied and by that time, they may be ready for the next application. We are very quickly running out of time. You better call everyone. This thing is going to have to go down very soon!"

"I'm on it! Go get Kassidy, Luke. Andre, cover his butt, please!" Rick was already calling the women.

"Hey, if I'm supposed to be covering your butt, shouldn't I get the gun?"

"Can you shoot it?"

"Are you kidding? Of course I can. I prefer a little larger piece, but it will do."

"Great, it's yours; I can't seem to hit the broad side of a coconut anyway!"

"Cool, can I keep it?"

"No, Kassidy would have you drawn and quartered. It's not paid for. We have to return it!"

"Oh, too bad!"

"Let's go."

Cecil had entered the room; she kissed her husband, wished him a 'bonne chance' joined hands with him briefly and sent him and Luke on their way.

The two arrived in the dissection room they had been in before. This time they were not alone. Luke and Andre went to work augmenting the three technician's minds immediately. *"I sure hope this room has not been covered in that rock yet!"* Luke thought.

"It must not have been, because we didn't hit the roof and the technicians have bought the little lie we gave them. By the way, what little lie did you give them?"

"I told them we were with management and just checking on their progress."

"Good, I told them to keep on working; we had just entered to check out the facility rooms."

"We might want to work out what we are going to say. Next time we might not be so lucky!"

"Good point. What are we going to say?"

"*Well, maybe we want to start turning this place into a cancer treatment center now. We could start telling them to keep working on what they are doing; we are just management checking up on their progress on cancer research.*"

"*Can't hurt, let's get looking for Kassidy.*"

Luke sent the part about cancer research to the men in the room. They didn't seem to even blink when the new thought hit their minds. Usually there was some reaction. Luke took a quick peek into the closest one's thoughts. "*They are prepping this room for a surgery! It's an exploratory on a new patient they just brought in. These guys didn't even know what they were researching here! They were just set up and clean up guys!*"

"*Well, looks like LeBeau is going to make our jobs much easier than we thought!*"

"*Yeah, but if they are prepping this for exploratory, it could be for Kassidy.*"

"*If that's the case, we could just wait here until they bring her in!*"

"*But we don't know for certain if it's for her!*"

"*Should we divide and conquer?*"

"*I like the conquer part, but I don't think we should divide.* Gentlemen, what time is the exploratory to begin. We might like to observe."

"It was scheduled to begin in about thirty minutes, sir, but some emergency messed up the time schedule. The exploratory has been delayed until this afternoon at 1:00. You have time to look around before then."

"Thank you! You have been very helpful! *What do you think that is all about?*"

"*I don't know but let's not look a gift dog in the tail.*"

"*A what?*" Luke looked questioningly at Andre. "*That's not exactly the way I learned that saying.*"

"*Poodles . . . you know, docked tails . . .*"

"*Never mind, let's go!*"

The hallways were not as empty as they had been the last time they had been here, but no one seemed to notice them as they passed. The two augmented every mind they met, but no one really seemed to be affected one way or the other by the new knowledge that they were a cancer research facility.

The two men checked memories of passers by for any clues to Kassidy's whereabouts. They had not found any information and Luke was beside himself with worry when Andre came up with a pretty good idea.

"*Suppose we find a secluded closet and stretch out our minds again.*"

"*Won't do any good if she is in an area with that rock covering it. She won't be able to hear us.*"

"*No, but, Luke, there are people all over this facility. We can hear them* all *right now. We may be able to pin point her location by finding the place in this building where we can not hear* anything.*"

Hope exploded across Luke's face. *"Worth a try!"*

It took seven doors before they found an unlocked janitor's closet with no one in it. The two squeezed into the narrow room. Andre put his hand on Luke's shoulder and the two began to search for the spot in the building where they couldn't hear anything. It didn't take long. They each looked up at the other at the same time. "Found it!" they exclaimed together.

"Let's concentrate on the edge of the sound." Luke's mind raced with anticipation. He could feel they were getting close and he couldn't wait to have her back in his arms and under his protection.

It was a new sensation, concentrating on the sound instead of a place. Andre wasn't sure it was entirely safe. They could end up dropping in somewhere they really didn't want to be . . . like security's office. But he couldn't stop Luke now. The man was possessed. Andre pitied the one who got in the way of this man now. There was determination in the way he gritted his jaw and an intensity in Luke's eyes that could rival a hawk on the hunt.

They concentrated on the edge of the sound. It turned out to be a hallway. There were very few people around them. One was a janitor mopping up a spill, but facing away from them. There were two others coming toward them, a man dressed in an identical white coat to Luke's and Andre's and a young woman in scrubs, but they were deep in concentration as they discussed a chart they were sharing between them. They came right up to Andre and Luke but without even looking up, turned left down a hallway toward the silent part of the facility.

Luke and Andre followed them down the same hallway. They had only gotten about halfway down it when they came to an intersection. They stepped into it before they noticed what it was. Some commotion caught Luke's attention down the right hand hallway in the exact direction of the silent part of the wing. He saw a man crumple to the floor. A guard was standing with his back to Luke and Andre staring down at the man on the floor. Another man with a white lab coat on also, stepped out of the room and leaned down to check the man. He heard her voice then! That most precious of voices. His Kassidy! She was there! She was talking to someone about the guy on the floor . . . what was she saying?

"Yeah, you're probably right, might as well let the boss die. Then you can all go free."

Luke started to reach out to Andre to get his attention, but Andre had heard the commotion also and was already headed in that direction. It only took the two of them a few seconds to run the distance between the intersection and the man on the floor. Unfortunately, it took less time than that for the guard to hear them coming and turn around. The guard raised his gun, told them to stop and identify themselves. Andre slowed and put his hands up, but Luke never broke stride. Andre thought for sure that the guard was going to shoot and ask questions later as he swung his aim at Luke. The guard was confused for just a moment by the lab coat. It was just enough time for Andre to pull his own gun out and point it at the guard.

"I wouldn't do that if I were you! Yours probably has tranquilizers, mine has bullets!" The guard threw his hands up dropping his gun. At the same moment Andre spoke, Luke's foot connected with the doctor's head. The blow sent the doctor sprawling further down the hall way.

"Luke!!!" Kassidy was struggling with her bindings.

Luke was just about to beat the pulp out of LeBeau when he heard her voice again. He stopped before he had a chance to drop down to LeBeau's level and ran to her. He gasped when he saw her face. The angry bruise was covering half of her face. Her right eye was nearly swelled shut. He was torn between the need to release her and hold her and a need just as intense to smash LeBeau's whole face in. His mind was made up for him when he saw her struggling against the bindings. He moved like lightening to her side, unbuckling the straps and pulling her into his arms.

He picked her up and turned to carry her from the room. That was when he realized that he needn't have worried about LeBeau, because Andre was about to do the same thing to him that Luke had wanted to do. But before he could get the first real blow off, Kassidy stopped him.

"Wait, don't do it! We need him!"

"What?" both men looked at her in astonishment.

"He's being called to a crossroads. It'll take us a lot longer to find that path without him. He's being drawn to some rock, but he doesn't know where it is or he'd have gone. He's well past the part where you are just drawn there. He is totally incapacitated. This is the third time he's crumpled to the floor right outside this room."

At that moment, LeBeau started to come around again. His eyes flew open as he looked into the faces of both Luke and Andre.

"Yeah, you should look astonished," Luke's voice sounded deadly, "I'd have killed you just for what you've done to her face, but she stopped me. She says we won't find the new path without you. But I disagree. We'll find her; it will just take us a little longer. So the way I see it, you have a choice. You can come quietly with us. Or you can die right here, right now!"

"What are you planning to do with me?" LeBeau was still a little amazed at the turn of events.

"The plan will be revealed on a need to know basis. Right now, all you need to know is that you have a choice. Die now or maybe die later." Andre's voice wasn't much less threatening than Luke's.

"I guess I'm with you for the time being!" LeBeau looked away from them then, his eyes resting on the gun that the guard had dropped.

"Don't bother thinking about it. Your hired hands on the roof, . . . you know, the ones who are wondering what kind of a raving lunatic would hire them to spray black rock all over a roof in the middle of a desert, they have reached this part of the building and you do not have the power to do anything telepathically. Why do you think you are conscious? Oh, and I'd get a bullet off before you could even get to the gun, so maybe you might want to think it through a little bit more slowly." Andre was smiling down at LeBeau, but there was no humor or well wishes in the smile.

"Luke, put me down. I can walk. Let's get going. I've had all of this place that I can stand!" Kassidy was ready to get going.

Luke reluctantly set her down on her bare feet. Then noticing the tie-in-the-back hospital gown, he took off his lab coat and wrapped it around her. "Let's go!"

LeBeau stood up and began walking down the hallway. Andre kept a close eye on him. Luke stooped down and picked up the tranquilizer gun, shot the guard to put him to sleep, and followed after holding tightly to Kassidy's hand. As soon as they hit a rock free zone, LeBeau started to crumple again. Andre and Luke caught him and immediately 'saw' the place to which LeBeau was being drawn. LeBeau's conversation telepathically had deteriorated to one sentence which he thought over and over again. *"I have to go!"*

"Kassidy, we know where we're going now, can't we just kill him and go without him?" Luke pleaded.

Kassidy looked at him, mortified! *"No, you can't just kill him! I know he's a worthless murdering monster, but we can't become what he is. Let's go. Maybe a miracle will happen and he'll fall so in love with his path mate that he will no longer be a threat to us. If not, you can do what ever you want with augmentation . . . but you can't kill him!"*

"Well, if you won't let Luke kill him, can I? I owe him for all the crap he put Cecil and me through. We really can't trust this guy. And think what he did to Derrick . . . just a little bitty guy. He held his parents in an unconscious state and did what ever he pleased with that defenseless innocent child. What ever else he did to him scared him so badly that he was in hysterics the night they kidnapped you!"

Kassidy's love for children nearly won the argument. She paused for a moment.

"I promise that for you, I'll make it quick and painless!"

He lost the argument right there. Kassidy did not want anyone killing anyone for her! *"No, he does not die by our hand! Let's go!"* She started praying right then. *"Please, God, honor that act of mercy. Don't let this become a mistake that will cost us someone later! Oh, and help us find the path that LeBeau has been ignoring.*"

"*You are such a softy.*" Luke pulled her to his side and kissed the top of her head. The group concentrated on the rock in LeBeau's thoughts and was gone.

The 'rock' turned out to be more of a cliff. They were standing at the foot of it, looking up. There was a rope dangling from somewhere higher up, but there was no one on it. Kassidy was the first to look down at the foot of the cliff. A woman lay sprawled on the ground. There was blood pouring out of her head and she had sustained multiple other injuries as well. A young man was crouched by her side, tears streaming down his pale face, calling her name. "Laurie! Oh no, please Laurie! What am I going to do? Laurie, wake up!"

LeBeau was awake and at her side in a second. He couldn't take his eyes off her. "What happened?" he asked the man beside her.

"We were climbing together. We always climb together. She slipped . . . I guess . . . I don't know. I was above her and didn't see it happen. I just heard her scream and then she was down here. You gotta help her. She's all I have."

Luke looked over at Andre. "Kassidy and I have to get Mark. Can you handle LeBeau by yourself?"

"Yeah, but you better hurry. I don't know if he's back at the beach house now, or still at Lakenheath. I'd try the beach house first."

"Thanks, we'll be back as soon as possible."

Luke tucked the tranquilizer gun in his belt and took both of Kassidy's hands in his. He pulled her close, noticing that her face had made a marked improvement since they had gotten her away from the lava rock. He thought of the beach house and they arrived on the deck seconds later.

Their arrival started a panic for a moment when Cecil noticed that Andre was not with them. Luke quickly shot her the Reader's Digest version of what had happened. She reached out and touched him, picked Luke's brain for the place where Andre was and sling shot herself to the rock. She had moved so fast that Luke was surprised by her and stood stunned for a couple of minutes after she left. Kassidy had recovered more quickly than Luke and reached up and touched the side of his face. "Hey, we have a mission, remember?"

As it turned out the only people at the beach house were Lisa and Sandy. They explained that Jonas was having some trouble getting Jennie and Mark back. He had managed to let Cecil know that they had been delayed, but that was all. Everyone else had gone to the agency. The attack was on!

"*We have to talk to Jonas!*" Luke was already concentrating." *Jonas?*"

"*Luke? Would you check her out? She's beautiful!*"

Luke and Kassidy could see Jonas' attention completely taken by a beautiful face. She had long dark hair and blue eyes that bordered on violet.

CHAPTER 33

Back to Back

Luke rolled his eyes, *"Jonas, get a grip! Is Mark with you?"*
"He's right here."
"Is anyone else with you?"
"Uh, yes, actually, that's the problem."
Luke thought for a minute, *"Jonas, go find an empty room and give me a visual of it."*
"Uh, O . . . K . . . um . . . but . . ."
"What's the problem?"
"Well, I just wasn't ready to leave her alone, just yet."
"I thought you just told me that people were there with you."
"Well, yeah, but they can't get inside her head and hold back that black thing."
"Tell her you'll be right back and go! NOW! Another path needs Mark!"
Jonas was going to relay the message to Jennie, but she was already telling him to go.
"I'll be right back, I won't leave you with it for very long."
"I was fighting it by myself before you got here. I can do it again. Now, go!"
Jonas very reluctantly let go of her hand and looked around the room. When he caught Mark's eyes, he asked him to come with him. The two walked quickly down the hall until they found a vacant room. Jonas was explaining the whole situation to Mark on the way.
"Oh great! I just finished with Jennie's surgery. I don't know how I'm going to make it through another one so soon! It takes a lot of concentration!"
"Doc, you're all we have. You have to try."
"Of course, I'll try. I'm just not as alert or relaxed as I like to be when I go into surgery."
"Jonas, where are you now?" Luke was getting impatient.
"OK, Luke, here's the room." Jonas looked around the room giving Luke a good visual and before he even finished scanning, Luke and Kassidy stood before him.

"Wow, Kassidy, great to see you're back! You had us all worried! Uh, nice outfit! I bet there's a great story to go with that."

"If you like it, you can borrow it anytime!"

"Mark, we need you. Believe it or not, LeBeau was drawn to a crossroads. She looks pretty bad. We have to go." Luke looked impatient.

"Get my bag, Jonas." Mark sent him back to the room where Jennie was.

"Jonas, we'll be back to get you after we get Mark to the path." Jonas 'heard' Luke tell him as he ran back down the hallway.

"OK, but we may have a problem. Jennie's family won't leave her side for anything! I've tried to get them to go eat or something, but they aren't budging . . . close family!"

"We'll work that out later. Hurry!"

Jonas was back in a moment with Mark's bag and the three were gone before Jonas could walk back out of the room.

They arrived back at the cliff and Mark dashed over to the path on the ground. He was examining her wounds, taking vitals and assessing her condition with a speed that Luke and the others had not seen before.

The young man who was still wailing beside her was confused. Where had this man come from? Why was he pushing him out of the way?

Luke heard every thought and went to pull the man away so Mark could work. The man resisted, but Luke began to explain who Mark was and to augment the young man's mind to believe that they had just happened on the accident. Unfortunately, Mark was still in scrubs and a doctor's coat. Luke found that as he augmented one correction to the man's memory, he had to come up with another one. *"It's just like they say,"* he thought, *"one lie leads to another!"*

Kassidy finally came to Luke's aid, helped him get the man seated on a large boulder and began to ask the young man questions to get his mind off the immediate. "What is your name?"

"Eric Trainer."

"Eric, what is the name of the woman you are with?"

"Laurie. She's my older sister."

"Were you rock climbing when this happened?"

"Yes, we climb here a lot. We're so good at this particular cliff that we could probably climb it with our eyes closed. That's probably what happened. She was too confident. She made a mistake!" Eric threw his head in his hands and he began to rock back and forth a bit as he watched Mark work. Nervous energy seemed to ooze out of him and spill down the rock they were sitting on.

"Eric, the man working on your sister is a very, very good brain surgeon. He'll take very good care of her. But maybe you can help us. Where are we?"

Eric looked at her like she was nuts. "You are here and you don't know where this is?" But then he noticed Kassidy's hospital gown and doctor's jacket at the same time. His mind began to reel again. This must be a dream, it was too weird to be real.

"Look, Eric, I don't have time to explain, but how far from a hospital and an ambulance are we?"

"Oh, about 50 miles . . . . one way." He still looked pretty confused.

"How long ago did this happen?"

"It happened just before those other guys showed up. I had just gotten back down to her when that blonde guy was hovering over us."

"Good. Mark, did you hear that?"

"Yes, thanks. She's in pretty bad shape. We can't wait for an ambulance. We need to get her to my surgical unit as soon as we can. Luke, can you check it out to see if it's empty for me?"

"Sure. Show me what the room looks like."

"I'm going to show you to the outside of the door; then you look in the door window and see if it's empty. That way you won't contaminate anything if there is a surgery in process. Don't forget to come right back!" Mark thought of the little room just outside of the operating room. Luke and Kassidy picked up the visual and left immediately. They were back in an instant.

"It's in use. What now?"

"I'm not sure, but we need somewhere fast!" Mark was thinking frantically.

"Let's just pick another hospital and go!"

"If we're caught before the surgery finishes . . . ." Mark was clearly uncomfortable with the possibilities.

"Take her to the facility!" LeBeau had not spoken much since their arrival and his suggestion now made Luke take a step toward him with the intent of quite possibly grabbing him around the scruff of the neck and shaking him around like a dead rat. But Andre protested just in time.

"Get out of the line of fire, Luke. I'll take care of this!"

"Stop it everyone!" Kassidy yelled. "We don't have a lot of choices here." She was thinking furiously. "Luke, you couldn't resist the call, could you?"

"No, but Kassidy, we don't know how strong LeBeau's connection is. He's only about one eighth path!"

"So maybe it's even stronger with him . . . less resistance. I watched him crumple three times in the hallway, before you two got there. If we find a place in the facility where they haven't put the rock on the roof, we would still be able to protect the area. It could be Laurie's last hope. We need to go. You still have the guns. If LeBeau doesn't do everything we say, then I'll let you shoot him! In the knees!" Kassidy had her back to LeBeau; she was glad he couldn't see her face. She hoped he couldn't tell by her voice just how abhorrent she was to that idea. Still, if he threatened any of them, she vowed to herself that she would not get in the way of Andre and Luke if they shot at him.

Luke and Andre both smiled at the idea of shooting at LeBeau. They both looked down at him. LeBeau had sweat dripping off his forehead. His complexion was waxy and pale. His blue-green eyes pleaded with them.

"Please, I won't let anyone detain you. If you just get us there and allow Dr. Johns to do his thing, I will do anything you wish."

"OK, and what happens after? You keep Laurie and experiment on her? I don't think so. You will allow us to take her with us. You will not interfere."

LeBeau looked like he was trying to swallow a bite that was too big, or too dry. But he nodded his head in agreement. "Just save her, please!"

Luke moved to his side and dragged him up on his feet. Kassidy went to stand between Luke and Eric. Cecil stood between Mark and Laurie and Andre closed the circle. The paths held hands while touching their charges.

"LeBeau, picture a surgical room that has not been covered by the rock. We've experimented with the stuff and if you try to take us to a room that has been covered, we are going to hit it like a wall. Laurie will not survive the jolt, so make sure you aim carefully. As soon as we get there, call off the roofing crew!"

"OK, I've got it." Luke said out loud as he got the picture in his head. LeBeau was showing them the same room that Luke and Andre had been in on their way to get Kassidy. Luke was pretty sure that it had not been reached yet by the rock. There had been a lot of rooms between that unit and Kassidy's room. He took a deep breath, said a short prayer and looked at his friends. He sure hoped they were not making a colossal mistake.

It will be all right. Kassidy reassured him.

Eric wasn't sure what was going on. He was in shock himself which was probably a good thing for the little group. He was in no condition to question anything, or to stop what was happening. The teleflight did not even register in his brain. By the time they reached the facility, he needed attention as well as his sister.

Mark had them put Laurie on the operating table in the middle of the room. The technicians who had been present before were no longer there. The room was completely empty except for the little group. Mark was prepping the girl for surgery and yelling out instructions as he went. He already looked like he'd been through the surgery. He had Laurie's blood all over his hands and shirt. He had mud and debris stuck to his knees and he looked very, very tired.

Luke had LeBeau call in the order to stop the roofing project.

"Uh, yes sir," came an unsure reply from the man on the other end of the phone call, "but, sir, we stopped it over an hour ago. It was disturbing the other patients."

"What other patients?" asked a confused LeBeau.

"The other cancer patients, sir!"

"Cancer patients?"

"Yes, sir, what other kinds of patients would we have in a cancer research facility? The new patients arrived an hour and a half ago. We've started the preliminary tests on them to get us a base line. You know, the routine, sir."

"OK, thanks!" LeBeau turned to look at Luke and Andre suspicion etched on his face. The two were smiling back at him. They had heard the entire conversation via LeBeau's mind.

"I guess our boys and girls have met with some success!" thought Andre.

"I guess so!" agreed Luke.

Mark was getting more and more frustrated with having to describe things because no one in the room had any idea about medical jargon. Finally, he addressed LeBeau in frustration. "I need a surgical nurse. I need one right now! Oh, and find someone to take care of Eric. He's gone into shock."

LeBeau was back on the phone in an instant and calling for a surgical nurse on the double. There happened to be one waiting for an exploratory in this very room. She hustled into the room, surprised and a little miffed that no one had called her prior to this! She had had to scrub too quickly. She didn't like to hurry when it came to scrubbing. She was griping about this to herself when she entered the room. What she saw nearly rocked her off her feet. Two men were standing near the door holding guns on another man . . . . that man was the owner of the hospital!! She had only seen Mr. LeBeau a couple of times, but she would know him anywhere. What was this? A hold up? At a hospital? She knew that medical insurance was a bone of contention in the United States, but had it come to this?

LeBeau motioned for her to proceed over to the table and help out the doctor. Then she saw the doctor. He was standing there in scrubs, but the knees were filthy and he was covered in blood. He had bags under his eyes and looked as though he hadn't slept in a week. As soon as she was beside him, he started throwing out orders. She stepped right in, assisting him as if she had been assisting him all her life. She was smooth and adept at her chosen career.

A second nurse entered the room. He was told to care for the young man sitting in a heap in the corner of the room. The nurse helped Eric up and took him to a room across from the surgical unit. Kassidy and Luke followed them out.

"We'll stay in touch incase we need you or vise versa." Luke told Andre.

"OK, and don't worry, if LeBeau so much as thinks about being anything less than hospitable, I'll make him wish there was a brain surgery that could save him."

Mark began to relax a little as the surgical nurse worked with him. She seemed to know what he needed before he even asked for it. He felt his muscles relax and a sort of rhythm develop between them.

"Well, Radar, you are good at what you do." He complemented.

"Thank you, so are you. But, Radar?"

"You seem to know what I need before I need it . . . like Radar from the sitcom M*A*S*H."

"Oh, thanks! I guess . . . wasn't he a short guy who slept with a teddy bear?"

"Yes, but he was great at his job and that is where the resemblance stops."

"Thanks for clarifying. I'm curious. Did John Q start this?"

Mark smiled. "John Q?"

"You know, that movie about the man who forces a hospital to operate on his . . . what was it, his son? He didn't have insurance or the money to pay for a needed operation."

"I know the movie."

"So, why are we doing a brain surgery in a cancer research hospital on a patient that appears to have no cancer, but obviously has a few broken bones? As a matter of fact this woman seems to be the victim of an accident. Why was she brought here? And while you're answering that . . . . why is there a man holding a gun on my boss?"

"It's a long story. One better left for after we finish putting this young lady back together."

"Yes, Master!" The nurse produced an extremely good impression of Igor from the movie Young Frankenstein.

Mark was in seventh heaven as a smile broke once again across his lips. "You wouldn't happen to be looking for a change in job location, would you?"

CHAPTER 34

The Gift

LeBeau sat quietly beside Laurie's bed. His eyes hadn't left her face since Mark, now crashed out entirely on a gurney they had pulled in from the room across the hall, had finished the operation and set her broken bones. Kassidy had produced a sleeveless dress and sandals and had changed out of her hospital gown. Luke was admiring her choice, noticing how the dress flattered her already exceptional figure, but finally turned to check on LeBeau. LeBeau held Laurie's hand, but there seemed to be no communication going on between them. Luke wondered how this particular relationship would pan out. Eric was sitting on the other side of Laurie's bed. He held her other hand and waited with LeBeau for any sign of improvement. It had taken some time for him to come around after the unbelievable adventure he had had that day.

Since he had lived through the accident and been whisked away by teleflight, it took him a while to wrap his mind around the whole situation. Luke and Kassidy had been with him for several hours, trying to explain what was going on. They weren't sure what they were going to do about him. They couldn't leave his memory entirely untampered with. That was just what they were trying to avoid. The fewer people who knew about paths the better. They would have to wait until Laurie woke up . . . if she woke up . . . . to figure out what to do with him.

LeBeau was also going to be an issue. In the event that she did survive they couldn't really leave Laurie with him. They didn't trust him. But it was going to be difficult to get her away from him. They couldn't take him to their safe houses. Though it appeared that his talents were very limited, who knew what would happen after Laurie was conscious.

Kassidy's giggle brought Luke back to the present. He tuned in to her thoughts and got a very clear picture of a besotted LeBeau, bending over backward to keep 'his' Laurie safe from harm. *What if he has to change his ways to keep her?!*" Kassidy's musings made Luke smile. But it also gave him an idea. He remembered how Mark could 'hear' them when they were holding hands and touching him. He looked back at LeBeau who had left Laurie's side and was pacing the length of her bed. He stopped and sat back down, but he didn't pick up her hand again. It was worth a try.

Luke took Kassidy's hand and led her to LeBeau's side. Then he put his free hand on LeBeau's shoulder. *"Touch her!"* he told LeBeau.

LeBeau jumped at the voice in his head. He looked up at Luke, a question in his eyes.

"Reach out and touch Laurie."

LeBeau did as he was told. The pain was excruciating and he drew hack.

"Put your hand back on her and face the pain. It will recede if you face it."

LeBeau did as he was told again. All three of them felt the pain, but as LeBeau faced the source, the pain receded as Luke had said it would. *"Walk toward the pain."*

LeBeau faced the pain and began to walk toward it in his mind . . . . was this his mind?

"No, this is Laurie's mind. Walk toward the source and you will find Laurie. Help her fight the blackness."

LeBeau paused, *"How do I fight the blackness? What is it?"*

"You'll feel the fight and you'll fight beside her. Just go!"

LeBeau walked toward the source again and before he'd taken two steps, he saw someone standing in front of him. She was facing away from him. He could see her fighting the blackness but she was faltering. She was too weak. The fall had taken its tole. She had been weak to begin with. Now she fought for her mind as well as fighting the pain of a couple of broken bones.

"Take her hand, fight beside her."

LeBeau took her hand and the power of the four paths fought together; Kassidy and Luke augmenting LeBeau's power as they fought together. The blackness was receding quickly. Luke was amazed. It was receding much faster from Laurie than it had from Kassidy.

"There were only two of us then." He heard Kassidy clearly in the blackness.

The electricity began to ignite the air around them and all four paths were caught up in it; their hair flying around them. The blackness was nearly gone. LeBeau looked over at Laurie. She still faced forward, but he turned and reached for her other hand. He turned her around to face him. The electricity dissipated and their hair began to settle. Laurie smiled. Her smile made LeBeau's knees weak. If he hadn't been physically sitting at the time, LeBeau was sure he'd have fallen to the floor. He was absolutely taken by her incredible beauty. Her blonde hair hung in ringlets to her waist. Her eyes were dark brown around the inside gradually changing to a topaz gold around the outside. She had a sprinkle of freckles across her nose and a smile that dazzled him.

"Beautiful!" was the only word that reached LeBeau's thoughts.

Eric watched the strange behavior on the other side of the bed. He saw Luke take LeBeau's shoulder and thought for a minute that the three were going to pray or something. Then he saw LeBeau reach out and take Laurie's hand again. Eric was struck with the pain at the same time as the paths. Not knowing that to avoid it he only had to let go, he endured it as he watched. He saw the blackness and watched as LeBeau walked toward it. He stood mesmerized as the four paths fought the blackness and he watched it recede to nothingness. He saw his sister turned toward LeBeau and watched as she looked up at him with a bit of awe in her eyes. Then she smiled and any blackness that had been hiding out in the recesses of this place was chased away.

As Eric watched the dark haired path standing behind them turned to the girl with him and smiled. Did Eric hear him talk to her? It sounded more like an echo in his head. *"Kassidy, let go and let's see if LeBeau can keep the connection."*

Kassidy let go and disappeared from Laurie's mind. Eric saw her standing there one second and then she was gone. But the other two guys were still there with Laurie. Then the dark haired guy was gone and only the blond guy was left. Eric watched wide eyed as the blond guy leaned down and kissed his sister! Damn, he kissed her! Who did he think he was? Eric tried to run to him, but he couldn't seem to make any progress. Something was holding him back. Then his sister turned to look at him. *"Eric, I got this. Let go of my hand and give me a little privacy, please!"*

Eric wasn't sure what to do. He wasn't holding her hand, he was standing way over here away from her. Just then, someone touched him. He felt them touch his hand and then he was back sitting in the chair beside Laurie looking at her unconscious face again. The big dark haired guy was standing beside him. He had pulled him away from Laurie's side.

"Give them a little privacy, kid." Luke was smiling kindly at him.

"He was kissing my sister," Eric pointed at LeBeau who sat serenely beside Laurie, still holding her hand and totally oblivious to the rest of the room. He had a stupid grin on his face and as Luke looked more closely, he noticed LeBeau's scar had begun to heal!

Luke and Kassidy were passively listening to LeBeau's thoughts. It had taken him a long time before his mind began to work again. He had gotten lost in her beautiful face and as Luke and Kassidy listened, they thought they would probably have every detail of her eyes memorized before she had even gotten a chance to open them physically.

"Who are you?" they heard Laurie ask him.

"I'm . . . Todd . . . LeBeau."

"Where am I?"

"You're in my hospital."

"Why am I here?"

"You fell while you were climbing. I was drawn . . . I was there. My . . . friends . . . and I brought you here. A surgeon worked on you. You were pretty messed up. But don't worry; you're going to be all right now."

"Where's my brother?"

"He's here in the room with you. As soon as you open your eyes you'll be able to see him."

Luke cut into the conversation. *"Todd, ole buddy,"* he said sarcastically; then more seriously, *"look at her brother, she should be able to see through your eyes."*

LeBeau dragged his eyes away from the woman's unconscious body and looked at Eric.

Eric was glaring at LeBeau.

"What's wrong with him? Why is he looking at you that way?" Laurie asked.

"He's just a little miffed that LeBeau kissed you and then you told Eric to give you privacy. He'll be all right . . . later."

"Oh, who are you?"

"Luke Matthews"

"So how many people do I have in my head right now?"

"Besides Todd, here, you have me and my path mate, Kassidy."

"Hi, Laurie. I can't wait to meet you when you wake up. Sorry about intruding, but LeBeau needed a little help."

"He needed help to talk to me?"

"Yes."

"Oh!" Laurie began to listen to the other's thoughts more intently, *"Todd, you aren't as strong a path as these other two? . . . You didn't like them before . . . no, they didn't like you . . . they still don't like you. Why?"*

"Well, I'm a scientist . . . this hospital is a research hospital . . . I . . . we . . ." Todd cut off. How would he explain to this incredible woman what kind of research hospital it was? He had spent all these years trying to uncover the secrets of the path mind. It had begun as a defensive mission. He needed to keep regular people safe from the powers that were manifesting in the lives of these few. But it had become more than that. Oh, he had used his own body for experimentation supposedly for scientific purposes, but that hadn't been entirely his whole motivation. He had wanted the powers himself. His selfish desires had hurt and even killed others . . . . Regina . . . . she really hadn't needed to die. She was willing to work with them. She had never fully realized the danger she was in, just by working with LeBeau. As he began to really look into his past, his decisions, he discovered a truth about himself that he could barely stand to acknowledge. Yet, he made himself look. He made himself see the man that he

had become and tears began to cascade down his face as the realization of the magnitude of evil he had been pushing began to scroll through his mind. He couldn't seem to control the thoughts as they rushed like water from a broken dam. Though he could clearly see how they were going to devastate the life he now wished he could keep, he couldn't seem to get control of the raging waters. His eyes sought hers trying to explain, or to communicate the deep sorrow he now felt. His whole adult life seemed to be one self centered act after another. He buried his head in the bed beside Laurie. *"I'm sorry, I'm so, so sorry! Luke, Kassidy,"* his thoughts were agonized pleas now, *"can you ever forgive me?"* He didn't wait for an answer before he was pleading with the woman whose hand he still held. *"Laurie, I'm so sorry!"*

Laurie stopped talking. She stopped thinking. She saw everything that scrolled through his mind. There was deceit, hate, jealousy, anger, and . . . murder! Well, it wasn't totally planned murder. He had tried to keep the other paths alive, but he knew the risks and had operated on them anyway! She could take no more. *"You hunted these people and then did tests on them?"* Laurie was having difficulty reconciling the truth with the anguished eyes she was staring into. *"They died!"* The horror of the realization swept over her. *"You were responsible for killing them!"* Disbelief and denial layered the last statement, but his thoughts betrayed him and Laurie saw the truth for what it was, ugly, mortifying, disgusting. *"How could you do that?"* Now the woman before him in her mind began to cry also. Anger flooded her thoughts. *"Let go of my hand."* LeBeau made no move to let go of her hand. *"Todd, leave me alone!"* Her scream echoed loudly in everyone's mind. LeBeau let go of her hand and the visual connection was broken. Unfortunately, for LeBeau, he had no idea how to turn off her thoughts now and her sobs reverberated through his mind.

Luke and Kassidy blocked her thoughts from theirs to give her some time. Luke was enjoying the anguish that LeBeau was experiencing. Despair rocked across his face as he experienced total loss of control for the first time in his life. LeBeau had hit bottom. Here he was drawn to this one woman. He had made contact with her and the connection was already more than any relationship he had ever experienced. How would he ever make up for all the evil he had instigated? There was no way to make up for his wrongs. There was no hope for him. He couldn't go on without her and he couldn't possibly make up for his past.

Eric was at a loss. The whole scene was just another weird thing going on in the middle of the weirdest day in the history of his life. There was no communication going on that he could hear, but the man sitting on the other side of his sister's bed was bawling like a girl! The big dark haired guy was obviously enjoying it and the pretty lady with the exquisite green eyes was looking thoughtful and . . . . what . . . . was it pity he saw in her eyes when she looked at the blond guy? Something was going on, but he didn't know what. All he wanted was for his sister to wake up. Maybe once she was awake, he would find out what was happening.

It was Kassidy who took pity on LeBeau. She had been listening to his thoughts as she watched him spiral downward. *"LeBeau, everyone messes up. Everyone makes mistakes. Are you truly sorry for the things you did to me?"*

"Everyone does not *mess up like I did.* You *didn't get anyone else killed! I did."*

"Are you sorry for what you did to me?"

"Yes, yes, I'm so sorry! Please forgive me!"

"I forgive you. But I am not everyone else. You will have to talk to the others. You will have to ask for their forgiveness. Some may forgive you and some may not, but from here on out, you have a choice to make. You have a wonderful place here. You have built an incredible facility. You can choose to use it for good, or use it for evil. That is your choice. Which ever you choose, please know that we will be watching you. The files in your computer lab have been changed. This place is now a cancer research facility just like your stationery proclaims. The rock on the roof will be removed. We will know if you revert back to your old ways. Also, I forgive you for all the things you did to me, but I'm still a little angry about the shots your guys fired at Luke and the anguish you put Derrick and his parents through. I choose to forgive you for that, but my feelings are not totally aligned with my choice yet. That's something I'll have to pray about. Still, as far as I'm concerned, you have a fresh start from here on out with me."

"Thank you, it's more than I deserve."

"Well, I'm not sold on all this forgiveness stuff, yet." Luke was thinking about the bruise that had covered half of Kassidy's face when he had rescued her from LeBeau's clutches only a few hours before. He was a little ashamed of himself that he thought first of a bruise across Kassidy's face and only second about the lifeless face of Regina on the day they had found her in a room just about like this one. Luke looked up at Kassidy and was happy to discover that her face was completely back to normal. He reached out and ran his fingers over the now fully repaired cheek.

"I'll work on him, LeBeau." Kassidy moved closer to Luke and wrapped her arms around him.

CHAPTER 35

The Cave Revisited

Luke and Kassidy brought Laurie, Eric and Mark back to the beach house with them. True to his word, they had had to throw a glass of water on Mark to get him to sit up long enough for the teleflight back to the beach house. He had only been asleep for about five hours and was still a little groggy. He had checked Laurie and deemed her healthy enough to move. LeBeau was not happy with her leaving, but understood that he couldn't keep her unless she wanted to stay. Kassidy suggested that he demonstrate his change of heart. They would be watching his progress and they would keep Laurie up to date on it. If she chose to come back, she would. If she didn't, he would have to live with it. LeBeau agreed.

When they arrived at the beach house, they were surprised at the number of people who were there. There was a celebration in full swing. Jonas sat in the center of a group of people that Luke and Kassidy had not met yet. He waved them over and they walked toward him with some curiosity.

"Luke, Kassidy, this is Jennie." Jonas had an arm around a very beautiful girl. Her eyes were an amazing shade of violet-blue; her dark hair was about waist length and hung loosely around her shoulders. Kassidy thought that the hair was probably helping to hide a scar that could not possibly be completely healed yet. Jonas seemed to glow. His eyes seemed to not be able to stray from her for long at all. With each introduction, he glanced away from her for only a moment and then his eyes were back on her.

"Nice to meet you, Jennie." Kassidy spoke first.

"Yes, we are very, very glad to see the two of you together!" Luke agreed. He was more than happy to have Jonas focused on a different girl than his! Kassidy stuck an elbow in his ribs. He got the clue and closed his mouth, but kept a very pleased smile on his lips.

"Nice to meet you too!"

Jonas didn't seem to notice and proceeded to introduce Jennie's parents, Colonel Robert Scott and his wife Marcia. He then continued on through Jennie's brothers, starting with the oldest and working his way down, Jake,

James and Jared. The boys had one major thing in common. They were all three over six feet tall! They even towered over their father. Col. Scott had an easy smile and even seemed to be all right with his daughter's new boyfriend. Clearly, Jennie took her looks from her father. He was the one with the light skin and blue eyes. Marcia was a small woman, with dark skin and dark eyes. Her hair was cut in a cute style that wrapped just under her chin. Her boys looked more like her, height not withstanding, all of them with olive to dark skin and dark curly hair. Two of the boys, the older two, had very light eyes, but the third had her dark beautiful milk chocolate eyes. It was a closely knit family. Luke discovered that the older two were home from college on summer break. The youngest boy had just graduated from high school. Jennie was the youngest child having just finished her junior year of high school.

Jonas looked a little sheepish about having brought the entire family to the beach house, but he explained that they wouldn't let him out of their sight with their daughter. When Rick and Sophia came back to the hospital because Jonas had not returned by the deadline, they were surprised to discover the reason why. Jennie was never left alone. There was always one or two of them with her. They were amazed by her speedy recovery and even more amazed by her eye color change and the fact that when she needed something, it somehow made its way into the room. Jonas had been floundering as he tried to explain the unexplainable until Rick made his entrance. It was decided that the Scott's needed to be brought in on the secret.

It had taken some time to convince the Colonel that Jonas was not a stalker, but had been drawn to the accident. It took a miracle, and very open minds on the part of the Colonel and his wife, to explain the path life and why Jonas was probably stuck in their lives forever. That might have been a real problem, except that Jennie seemed just as stuck on him, as he was on her. It also didn't hurt that Jonas was already going to the very college that Jennie wanted to attend after she graduated and he was a star athlete and scholar at the college.

Luke and Kassidy enjoyed the short time they spent with the Scott's and then made their way through the other partiers. They ran into Uri and Ute as well as Andre, Cecil and Demetri. Demetri went on and on about the great raid on the facility. His Russian came speeding out of his mouth at a rate that kept everyone on their toes as they listened to him. He told of all the paths who had worked to the fruition of the plan all over the world. Some of the names were familiar to Luke and some were new, brought on board by Uri, Ute and another couple who had arranged for the augmentation of operatives abroad.

Rick had already heard from LeBeau who had vowed to give them information on any operative that he discovered who was still under the impression that the facility was hunting paths. Though LeBeau's abilities without Laurie would inhibit him from augmenting memories, he promised that he would tip the path network off, so they could take care of it. Rick was skeptical at first, but as he delved deeper into LeBeau's mind, he could find no indication that the man was not telling the full truth. The only thing LeBeau requested in return was an update on how Laurie was doing.

The raid on the facility itself had been easier than first anticipated. Since it was true that LeBeau had kept most of the employees in the dark about the agency's real mission, their minds took very well to the new purpose of the facility. The employees who were up high enough in the organization to know what was going on were a little more difficult, but with the combined efforts of all the available paths, not already pressed into duty elsewhere, the augmentation was successful. There were still a few paths on guard duty at the facility. They kept a close watch . . . . or rather they kept a mental ear out for personnel entering or exiting the facility to make sure that no stragglers had been missed.

Bonafide cancer patients had begun to arrive at the hospital within hours of the change in the computer lab. That was Satoro's gift to the facility . . . real patients! That had stopped the rock spraying on the roof. The noise and the smell did not set well with patients who were going through chemo therapy.

Fortunately, the transition had been complete before Luke and Kassidy had taken Laurie back to the facility for the operation. Had that not been the case, they could have been in for quite a surprise when all of the sudden Mark had begun to think like a Cancer surgeon instead of a brain surgeon. There was an audible sigh of relief from both Luke and Kassidy at that realization. It had not occurred to them to check out their timing before they arrived at the building.

When it was all said and done, the take over had only taken about a half an hour to forty-five minutes after the downloading and subsequent uploading of the computers. It had been most tricky getting the lab technicians out of the way and occupied until the transfer of information could be accomplished. Once the paths deleted the old computer information and up loaded the new cancer information, it was only a matter of minutes before everyone at the facility was working on a whole new agenda.

As Demetri began to run out of story, Luke's mind wandered to more interesting possibilities.

"Kassidy, come with me."

"I'm all yours!"

"Yeah, that's what I want to talk to you about, but not here. There are too many open minds around here. It's hard to concentrate and just as difficult to block."

He took her hand and led her slowly down the little brick path to the beach. They weaved in and out of people and lights. The music was loud down here and many couples and even groups of people were dancing in the moonlight. He wondered what time it really was. He turned toward the cave at the bottom and pulled her into his side as they walked, now arm in arm. He paused for just a moment in concentration, but Kassidy was not paying attention to his thoughts, because his lips had taken her by surprise as he nuzzled into her neck and kissed his way up to her lips. He turned her toward him and pulled her more tightly to his chest. She found herself losing her breath when he stopped kissing her and his hand suddenly ran down her back and pulled her back to his side. He smiled and continued steering her toward the cave. Kassidy wasn't sure if she should be disappointed at the interruption or pleased with their destination. Luke produced a lantern and the two slipped unnoticed into the cave. They made their way toward the little beach lounge that was still there, but before Kassidy could sit down; Luke pulled her into his arms and kissed her sweetly on the lips.

"Kassidy, we've known each other for only a couple of months," Luke's hands were shaking on her waist as he organized his thoughts. He was hoping that she wouldn't notice, but he was sure that she would because he could feel the warmth of her body through the thin material of her dress. "But I know you better than I've ever known anyone in my life. And you know me better than anyone has ever known me before." He took a deep breath then. "When you were kidnapped . . . . I couldn't . . . . I wanted . . . ."

"Luke, could we talk after you kiss me again?"

"No, talk first, then comes the kissing." He smiled a mischievous smile.

"Talk fast, please!"

"Kassidy, you have a one track mind."

"We just got rid of the bad guys . . . . we're free and clear! We can start concentrating on ourselves for a while!"

"That's what I'm trying to do. Now, be quiet. I'll tell you when it's your turn to talk." He said playfully.

Kassidy groaned but she quieted and listened. Of course, that didn't stop her from running her hands up his arms, around his neck and into his hair.

"Kassidy, honey," Luke caught her hands and brought them back down to hold in his. He pulled them up against his chest. He closed his eyes, took a breath and opened them again. He looked into those incredible green eyes, leaned his forehead against hers and finally finished his thought. "I couldn't breathe right without you. I want you with my entire being. I need you more than I've ever needed anyone, but most of all, I love you with all my heart. Will you marry me . . . like, oh, I don't know . . . tomorrow?"

She stood in his arms totally taken by surprise. She didn't move or breathe for what seemed to Luke to be forever. Maybe it was a poor choice to bring her into the cave. He knew he wouldn't be able to hear her answer before she spoke it, but he had wanted to hear her say it first, before anyone else 'heard' it. Right about now, though, he was wishing he had asked her out on the beach, or taken her home to the cabin and asked her on the deck. The wait was unbearable.

"Kassidy, now it's your turn to talk!" When she still didn't respond, Luke pressed her further. "Kassidy . . . . you are killing me, sweetheart."

Kassidy was stunned and frozen in place. Hadn't they already decided on this? It wasn't that she would even consider saying 'no' even for a moment. She was just . . . well, he had taken her breath away. She smiled and then interrupted his complaint as she reclaimed her hands and slid them back up to his hair. She stood up on her tip toes and kissed him. It started out as a sweet peck on the lips but she didn't stop there, she turned her head slightly to the side and kissed him deeply. She still hadn't taken a breath, but when she did it was more of a catch in her throat. The tears began to role down her cheeks and the smile on her lips was easy to distinguish as Luke kissed them back.

"So . . ." Luke was interrupted by a kiss, "yes . . ." another kiss, "then?"

Kassidy moaned in answer.

"In that case, Kassidy, I have something for you." He managed to get out between kisses. "Honey, you have to stop kissing me for just a moment so I can give it to you."

"What ever it is, it can wait for a few minutes; I'm not finished answering you yet."

"OK," Luke squeezed in between kisses. "Just give me your hand then."

She slowly unwound her hand from his hair and dragged it down his chest as he brought his hand up to meet hers. He placed a small velvet box in her palm and closed her fingers around it. Though she had not broken the kiss to this point, her eyes flew open. That brought her up for air! Luke had a hesitant smile on his lips as if his happiness rested on her reaction to the contents of the little box. *"Well,"* he thought, *"it did actually!"*

She swallowed and brought her other hand down to open it. Luke wrapped both arms around her waist and waited with baited breath.

The ring was beautiful. It had one large diamond in a gold setting that raised the stone gracefully up with a slight twist. It looked delicate and sparkled beautifully in the soft light of the lantern. Luke let go of her waist, took the ring in one hand and her left hand in the other. But before he slid it on her finger, he looked back into her eyes and said, "You never answered me, sweetheart."

"Yes, Luke, I'll marry you," she whispered up at him. The tears started again, as he slid the ring on her finger. "When did you have time to get this? We have been so busy."

"That's my secret."

"Until we step out of this cave, it is."

Luke laughed and then he was kissing her. He held her head in one hand and pulled her closer with his other. She would be his as soon as he could arrange it. He sure hoped that her parents wouldn't insist on a two month wait, as Anthony's in-laws had. He wasn't sure he could stand another two month delay. He left her lips and kissed her forehead and hugged her closer.

"Luke, you surprise me. Your patience was commendable."

"What patience?"

"You waited for all that time after you proposed while I stood there in shock and you didn't even use your secret weapon."

"Oh, it was shock was it . . . didn't you see that coming?" he laughed.

"No, I was a little preoccupied. So how come you never used it?"

"Well, I know how potent that secret weapon is and I wanted to make sure it was you saying, 'yes' and not your hormones."

"Well, just so you'll know. Your secret weapon doesn't work solely on hormones."

"Really, are you sure?"

"Positive!"

"How can you be sure?"

"Because it doesn't work for anyone else. It only has power coming out of your mouth. If it were just hormones then any old fairly attractive guy should be able to wield its power."

"Mmmm, that's good to know." He kissed her again. "Shall we go home?"

"MmmHmm. You need your rest; you get to meet my parents tomorrow!"

"I already met your parents."

"Yeah, but they didn't know you were going to be their son-in-law then."

"They aren't going to be very happy with me. I took you from them, remember?"

"Well, it was either that or lose me forever. I think they'll be more forgiving than you think."

"I hope so!"

"Do we need to give Mark, Lisa and Sandra a lift home?"

"Not tonight. Let Mark sleep. We'll pick them up tomorrow!"

The two turned to stroll out of the cave, arms around each other. As soon as they cleared the cave, Kassidy looked up into Luke's eyes. "You got the ring just before we entered the cave. That was why you stopped and kissed me . . . to keep me preoccupied while you found a ring!"

Luke just smiled down at her. "Pretty sneaky, huh?!"

"Very sneaky! So, that's how you do it! It's all slight of hand. Or mind, I should say. You are able to keep stuff from me by distracting me with one side of that male brain of yours, while the other side is up to something."

"Well, you know guys . . . we compartmentalize everything."

"That explains a lot." Kassidy's brow suddenly wrinkled in thought, "Uh, Luke, honey . . . you did pay for it, right?!"